For A Friend

Mark Lenard

Heads Up Publishing

For A Friend Copyright © 2016 by Mark Lenard

All rights reserved. No part of this book may be reproduced or transmitted in any form or by any means without written permission of the author.

Edited by: LeeAnn Riley
Cover Design by: Gregory Graphics
Interior and Typesetting by: InteriorBookDesigns.com

Published by:

Heads Up Publishing

www.facebook.com/mark.d.pratt.3

marklenard@ymail.com

ISBN 978-0-692-71155-2

I want to dedicate this to my supporters and to anyone that's chasing their dreams. Don't ever give up until you catch what you're reaching for.

Acknowledgments

I've been waiting for a long time to write one of these, lol. First off, I have to thank God for blessing me with the ability to put together words as a way to entertain others and myself as well. Without him, there could never be me! I want to thank my mom, Barbara Pratt, for giving me life, and for believing in me and these crazy dreams I have. I love you more than you'll ever know. To my kids, Carissa, Mark Jr., DeVaughnte, and Nicholas, I love you all to death, and my goal has always been to be the father that I know I can be to all of you. Hopefully, I'll reach that before I leave this earth. I want to thank my sisters, Nikeya and Naya Pratt for holding me down while I was away, and for being there when I called. Pamm Moore, I just want to thank you for everything. No matter what, I'll always consider you the realest friend I've ever had. I have to give a special shout out to my boy, Author King Benjamin, for opening the door for me to jump into this literary game. It's just the beginning, homie, and we have so much to look forward to in the future. VDS4L! Evette Newbern was the person I could call and ask the world of while I was away, and if she could do it, she did. I just want you to know that I love you, girl, and like I always told you, I'm doing this for us! To Jeffery White, my little man, my guy, the person who stays on my head to make sure I'm putting in that necessary work in order to succeed. I love you like a son, and this journey is ours even though you're not physically by my side. You motivate me like you could never imagine, and I'm making sure you reap the fruits of this labor we're putting in. I want to give a very special and heartfelt shout-out to my big cousin, the person who I want to be like when I grow up, Rodney Fresh Sr. I could say so much about such a wonderful, caring, and positive person, but all I'll say is that I love you, and I appreciate your encouraging words, your huge heart, and your crazy sense of humor. You're the best! To my in-house editor/wonderful friend/ #1 supporter, LeeAnn

Riley: You were there at the beginning, and I'm making sure you're there until the end. Thank you for believing in me and being the beautiful spirit that you are. Your words encouraged me to write from my heart, and I could never thank you enough. I want to also thank three special people who have supported me and my writing, the people I send my work to before it's published, whose opinions I value tremendously: Sharon Stanley Hillman, Yolanda Briggs, and Maureen Billings. I'm eternally grateful for you ladies, and I appreciate the interest and support you all have shown in this journey of mine. Thank you! I have too many family members to list, so I'll just say thanks to the Pratt/Fresh/Rambus family members that have shown their love and support. Shout-outs to my Decatur, Illinois family, my Van Dyke family, and also my Springfield, Illinois family, lol. Last but not least, I want to thank the person who became my best friend, the person who inspired me to write, my business partner, and one of the funniest people I know, Larry "Black Jus" Williams. It's just the beginning, bro, so come on and let's put this work in. We got people to feed and money to give away, and believe me when I say that if it wasn't for you, I would've never picked up a pen and sat at that iron desk for hours at a time. You lit the fuse that sparked it all, and I'll forever be indebted to you. We all we got!

    I know I missed some people, but I have to wrap this up. Charge it to the price of publishing and not to my heart, lol. If you rock with me, I know who you are, and I want to thank you for supporting, encouraging, and being in my corner. Oh, and let me thank all my Facebook friends, too, lol. Y'all are the best. Well, some of y'all. lol

CHAPTER 1

May 7, 1998 – Federal Courthouse, New York City
Devon Raines, aka "New York"

"Does the defendant have anything to say before I impose sentence?"
He didn't even look at me when he asked that shit. I was scum to him, the bottom of the motherfucking barrel. I knew it, my lawyer knew it, and anybody who had heard of Federal Judge Wallace McClain knew it, too. His daughter, dying with a pipe in one hand and a gram of crack in the other, had a lot to do with why his decrepit looking face was so familiar to the people of New York, and the rest of America. When you're a Federal judge and your daughter takes her last breath in a roach infested apartment somewhere in the middle of the Bronx, well, it's kind of hard to stay out of the spotlight. It had to be embarrassing for him, so I kind of understood why he felt that way about somebody in my profession.
It was all misdirected anger if you ask me, though. I didn't know the bitch, let alone serve her some high-quality dope that was strong enough to cause her heart to give out. He should've been mad at the very government he was a part of. They let that shit get over here, and had been keeping the black community doped-up for decades. But once crack started affecting white America, they kicked off the "war on drugs" in the hood, killing us off by giving fed cases to street level dealers and hitting us with king pin sentences. Putting off on us a situation they had a hand in, but once it got out of hand, we were the ones to suffer the consequences. Niggas weren't growing coke in Harlem, and

every real contact I knew had a Spanish accent. But we were the ones getting basketball numbers in the court system.

And, here I was, about to get my number, about to get penalized for my participation in a game that was played on an unleveled ass playing field. And who better to dish out the punishment of slapping me upside the head with the good ole hammer of justice than a judge who was on a mission to avenge his daughter's death, equipped with laws made by motherfuckers who didn't like us in the first place. Shit was crazy.

She had been gone almost a year, enough time for the feds to go out and round up enough drug dealers to feed McClain when he came back from a self-imposed hibernation following the death of his only child. His appetite for some sort of revenge was in his eyes when he held a short press conference announcing his return, and he made it clear to everyone that he was out for blood when it came to crack dealers. I was sure that I wasn't the only inmate in the Brooklyn Metropolitan Detention Center who was shaken up after watching that broadcast.

Bert stood up. "Yes, he does, Your Honor." He nudged my chair as I sat next to him, letting off a sigh before nudging it again.

"My client would like to address the court."

The thought of Bert telling me *"That speech shit don't help with this motherfucker"* crossed my mind. *But do it anyway, for Christ's sake.*

My small chuckle caused a jack-in-the-box reaction from McClain. His long wrinkled neck extended when he spoke. "I won't tolerate foolishness in my courtroom."

Bert nudged me again. I stood up, figuring I might as well get this shit over with.

I walked toward the podium, meeting eyes with U.S. Attorney Elwin Hodge, as he sat at the prosecutor's table. He shook his head as he tapped his fingers on a stack of papers, holding the stare long enough to relay his silent message: You had your chance.

Yeah, I could have cooperated with the feds, gave up a few names. Shit, they were even willing to let me out to set up one of my contacts – a Spanish guy they had a hard on for – after they somehow found out I copped from him on occasion. They were acting like they wanted to give me a free pass and a badge. Fuck that shit, though. It wasn't in me to throw another nigga under the bus as a way to save my own ass. I put myself in the position to be set up by a motherfucker who didn't have the balls to take his own weight. Now I had to stand up and take what I had coming.

I didn't realize my palms were sweating until I touched the wooden podium. It was quiet as hell, and McClain eyed me over horn-rimmed glasses that rested on the tip of his pointed nose. If he was trying to hide the disgust and contempt he had for someone in my line of work, he damn sure needed years of acting school to pull it off.

"You may proceed, Mr. Raines," he said, sounding as if it hurt him to refer to me as "Mr." Under any other circumstances, I would've come back with some smart ass remark or straight up cussed his ass out. Taking shit from people had never been my thing. But the circumstances were different now, and even though I knew it was a long shot, I was hoping to get twenty years instead of twenty-five. Still, it was tempting.

So, I started reciting some shit I had been practicing for the last few weeks. Basically, I accepted my responsibility and acknowledged that what I did was wrong. I confessed to making a bad decision and apologized to the community. It lasted all of three minutes. Judge McClain looked like he was reading an article out of *Field and Stream* the entire time.

When I finished, I turned to go back to my seat, giving Elwin the finger as I passed him. I made sure McClain didn't see me, and all Hodge did was smile and adjust his tie. Bert saw it. He shook his head as I walked over to him.

The judge began to speak even before I could sit down. From the harsh tone of his voice, I quickly realized that the slim chance of me getting the twenty years was out the motherfucking window.

"Mr. Raines," he said, his stare hard and burning. "You're right when you said you made a bad decision and you must now pay for that bad decision. You're twenty-two years old, so you're at an age where you should fully understand the harm and destruction drugs cause in the community." He sat back like he was at home chillin' in his Lazy-Boy. "And I think you should also understand why I am sentencing you to three hundred months in the Bureau of Prisons."

At that point, I blocked out all the other shit he went on to say. Nothing else mattered. And really, his announcement didn't surprise me. I knew it was coming. I just didn't know how I would react; didn't know how I would feel. And, as I sat there, I didn't feel anything. No sadness. No fear. No disappointment. I was numb, which was a good thing at the time. If only that numbness could last for twenty-five years.

A hand on my shoulder brought me out of my trance. It was Bert.

"I'm sorry, kid," It was a sincere whisper. "We got the bad luck of the draw. Fucking judge."

"Tell me about it." I stuck my hand out and shook his. "Thanks anyway."

"I'm here for you if something changes."

Bertello Cardoni probably would've been a Mafia underboss in another life. He talked like a mobster, walked like a mobster, and had the short barreled frame of your average Italian with pasta-based eating habits. His dislike of "rats" was also something he had in common with the mob.

I met him when I caught my first drug case after somebody recommended him. It was a state case, though. Bertello eventually got me a year of probation, and I'd had him on retainer ever since, dropping him off money here and there just in case I ever needed him again. But dealing with the feds was a different monster. After reviewing the evidence against me, his only advice was, "Either you bend over and get ready for them to fuck you in the ass, or, you rat. I can't represent you if you rat. But, if you wanna take this fuckin', I'll hold your hand." He was a good guy.

I nodded my appreciation to Bert as two marshals came over and stood behind me, ready to escort me back to the detention center. Judge McClain was talking to his clerk and court recorder. It didn't surprise me to overhear him telling them a joke. When they laughed, I did, too. Loudly.

The judge looked in my direction, coffee-stained smile still intact. Smiling along with him, I flipped him the bird. "Fuck you, too, Your Honor."

I felt much better.

After the marshals grabbed me by both arms and ushered me out of the courtroom, I sat shackled from head to toe as I rode in the back of a van. The numbness was gone and reality had me in a headlock, choking out any life that was left. Regret was beating the shit out of me, too.

I was regretting everything. I regretted not listening to my mom and dad when I was younger; I regretted dropping out of high school just so I could hang out to do much of nothing; I regretted selling dime bags of weed on my block instead of getting a job to support myself; and I most definitely regretted giving up the weed after finding out that crack brought faster money. No amount of money was worth losing twenty-five years of my life.

As the van exited the expressway, I leaned my head against the tinted window and watched people do regular everyday shit. Some sat around on park benches, feeding pigeons and enjoying the afternoon sun. Some moved through the crowded streets like they had places to be. Others pumped gas while fending off homeless people in need of spare change, while a guy in dirty and torn clothes stood on a corner. He was holding a sign declaring that he was the Son of Man. What I would have done to switch places with any of those people.

I swam in my pool of self-pity for the entire ride. Not until the van pulled into the garage of the detention center, did I attempt to shake it off. It helped a lot when I thought about giving the judge the finger; a whole lot. I sat up and took a deep breath, blowing out the last of any sympathy I had for myself. The marshals opened the van's door to let me out, and I smiled as I penguin walked up to the building's entrance.

CHAPTER 2

January 25, 2004--Federal Court, Urbana, Illinois
Kabazza Wright, aka "Kay"

"So what am I facing?"
I knew the answer. The "Federal Sentencing Guidelines" book had become a favorite read of mine. I found it in the library on my second stint in the county jail, opened on a table like a Bible in an old Christian woman's home. It basically explained the punishment you could get for breaking laws on the federal level. My mandatory minimum was ten years. I asked my court appointed attorney, Chazz Blakely, the question anyway.
"I believe it's ten-to-life," he said while rummaging through a leather legal folder. After finding what he was looking for, he opened a file. My name was on it.
Scanning pages, he said, "Yeah, ten-to-life. No criminal history, so you may be eligible for a reduction if the judge grants it. Either way, you're facing considerable time in prison."
He sat the file down to the side and leaned back in his chair, not doing more than what was expected from a public defender. Going out and hiring an attorney was my first choice. Money wasn't a problem. But when I found out the evidence against me was solid, I changed my mind. It didn't make sense to spend a lot of money just to plead guilty.
The feds picked me up four months ago. I'd been sitting in the county jail ever since. Bond was denied at the request of the U.S. attorney who prosecuted my case. He labeled me as a "flight risk" and a "danger to the community". The judge agreed.

I was originally from Detroit, so I somewhat understood why they believed there was a chance of me taking off if given a bond. But a "danger to the community" was beyond exaggeration if you asked me. I was a drug dealer, not a murderer. The one time I did kill someone, it was a clear case of self-defense.

Today was the day when I was supposed to plead guilty to my charge. The guy who was sitting in front of me, who looked more like he was straight out of a Calvin Klein ad, was advising me of my options. We had spoken twice before and we both knew what those options were.

"What do you think I should do?" I asked, smoothing the legs of my orange jumpsuit.

Blakely appeared more interested in his reflection cast by the glass and wire partition that separated us. Fingering a few out of place hairs, he said, "It's your call."

Noticing my hard stare, he assumed a professional manner. He inched closer to the partition and spoke in a conspiratorial tone. "Look, Wright, I know you're in a tough situation, but there's not much I can do. Unfortunately, I'm just a guy they throw these types of cases to. Drug cases rarely go to trial, so in this arena, I'm nothing but a plea deal defender. And like I told you before, the feds only deal with you when you have something for them. Other than that, you get what the guidelines call for."

He let his words hang in the air, never taking his eyes off me.

"The U.S. Attorney on your case is willing to recommend that you get three years," he said, holding up a plea agreement. "All you have to do is give up what you know about a..." He removed an index card from his shirt pocket and studied it for a moment. "Khalid Morgan. You know the guy?" I gave him a slow nod.

"Yeah, I understand this isn't an easy situation to be in." He let out a sigh, laying the papers to the side. "But this is how it is. You can either take the ten years, or we go upstairs and sign the papers stating that you will cooperate. Your choice."

He did a good job of making it sound so easy, but this was the toughest decision I ever had to make.

When I first decided to step into the drug game, I never once thought about getting caught; money was my only focus. I guess that blinded me from seeing all the other aspects of being involved in something I really knew nothing about at the time. The possibilities of getting robbed, killed, or arrested, never entered the equation, even though those were real consequences a lot of people encountered. I was naïve of course, believing everything was all glitter and gold in the game, and riches would be my only return. On the outside looking in, it appeared that way. But once inside, the truth was revealed. And the truth was, there was nothing good about risking your life or your freedom just to get ahead.

I found this out the hard way, and now my freedom was about to be snatched away from me, regardless of what I did. The only comfort I had, was knowing that I could decide how long it would be for.

For some reason, an old mob movie played in my head as I continued to contemplate my decision. I couldn't recall the name, but there was a scene where a mob boss was referring to someone who had cooperated with the police. He called the guy a "rat". When asked by an associate why was the guy a "rat", the mob boss replied by saying, "When a rat is cornered, he will do anything to save himself."

A marshall came through the door and told Mr. Blakely that it was our turn to see the judge. Blakely turned to me. "What's it going to be, Wright?" This was it. I had to make the call. An image of my family flashed in my mind. My wife, Taj, my four-year-old son, Dante, and my mom. They meant the world to me. "Okay," I said, rising slowly from my chair. "Let's go sign those papers."

Three days later – County Jail

I was staring up at the television when a C.O. called my name over the speaker. "Step out here," he ordered. Walking up to the door, I glanced over my shoulder. Four sets of eyes were on me.

They knew how it worked. It wasn't visiting day. I didn't care what they thought, though.

A buzzer sounded, letting me know the door was unlocked. I stepped out and closed it behind me. "What's up?"

The C.O. came from around the control desk. "You have some visitors."

I followed him to the exit of the housing area. The door buzzed and he led me to the prisoner's library. I wasn't surprised to see two of the agents who arrested me sitting at a table: Hudson and Fraser. I would never forget those names.

The two agents stood when I came in. Both were clean cut and casually dressed in khakis and button down shirts. After assuring the C.O. that his services were no longer needed, he pulled the door closed. The turning of the lock signaled it was time for business.

We exchanged handshakes as they reintroduced themselves. Smiles even accompanied the handshakes. I wasn't stupid, though. They were just trying to make me as comfortable as possible before I turned into a snitch. The greetings ended and we all took our seats.

"You doing all right, Kabazza?" Hudson asked. He was the younger of the two. About thirty-five, I would've guessed.

"I'm good, under the circumstances." I watched as they began to remove pads of paper from folders.

"How are they treating you in here?"

"Like a criminal."

They both laughed, reaching for pens and pads as they did. The small talk was over. Fraser was the older guy. Late-forties, hairline looked to have receded when he was a teenager. I noticed the lights glaring off his head as he started the questioning.

"What can you tell us about Khalid?"

I felt my heart accelerate a bit. "What do you want to know?"

They asked me all kinds of questions about Khalid; how long had I dealt with him; how much dope did I get from him on the average; did I know who he got his dope from. I told them everything I knew about the guy. During the hour-long session, I realized a few things also. For one, I realized I was helping to destroy another man's life as a way to make my situation better. Khalid's time on the streets was probably limited anyway, but I was playing a part in speeding up the process.

I also realized that I was not made to be part of something that some people involved themselves in as a way to survive. I didn't grow up poor, going to bed hungry. I could have done a lot of other things to support myself. I had opportunities while others didn't. I basically tried to use the game, and it showed when I couldn't stay true to it after I got busted.

The last thing I realized was that when I was forced into a corner, I was willing to do anything to save myself.

It was now over. Hudson and Fraser seemed satisfied with all I gave them. The pens and pads were put away, but Fraser had one last question. "Would you be willing to swear your statement in by going in front of the grand jury?"

I stared at him. "I don't have much of a choice, do I?"

"Yes, you have a choice." He picked up his briefcase. "You can be back home with your son before your twenty-seventh birthday or your thirty-fourth birthday."

CHAPTER 3

Four months later

Being confined to one area for nine months was tough. If a person wasn't mentally strong, the situation could become overwhelming. Until I experienced this for myself, I never could understand why someone would choose to tie a bed sheet around their neck as a way to escape the reality of it all. I understood now. Luckily for me, though, my situation wasn't nearly as bad as some. I had a supportive family behind me, and my mind was in a good place for the most part. The three years I got played a big role in that.

Obviously, the feds wanted Khalid in a major way if they were willing to knock my time down from ten to three years. I guess I was really nothing to them but a small fish in Khalid's pond, and they used me to help catch the big prize. But if you ask me, I did get something out of it.

Snitching on Khalid wasn't easy for me to do, nor did I feel good about my three years. In fact, the thought of it caused me to stay awake at night. I would stare at the ceiling for hours wondering how I even went through with something I considered to be a cowardly act. That's what I thought until it happened to me. It then became a matter of using man's first instinct: self-preservation.

It was only natural to feel guilty about it, and it was that guilt that caused me to have the same dream more than once while in the county jail: a crowded courtroom. Khalid would be the defendant, and I would be sitting in the witness box, arm extended, a finger pointed in his direction. I would wake up when he and I made eye-contact.

The guilt was strong, but family became my coping mechanism when the bearing of that feeling became too much. "I did it for them," I would tell myself. "They need me," became my fight song. It began to make me feel like I was less of a man by cooperating with the feds, but I would then tell myself that a real man would do whatever he had to do to get back to his family as soon as possible. It worked sometimes.

The only bright spot during those nine months were the twenty-five-minute visits I had with my wife, Taj, and my son, Dante. My mom lived in Detroit, but she came for all of my court dates and visited me while she was there. The visits kept me going. If they could have snuck in our Teacup Chihuahua, Shorty, it would have made it even better.

At the beginning of all of this, the visits were very hard for Taj and I. The first couple of visits were spent with her wiping away tears as Dante sat quietly beside her. He would reach into his pocket and hand her a crumpled up piece of tissue, doing all he could to stop the tears.

It was heartbreaking because I wasn't able to hold her and promise her that everything would be all right. It got to the point that I told her not to come if she was going to cry. Not that I didn't love her or anything; it's just that since I'd met her, I never wanted to see her sad. I made it my mission to keep her happy. And I had accomplished that until this happened.

Our son was the pillar we leaned on during those visits. His cheerful nature and constant smiles held us up at times when we would have, otherwise, broken down. His insisting that he gets to hold the phone to his ear for at least ten minutes during the visits was one of the things that made us laugh instead of cry. Taj never told him Daddy was in "jail", "off to school" or "gone away because he did something bad". She told me she didn't have to say anything. When I missed our nightly bedtime story the day I got arrested, he knew something was wrong. He didn't cry, he didn't ask his mom where I was. And when he saw me the next day dressed in an orange jumpsuit, on the other side of a bulletproof glass that prevented us from sharing a high five or a hug, all he did was wear an encouraging smile.

He would spend the visits sitting in a chair next to his mom, using the small counter as a wrestling ring for two toy figures he would bring with him. We would trade winks and thumbs ups while I spoke to Taj, and he would periodically ask for the phone to tell me about something he had forgotten to mention during his mandatory ten minutes. The ending of each visit was always concluded with him climbing up on the chair, leaning in as close to the glass as his short frame would allow. He would put his small hand on the bullet proof barrier, encouraging me to do the same, while he spoke words into the phone a father would say to his son instead of the other way around.

"Be strong, daddy. We'll make it through this. I love you."

I would hold back the tears until I got back to my cell.

Dante was wise beyond his years, by far. He was nothing short of amazing. We never referred to him as a prodigy, not even during late night conversations while we'd lie in bed and marvel over some of the things he had said or done earlier in the day. As parents, we only wanted to see him as our cute and adorable son, and to shield him from anything that would have deprived him of a happy and normal childhood. But we knew he was special.

At fourteen months, he was talking like he had been here before. It had become a common occurrence for Taj and me to sneak shocked looks at one another when he would come in the room expressing his views on things from the weather, to how many pieces of tissue it takes to adequately wipe after using the bathroom. That topic was inspired by an over-flooded toilet. He stood outside of the bathroom door, Shorty at his side like always, while I scrambled for the plunger, as water and used tissue rose to the rim of the toilet. I didn't find it in time, and he then offered his input while I cleaned up the mess.

"Over in Europe, they use an average of four sheets to clean up after doing number two."

Confused, I looked over at him. "What? Who told you that?" I noticed Shorty look at me then glanced up at Dante as if he was interested in his response.

"I saw it on the news. I would say it depends on what you ate, though." Shorty turned back to me.

I didn't know what shocked me most; the fact that he watched the news, or knowing that Europeans thought four sheets was enough. How they actually performed the research was something we never got into.

By the time Dante was two, he had mastered the alphabet, and took a fascination to the letter "x". Words like "exciting" and "excellent" rolled effortlessly off his tongue at every given opportunity.

"Dad, this pizza is exceptionally good!"

"Dad, can you examine this mosquito bite?"

So when he came to us one evening saying he wanted a xylophone, of all things, we figured it was just another part of the fondness he had for our twenty-fourth letter of the alphabet. But, it turned out to be a little bit more than that.

Dante beamed when I came into his room carrying a colorful box that held his toy xylophone. He had been reading one of the many children's books from a collection of over a hundred that were stockpiled in two bins under his bed and in his own personal library. Yes, he could read. He had even taken over as the reader of bedtime stories, and he was far more animated than I'd ever been while telling them.

"Thank you, daddy," he said, opening his little arms to receive his gift. Once he got it out the box, it was like he had forgotten all about me.

The xylophone was placed on the bed while he retrieved a chair from his play set. He made himself comfortable like he was sitting at a piano, running a small hand through his curly black hair before taking hold of the two plastic mallets. I guess Shorty wanted a view better than the one he had from the floor. His bark caused Dante to reach down and pick him up. He put him on the bed, and Shorty turned around in circles a few times before finding a resting place right next to the xylophone. His ears perked up like he was waiting to be entertained.

"I'll be right back. You want some juice or a snack?"

"No, I'm fine, Dad." He was slowly running the mallets over the keys soft enough not to make a sound.
"I'll be down when dinner's ready."
"Sounds like I'm not welcomed here."
"I expected you to say something like that," he replied, smiling down at his new toy.

His smile was like gold to me. "Okay, I'll be downstairs with your mom."

I left out and walked toward the stairs. A faint note traveled through the hall. Then another.

Kids sometimes get a new toy, and three days later it would be off in the corner, only to be touched again by us parents who stored away almost anything that held memories of our child's first years. Well, the xylophone lasted about a week, and Dante spent almost every waking hour on the thing. His room had become his little studio, the constant pinging of xylophone keys muffled behind a closed door. It had gotten to a point where we had to knock so that we wouldn't, in his own words, interfere with his exploration of his new instrument. A trip to the lake to feed the ducks was the only thing that lured him away from his new hobby during that week. One day, I was downstairs in the kitchen eating a sandwich when Taj came in and grab me by the wrist and started leading me upstairs in a hurried fashion.

"Can I finish my sandwich, horny lady?"

"Shut up, silly," she whispered as we made it up the flight of stairs.

Taj released my wrist and walked slowly over to Dante's closed door. She leaned against it and took an eavesdropping position, waving me over as she did so. "Get over here," she mouthed silently. I took a bite of my sandwich and walked over to her, settling in on the other side of the door.

"You hear that?" she asked, whispering with a look of excited disbelief on her face.

"I've been hearing it for the last week. It's called xylophone noise."

She put her finger up to her lips. "No, just listen."

Turn a fan on and leave it running for a week straight, and it becomes just another sound we take for granted, like the continuous hum of a running refrigerator; the only time you notice it is when it stops. Dante's xylophone was no different. As long as I heard the pinging, I knew that everything was fine. When it stopped, I would be at his door checking in on him.

"Can you hear that?" She looked as if the notes were soothing her soul as she stood there. I satisfied her by getting closer to the door. A dust build-up on the hallway ceiling fan caught my attention.

"Yeah, 'Itsy Bitsy Spider'." I gave her the "duh" stare.

She continued to listen, the love of a mother in her eyes. In her soft whisper, "That's our son in there, Kay. Our two-year-old amazing son is in there playing that music."

The children's song that we all have sung once or twice in our life was repeated a few times as we stood there. I remember being in kindergarten, singing along as the music teacher played the piano. There were times when I would hear my high school marching band practice the tune out on the football field. But nothing came close to the version my son played beyond that door.

"He's a smart kid, baby." I don't think my nonchalant answer was what she was looking for.

"So you're telling me it's normal for a two-year-old to pick up an instrument and basically master a song in a week? Sounding like that? A toy?"

"It's a simple song to learn." I shrugged her off without saying anything.

She was right, of course. What was playing wouldn't have been a big deal had a trained percussionist, or somebody with musical experience, had been in control of those mallets. But the crisp notes, wrapped in a melodic rhythm, were being produced by a curly-headed toddler who just so happened to be our son.

Exactly a week later, Dante and Shorty came downstairs and made a rare appearance in the living room. Taj and I were on the couch wrapped up in a game of Jeopardy, her favorite show, which eventually became mine. Until I'd met her, I thought only old people tuned in to watch Alex Trebek call off answers for people to question. But that was just another side of Taj that drew me in from the beginning. She was as smart as she was beautiful, my daily double of a lifetime.

"...What is the Liverpool, Alex?"

"Oh, I knew that!" She slapped my leg in frustration.

"Well, you should've slapped your own leg."

"...I'll take World Capitals for one thousand, Alex."

"...This is the most northern world capital. Brrrr!" Taj blurted out, "What is Reykjavik?"

"Rayka-who?

"...What is Reykjavik, Alex?"

"...That is correct. Go again."

"Geography isn't your strong suit," she teased.

"I can point you to the bedroom."

I leaned over and let my tongue brush her ear. The bark from a feisty four-pound Chihuahua interrupted me as Mr. Trebek gave up another question. "What is it, Shorty?" I turned around and he and Dante were standing in the doorway, the xylophone on the floor in front of them.

"There's a key on here that sounds excruciatingly off. I think I need another one."

We would hear that more than twenty times over the next two years. Dante's walk-in closet would eventually become a xylophone graveyard, neatly stacked rows of colorful toys deemed unplayable by a kid who transformed into a superhero whenever he put on his Batman pajamas. They were "out of tune", according to him. He'd always sounded very convincing when he said it, too. So much so, I would be at the toy store fifteen minutes later, following him around until he found what he was looking for. He would point and I would grab. A brief inspection of the box would occur, spearheaded by him, of course, and minutes later "Itsy Bitsy Spider" and other childhood tunes would be bouncing off walls of the second floor of our home.

It didn't always happen like that, though. Sometimes he'd fall asleep on the way home, and I'd get the chance to experience that warm and cozy feeling of picking him up and having him latch on to me like a magnet as he continued his nap. We'd make it to his bedroom, and he'd only loosen his grip when he'd feel the comfort of the bed on his back. I would then slip off his shoes and gently undress him; a slightly opened eye would peek up at me accompanied with a sleepy smile. He would then drift back off to dreamland, taking a kiss on the cheek from me with him.

A xylophone was never touched again by Dante once it was exiled off into that pile in the back of the closet. He did stop collecting them once we found a real xylophone while on vacation, though. It was a gift from an old wood carver, and it seemed to propel Dante's ability beyond anything we could ever imagine. But still, he wasn't quite ready to depart with the other ones when his mom suggested he give some to a charity toy drive.

"Please, mom, can I keep them?" He was hip-high at her side, his hand reaching for hers as they stood in the closet door.

The power of the word "please" was something Dante understood fully and used it strategically, it seemed like. It never sounded whiny coming from him, either, making it even more effective on us mere adults.

"Dante, they're just collecting dust. Let's give them to some great kids and put a smile on some faces. It can be your first EXperience at giving back," she playfully teased, running a finger across the tip of his nose.

"OK," he replied, smiling up at her. "But not today, please-e-e-e? Not just yet."

Like I mentioned before, the only thing that could entice Dante away from his xylophone was a trip to feed the ducks. With a loaf of bread in hand, we would go down to the lake and instantly be surrounded by a herd of the quacking little animals. Dante would squeal and shriek with delight as they would come closer and closer, their beady little eyes focused on their meal for the day. We were frequent visitors to the lake after I gave up selling drugs, so when the flock of ducks would see us, they knew that their little bellies were about to get full. I would give Dante a few slices of bread and he would begin his "here ducky, ducky" call, his puffy little cheeks raised by a giggling smile, and an innocence that even the ducks could sense. I lived for times like those, and now it was killing me not to be able to do those same things with my son.

I had been waiting to get transferred to wherever I was going to do my time. I was tired of the county jail; tired of being stuck in a dorm that housed six other guys at its capacity, tired of the food we were served that was always lukewarm by the time it was transported from the local hospital, and tired of not being able to have contact visits. It was strange to be in a hurry to go to a real prison.

The majority of my time was spent reading books. There was a television hanging up on the wall that we all shared, but majority ruled, and I wasn't a big fan of soap operas and drama series. I played spades a few times, but after two of the guys got into a fight while we were playing, I left the card games alone. Paperbacks then became the only thing I held in my hand. I would consume a book in one day, getting lost in between pages of tales based all over the globe, and reading became my lawful escape from a place that was a world of cement, steel, and cold reality.

Ten o'clock in the evening was a time I welcomed every night. That was the time when they would let us back in our one-man cells and put us on lockdown until five the next morning. I would respond to letters from my family and then eat Oreo cookies and Jolly Rancher candy while I read until I fell asleep. Sometimes I would even write down my plans and goals for when I got out. I wasn't exactly sure what I wanted to do, but I knew selling drugs wasn't an option. I would cringe just at the thought of going through this again.

CHAPTER 4

"Wright, pack your stuff," a C.O.'s voice echoed over the intercom. "You're outta here in twenty minutes."

With those words, I was instantly roused from one of the soundest sleeps I'd had in the nine months of my stay. I sat up and ran a hand across my face. Prison was the agenda for the day, and I was ready.

I was escorted into the back of a white van, which was nothing more than a steel box with two steel benches on each side. Its only occupant was a frail looking guy sporting dreadlocks that hung down his shoulders and hid his face when he looked away. He watched me as I slid down the small bench and took the position against the wall of the van.

"What's up, Joe?" he said with a slight tilt of his head. I assumed he was from the Windy City. "Joe" was Chicago's trademark saying, their version of Detroit's "what up doe".

"Not too much up in here," I replied, slightly brushing my head against the van's roof.

"Shit's tight as a mothafucka." He cracked a weak smile and lowered his head. The thump of two slamming doors shook the van. The engine roared to life and the transmission shifted into gear. Daylight was revealed as the garage door rose slowly. The van pulled forward causing the dreads across from me to sway from side to side. I looked to the back door of the van. A barred set of windows offered me a view. I watched as the county jail disappeared into the morning sunrise, and I realized I was on my way to prison.

"Where you from, cuz?"

My gaze stayed on the window. "Decatur."

"Oh, yeah?" It sparked his interest. "I know some chicks down there."

Before I could say anything, he started rattling off names of girls we both knew. He mentioned almost every girl that was known for doing something strange for some change. And there was no shame in his game when it came to his fetish for pay to play women.

"Everybody tricks," he proclaimed. "Either you're spending time or money on them, and I ain't got time for these hoes. I let them hoes chew me up, hit that pussy, and then send 'em on their way."

He went on for a while as his words drove time by. I just sat back and halfway listened, letting him reminisce about his past adventures. I would give him periodical nods, head shakes, and occasional "straight ups" as a way to let him know that I was paying attention. But then he changed the subject.

"What they got you for?"

No eye contact. "Drugs."

"Shoulda' known." I could feel his stare. "How much time they hit you with?"

"I got off easy. Only three years."

"Hell yeah, you got off easy!" His voice hit a high pitch. "These people bustin' nigga's heads. They gave me fifteen years like it wasn't shit."

"For drugs?" I acted surprised, but I really wasn't. I knew what the feds were capable of.

"Yeah, Joe, they fucked me around. And then they get these snitch-ass niggas out here helping lock a real nigga up and they stay on the streets." He let out a heavy sigh. "Man, fuck a snitch!"

The van was quiet for the remainder of the ride.

Our journey came to an end at an airport of some sort. I didn't know where I was headed, but I assumed a flight was needed in order for me to get there. Dread was twisting a braid as he glanced out the back window.

"We in Terra Haute."

"Indiana?" I asked.

"Yeah. I'm going right up the road to the medium-security spot. No plane ride for me. They can keep that shit."
"Tell me about it. I wonder where I'm going?"
"Ask the Marshals. They'll tell you."
I rapped lightly on the steel cage. A marshal slid back a glass divider and then put his ear to the small opening. "What's up?"
"Could you tell me where I'm going?"
"Your name's Wright?" He looked down and I could hear him rifling through papers.
"Forrest City is where you'll be staying." He slid the opening back closed.
Dread must have noticed my puzzled look. "Arkansas," he stated. "Ain't nothing down there but a bunch of Mexicans and big-ass bugs."
The sound of a plane's engine could be heard in the air. "That's your ride," one of the marshals sang.
Their doors opened and both men exited the vehicle. We could hear them talking until the sound of a plane's engine slowly drowned out any noise in the nearby vicinity. It got closer and closer until I could barely hear the sound of my shackles whenever I moved my arms or legs. The van then began to vibrate, and I looked up at the roof expecting to see the blade of a giant can opener making its way in. Rattling came from the back door, then daylight.
Both doors swung open. Two men in blue U.S. Marshal's jumpsuits glanced at us as they traded paperwork with our transporters. "Step out here, Wright."
"Stay up, Joe," Dread called out as I slid across the bench. "Have a safe trip." His Tony Montana impression wasn't too impressive.
"You too, Joe."
One of the marshals held onto my cuffed hands and helped me as I stepped down out of the van. A small rock almost pierced the thin rubber sole of the county issued shoes I was wearing, causing me to instinctively lift my right foot up. Had I not been shackled, I would've avoided stumbling awkwardly into the alert arms of two of the marshals, and the cuffs on my ankle wouldn't

have dug so far into my skin that I was sure they had drawn blood.

"It's too early for hooch," one of the marshals yelled, joking as the plane's engine hummed mightily around us. "Name and number!"

"Kabazza Wright and I don't know my number!"

He scanned the papers he was holding. "Just got in, huh. You better learn it quick! Birthdate?" I gave him what he asked for and then was ordered to stand against the van.

I hadn't actually been outside since being locked-up, aside from going to court three times. But even then, I never got the chance to smell the fresh air. We were always delivered through underground garages – the order of operation by the feds – so it was almost surreal that I was basking in the morning sun as it rose above the eastern horizon. Not even the fumes from the van's exhaust system could spoil the fresh spring air that smelled just like I'd remembered. And weirdly enough, I found myself thinking about how beautiful of a day it was, the perfect day to go on a forced vacation to an undesired destination.

The airplane was taxied about a hundred feet away from where I was standing, engine running. A steep flight of stairs extended out the tail end of the plane, and a crew of blue jumpsuits was gathered around at the bottom, all wearing black gloves and on full alert. The van I arrived in was part of a caravan of vehicles that made a semi-circle around the plane. Two white charter buses were bookends to several unmarked police cars, more windowless vans, and an Illinois State Patrol car that was parked about ten feet away. I could see a black man in the back seat, his face pressed against the glass, his expression leaning toward depressed. His bright orange shirt was clear evidence that he was also on his way to prison. He looked over at me, and we found ourselves giving each other slow shakes of the head, a mutual understanding of the reality of our situations.

No other planes were in sight. The runway was occupied by two men distances apart. Both were wearing black military-style gear, a bulletproof vest and high-powered machine guns included. A look to my right revealed a few more scattered around the perimeter, including a sharpshooter planted on top of a control tower. The left revealed more masked gunmen scattered along the barbed-wire fence that surrounded the small airport. It was like being in a movie and, at any moment, a jailbreak attempt was about to go down.

Other marshals were exchanging paperwork with the transporters, and then the bus on my left started to unload its cargo. A continuous line of khaki-clad inmates of all shapes and sizes, Afros and braids were the favored choice of hairstyles. They followed two marshals toward the plane while two other marshals trailed at the end of the line, coming to a stop once they reached the crew waiting at the bottom of the stairs. I could see guys bending over and running cuffed and shackled hands through Afros and dreadlocks, all under the watchful eyes of marshals, before being allowed to board the plane. My short tapered fade allowed me the luxury of just having my mouth checked like I was at the dentist, and a brief examination of my hands. The challenge of climbing the stairs while shackled was the worst part of the whole thing, until I noticed layers of duct tape on the wing of the plane. I thought maybe I was just seeing things, so I stopped just short of the top of the stairs and looked again. And, yes, the wing was bandaged-up in duct tape.

"Don't hold up my line!" a voice boomed over the sound of the engine. A glare from a jump-suited marshal was waiting for me when I looked up. He and one of his counterparts stood at the entrance of the plane looking like some bad guys from WWE wrestling. I made my way up to them and expressed my concern.

"Man, is that duct tape on that wing?"

"Yeah, so?" said the yeller as he gestured to his friend. "WE got parachutes." They laughed as they guided me onto the plane. When it was all said and done, approximately one hundred people had been searched thoroughly and herded onto the 737 as if we were cattle. By the time I was directed to my seat – in which I had to sit in between an old Mexican and a black kid around my age – I was beyond blown away. It wasn't just the fact that a crew of U.S. Marshals was posted up outside armed with heavy artillery. Nor was it the fact that there was another crew aboard the plane, strategically placed and watching our every move. And considering I had heard about the staggering number of minorities in prison, the fact that I only managed to see two white faces in the crowd of a hundred or so men didn't really catch me by surprise. But witnessing the accuracy of those statistics, first hand, well, that's another story in itself.

The one thing that overwhelmed me more than the scent of the old Mexican guy next to me and the scene that was taking place as if practiced a million times, was the fact that I was in the dead-center of it. Me. On a plane. In shackles. U.S. Marshals. I grew lightheaded as I sat there. The only thing that prevented me from fainting was the thought of my head resting on my old grungy travel companion's shoulder.

The marshals that handled the paperwork were the last to board the plane. Once they were seated, another marshal stood and began to shout the rules for "Con Air."

"You move when we say you move," he said, jabbing a finger in his chest. "Keep your feet out of the aisle. You have to piss or take a dump, you go when we say go."

"I gotta shit!" a voice yelled from the back of the plane. The cabin of the jet filled with laughter.

"Hey, asshole," the marshal screamed over the chuckling crowd, focusing in on the heckler. "You go when we say you go! You can't wait until then, too fucking bad."

A chorus of "fuck you's" and "bullshit's" followed.

The marshal quickly regained everyone's attention by shouting, "Next motherfucker says a word, goes to the hole when we get to our last stop!" Instant silence. He finished his speech without interruption. Once he was done, he sat down. The plane began to move seconds later.

Flying wasn't a big deal for me. I had flown a few times before. The only difference was I didn't have Taj holding my hand, curled up next to me. Instead, I had a guy who was in desperate need of a hot bath on one side of me, and a young kid, who obviously didn't agree with flying, on my other. He called out to one of the marshals and asked for a barf bag as the plane taxied onto the runway. And when the pilot announced, "Prepare for take-off", the kid made really good use of that bag.

We were in the air for about twenty minutes when the marshals allowed us to use the restrooms. And, as the loud-mouthed marshal said, we didn't go until they told us to go. One by one, each prisoner was asked if they had to relieve themselves. If that was the case, you waited until you were directed to do so. I had to go, but after watching shackled inmates struggle to make it down the aisle, bouncing off seated inmates' shoulders as if they were pinballs, I decided to hold mine a little longer.

Obviously, everyone understood how cramped the conditions were, so no one seemed to get too upset about being used as a bumper. A fat white guy did get a few angry glares directed his way after he wobbled down the aisle and made dominoes out of anyone with an aisle seat. They all ended up in the lap of the person next to them. And judging from those glares, it was pretty safe to say that if we weren't ten thousand feet in the air and surrounded by marshals, he would have been in a little bit of trouble.

My Mexican companion stood when the marshal made it to our row, causing the funk from his seat to rise and slap me dead in the face. I turned my head and held my breath as he stepped over me. I watched the kid next to me do the same.

"Move over," the marshal ordered, glancing down at me as he frowned at the Mexican.

"In that seat?" I asked as I stared down at the seat the smelly guy had just occupied.

"The one on the wing, smart-ass! Yeah, that seat."

"Mannnnn."

I stood up slowly and prepared myself, and my ass, for something that instantly made me sick to my stomach. I then eased down onto the cushion as if I was about to sit on an embedded needle. I took a deep breath and held it, knowing that the remnants of his body odor were still lingering. The seat was still warm. I was about to call for a barf bag.

After I got over the shock of having to sit in the seat, I peered out the window and stared into the clouds below. All I could think about was my family. I wondered what they were doing. I wondered how they were feeling. I wondered if they missed me like I missed them. I wondered if we could be the same family we were before all of this happened. I didn't have a lot of time to do compared to others, but it was enough time to test the stability of any family.

CHAPTER 5

Con Air made three more stops before we arrived at our final destination for the night. Each was in places I would have had trouble pinpointing on a map; Rochester, Minnesota; Sandstone, Minnesota; Yankton, South Dakota. Three different cities, but the same identical thing happened at all three stops: prisoners got on, prisoners got off. I watched the process each time, carefully putting crimes to faces as they shuffled past. Drug dealer. Child molester. White-collar criminal. I'm pretty sure I got one right out of it all, but I couldn't help but wonder what they actually did to end up in prison. Some looked too young to have committed a crime, and some looked like they should have been home reading bedtime stories to their grandkids.

There were even a few women on the plane, and that really made me wonder what they could've done to be passengers on Con Air. They were seated at the front of the plane, away from the male prisoners, but were basically gang-raped by the eyes of drooling sex-starved inmates as they passed to exit and board the plane. One thing was clear to me, though: the feds didn't discriminate.

There was quiet chatter during the entire ride. Most of it seemed to revolve around prison life. I overheard veterans as they schooled rookies about everything from security levels to what not to do while doing time. One prisoner told another inmate that prison was all about giving and receiving respect.

"You do that, and you have nothing to worry about," he said like it was law.

Another guy in front of me warned a rookie about the dangers of worrying about what was going on in the "free world".

"It will drive you crazy. You in anotha world now, youngsta, so you gotta keep your mind on doin' this time."

The rookies weren't the only ones soaking up the vets' game, and it was inevitable that I would witness the testing of some of their theories firsthand.

The pilot announced our approach to Oklahoma City as I watched the clouds give way to squared-off acres, upon acres, of dirt-brown southwestern real estate. The landing was always the best part for me. The view from a plane was something a lot of people didn't see every day, and I was fascinated each time I witnessed it. But it wasn't the same. I wasn't on my way to an exotic and tropical location with Taj. She wasn't cuddled up in the seat next to me, head on my shoulder, face in a book. Her customary "I love you's" didn't accompany me on the trip. Instead, I listened to the silence grows louder.

The city below became visible as the plane angled off into a turn. The hum of the engines was all I could hear. I turned to my left and the young kid next to me was looking over my shoulder. The smelly Mexican was looking over the kid's shoulder. I turned back toward the window. Every inmate on that plane probably peered out and saw the freedom they once had, just like I was.

"Los coches se ven como hormigas."

"Si," The young kid chuckled and offered the translation. "He said the cars look like ants."

I was impressed by his bilingual skills; the view, not so much. "You know Spanish?"

"Yeah, a little bit." Endless skies appeared as the plane dipped into a deeper turn. His voice softened. "You learn all kinds of shit in here."

The plane pulled into the Oklahoma City Transfer Center. It was a federal prison/layover stop for inmates headed to different facilities in the Bureau of Prisons, which had prisons located throughout the United States. Forrest City, Arkansas was my destination, so I figured I would spend a few days in good ole Oklahoma City. Before the plane could come to a full stop, the marshals were already in action. They took up their positions and started the process of unloading their cargo. Row by row was emptied, as we were ushered off the plane and down the corridor. We were greeted by another crew of marshals as we stepped off.

"Stay inside the yellow line!" a marshal's voice boomed as he lifted his belt over a hanging gut.

Three of his counterparts split away from the group and directed traffic. We were ordered to walk along the left side of the hall. The aforementioned yellow line gave us just enough room to walk straight ahead. Considering we were shackled at the ankles, wrists, and basically handcuffed to a chain that was wrapped around our waists, that amount of space just didn't seem to be fair.

"Inside the yellow line!"

The clanking of steel against concrete provided our soundtrack as we marched down the very long hall. I winced with each step because of the angle the cuffs came down on my ankles. Nothing I did could stop it. Every move caused steel to rub against skin, and the steel always won. The cuffs around my wrists weren't as tight, but I could still see the red marks brought on from wearing them all day. My whole body breathed a sigh of relief when the line slowed. The welcoming committee was ahead, grouped around a raised platform, keys in-hand.

"Listen up!" It was the guy with the big belly.

"Step up on the platform in a nice and steady fashion so that we can get upstairs as soon as possible."

That "as soon as possible" turn out to be about six hours, as we went through what was basically a very long check-in into Club Fed. We were crammed into a cell that was forced to hold every inmate from the plane. The noise of a hundred guys talking was almost deafening, but after sitting in there for a while, it became like the sound of a steady wind.

I was lucky enough to get a seat on a bench, while other guys made themselves as comfortable as possible on the concrete floor. Some stood up and held more prison related conversations. I assumed the inmates who joked and laughed like we were at a social function, had been through this before. They gave each other a fist-bump as they spoke, and didn't seem to be phased by the crowded conditions or the fact that we were in prison. As hard as I tried, the first-timer in me just couldn't ignore the situation.

The once cold cell had turned warm and funk-scented as time went on, which made me yearn for a little fresh air. It didn't help when a heavyset older black guy calmly excused himself through the crowd and headed over to a steel toilet that sat against a wall. In a very nonchalant manner, and without hesitation, he gently let his khakis fall to the floor and took a squat. Before the familiar sound of bubble guts echoed throughout the cell, he had already created a six-foot perimeter around him and that toilet.

The majority of the crowd returned to the conversations they were holding, some speaking with their shirts covering their mouths and noses. I assumed the consensus was that no matter the circumstances, a dump waits for no man.

Minutes later, the rattling of keys demanded everyone's attention. The cell door opened and a C.O. instantly took charge.

"Shut up and step out when I call your name!"

I found myself standing up and easing toward the door like everyone else. He called off fifteen names before he got to mine. I brushed a few shoulders as I made my way to the door.

"Name and number," the C.O. said, looking down at some papers. I quickly ran off both, my federal inmate number fully memorized over the plane ride just like my date of birth. We spent the next few hours getting mugshots, humiliating cavity searches, and receiving a fresh change of clothes. It was all done in assembly line fashion, the finished products decked out in more khakis and flimsy white tee-shirts. We were then stuffed into another cell, where we were served dinner out of brown paper bags. A smashed bologna sandwich was the special for the night, complemented by an apple and a small box of juice. I saved the apple for last, crunching into it until the core was left, my eyes shifting whenever someone made a move.

Soon after, I was called out the cell along with some other inmates. Two C.O.s tossed us all a pillowcase. I looked down at mine and saw two very worn-looking sheets and a folded piece of sandpaper that they were passing off as a blanket. All I could do was shake my head for putting myself in a situation like this.

The ten of us were led to an elevator and taken up to the fourth floor. The door slid open and another C.O. stood on the other side. "New tenants for you," the C.O. on the elevator said. He handed his coworker a stack of index cards. "Step off the elevator and line up against the wall, you convicts." He let out a chuckle as he said it. Stepping back onto the elevator, he gave a military salute. "I'm gone, Charlie. Watch these assholes." The elevator slid closed.

"Okay, fellas, this is your new house until further notice."

He recited his "house rules" and ended it by saying, "Don't fuck with me and you give me no reason to fuck with you." He received a few nods of agreement and then turned and unlocked a door. "These are the bed assignments. Wright, four twenty-three upper."

I came off the wall and walked through the door. "Second tier," he said, behind me. A few guys were standing to my right, talking as they watched me make my entrance. I surveyed the whole layout as I followed the numbers on the wall. There were two floors with at least thirty rooms on each level. Some inmates were perched on the second-floor railing, checking out who was checking in. A number of others were sitting around tables on the first floor, hands clutched around cards, dominoes or chess pieces. I came to the steps and took them two at a time.

Doing nine months in that county gave me time to pick up a few prison rules from people who had done a bid or two. The thing that really stuck in my head was, always look a man in the eye. This was what convicts would call a "mental chin-check". Look away as someone looked at you, and that could instantly label you as potential prey. So as I walked the second tier, I gave everyone I passed a brief shot of direct eye contact. Not too much, but enough to let any vulture know that there wasn't going to be any taking of food or manhood this way.

I came to the room assigned to me. The door was closed and a piece of toilet paper was hung on the small glass window, not allowing me to peek inside. I grabbed the knob, turned it and pulled the door open. Before the fat Mexican, who was stooped down on the toilet, could say a word, I pushed the door closed.

"First time, huh?" The voice came from the room directly next to the one I was going to be staying in. The door was cracked and an old black guy was laid on the lower bunk. "The toilet paper to the window is the "do not disturb" sign." He let out a chuckle.

"Yeah, I see." I dropped the pillowcase and leaned on the railing.

The scene was depressing. Guys sat around playing games and doing whatever they could to kill time. There was a small crowd of guys standing around a desk in the middle of the room. One guy was holding a Bible and quoting verses while the others listened. When he finished, another guy wearing Muslim headgear took over and attempted to dispel everything the other guy had just said. I soon found out that, amongst the prison population, religion is the most debated topic hands down. I guess it was just another way to pass time for some.

The phone area caught my attention as I scoured the rest of the place. There were five phones and all of them were occupied. I was yearning to hear Taj's voice just so that I would feel a little better. Talking to her was the cure for my prison blues since day one because she would only have encouraging words to offer me. My heart always smiled when I thought of her and my son.

One guy stepped away from the phone after cursing into it and slamming it down. Obviously, he didn't like what was said on the other end. I headed toward the stairs. My mood instantly changed, anticipating speaking to the people I loved with all my heart. The heat from the mad guy's hand was still on the handle of the phone. I put the receiver to my ear and almost choked when I got a whiff of the mouthpiece. I wanted to call him back and tell him he forgot to take his breath with him. My flimsy tee-shirt was used to wipe away whatever it was that contaminated that phone. I poked at the keypad, making sure the mouthpiece didn't rub against my lips.

After a couple of rings, Taj's voice came on the line. Her "hello" was interrupted by a recording advising her that the call was from a federal prison and the call was being recorded. Before the message was over, the line clicked.

"Hey, baby!" she cried softly into the phone. "Where are you?"

"Oklahoma City, baby, and somewhere I'll probably never ride through or visit ever again in life."

"It can't be that bad." She sighed heavily into the phone. "I saw on the BOP's website that you're going to Forrest City, Arkansas, so that means I will be able to hold you in my arms in a week or so."

It had been almost ten months since I had last touched my wife. During my time in the county jail, we communicated through a phone while on visits. Plexiglas separated us. No holding hands, no hugs, no kisses. It was a torture I could never have imagined, and I anticipated our first contact visit like a kid on the night before Christmas.

Our conversation was interrupted by a voice I had come to despise since the beginning of it all.

"You have one minute remaining," the operator advised.

Taj let out a sigh. "Ooooh, she makes me sick!"

Her soft laughter drew a smile from my face. "Yeah, well, we have to tolerate her for a minute, baby."

The silence on her end told a story, and even though I was the one whose freedom had been taken away, in my heart, I knew that my wife was also doing hard time.

"Kiss my son goodnight for me." I took a deep breath. "I love you."

"I love you more."

"Impossible."

Those were three lines we shared for years. We had spoken them religiously, day-in and day-out. Our days began with them, and our nights were ended with them. But the real beauty of it was that whoever said "I love you" first, always got to say "impossible". Taj hadn't had a chance to say "I love you" first in nine months.

No words passed until the operator gave us a ten-second warning. My eyes fell to the floor. "I'll call you tomorrow."

"Okay, baby, talk to you later."

The line went dead. I hung the phone up and headed back up the stairs.

"Lockdown, fellas!" a voice yelled.

The C.O. was on the first floor shooing guys to their cells like they were little kids. An intense card game ended when one guy stood up and slammed the last few plays of his hand. After he gave his partner a fist bump, he jokingly insulted the two other guys at the table and didn't stop until he made it to his cell on the first floor.

Pillowcase in the same place it was when I dropped it, I scooped it up and made sure it was safe to go into my cell. I could hear what sounded like a growling bear as I turned the knob, and it got louder and louder with every inch I opened the door. I shook my head and prepared myself for a long stay.

CHAPTER 6

I spent three days in Oklahoma City. The last two weren't so bad. The bear was shipped out the second day I was there, so I had the room to myself for the remainder of my stay. I only came out of my cell to eat, take a shower, or to use the phone. There were three rooms where inmates watched TV, but I preferred to read. When I wasn't reading, my thoughts were consumed by getting through the time I had to do. I felt like the end was never going to come.
It was in the middle of the night when keys were rattling at my door. I turned over to see C.O. stick his head in. "Wright, time to go!"

<><><>

Con Air touched down in Memphis, Tennessee on a delightful spring day. The pick-up-drop-off routine took place and my name was called over the intercom. I got up and made my way to the back of the plane, where I recited my name and inmate number to a woman in a Bureau Of Prison's uniform. Once off the plane, I was patted down and yelled at. The noise from the engines made it hard to hear anything, so the C.O.s had to holler out their commands.
"Line up over by that bus!"
Another BOP officer was giving orders. He pointed to an area where several other inmates stood along the side of a white passenger bus. I shuffled over and reached the end of the line, glad not to have to take another step. A sunburned C.O. in Oklahoma obviously wanted to inflict pain on me in some way. I told him the shackles were too tight when he put them on, but all

he said was, "It won't kill you," and went on about his business. I gave him the benefit of the doubt and assumed he was an asshole to all inmates and not just some racist ass cowboy.

The line grew longer, almost out-stretching the lengthy freight. Two white guys were talking about what they had heard about doing time in Forrest City.

"It's supposed to be a low-security prison, but they run it like a medium," one of them complained.

"The food is horrible, I heard."

The other guy shook his head at hearing that news.

That went on for a few minutes, and I just assumed that the two guys spent a lot of their time talking about what could make prison a little more bearable. Throw in more amenities and a few more privileges, and they would gladly do time.

A BOP uniform broke away from a meeting with his counterparts and stepped up onto the bus. Moments later, inmates began to file from the bus and into a line destined for Con Air. Faces of all races, but, by far, predominantly black. I lowered my head and studied my shackled wrists.

"Kay, what up!"

I was startled to hear my name called, loud and clear, even over the sound of the plane's engine. I looked at the line about to board the plane. It belonged to Wes, a guy I had dealt with in Decatur. He got knocked off on the highway with five kilos, but I hadn't seen or heard anything about him since that incident. It was like he just fell off the face of the earth. He was one of Khalid's workers, so I was kind of sure who the dope belonged to. He was also the person who introduced me to the informant. The same one I had sold three ounces of crack cocaine.

"You headed to Forrest Shitty?" Wes asked.

The two white guys in front of me found it funny.

"Told, ya," one said to the other.

"Yeah." I was tuned into Wes' demeanor.

"I'll holla at you when I get back." His line started to move. "I gotta kick it with you."

I had a lot of questions, but no time to ask. And, I was pretty sure that Wes had all the answers.

Once the bus was empty, we boarded and got treated to a brown paper bag lunch. A cold chicken sandwich and an apple were its contents. I offered the sandwich to one of the white guys after feeling how cold the wrapper on the sandwich was. I settled for a few bites of the apple. Stretched out as good as anybody could manage with shackles on, I made good use of the headrest and gazed out the window.

Con Air was loaded and rumbled over the tarmac, tail, and wings shaking as if they would fall off at any time. A few machine-gun holders gave the plane a salute and then walked over to a black van. They stood there until Con Air took flight, black smoke left in its wake. The bus shifted into gear. Moments later, I found myself fascinated by the sight of people driving by in cars. The time in the county jail had taken its toll on me.

The muddy waters of the mighty Mississippi River didn't appear to look safe for fish or humans, and I declared that the "dirty south" had earned its name legitimately. A "Welcome to Arkansas" sign was posted on the bridge we drove over. After the bus crossed that bridge, cows outnumbered people ten-to-one until an hour or so later when the town of Forrest City made way for us. A statue of a man on a horse stood high on one side of the road. Civil War hero was my guess, but a guy seated somewhere in the back of the bus shared a piece of American history with everybody.

"That's Nathan Bedford Forrest." He had a hillbilly accent. "He was the Grand Wizard of the Ku Klux Klan."

"Shut the fuck up, honky!" someone yelled.

A rumble of laughter was interrupted by a voice over the intercom.

"No racial slurs will be tolerated on this bus."

I looked toward the front where three C.O.s were stationed. A steel cage protected them from a possible hijack attempt by anybody who decided that they wanted to delay their trip to prison. And if that didn't work, the guns holstered at their sides were adequate enough backup plans. At the sight of upcoming cars and obvious citizens of the small town, everyone's attention seemed to turn to the activities that were going on along the street the bus was riding down. And as soon as women were spotted, they were unknowingly gang raped by the eyes of a busload of sex-deprived hounds.

"Damn, look at dat ass on her!" One guy squealed. "I would fuck her fa' days!"

"That's what I'm talking about." Another horn-dog said. "You see those tits on that cow?"

An old lady with a hunchback wobbled down the sidewalk with the help of a cane.

"I would bang her out right now!"

Suddenly, the town turned into flat land and nothing but blue skies for miles and miles. The place had to be about two blocks long and a block wide, at the most. The bus made a right turn a few minutes later, and I saw what looked to be larger than the town, itself, on the horizon. It was fortress-like, with tall fences and plenty of barbed-wire. A number of buildings made its own skyline, and I realized that it was going to be my place of residence for a while.

CHAPTER 7

We stood around in a holding cell after going through the prison check-in. They stuffed close to forty of us in a cell probably made for five people, and we all were decked-out in cucumber-green jumpsuits. The only fresh air we got was from the slot in the door where food trays were passed, and that wasn't opened until a Bernie Mac look-a-like complained about the lack of oxygen. He cursed a few times and talked about writing people up, and how he had just come from a medical facility. He even went so far as to ask for the lieutenant, and that's when they opened the slot. The lieutenant was obviously capable of making heads roll if inmates were treated unfairly, and Bernie probably had a few years under his belt to know that. I just hoped the sweat that poured from his forehead wasn't a sign of an oncoming heart attack.

When a C.O. swung the cell door open, I was more thankful for the air than the fact that a very attractive young black woman stood there with a clipboard in her hand. Whispered "damn's echoed off the cell walls.

"When I call your name, step out, grab a bedroll, and line-up by the door." Her tone was business-like. "Name and number before you go through this door. Lucas is first."

We were met by more guards as we came out the cell, who directed us to a stack of bedrolls. Then we were given a speech by a cowboy boot-wearing lieutenant, whose closing line was, "Don't get in no shit, and you won't be in no shit."

He let it linger as he gave everyone a once-over. Walking away, he reached a sun-tanned hand into his shirt pocket and pulled out a pack of Marlboros.

Two C.O.s headed the line as we filed out the door, bedrolls under our arms. I didn't know what to expect as I came through the door and observed the neatly cut grass with paths of concrete trails that veered off into different areas of the prison. I then noticed the absence of trees. The sun was directly overhead and the thought of relaxing under a shade tree crossed my mind. But the only shade that was cast down came courtesy of forty-foot high light poles that were positioned throughout the immense prison yard.

Concrete dominated the architecture of the entire complex. Three buildings stood tall over a plaza-like layout, complete with a prison strip mall. But instead of House of Fades, Singleton's Cleaners, or Coney Island, the plaza was home to BARBERSHOP, LAUNDRY, and COMMISSARY. There were other offices and departments stationed in the L-shaped block of cement, and I was sure I was going to find enough time to visit each and every one of them.

"These are the living quarters," one of the C.O.s said, as he gestured to Forrest City's skyline. "Stay in your own unit. Get caught in the wrong unit and you're going to the hole."

The three buildings were identical in structure, two stories tall with barred windows. Huge block letters hung high on their sides. We were officially introduced to our new homes; WYNNE, MARIETTA, and HELENA.

Heads were posted in the windows of the buildings, while two C.O.s stood on the steel balcony of the building we were approaching. One was puffing on a cigarette and talking at the same time. His buddy was leaning on the rail, shaking his head as he looked in our direction.

"Some of those for me, Blaine?"

"A few," one of the C.O.s leading us replied.

If it weren't for the fact that the officer who asked the question was running neck and neck with Wesley Snipes on the complexion side of things, I would've taken his remark as being racist. It sounded like something one slave owner would've said to another. But he still managed to make me feel like I wasn't anything but a body in a green jumpsuit.

Blade led the way as the two officers came down the steps and greeted their co-workers. Index cards exchanged hands while Blade ran his mouth about some chick.

"Yeah, she came to the crib for a minute," he said as he laughed. "And with a head on her shoulders like that, that's all it takes!"

They laughed as if they were just hanging out, shooting the breeze, talking about what normal people do. One of the guys mentioned something about how he went to the store, which to me, sounded like the greatest thing in the world.

"Freedom is sweet," I whispered. I then resisted the urge to punch myself in the eye.

Their chat ended and Blade's partner called names from the index cards he was handed. When he finished, he and Blade marched up the steps followed by a row of green suits and disappeared through a steel door. We continued on our way to the next building, where two more C.O.s were waiting. Index cards exchanged hands and my name was called shortly after. I didn't know what to expect as a linebacker-sized C.O. opened the first-floor door and led us into our "living quarters."

The distinctive smell of feet hit me when I entered. Four inmates were assuming different positions as they held phones to their ears at booths set-up in the entryway. Two other inmates leaned on the opposite wall, waiting for the phone, I assumed. The line took a right turn and slowly stopped as the C.O. stood at a door to a small office. In the office were a desk, chair, and microwave that sat on a mini fridge.

"I'm Officer McKinney," he said in a nonchalant southern drawl. "All I wanna do is my eight hours. Anything else makes it hard on all of us." He went into the office and grabbed a folder off the desk. "I don't wanna have to do any paperwork. If I gotta do paperwork, somebody's going to the Special Housing Unit. That's the 'hole' for you first-timers that watch a lot of movies."

I chuckled along with a couple of others. That must've been every C.O.'s go-to threat when it came to keeping inmates in check. He went through the index cards and called names, giving us our cell numbers and further instructions. My cell was 148 upper. The top bunk. That meant somebody would be sleeping on the bottom bunk, my cellmate.

"This is my dorm when I'm here," McKinney said, poking a finger into his barreled chest. "And I like my dorm quiet. That's all I ask." His lip curled into a small smile. "That's it, fellas. Your cubes are that way." He pointed behind us. "Enjoy your stay at Forrest City." The office door closed behind him.

Our group did an about-face into McKinney's dorm. No barred cells with locks on them. Instead, there were concrete walled cubicles lined up and down a long aisle. Numbers were printed on each one, so I went out searching for my cell as our group split up.

Everyday jail life looked to be taking place as I walked down the aisle. I passed an activity room where guys sat around tables playing cards and chess. Others had on headphones while they stared up at televisions that were mounted on walls. Some guys lay in their bunks, some taking naps while others read books or magazines. Whenever the door to the activity room swung open, the sound of loud trash-talking rushed out into the otherwise peaceful dorm area.

The cubicles housed a bunk bed, two three-foot-high lockers and a small steel desk that hung from the concrete wall. An uncomfortable-looking steel chair was attached to the wall also. The cubes were about the size of a spacious bathroom, and I realized that I was going to have to share a very small amount of space with another guy.

I was near my cell when a lanky bald guy in a gray sweatsuit came out of a cubicle. He had a broom and a dustpan in his hand as if he had just cleaned up, and toted a spray bottle that dangled from his hip. "Where you from, shawty?" he asked in a friendly manner. The accent was countrified and instantly recognizable as being from Atlanta. "Shawty" was the dead giveaway.

I tucked my bedroll in a little more as I glanced at the numbers on the cubicles. "Detroit."

A smile came to his face and he got a little animated. "Motor City! Oh, yo' boy done had some good times in the D!" His smile convinced me. "I thought the "A" had all the baddest broads, but y'all got it goin' on up north." Pause, then, "What cube you in, shawty?"

"One forty-eight upper." His southern hospitality was welcomed under the circumstances.

"Oh, that's on the otha side," he said as he gestured over his shoulder. "You in there with New York's crazy ass."

His burst of laughter caught me off guard.

"Is that good or bad?"

He continued laughing as if a funny joke had been told. "Nawl, shawty," he said, waving a hand and calming himself. "You cool. That's just a funny ass nigga."

Right there on the spot, I prayed that the guy meant Eddie Murphy-funny and not funny in a strange kind of way. But whatever it was about this "New York" guy, it really had him cracking up. A glimpse of his watch changed the conversation.

"If you wanna go somewhere, they about to call the ten-minute move." He went back into his cube and put the cleaning supplies away. With a pep in his step, he rushed past me and said, "Holla at me, shawty, if you need something."

Before I could say anything, ATL was gone. I turned down the aisle that led to my cube, somewhat relieved that my first prison encounter wasn't with a six-eight dude wearing Kool-Aid as lipstick with a shank in his hand. I made it to my cube and stood there as I looked over my new home. Two pairs of shoes were under the bottom bunk. A couple of plastic chairs were stacked in the corner next to one of the lockers. No sign of my cell mate. His bunk was neatly made and the floor had a shine to it like it had been recently waxed. A bare mattress waited for me on the top bunk, so I took the bedroll and started making my bed, wondering how I was going to make it for two years sharing an 8-by-8 cubicle with a guy named "New York".

I used one of the chairs as a stepping stool to get my bunk in order and was able to scan the whole dorm from front to back. Four rows of cubicles lined the dorm, with two against each wall and the other two in the middle of the dorm, back-to-back to one another. A five-foot high block wall was the only thing that separated the middle cubes. My bunk was only inches away from the top bunk in the cube on the other side of the wall, meaning that if I slept at the head of the bed, I would only be inches away from the guy who slept there. I prayed that he was somebody with very good hygiene.

My bunk was made, so I stepped down off the chair and took a seat, not really knowing what my next move was. I felt lost as I sat there, confronted by a locker that a midget would have a problem fitting into. I assumed that whatever belongings I accumulated during my stay would go there, my life downsized tremendously in every aspect. The front of the cubicle's wall was only a few feet high, so there was no privacy as the traffic in the aisle got heavy all of a sudden. I heard the trash-talkers exit the TV room and continue their conversation.

"Nigga, yo' game weak as hell!" one of them yelled. "Get yo' bitch out the game and it's over fa you!"

"Whateva, nigga!" His voice echoed throughout the dorm. "I'll be back on the next move!"

I didn't pay any attention to the guys that passed by until, out the corner of my eye, I noticed a guy go by and then stop. After he took a few steps backward, I turned to see what he was up to.

"What up, homey?" he said, resting his hands on the block wall. He was nowhere near intimidating. His slim frame and short stature didn't send any alarms, nor did his cocked-eyed stare. A mouth full of gold teeth and a du-rag that was tied tightly on his pea sized head, his appearance more comical than menacing. He showed more gold as he said, "Where you from, homey?"

I stood up, giving him a chance to see that he didn't stand a chance against this solid one-hundred and ninety pounds, just in case he was thinking about trying me, a skinny guy with gold teeth wasn't going to get the jump on me if something went down.

"Detroit," I replied with a little extra bass in my voice.

The little guy held a balled fist to his mouth and started turning in circles like he was doing an Indian rain dance. I assumed the screeching noise he made was laughter.

"Mane, I got plenty hoes in Detroit," he said as he came to a stop. Dark brown gums accompanied his golden smile, and if I had ever seen him once – if only for a split second – in the D, I most definitely would've remembered a spotting of his sort. And the way he said "man" I knew that he was from Memphis.

The accent was southern, and so was his hospitable manner, something I had welcomed since my days of traveling outside of the Motor City. Walking up to a stranger and starting a conversation that didn't involve "Can you spare some change?" was very rare where I was from. And even though Decatur wasn't considered south, the people there didn't have a problem opening up to people they didn't know.

I held off laughter as I reached over and swung open both doors to the locker that I assumed was mine. It was empty except for a plastic mirror that was stuck on one of the doors. I was pleasantly surprised by the smell of cologne that lingered in such a place as a steel prison locker.

"Yeah, mane, they love a real playa' up in Detroit," he commented as I turned to him. "I still got a crib up there, mane. Five bedrooms, marble throughout dat bitch and er'thang."

"Oh, yeah?" It was starting to become a little entertaining. "What part of town is it on?"

It took a second before he replied. "The west side...yeah, the west side."

"What street?" I shot back.

He looked as if I had asked him what the capital of Mars was.

"Mane, I ain't been up der' in a minute, but I'ma call one of my hoes and ask her. She still livin' in the crib with three of my otha' hoes."

So he was one of those types. It was cool, though, because he was kind of amusing and I had nothing else to do.

Guys were shuffling through the aisle while we stood there. Some acknowledged me with words, while some gave a brief glance as they went on their way. But when a stump of a Mexican guy waddled past and waved my golden cohort off, accompanied by a shake of the head and a chuckle, I knew that my assessment was not too far off.

After mentioning something about a Range Rover, two BMWs, and a winter crib in Utah, he reached into the pocket of his three sizes too big sagging gray jogging pants. He came out with a green pouch of tobacco.

"You smoke, Detroit?"

"Nah, man," I said, looking down at the offering. "Thanks, though."

He shook his head as he began the process of rolling up his cigarette. "A nigga hurtin' right now, mane. They gotta pimp smokin' roll-ups and shit. But a true playa always come up."

A laughed escaped me when he looked over at me as he swiped the cigarette paper with a saliva-soaked tongue. I think if he hadn't been cock-eyed, he would've been just as funny.

"TEN MINUTE MOVE, TEN MINUTE MOVE"

The announcement over the intercom caused traffic through the dorm to pick up even more.

"What does that mean?" I asked him.

He gave his creation a final twisting suck. "If you tryin' to go to the yard or somewhere, you betta go now. I'm headed to Wynne Unit to grab somethin'. Get at me, Detroit."

The cigarette hung from his lips as he turned and sagged down the aisle, everything but the soles of his shoes hidden by his long pant legs.

Passing up an opportunity to go outside and breathe in some fresh air, was something I couldn't see myself doing in the foreseeable future. So, I figured I would take a trip to the yard. I didn't know where it was exactly, but I was pretty sure it wasn't going to be hard to find. For insurance, I trailed behind two older white guys as they passed me and headed to the exit. They were wearing headbands and prison active wear, everything in some shade of gray. A mention of running a few miles caught my ear as I followed a few feet behind.

Before getting to the exit, I had been asked the question "Where you from?" way too many times. I switched up the answer just to take the repetition out of it. "Detroit", "The Motor City", "Motown", I called out as I stayed in stride. Why it seemed to be such an issue was beyond me. I chalked it up as the southern hospitality thing, and for a second I felt guilty about not stopping and asking each person how was prison treating them.

<><><>

I came out the door and had to navigate through a crowd of guys as they stood out in front of the building, some talking while others smoked cigarettes, staring off into nowhere. The rest of the compound was alive with inmates coming and going, the two joggers lost amongst a sea of men wearing the exact same sweat suits. I could see the basketball court from where I was standing, so I started walking and took in the scenery.

"Any rastas on de bus, mon?" a Jamaican guy asked as I passed him in traffic.

"Not sure, mon." I continued my stride while hoping the guy didn't take offense to my mocking him.

I made it to the gate just as the same voice came over the intercom.

"THE MOVE HAS ENDED. THE COMPOUND IS NOW CLOSED"

A black guy abruptly stopped as he made it to the gate, apparently disgusted at the announcement.

"Shit," he yelled, sweat drenched tee-shirt plastered to his chest.

He leaned against the fence, hands on his knees, bent over like he had just ran a marathon. I made my way through a small corridor that connected two small buildings. The traffic in and out of each was heavy with guys clutching rec equipment of all sorts: basketballs, soccer balls, baseball equipment, and even horseshoes. A group of shirtless guys filed out one of the doors, each holding onto blue exercise mats and an ab roller wheel. They disappeared around the corner at the end of the corridor while I picked the door on the right to start my investigation of life behind "the fence".

The sound of clashing pool balls would've usually been music to my ears, especially after I walked into a room filled with eight pool tables and a bunch of inferior pool players. But not even the game I enjoyed most was capable of winning my attention at the moment. Guys were sitting around in chairs while battles took place on every table. Insults were exchanged between players and onlookers after easy shots were missed, causing the room to fill with a burst of loud yelling. Piano music spilled into the mix when a guy opened a door on the other side of the room, revealing an old white guy as he sat at the keyboard. Another door swung open and the rhythmic sound of beating drums could be heard over somebody rapping. There was a lot going on in the building that I never expected to see or hear. There was even a posting on a bulletin board for a yoga class. I found it kind of comical considering where we were.

My investigation continued in the building next door, where exercise bikes and treadmills were occupied by sweaty guys of every shape and color. The smell and humid temperature of the room drove me back out the door and onto the patio area of the rec yard. Shirtless guys were laid out on their mats doing abdominal exercises, a dread-locked inmate leading the workout. Picnic tables took up the other side of the patio. Card games and chess were being played by others who preferred to exercise their minds instead of their bodies. I strolled pass the activities and headed down a set of steps that overlooked the entire yard.

Two baseball diamonds and a football field made up most of the yard. Scores of guys walked or ran on a track that looked to have been man-made from years of being tracked over. It outlined the whole perimeter of the yard and was big enough to allow a guy to walk in peace, and in an attempt to get a piece of mind. I took the steps in search of some of my own. Once I passed the heavily populated basketball courts, I was able to see land beyond the heavily barbed wired fences. Not a farm or house was in sight from where I was. If somebody did escape from the prison, there weren't a lot of places where he could hide. I assumed that was one of the purposes of putting the place out in the middle of nowhere.

Footsteps caused me to turn around as I made it further away from the noise of men at play. A jogger wearing headphones side stepped me and continued around the track, dust kicking in the air with his every stride. I assumed that while doing time, everyone had something they did as a way to make the days go by.

The track was peaceful for the most part. And, after a few laps, I saw myself spending a lot of time going around in circles on the this dirt path. I was able to think without being bothered even though there were others out there with me. Everybody seemed to be in deep thought as they did their laps, and most were probably thinking about everything that was outside of the fences that surrounded us.

I didn't bother to keep up with how many times I went around that track. My mind was on my family, and I couldn't break free of the building anticipation of finally being able to hold Taj's hand and give Dante a big hug. C.O. McKinney advised us that the unit counselor would be in the next day. He was responsible for things like adding my family to my visiting list and other inmate matters. So, I was going to make sure I got in touch with him as soon as possible.

I'd grown immune to the patter of feet coming up behind me after a while. Some of the same joggers had passed me numerous times, so I was used to the flow of things on the track. On the first couple of laps, instinct caused me to turn around to see who was running up on me. I would glance back to make sure everything was cool before continuing ahead. After snitching on Khalid, I felt like I would always have to watch my back.

I had sat in front of nearly two dozen citizens of the United States, one hand on a Bible, the other raised in sworn oath. A U.S. prosecutor stood at my left as he ran off question after question concerning my involvement with Khalid Cartwright. The questions were similar to the ones that agents Hudson and Fraser had asked me when I talked to the Feds, so I gave my previous answers. I never raised my head during those fifteen minutes. I saw none of the faces that sat out in those seats as they listened to a government witness help bring down another man with him. Guilt wouldn't allow me to look them in the eyes. Fear of seeing disgust on their faces caused me to stare blankly down at my hands. And I knew that those two emotions would torment me for as long as I lived. It was my decision to do what I did, so I had to live with the consequences.

I resisted the urge to glance back when I heard the slow trot of a jogger that came up from behind. Instead, I moved to the side to make way for the oncoming runner, but was surprised when a voice accompanied the trot.

"Hey, you in the pickle suit!" the voice called out.

I had on a green jumpsuit, but wasn't sure if the remark was aimed at me.

"Hey, my man in the pickle suit!" the guy yelled louder.

There were other new guys on the track, but none were in earshot of the guy's call. So I stopped to see who was making fun of my uniform.

"Hold up a minute." It was a guy I had seen on the track while I walked. After a few trots, he was close enough for me to notice a gapped-teeth smirk. His drenched sweatsuit told me that he had put in some serious time on the track. But when he used his shirt as a towel to relieve the sweat from his bald head, I could tell that he needed to put in even more miles before he could do the shirtless thing with pride. His trot turned into a swift stride as he came nearer.

"Where you from?" he asked.

Another nosey guy, I thought to myself. "Detroit."

"Word up?" The phrase and accent had New York written all over them. His smirk never left. "What unit they put you in?"

For some reason, I began walking along side of him as he picked up his pace.

"The one with Helena on it," I replied.

"Yo, it's four units in that building," he stated. "Upstairs or down?"

"Down. It had HB on the door."

"We in the same unit." He paused as he nodded his head. "What cube you in?"

"One forty-eight upper."

He came to a stop. I took a few steps and turned to him. That smirk was still in place. He closed the distance between us and, before I could react, he had his hands up as if he was about to give me a hug.

"Whatsup, celly!" he said in a joyous tone, arms spread out like I was supposed to willingly fall into his embrace. I leaped back and prepared to fight for my manhood.

Arms still extended, he let out a burst of laughter and bent over, resting his hands on his knees. I kept my eyes on him, looking out for the old scoop-slam move. When he straightened up, tears were running from his eyes. He managed to suppress his laughter and said, "Yo, you shoulda' seen the look on your face!" More laughter. "You was spooked, son!"

"I wasn't spooked." I replied as I laughed off a sigh of relief. "I just didn't feel like knocking anybody out on my first day in here."

"I was just fuckin' with you. Shit gets boring around this mothafucka." He started walking, with me following his lead.

I thought about what ATL had said. "You must be New York,"

"Yeah, that's me. Which one of them fake ass niggas told you about me?" That smirk wouldn't leave his face.

"Tall guy named ATL."

"That country ass nigga." He chuckled. "He cool, though. Who else you meet?"

"Some cockeyed pimp..."

"Awww shit," he said, stopping me before I finished. "Stop Playin'."

"I'm not playing."

"Nawl, nawl," he replied, shaking his head. "That's the nigga's name."

"Are you serious?"

"Yeah, the nigga always talkin' this big money shit, but ain't coped a noodle from commissary in damn near two years. We started callin' him that 'cause he had to be jokin' about that shit he was talkin'."

New York continued to fill me in on Stop Playin' and some of the other guys in the unit while we circled the track again and again. I laughed more than I had in a very long time as I listened to him make fun of everybody he spoke about. His comedic personality, combined with his accent, made me feel as if I had front seats at a comedy show. I then understood why ATL reacted the way he did when he talked about New York. Not only was he funny, but just for a minute, he was able to take my mind off the time I had in front of me.

An announcement came over the speaker system.

"YARD RECALL!"

"It's time to ride." New York cut off his route and headed toward the exit like everyone else looked to be doing.

"Oh, we have to go now?"

"You can stay out here if you want to." He turned and walked off. "But yo' ass going to the hole."

I heard him giggling. He was being entertained at my expense again. I caught up to him, that smirk was in place as he extended his hand.

"What's your name anyway?"

I glanced down to make sure he didn't have a surprise waiting in his palm. "I'm Kay."

"Alright, Kay," he said, exposing a gap-toothed smile. "Let's get out of here."

When we made it back to the housing unit, the idea of sleeping in a dorm with one-hundred and fifty other people crossed my mind. It didn't seem too appealing. I didn't know how I was going to make it, but, obviously, I didn't have a choice.

New York stopped in the hall where the phones were and told me he had to make a call, so I found my way to my cube amidst the buzz of yelling, running showers, and the slamming of locker doors. I instantly caught the blues, which usually would've been cured by a phone call home. But that was impossible until I saw the counselor. With nothing else to do, I climbed up into my bunk and tried my best to block out all that was going on around me. It was virtually impossible.

New York came into the cube and opened his locker. I broke my stare with the ceiling and glanced over. He was stripped down to his boxers, a towel thrown over his shoulder. It kind of caught me by surprise until I realized the cubicle was both our home for now.

"Hey, if you need something my locker gon' be open. Don't eat all my shit up," he said, before holding up a radio. "You need these to watch TV, so you can use mine 'til you get some."

He picked up his shaving bag and left out the cubicle. I sat up and jumped down onto the concrete floor, picking up New York's headphones as I made my way to the TV room. I wasn't really interested in watching anything at the moment, but I needed something to do just to hold off the looming depression. Lying down always brought it on.

There were plenty of nationalities represented in the dorm. Some Mexicans sat in one cube speaking in their native tongue and sounding more like they were arguing than having a civil conversation. Two cubes away, a lone Arab guy was kneeled over on a prayer rug, bowing repeatedly like an obedient servant. A chess game was being played in a cube near the entrance of the TV room. A dreadlocked guy wearing a big red, yellow and green hat shouted, "Bumbaclot!" as his opponent picked up a chess piece and slammed it down. He turned to me and shook his head before I pulled the door open to the TV room.

I got a few stares from some of the guys sitting around in plastic chairs as I stood inside the door. Their attention then went back to programs that were playing on the six televisions that hung from the walls in various locations around the room. Almost everyone had headphones on except for a couple of guys who were seated at tables playing cards or other board games. I walked over to an empty chair and took a seat.

Each television played a different program, but only one caught my attention. Shaq was dunking on Tim Duncan as I put the headphones on and fumbled with the buttons. I got the radio on but only heard the sounds of rap music playing. Confused, I turned to a head-bobbing black guy sitting a few feet away from me. It took a second for me to catch his attention. He removed an earplug and instantly realized my situation.

"Whatever TV you want to listen to, tune in to the station on the TV." He pointed up to the television that the game was on. "That's ninety-two point five."

I gave him a nod of appreciation and found the station on the radio.

The game ended without me knowing who had won. I was lost in my own thoughts, homesick. I returned to my cube, where I found New York seated at the steel desk. His face was glued to the paper he was gliding a pen over. I assumed he was writing a letter to someone. I returned his headphones to his locker and climbed back up on my bunk. I knew what would happen if my head hit the pillow, but I did it anyway.

"This is a no stress cube."

I rolled over and New York was still writing. "Just thinking," I said, looking down at him.

"Well, tell me what you think about this."

He moved away from the desk and began to use it as an instrument, tapping lightly on it to create a smooth beat. His shoulders began to get into the groove, and then a soulful voice joined the beat, a voice that I never would've expected to come from such a comical guy. He sung about a runaway love as I sat there mesmerized by what I was hearing. I was caught-up in the beat and his vocals. An audience of two guys stopped outside the cube and listened in.

"He the truth," one of them said, shaking his head.

We continued to listen until New York ended the song with a blending of a soft drum roll while carrying a note. The two guys came inside and gave New York well deserved praise, exchanging fist bumps and pats on the back. When they walked off, New York turned to me. "What you think?" he asked, shifting papers in hands.

I told him the truth. "That was good, man. Real good. Did you write that?"

He put the papers in a folder, stood up and put it in his locker. "Yeah, I write a little bit."

"You have some more?" I really wanted to hear another one.

He pointed to his locker. "I probably got a few hundred in there. Been writing since I got locked-up."

"Are you thinking about getting into the music business when you get out? You just performed a hit song right there."

He closed his locker. "I don't know," he said, disappearing in the bunk below. "I got fifteen years left."

A voice yelled "count time", causing me to look to the front of the dorm. Two C.O.s were walking around herding inmates out of the TV rooms and bathrooms. Everyone returned to their cube as the C.O.s stood at the front. Once every inmate was in their cube, the officers came down the aisle and did a headcount. There was total silence as they did their job, something I assumed was a rule. After they finished counting, one of them yelled, "Count clear! Quiet time!" The dorm went completely dark seconds later.

Once my eyes adjusted to the darkness, I saw New York get up and go into his locker. He came out with a pack of cigars. "You smoke?"

"Nawl," I said, rolling over on my back.

I heard his locker close and watched him walk toward the bathroom. I found myself repeating the hook of New York's song as I laid up there in the dark. After only hearing it one time, it was stuck in my head. It was clearly a song that could find heavy rotation on the radio, one of those songs that you would unconsciously find yourself singing along with even when it wasn't playing, just like I was doing. It was that good. My new celly had some talent, but it was unfortunate that he had a lot of time to do.

The bathroom was calling me, so I got off my bunk and navigated my way to the only lighted area in the dorm. As soon as I got near it, I could see and smell the stench of cigarette smoke. One guy was at the entrance puffing and passing a cigarette to another guy. More smokers were hanging out in the bathroom, talking and laughing as they filled their lungs with nicotine. I found an empty urinal amongst the heavy traffic and clouds of smoke. After taking a few whiffs, it was evident that cigarettes weren't the only thing being smoked.

I flushed the urinal and turned to see New York leaning against a stall door.

"What's up, son?" He took a puff of his cigar.

"Nothing really. I guess go to sleep."

"Word." He released a cloud of smoke. "I know how that first night is but you'll get used to it."

I let out a sigh. "You think?"

New York pointed over toward the shower stall, where Stop Playin' was in a conversation with a guy that came on the bus with me.

"Hey, nigga," he called out to Stop Playin'. "Stop all that damn lyin'! Nigga's gon' still fuck with you."

Stop Playin' excused himself and walked over to us. His du-rag was tied tightly over his head and a rolled-up cigarette dangled from his lips as he began to speak. "Mane, there you go with that bullshit. You New York niggas always got something to say."

That smirk appeared on New York's face. "That's 'cause you Memphis niggas always comin' up in here talking 'bout y'all coppin' candy-coated helicopters and shit."

I laughed along with my celly while Stop Playin' shook his head. Another guy with a mouth full of gold teeth came over and stood next to Stop Playin'. He smiled as he took the rolled-up cigarette from his comrade.

"Mane, we can't help it 'cause we get money down south. You niggas in the north only get money in the summer 'cause it's too cold to come out in the winter." He turned to his boy. "See, down here, we get money all year round," he said as he twirled a skinny finger in a circle. He gave his boy a fist bump.

New York shook his head as that smirk turned into a laugh. "Yo, take y'all country asses in there and polish them damn golds and go to bed."

I was hoping nobody was offended by me laughing. Stop Playin' turned to leave as his buddy followed. New York stubbed out his cigar and was still chuckling as we returned to our cube. He sat down on his bunk and slid off his shoes while I returned to the place I had been avoiding all day. The flimsy pillow did nothing to support my head, so I doubled it over and tried to get as comfortable as possible.

"Don't let me hear you up there cryin' and shit."

I smiled, appreciating the humor at such a dark time. "I'm cool, man."

"Just fuckin' with you." He tapped the bottom of my bunk. "See you in the a.m."

I was tired, depressed, and homesick. New York helped me in a way, but I needed sleep. It was the only way to escape the situation, even if it was just for a few hours. My eyes grew heavy as I stared through the darkness up at the concrete ceiling. Pictures of Taj, Dante, and my Mom flashed through my mind. I then looked back into the past, and how I'd made my own path to prison.

CHAPTER 8

From The Jump

I was born and raised in the Motor City, Detroit, Michigan. The only child of parents who were also only children, I didn't have much of a family while growing up. It had always been just us until my dad decided he had somewhere else better to be than at home with his wife and son. After he left, I didn't see much of him at all. The only time his presence was felt, was when my mom received the monthly checks he sent through the mail. He never even had the decency to at least drop them off, something that caused me to despise him at times. Even before he left, we had never bonded like a normal father and son. He would come in from work and walk past me like I was just a fixture in the house. Whenever he talked to my mom about me, which was not often, he referred to me as "that boy", like I was some kid down the street instead of his son. He died when I was fifteen, and the only reason that I did shed a tear was because my mom cried endlessly at his funeral, something that hurt me more than anything. My mom was my everything, and to see her cry the way she did, only caused me to dislike him more, even in death.

I can't say that I was an average kid. Being an only child caused me to believe that I didn't need anyone but my mom and myself. She was my best friend. If I needed someone to talk to, she was always there, no matter how small it was. Her job as a registered nurse took up most of her schedule, but she always made sure we spent quality time together whenever she got the chance. Dinner at the kitchen table was our ritual unless she worked overtime. A hug and kiss was always required before leaving the house. My mom loved me, and a day didn't go by when I didn't feel that love. I'll be the first to admit that she had me spoiled, as well.

What she didn't have in time, she made up for in acts of kindness in the form of almost anything I wanted that was in reason. The newest toys I received as a child, turned into the latest game systems and name brand clothes as I got older. As long as I got good grades in school and took out the garbage, I had it made. She was a strong believer that education was the key to living a successful life, and didn't tolerate bad grades or bad grammar. Reading books were mandatory while I was growing up. Before I touched a game controller, some chapters had to be read. If I slipped and used "ain't" or "cain't", chapters had to be read. I used to catch hell from kids in school about the way I talked, but it never bothered me because I thought it was kind of lame to tease somebody for doing something correctly.

There was a time when I did try to be sociable to a few kids in the neighborhood by inviting them over to play with me. But after the first time, they wanted to come over every day. I then felt like my space was being invaded, so I quickly brought that to an end. It was then that I realized I was a loner, and I liked it that way.

My loner ways continued through high school. I was the kid you'd always see by himself, not quite a nerd, but not popular by any means. I wasn't interested in hanging out with the "in crowd", even though I held my own when it came to fashion. Sports didn't catch my interest, so I never attended football or basketball games. Once I was done with my last class, I would high-tail it home and seclude myself in the comfort of my bedroom. Mom never encouraged me to get out and hang with other people, and because of the violence that took place on a daily basis in the city, I believe she felt more secure with me being in the house and not out in the streets.

As for girlfriends, I had a couple while in high school. There was nothing serious going on but a lot of tongue kissing and titty-sucking. Having sex had never entered my mind, and I believe it was the reason the relationships didn't last. Instead of getting butt-naked after hours of making-out, I would grab my book bag and head straight for the door, completely satisfied. After doing that a few times, I would usually see them the next day holding hands with some other willing participant. It was cool, though, because I had gotten what I wanted. Graduating high school, still a virgin, didn't bother me at all.

The day of my graduation, my mom told me something I had no knowledge of. To my surprise, I was the beneficiary of a trust fund started by my father when I was born. It was the only gesture from him that caused me to think of him as a real father, and greatly appreciated. After getting access to the one hundred thousand dollars, I went all out.

Mom really didn't mind me buying a brand new convertible Mustang 5.0 with all the accessories. Nor did she make a big fuss when I came home with a carload of new clothes on an almost every day basis. She made it clear that the money was mine to do whatever I pleased. But when she laid eyes on a diamond-flooded medallion and gold chain that I spent close to seven thousand dollars on, well, that was a little too much for her.

"I don't like it," she said in a calm manner. "You look like a drug dealer."

Never wanting to disappoint the one person that I could just look at and feel loved, I returned the chain. I replaced it with a bracelet that had a few diamonds in it, but a little less flashy. I could have imagined what she would have said had she known about the forty-four snub-nosed I bought that same afternoon.

If a guy from my neighborhood hadn't basically walked up to me and insisted I buy a "small revolver with plenty kick", I never would have thought about owning a gun.

"You need this for them jackers!" He spoke adamantly. "Niggas would love to catch you slippin' in this 'Stang!"

He sounded like a concerned relative, and by the time he was done, I was holding a forty-five snub-nosed in a very nervous and trembling hand.

It took a few days before I got over the fright of actually taking aim with the gun. I would wait until mom was asleep and then practice shooting at imaginary targets in my room. Posters of Detroit Pistons stars turned into gun-toting bad guys, and after a couple of weeks, the feeling of that gun in my hand became as natural as lacing up my shoes. I didn't want to take the chance of my mom finding the gun, so I kept it snuggled in between the seat in my car. I rode with it faithfully, sometimes even forgetting that it was there. Little did I know, it would eventually save my life, and while doing so, take one in return.

CHAPTER 9

A Summer To Remember

Twelve years of school had taken its toll on me, but because of my mom, I continued my education immediately after graduating. I knew I wasn't ready for any kind of four-year college. I escaped high school with a B-minus average, but only because I didn't fully apply myself. So, I had real doubts about surviving four more years in college. After convincing my mom that I wasn't ready to do the full-time college thing, I enrolled in Wayne County Community College and spent two years chasing an associate's degree in business management. Once that was accomplished, she gave me a year off to get my head right, letting me enjoy myself before I headed off into the real world. I didn't really know what I wanted to do, but I figured I had enough time to come up with some kind of plan. I was only nineteen so I had plenty of time to get a career, so I thought. But before I knew it, my year was up, and summer had come around again. I was still clueless about what I wanted to do. I knew that I didn't want to work for anybody, so starting my own business of some sort was the obvious choice. I had the money, and all I had to do was find out where to invest. Little did I know, I would invest it, but not how I thought.

<><><>

It was a beautiful summer's evening, and the streets of downtown Detroit were filled with people enjoying the nice weather. Like a lot of others, I drove around and took in the sights and sounds of summer in the city.

Traffic was thick with guys showing off in shined-up cars with big rims, and women in clothes that barely left anything to the imagination. Loud music blared from passing vehicles, and the smell of marijuana was in the air. Jefferson was the place to be if you were young and black.

As I came to a stop at a traffic light, I saw the woman that I fell in love with the moment I laid eyes on her. She was riding shotgun in a white luxury sedan. Her focus was on the passenger in the back seat, laughing as their car came to a stop alongside of mine. The woman in the back glanced over at me as I played it cool and turned the volume up on the Jodeci CD. Then, just as the light turned green, her friend looked over in my direction. Our eyes locked for a brief second. She flashed a smile as the sedan pulled off.

My foot tapped the gas pedal enough for my back-end to fish tail. A half block later, I was staring back into the eyes of the most beautiful woman in the world. "Could you have your friend pull over for a minute?" I peeked at the traffic ahead.

She turned to the driver, then back to me. "Follow us."

I pulled into a gas station and parked alongside of them. They were talking and giggling as I made my way around to the passenger side of the car. The lights from the overhead canopy allowed me to see that she was as beautiful as I'd first thought.

"Miss, could you please step out the car." I stood at her window and offered her a pleasant smile.

The driver laughed. "Are you the police?"

"Yeah," I said while reaching for the door handle. "And I'm arresting your friend for being too pretty in public."

Laughter erupted from the car, and the woman in the back gave the driver a high five. Their friend continued to laugh as she watched me open the door.

"Girl, you better get out before he put his handcuffs on you."

Soft brown eyes stared up at me as she stepped out the car, teasing. "Do you have handcuffs?"

"She's a fool!" one of the women yelled.

A slight breeze pushed a few strands of hair into her face as she leaned against the car. Removing the hair with a manicured hand, she said, "So, Mr. Smooth, what's your name?"

"I'm Kabazza, but you can call me Kay."

"Is that a Muslim name?"

"No," I replied while sneaking a peek at her half shirt that exposed a perfect stomach.

"It's a funny story how I got it. I'll tell you about it when I call you." I watched for her reaction.

"And how do you plan on calling me?" She playfully rolled her neck. "You don't have my number."

"I will when you give it to me."

Her smile told me that I was saying all the right things.

The two women got out the car. "You want something out of here, Taj?"

Without breaking eye contact with me, she replied by saying, "Bottled water is fine."

It seemed as if we both were caught up in a trance as we continued to stare into each other's eyes. Jefferson was filled with cruising cars and rubber-burning motorcycles, but for that brief moment, I didn't see or hear anything but her.

"Taj, huh?" I said, breaking the silence between us. "A beautiful name for a beautiful woman."

She reacted to what I'd said with a blushing burst of laughter. "You swear you're smooth, don't you?"

By the way she was carrying on, you would've thought she was at a comedy show and I'd just hit her with the joke of the night. Her arms flailed and shoulders bounced with enjoyment, accompanied by a laugh that caught me by surprise from its loudness. All the while, I was actually falling in love with her by the second, and it was at the very moment that I knew that I didn't want a minute to pass by without her in my life.

She managed to pull herself together, my shoulder used a leaning post as she suppressed the last of her chuckles.

"I'm glad you liked that one," I replied. "I got a few more if you want to hear them."

"No." She let her hand fall from my shoulder. "I'm fine, Kay."

We were interrupted by the return of the two women. "You done interrogating my girl?" the passenger joked as she ducked into the car.

"Not quite." My eyes met Taj's. "Can I call you so that we can finish?"

The passenger's face appeared at the rear window. "He seems alright, Taj." She gave me a once-over and said, "Give him the number."

"You think so?" Taj joined in on her friends' silliness, but her head-to-toe stare-down was sexy, seductive. She came back to my eyes and held them momentarily. "Okay, I guess I can do that."

Numbers were exchanged and Taj was back in the sedan. Even her wave was cute.

"Bye, Taj." I gave her a wave of my own and started to my car. Her voice turned me around before I could take another step.

"Bye means I'll never see you again." A look of seriousness came over her face.

I digested those words and quickly erased the thought from my mind. "See you later, Taj."

The smile returned. "Later, baby."

CHAPTER 10

I managed to hold off from calling her until the next day. The number she gave me started with an unfamiliar area code, and after asking her about it, I felt like fainting after hearing her response.

"I'm not from here."

Words most definitely could hurt.

"I'm from Illinois. I rode up here with my best friend, Kim. She was the passenger. The driver is her cousin, Mona; she lives here."

It was just my luck that the woman of my dreams lived two states over.

"Kay, you still there?"

"Yeah, I'm here." I cleared my throat. "So when can I see you again?"

"Whenever you want."

I pulled up to Mona's house later on that afternoon. The white sedan was in the driveway, along with an old school Chevelle. The pearl-white paint job and matching interior had it looking like a cloud riding on shining rims. It was immaculate, with that "dope-boy" feel oozing all out of the custom-leather seats. Whoever owned it, had to have some real cash invested in the classic muscle car, and my Detroit-state-of-mind quickly assumed that somebody was getting money in the streets on the west side of the D.

I walked up to the house, admiring the car as Kim ended a phone call she was having while sitting on the steps of the porch.

"Where are you taking my girl?" she asked, playfully pointing with her phone.

"Excuse me?"

"You heard me. I'm getting your license plate number before you leave."

"I think you're just nosey."

She put a hand to her chest. "Me?"

Mona came out the door looking like the spokesperson for "Sac Chasers" magazine, equipped with diamonds on hand, neck and ankle. A tight denim jumpsuit caressed a body that was a black man's dream. She looked to be the oldest out of the three, and there was no doubt that she was either about her money, or someone else's money. She took a seat on the steps across from Kim and pulled out a bag of weed.

"So where you taking her?"

Before I could say anything, Taj rescued me from any further questioning. All thirty-two of my teeth had to show when I saw the door swing open. Class was written all over her outfit of a sundress, sandals, and a very cute straw hat. She gave me a smile and removed a pair of sunglasses from her purse. "Where are we going?"

Taj and I arrived at one of the best seafood restaurants in the city. During the drive I found out that she loved crab legs and shrimp just like I did, and it was just one of the many things we had in common. We also shared the same birth dates, which was even more surprising since I'd never known anyone other than myself who was born on Christmas Eve. Taj was four years older than me, though, something she found hard to believe after I'd opened car doors and pulled her seat out for her when we made it to our table.

"You're such a gentleman to be so young." She seemed to be flattered by my manners.

"What does age have to do with being a gentleman?"

"Nothing." A pause. "I guess I'm just not used to the treatment I'm getting."

That led into a conversation about her past relationship, one that was abusive, filled with deceit, lies, and a boyfriend she ultimately got away from by moving from Atlanta to Decatur,

Illinois. As bad as she hated to leave her little brother and the grandmother that raised them after her mom fell victim to a serious crack addiction, it was the only way she thought she could get away from such a toxic relationship. Kim was also from Atlanta, but had moved to Decatur a few years before she did. So, Taj packed up and decided to move in with her best friend. Two years had passed, and according to her, the dating situation in Decatur was one that she wasn't even about to get involved with.

"So this is my first date in a very long time," she said, reaching for a menu and giving me a smile.

I took that as being a challenge to make it a very good date, and I planned on doing just that.

We went back and forth finding out more about one another during dinner. Taj was a beautician back in Decatur, working alongside Kim at a salon of a woman she spoke very highly of. Barbara was the owner, and Taj referred to her as the mom she never had. Like Barbara, she wanted to have a salon of her own one day, something she seemed to feel very passionate about. She had ambition, something I lacked when it came to my own future plans.

I filled her in on what my life had been like up to that point, leaving out the money I had gotten from the insurance policy. She didn't come off as being a materialistic woman, but I wanted to be careful just in case. Eventually, the subject was brought up anyway.

We'd finished eating when Taj gave me a long look as I sat across from her. I took a sip from my glass of pop and returned her gaze. "What's the matter?"

"I don't know, Kay." She continued her stare. "There's something about you."

"Something like what?"

A puzzled look. "I don't know."

Our waiter came over and placed the check on the table. Before I could reach for it, Taj grabbed it and proceeded to go in here purse.

"You better not even try it," I said, reaching over the table and gesturing for the check.

She continued to pull out some bills. "This is our first date, so I think it's only right that we go half."

"I got it," I insisted, unprepared for the glare she gave me.

"So where do you get it from, Kay?" Her stare was intense as if she was trying to read my mind. "Let's keep it real with each other, Kay. You're twenty years old and you drive a brand new convertible. You dress in very nice clothes, and that bracelet you're wearing says either you're a drug dealer or your mother takes real good care of you. I know registered nurses make good money so maybe that's the case." She sat back in her seat. "So tell me, Kay, what do you do for a living?"

She was even more beautiful when she was serious. All I could do was smile as she sat there and waited for my response.

"Kay, I told you the situation with my mother, and the one thing I can't do is date someone who's involved with drugs." She counted out her half of the bill and put it with the check. "I'm enjoying myself so far, but if you sell drugs, this will be our last date."

With nothing to hide, I filled her in on the insurance policy, and was satisfied that she actually cared about how a brother got his money. She seemed relieved after I told her, smiling and returning to her beautiful, bubbly self, even when I basically forced her to let me pay for dinner.

On our way to the car, she took hold of my hand as we walked. Her touch was warm, caring, and I felt as if I was floating on a love-filled cloud. The joy I felt must've been apparent, because she looked over at me and giggled.

"What's the big goofy smile for?"

"Nothing," I replied. "Just thinking."

"You're not going to share?"

I resisted the temptation to stop right there in the parking lot and tell her that I would share any and everything I had with her. I fought off the urge as I walked around to the passenger side of the car. My opening her door was met with a soft peck on my cheek.

"What was that for?"

"For being such a gentleman, Kay. You're a very nice guy." She gave me a wink and got in the car.

We spent the rest of the evening in downtown Detroit, maneuvering our way through the crowded sidewalks of Greek Town, taking in the festive activities in Hart Plaza, strolling the Riverwalk as the sun set over the Ambassador Bridge. And with every laugh, with every hold of hands, with every step we took together, I was falling deeper and deeper in love. It was something I couldn't stop. Something I didn't want to stop. I was just hoping that Taj felt just a fraction of what I was feeling.

The moon was shimmering off the waters of the Detroit River. Sitting side by side on the steps on the waterfront, Taj let out a sigh as she leaned her head on my shoulder.

"This is beautiful, Kay."

"This is the best part of Detroit," I said, surveying the gorgeous view.

"I'm not talking about the scenery, silly." She elbowed me softly in the ribs. "I was referring to the whole day."

She let out another sigh and cuddled up to me a little more. Instinct caused me to put my arm around her and pull her even closer. I ran my chin across her silky hair and wished we could stay that way forever.

"I know I'm going to hate to leave you, Kay," she whispered softly. "I just know it."

Those words brought me back to reality, a reality that I didn't want to face. Our time together was limited because she had a life in another state. A feeling of panic came over me. "When are you leaving?"

She raised her head and stared out into the river. "We're leaving Wednesday. The majority of our clients come at the end of the week and I can't afford to miss them."

My mood had dampened, and I could tell that those words had caused a change in hers as well. She sat quietly, as I thought about what I would do without her being in arm's reach of me. I knew that she was meant for me and I intended to do whatever I could to make sure that we were together.

The crowds had faded, and we looked to be the last occupants of the Riverwalk. Taj took my hand and playfully pulled me to my feet, the smile that I had come to love, intact and glowing in the darkness.

"Come on, boy. It's time to go."

We walked back to the car in silence as we let the breeze from off the river carry us to the car. Our hands seemed to have a firmer grip during the walk, a sign that neither one of us wanted to let go. Once we were in the car, Taj let her seat back and kicked off her sandals. "Drop the top, baby." She was laid back as if she was ready to fall asleep. Her being in my company was all I needed.

I took the scenic route back to Mona's, stopping at every yellow light along the way. But, inevitably, we made it there a little after midnight. Taj started a conversation when I turned the car off and it didn't stop until almost four in the morning. I still wasn't ready to leave her. She yawned between sentences, so I knew it was time for her to get some sleep. Reluctantly, I got out and walked her to the front door, where I gave her a hug and trotted back to my car. Before I could crank the motor, she came running down the walkway, and over to my door.

"Get out for a second," she said, pulling her hair back into a ponytail and applying a ponytail holder.

I did as I was told, and was met with the most sensuous and passionate kiss known to man. When it was over, she gazed into my eyes and said, "I couldn't end the best date I've ever had without a kiss."

Speechless, and savoring the taste she left on my lips, I watched her walk off and disappear into the house.

CHAPTER 11

I woke up with a smile on my face during the next few days. She had that effect on me, and had become the inspiration for me to get out of bed earlier than usual. The lingering thought of her going back to Illinois was always an afterthought, but it could never steal the joy I had while I was with her.

My life also took on new meaning after we met. Falling in love and making someone happy never crossed my mind, but Taj changed all of that.

My mom was interested in meeting the woman who I'd been spending all my time with. I was never there when she came home from work, and when I told her I'd met someone, she couldn't wait to meet her. So, on Taj's last day, I invited her over for dinner so that the two women in my life could meet. They hit it off from the beginning, talking to each other like I wasn't even at the table. Mom even gave Taj a hug before we left to go hang out, and it made me very happy to see that they got along so well.

Our favorite destination had become the Riverwalk. We both loved being near the water, so it was the perfect place to end any summer evening. It was also where we were spending our last night before Taj left for home.

"I really like your mom."

"She likes you, too," I gave her hand a squeeze. "You got a hug and she forgot about me."

"Aww, poor baby." She giggled. "So you're a momma's boy, huh?"

"I guess you could say that. She's all I got."

Taj nodded and gave me a smile. Turning around, she looked up at the towering building behind us. "So what's all in there?"

"A hotel, restaurants, and some stores, along with other stuff."

"Have you ever been on those elevators and looked out over the river?"

I turned around and watched an elevator shoot up the side of the building. "No, I've never been on one of those."

She stood up. "Can we go on it?"

"Now?"

"Please." She sounded like a little kid begging to go on a carnival ride.

We entered the building through the hotel's lobby, hand in hand. Before getting to the elevators, Taj excused herself to the ladies' room. I took a seat on a bench and was briefly entertained by classical music playing softly over the intercom system. A wishing well was stationed in the middle of the court. The tranquil sound of the waterfall lured me to the area, hand in pocket, searching for some loose change.

Coins of every denomination had been cast into the shallow pond, a hopeful thought probably attached to each one. I wondered if any had come true, and imagined some of the things a person would wish for. Happiness of some sort was probably high on the list for most people, and it didn't take me long to figured what was on top of mine. Closing my eyes, I tossed the coin into the pond and made my wish. A pair of hands came up from behind and went around my waist.

"What's your wish?"

"If I tell you it may not come true." I turned to her and kissed her on the lips.

"Well, in that case, keep it to yourself." Her hand came to my chest. "Come on, let's go."

I followed her lead to a set of elevators that weren't the ones that overlooked the river. "Is this the right way," I asked, looking around.

The elevator door slid open. "I got this."

The car started to rise, and so did a certain part of my anatomy. I was standing behind Taj while she playfully wiggled her butt on me, much to my satisfaction. When her wiggle turned into a slow and teasing grind, I was pretty sure she was aware of how excited I was. It was something I couldn't control. I was a virgin in an elevator with a woman who defined beauty. It took everything I had not to give her booty a few hunches like a kid in the fourth grade.

We arrived on the thirty-second floor, a few floors before I had to stop myself from exploding. I had to secure my hard-on in my waistband as we stepped out onto plush carpet. Taj gave me a giggle when she looked back at me. "It's this way."

She appeared to be following the numbers marked on each door we passed. At room thirteen twenty-five, she stopped and removed a card-key from her purse. "The lady said the best view is from this room."

I followed her into the room where we were welcomed by darkness. I found a light switch as she went over and fumbled around the curtain. A queen-sized bed and a roomy Jacuzzi dominated the spacious room. The curtains began to open, slowly revealing a star-filled sky and the Ambassador Bridge, as it floated magically over the Detroit River. The floor to ceiling windows offered the most spectacular view I'd ever seen of the city and its neighbor, Canada.

"Yeah, this is a something," I said in awe, while Taj walked over to the Jacuzzi and started the water.

"I told you I got this."

She tested the water's temperature and then found her way over to me. Arms draped over my head, she said, "Kay, these past few days have been the best of my life. I've never met anyone who's treated me like you have." Her stare intensified. "I like you, Kay. I like you a lot. And even though I've never been in love, I'm pretty sure this is what it feels like."

Her lips came to mine and I welcomed them. Our tongues began to dance a dance that we both had become familiar with during our short time together. But this time the kiss was different and held more meaning. It was as if she was trying to convey her feelings for me through the kiss. In return, I did the same.

The water continued to fill the Jacuzzi as she guided me over to the bed without unlocking the kiss. She let her body fall and I came down on top of her and planted kisses on her cheeks, down to her neck and back to her lips. She was panting heavily, lustfully.

"I hope I'm not rushing this," she whispered through the kiss.

Wanting to speak directly to her heart, I looked deep into her eyes, and said, "We can stop. We have forever."

Her lips curled into a smile that personified happiness, completeness. She had been through a lot in her life, and she deserved the happiness that every woman should have. I was willing to do whatever was in my power to give it to her.

We spent the rest of the night making love. It started in the Jacuzzi, where Taj took hold of my mind, body, and soul with each stroke she graced me with. I was in her control, and she showed me things I had only dreamt about. The bed was where she laid back and allowed me to please every part of her body. And even though I was a virgin, it was as if our bodies were made for one another, and I had no problem bringing her to the apex of ecstasy. She did guide me a little, though, whispering, and sometimes screeching whenever I had touched the right spot. And once I hit that spot, I continued until her legs trembled and shook, wanting nothing more than to let her know that I was there to satisfy her. I think I did pretty good for a first-timer.

We were cuddled together, our noses almost touching, the moonlight illuminating the room. Taj's eyes sparkled as she grazed my legs with hers.

"What are you thinking about?" I asked.

"You."

"What about me?"

"Just you." She closed her eyes. "You never told me how you got your name."

"It's a funny story."

She sat up on her elbow. "Well you know I like to laugh, so tell me."

"My mom had always teased me about how when she first saw the ultrasound of me in her womb, my head took up the whole screen. She would rub her stomach and say, 'Look at my, Head,' a nickname already given to me before birth. So, as I was about to come into this world, she was looking up at the mirror in the delivery room as my head came into view. She said as painful as it was, she still managed to laugh when she saw me coming. The female doctor who was delivering me just so happened to be Latino, and she shouted 'cabeza' which is Spanish for 'head'. After learning what it meant, mom decided that it was going to be my name but switched up the spelling to her liking."

Rubbing my head, Taj said, "My Kabazza."

"Well, I like it more than her first original choice," I replied.

"What was it?"

"Eugene."

Taj exploded in laughter. "Yeah, I like Kabazza better, too. You hardly look like a Eugene."

While picturing my life as "Eugene", Taj came closer and laid her head on my chest. My mind turned to what was next for us. She was leaving in the morning, and I felt like I would be lost without her. Obviously, she was thinking about the same thing.

"What are we going to do, Kay?"

"I don't know."

She ran her hand across my stomach. "I've never been in a long distance relationship before."

"Me either," I replied, wanting to tell her that I'd never been in a relationship that involved sex and such deep feelings.

She sat up. "Well, you start school in a couple months, so maybe you could come see me around the Labor Day weekend right before school starts."

I didn't know how I was going to make it that long without seeing her. "I guess I could do that."

"What do you mean, you guess?"

She climbed over and straddled me, her naked body warm and soothing.

"You know I will."

I tried to laugh to hide the fact that my heart was aching over her departure. But her playful manner helped ease the pain a bit.

"Don't make me drive back up here and kidnap your butt." She was staring down at me, her warmness causing me to rise to the occasion. She responded by lifting herself up and coming down onto me. Her hips began to roll and I fell over the edge, lost deep within her. After another lovemaking session, Taj was able to drift off to sleep. She had to start off their drive back to Decatur, so I didn't want her to be tired when she did. I couldn't sleep, though. I spent half of the time thinking, thinking about her. The other half was spent watching her as she slept beside me.

CHAPTER 12

We were at Mona's house the next morning, packing Taj's and Kim's luggage into Kim's car. Our night of passion was over, but Taj and I couldn't seem to stop holding and touching each other.

"Look at the lovebirds," Kim teased as she came out the house with a suitcase.

"Yeah," Taj said. "Look at us." She pecked me on the lips. "Take a picture, Kim."

Kim retrieved a camera from the car and snapped a few pictures of Taj and I posing like a married couple. We switched it up and I took a couple of Taj and her best friend together until Mona came out the house and joined in on the Kodak moments. All three women were very attractive and I was kind of honored to be in the company of such beauty.

Mona and Kim went and sat on the porch to smoke some weed that Kim claimed she needed for the road, while we sat on the hood of the car cherishing our last moment together. The Chevelle was still in the driveway, so I asked Taj who did it belong to.

"That's Jay's car," she replied. "He's Mona's brother. This is his house, too. He asked Mona to move in because it was a little too big for just him."

I surveyed the car and house. "Nice. What does he do?"

"He's twenty-six, never had a job and has a G.E.D., so you figure it out." She gave me a knowing look, and my earlier assumption seemed to be right on target. "Speak of the devil," she said, turning toward the sound of heavy bass coming from an SUV as it cruised up the street.

The black Range Rover on chrome rims pulled into the driveway, the music loud and vibrating the ground beneath us. A tall, dark-skinned guy sporting a bald head got out the driver's seat, leaving his passenger in the vehicle as the music continued to blare loudly through the entire block. The bald guy came in our direction, his eyes checking out my car first, and then me.

"Y'all about to leave?" he asked Taj.

"Yes, Jay. It's back to our little hick town." She grabbed my arm.

"Jay, this is Kay. Kay, this is Jay." She let out a giggle.

I reached to shake his hand and was almost blinded by his diamond-flooded Rolex. The chain he wore was also drowned in glittering jewels. He was most definitely a baller if I'd ever seen one."Nice ride, dog," he said, releasing my hand. "What side you from?"

"East. Van Dyke and Six Mile area."

"Oh, okay. You probably know my boy Big Rick from over there."

Big Rick was a known drug dealer in my neighborhood. "I don't really know him, but I see him around."

He paused for a minute. "That's what's up. Let me run in here real quick. Nice meeting you, Kay."

"Same here." I felt like I had just met an NBA player or something. I studied him as he ran up the steps and into the house after a brief chat with Mona and Kim.

Minutes later, he came out carrying a duffle bag. Mona followed him off the porch and spoke as he listened with an intense look on his face. When they finished, he came back over to us and gave Taj a hug.

"Y'all have a safe trip and bring me one of them Decatur broads next time," he said, laughing. "Let me holler at you for a second, Kay."

It stunned me to hear him say that. What did he want with me? I thought to myself. That was our first time meeting, so I was kind of puzzled. But instead of standing there looking crazy, I stepped off to the side with him after getting a stern stare from Taj.

"I got them good prices if you ever need something," he said, an arm around my shoulder as if we were old friends. "Get in touch with Mona if you ever need me."

Just like Taj assumed I sold drugs because of my car and the jewelry, here was, Jay, thinking that I was in the same business he was in, strictly based on my appearance. And instead of telling him that I was just a kid with some trust fund money, I let him continue on with his assumption. "Alright, I'll do that."

"That's what's up." He gave me a pat on the shoulder and walked to his truck.

The Range Rover backed out and took off down the block. Taj was standing by the porch as Mona and Kim took the last hits of the blunt they seemed to be enjoying. Both girls' eyes were low and bloodshot red.

"You don't smoke, do you, Kay?" Mona passed the blunt to Kim.

Taj answered for me. "No, he doesn't. Nobody's trying to look goofy like y'all."

"We might look goofy, but we feeling good!" Kim chimed in, exchanging high-fives with Mona.

"Well, I'm feeling good, too," Taj replied, her eyes on me. "And I don't need any weed."

"Oh shit!" Kim laughed. "It's time to go."

The girls got up and gave Mona a hug, my mood somewhat dampened after having the best week of my life. Taj then took my hand and we walked to the car. "You better come see me, Kabazza Wright." She gave me a sad puppy dog face.

"You know I am." I went in for one last kiss, which seemed to be a little too long for Kim.

"Okay," she said, loudly clearing her throat. "You can give my girl her tongue back now."

"She is so silly," Taj said, rolling her eyes. "Well, this is it. Make sure you call me later."

I opened the driver's door for her. "I will, and have a safe trip."

She started the car, giving me a last look. "See you later, Kay."

A wave was all I could give. "Bye.., I mean see you later, Taj."
She blew me a kiss and, like that, she was gone.

CHAPTER 13

The next month was a daily dose of two-hour phone calls between Taj and I. Nothing compared to physically being with her, but it gave us a chance to learn all we could about one another. And, though, we were separated by almost five-hundred miles, it didn't stop our feelings from growing for one another. And, at the end of one of our phone calls, Taj let it be known where her feelings were headed.

"I like-to-love-you-lot," she spoke softly into the phone.

My heart raced to hear her use "love" in a sentence that was directed towards me. It was the only word I heard. "What did you say?" I asked, sitting up in my bed.

"It's how I feel, Kay." A slight pause. "I mean, I really do like you, but I want to love you a lot."

I was speechless, overjoyed. She was feeling like I'd felt the first day I'd met her. Nothing could have pleased me more.

"I like to love you lot, too, baby," I told her before hanging up. I went to bed feeling like I had just won the jackpot of love.

<><><>

By chance, I ran into Mona's brother, Jay, the next day. He stopped by while I was shining up my rims on my car in front of my house. Big Rick was with him, in the passenger seat of a drop-top corvette.

"You not ready to holler at me yet, Kay?" Jay asked, a smile on his face and gripping the steering wheel with two hands. "Ain't nobody got the prices I got!" he said confidently. "Fuck with me!"

"Damn," Rick chimed in. "You low-key in the hood, huh?"

I went along with the program. "I don't do too much this way, Rick. I'll let you have the hood." I laughed it off. "Yeah, Jay, I haven't been doing anything, man, but when I jump back down, I'll be sure to get with you."

"That's what's up. As a matter of fact, put my number in your phone. You look like you get money, Kay, and I like to see a young nigga out here gettin' that paper, so holler at yo' boy. I got you."

Jay seemed to be a cool guy, regardless of his occupation. I took his number and watched as he hit the gas on the Corvette and burned rubber down the street.

A couple days later, I was at home doing my usual video game thing. Mom had just come home from work and decided that she wanted her crab legs for dinner, so she asked me to go get a few pounds for her. Without hesitation, I got in my car and headed to the fish market on Seven Mile.

Usually, I would have dropped the top on the Mustang, but it had rained earlier and I settled for letting the windows down to catch a nice breeze. I came to a stop at Nevada and Van Dyke, almost running the red light until a man pushing a grocery cart came into view. The cart was filled with nothing but junk, and the guy was wearing a trench-coat and a skull cap even though the temperature was in the low eighties. He was pushing the cart at a snail's pace, and I was tempted to go through the light before he made it halfway across. But instead, I waited, watching my rearview as I did so.

Stopping at red lights in the city was sometimes hazardous to someone driving a nice car due to the amount of carjackings that took place. The thought was always there, but I never thought I would actually be involved in one.

A blue four-door, rusted Buick pulled along side of me. As the car slowly came to a stop, I noticed it was only occupied by one person. I glanced over at the driver, who was staring at me when I made eye contact with him. He gave me a nod of the head. My attention then turned back to the traffic light, and that's when all hell broke loose.

Out the corner of my eye, I saw the rear door of the Buick swing open. Before I could react, a guy was standing outside of my car, one hand on my door, the other hand holding a black automatic pistol.

"Get out the car, nigga!" he yelled, spit flying from his mouth and landing on the side of my face.

I couldn't believe I was in the middle of a busy street, in broad daylight, about to become a victim of a carjacking. My mind flashed to the many stories I'd seen on the news about people who surrendered their car but ended up losing their life anyway. I couldn't take the chance of seeing if I could walk away with mine. It all happened so fast.

The guy continued to yell. I glanced over at his partner, whose head swiveled back and forth in search of police. If my top had been dropped, he would have been able to see my hand reaching for the forty-four snubbed nose that was tucked in between my seat. I never thought I would have had to use it.

"Get the fuck out now, nigga!"

"I'm putting it in park, man!" I yelled, nervously wrapping my hand around the pistol. The whole time I braced myself and prepared to be shot.

I guess I was taking too long for his liking because my car door swung open and I felt his hand grab hold of my shoulder. He was trying to drag me out, the hand holding the gun no longer aimed at me as he attempted to do so. His force pulled me halfway out the car, my body turned sideways, both feet on the cement of the street. Believing it was my life or his, I brought the gun across my body and aimed back and upwards in his direction. I can remember closing my eyes as I pulled the trigger.

The first explosion of the gun was deafening, and I barely heard the next five shots I let off. I was thrown back into the car by the recoil of the powerful gun, and shot blindly in his direction, the fear of dying heavily on my mind. The gear shift raked my back as I lay across the seat to avoid taking a shot in the head. I pulled the trigger until the gun was empty, each shot feeling like an M-80 exploding as it left my hand. A haze of smoke momentarily blinded me, and then panic took over. I was expecting the jacker to appear and finish me off. I turned and reached for the passenger door, my only means of escape. I crawled across the seat and jumped out, ready to run for my life, ducking low to the ground with my hands covering my head. That's when I saw the bum with the grocery cart staring motionlessly towards the back of my car.

The danger was over. I turned to my car, both doors wide open. The Buick was gone. The carjacker was laid out in the street, a stream of blood running from his body and down to the curb. It wasn't a sight I wanted to see.

Onlookers started gathering around, some parking their cars and coming over to get a better view. In a daze, I walked to the front end of my car and took a seat on the curb. As sirens wailed in the distance, I realized that I had just taken the life of another man.

I was arrested at the scene and taken to police headquarters, where I spent hours being interviewed by detectives. But after hearing my story and the stories of other witnesses, I was let go. It was a case of self-defense, plain and simple. The gun I used in the killing had been stolen from a suburban home, and fortunately hadn't been used in any other crimes. There was a possibility that I could've been charged with possession, seeing that I wasn't a licensed gun-holder. But, as one of the detectives put it, I had basically done the city a favor by taking out a guy who was the "worst of the worst".

Carlton Moseley was his name; career criminal and an all-around bad guy. He had been in and out of prison his entire life. Armed robbery charges littered his rap-sheet, and he'd probably had more unsolved carjackings under his belt. The detectives didn't seem to mind that he was no longer with us, one even assuring me that the gun charge against me would somehow disappear because of who the deceased was.

It didn't make me feel any better knowing I had killed someone who obviously didn't give a damn about his victims. Nor did I feel like some type of hero for taking out someone who helped make Detroit one of the worse places in the world to live. He was someone's son, and at the age of twenty-six, probably the father of a child or two. People were probably going to miss him, regardless of the life he led. And when it was all said and done, he would become just another statistic, another black man dead as the result of violence. That was the sad part.

My mom cried for two days after the incident. Almost losing her only child was a little too much for her to bear. She never asked about the gun or why I even had it; her only concern was my well-being. She had always smothered me with affection, but the hugs and kisses to the forehead were constant with the tears after the incident.

I felt kind of guilty for putting her through all of that. All she ever wanted was to see that I was happy. And when she asked me to trade in my car and the rims for something less flashy, I did it without hesitation. I even let her pick out my new ride, a Ford Expedition that sat up higher and offered a feeling of security.

That event caused mom to realize that the crime in the city was getting worse. She started her search for a new home in the suburbs outside of Detroit, closer to where she worked in Farmington Hills. She also recommended that I take my trip to Decatur sooner than planned, something that brought a smile to my face, as well as Taj's.

"You better do what your mom says," Taj joked when I told her.

"I just wanted to make sure it was okay with you." I waited for her response.

"Kay, I wanted you to come with me when I left. I miss you so much."

Those words were music to my ears.

Two days later I was packed and ready to reunite with my soul mate. I had lunch with mom before I left, and it was somewhat of a sad occasion. It was going to be our first time away from each other, and the only thing that gave her peace of mind was that I would no longer be in Detroit. She also knew how Taj and I felt about one another, so she took comfort in knowing that

I would be with someone who cared about me just as much as she did.

"Drive safe, honey," she said, giving me a big hug and kiss.

"I will, mom. And you take care of yourself, lady." I got in my truck and blew her a kiss.

"Call me when you make it." She wiped away a tear. "Bye, baby."

"It's 'see you later', mom."

She did her best to smile. "See you later."

I hit I-94 and started my journey to a place that held unforeseen consequences for me, some good, some not so good.

CHAPTER 14

Mary J and Jodeci got me through the seven-hour drive. It was relaxing to be out on the open road and to take in all that central Illinois had to offer. Farmland was in abundance, and cattle were grazing the fields. The air seemed to be cleaner, and I rode with my windows down and soaked it all in.

When I made it into town, it was nice to be able to stop at a gas station and not get harassed by panhandlers begging for some change. Nobody was posted up at the front door, letting me know that they had fat dime bags of weed. I started liking Decatur the moment I stepped into town.

I called Taj to let her know that I had made it, but Kim answered her phone. Taj had gone out to get something to eat, so I followed Kim's directions and arrived at their apartment complex. Kim was standing on the balcony waving at me with a smile on her face when I pulled up.

"She is going to be so happy to see you," she said, as I made it up the steps. "She should be pulling up any minute." Kim was leaning on the railing, looking toward the entrance to the complex. "Here she comes! Come on!" Kim grabbed me by the arm and took me into the apartment, where she stuffed me in a hall closet. "Stay put."

I stood in there and thought about how my game system would look on the big screen television in the living room until I heard Taj's voice. A chill went through my entire body.

"Did my baby call yet?" She walked right by the closet and into the kitchen. I was staring directly at her as she sat a bag on the table and stuffed a french- fry in her mouth.

"Not yet," Kim replied, pushing the closet door closed when she walked past. She went in and pulled some food out the bag, giving me a wink while Taj's back was to me.

I silently pushed open the door while Kim kept Taj's attention.

"Do you think this is a ringworm on the back of my neck?"

"Girl, it better not be," Taj replied, carefully inspecting.

I covered my mouth to stop from laughing and tiptoed up to Taj. She didn't even flinch when I gently caressed her around the waist and planted a kiss on her neck. "Guess who," I whispered in her ear.

"How many guesses do I get?"

"How many do you need?"

"Just one. But first I'm going to close my eyes, and then turn around and kiss you. I think I can guess better from a kiss."

"Fair enough, but no peeking." I turned her around and gave into her kiss, adding just a touch of tongue. "Are you ready to guess?"

Her eyes remained closed as she tasted me on her lips. "Umm...I think I need one more." Our lips touched again and she held on to me like she was never going to let me go.

"I'm out of here," Kim said, abruptly. "Love is in the air and I'm not about to breathe that shit in." She snatched up her food and headed to the door. "See you lovebirds tomorrow."

"Okay, girl," Taj mumbled, her bottom lip held captive by mine.

"Get that ringworm checked out," I said as Kim left out the apartment.

Our kiss continued until Taj broke it and stared me lovingly in the eyes. "Hi."

"Hi."

"It's only been a month, but it seems like years since I've seen you." She shook her head. "I don't know how much longer I could've gone without seeing you."

"Me either." I stroked her face. "But I'm here now."

"So, how do you feel?" she asked, wearing a devilish grin on her face. "Are you tired from the drive?"

"Not at all."
"Good." She led me down the hall and into her bedroom.

<><><>

I woke up the next morning feeling like a million dollars. I was in Taj's apartment, butt-naked in her bed, and her sweet scent was all over me. I was in paradise.

The smell of cooking food was in the air. I got out of the bed and went into the kitchen, where Taj was fully dressed while she tended to her breakfast creations.

"You're just in time." She took a pan off the stove and slid an omelet onto a plate. Fresh fruit and orange juice were already set up on the table. "Have a seat."

After a taste of the omelet, it was evident that Taj knew how to work magic in the bedroom and the kitchen. She was definitely wife material.

"I have to meet a client at the shop in thirty minutes, so call me when you're dressed." She came around and kissed my cheek. "I have somebody who can keep you company and show you around."

"Somebody like who?" I took a sip of orange juice.

"His name is Run." She threw her purse over her shoulder. "He's a couple years younger than you, but he's cool people."

I'd planned to spend my time playing video games while Taj was at work, but I was curious about the small town. With a population of about one-hundred thousand, it couldn't be anything like Detroit. And, seeing that Taj had picked someone out to hang out with, I was cool with the idea of getting out a bit.

<><><>

I finished breakfast and went out to my truck to get my luggage after Taj left. There was a pool in the center of the complex, and two white women were laid out in bikinis soaking up some sun. Obviously, Decatur was a diverse town where blacks and whites lived amongst one another, something that I didn't see much of in Detroit. One of them actually gave me a wave as I walked over to my truck, which was probably my first friendly interaction with a white person that I could recall. It was a nice change, though.

I opened the hatch and pulled out a suitcase when I heard the buzz of a remote control car. It sped over the cement and came directly at me, full speed. Before it crashed into my foot, it did a three-sixty and stopped a few inches away. Somebody was playing games. I scouted the parking lot, but didn't see anyone.

"Did I scare you?" It was the voice of a child. "Yeah, you were scared."

From in between the cars parked next to mine, appeared a grinning little boy who looked to be around seven or eight years old. The sun gleamed off his little pea-sized head as his little hands gripped the remote controller.

"No, little man, you did not scare me." I laughed. "But you almost got your car smashed."

"Shit, you woulda' been buyin' me another one." He picked up his car and looked it over.

I was shocked by his choice of words, but in a strange way, it was amusing. "What's your name?"

His chest puffed up a little. "I'm Baby Dee."

"Alright, Baby Dee, where's your mom?"

"In the house smoking weed with the girl's next door boyfriend."

I shook my head. The kid knew too much to be so young. I imagined what his mom was like as I reached for another piece of luggage. "You want to make five dollars?"

That got his attention. "Doing what?"

"Take one of these suitcases up those stairs for me."

"You ain't tryin' to trick me, is you?" He had a serious look on his small face.

"No," I replied with a chuckle.

He held his hand out. "Gimme my money first."

I went in my pocket and came out with a small roll of money. After giving him the five dollars, he held the money up as if he was checking to see if it was real. "You rich, huh?"

"Not at all." I handed him a suitcase.

"Man, this mothafucka heavy!" He yelled, letting it fall to the ground. "I'ma have to charge you five mo'dollars."

The kid's vocabulary was one that he probably got from his mom and from watching R-rated movies. I gave him the lightest bag I had, and he followed me to Taj's apartment. He began to case the spot as soon as he walked in the door.

"I sho' could use that big-screen," he said as he sat the bag down.

"So what are you saying?" I gave him a stern look.

He laughed it off. "I'm just playin'." Pause. "Hey, you Taj's boyfriend?"

I ushered him out the door. "You're awfully nosey."

"I'm just askin'." His little feet pattered down the steps. When he got to the bottom he stopped and looked up at me. "Ya'll be doin' the oochie-coochie don't y'all?" He balled up his hand and then inserted his index finger into the opening.

I was ready to take off my belt and give him a taste of leather. Instead, I sent him on his way after resisting the temptation.

<><><>

I got dressed and was kind of anxious to see what Decatur was all about. It only took me about ten minutes to get to the salon where Taj worked. She said it was across town, but being from a big city, it was more like a few blocks over.

On the drive there, I got more stares than a celebrity. People were driving by trying to get a glimpse of who was inside of the big SUV with Michigan license plates. Heads turned when I drove past a park that was crowded with kids and guys playing basketball. A car that was filled with four girls even pulled on side on me and blew their horn several times trying to get my attention. They followed me until I turned into the parking lot of the salon. When I got out, they drove past again, heads hanging out the windows of the car. The catcalls were flattering, but I was kind of embarrassed about all the attention.

The chattering of women's voices welcomed me when I entered the salon. A row of barber's chairs was filled with women getting their hair styled in various fashions. Taj and Kim, along with an older woman, curled and pressed as they talked and laughed while Brian McKnight's voice crooned softly in the background.

"Look who's here," Kim teased, reaching for a blow dryer.

Taj put a few finishing touches on her customer's hair and removed the cape. "You're right on time."

She came over and started introducing me to everyone. Barbara was the other beautician and also the owner of the salon. Still very attractive, I could tell she was a serious head-turner in her day.

"I've heard so much about you," she said, a warm smile on her face.

"I hope nothing bad." I glanced at Taj.

Barbara shook her head. "Not at all."

They were like Taj's family, and from the first day I'd met them, they opened their arms and treated me as if I was a part of that family. It was the only thing that made it easier to be away from my mom.

Taj and I were outside talking in front of the shop while she waited on her next customer. Not one car passed without someone blowing a horn or waving at Taj. She was obviously very popular in the small town, and it wasn't a surprise because she was just a very likable person.

"I can't wait to have my own shop one day," she said, looking over the building. "Maybe I could save up and buy this one when Barbara retires."

"That's what you want?" I asked.

She had a dreamy look on her face. "Yes, Kay. And one day I'll have it."

From the way she said it, I was convinced that she would get it, and I was willing to do whatever I could to help her.

"Here comes, Run." She was watching a car as it turned up into the parking lot.

A woman wearing a scarf got out the car. She was puffing on a cigarette. "Girl, you gotta do something to this head of mine."

"I didn't tell you to try the Erykah Badu look," Taj said, breaking out in laughter.

"Girl, shut yo' mouth." Tina flicked her cigarette. "I'm, Tina. Nice to meet you, Kay."

She rolled her eyes at Taj.

"Nice to meet you, too, Tina."

"Why is Run sitting in that hot car?" Taj asked.

"'Cause he crazy just like his damn white ass daddy." Tina turned and yelled. "Run, bring yo' ass over here!"

"You so ghetto," Taj said, giggling.

The car door slowly opened with a creak. A baseball cap, turned slightly to the left, popped out the car. And, with the speed of a caterpillar, Run began his trek over to us. Along the way, he pulled up his sagging pants to stop them from falling to the ground.

"Mothafucka' won't wear a belt to save his life," Tina said, angrily.

"Leave him alone, Tina," Taj said, meeting Run to seemingly help him move a little faster. "Run, I want you to meet, Kay."

We shook hands and he went back to the chore of holding his jeans up. Taj gave me a kiss and a playful "behave yourself" before going into the shop with Tina.

I got into my truck as Run climbed into the passenger seat and started checking things out, his once lackadaisical demeanor getting a boost of energy once I started up the engine.

"This you?" He rolled down his window and reclined the seat.

"Yeah, if you talking about the truck."

"This nice," he replied, digging into his pocket and producing a lighter and a blunt. "You smoke?"

"No, but I don't mind if you do."

Run lit up the blunt and exhaled after holding in the smoke for a second. "Let's ride."

<><><>

We cruised the town and listened to music as Run smoked his weed and let me know when to "turn right", "turn left", "drive slow past these hoes" and other comical requests. Whenever he saw someone he knew, he would stick his head out the window to make sure that he was seen.

"What up, nigga!" he would shout loud enough to be heard by whoever was around. He would also hold conversations with people as we drove side by side on a busy street.

On more than one occasion while we drove around, someone would pull up to the side of us and ask Run who had "work". I was kind of confused the first time it was asked, but I figured they were talking about drugs after hearing it so many times.

"It's fucked up around the town," Run replied whenever he was asked the question. He even turned to me and asked if I had brought some "work" with me, probably thinking the same thing Jay thought since I was riding around in an expensive truck. All I did was shake my head, and just like with Jay, I let him go on with his assumption.

I learned my way around the town in a matter of a couple of hours, thanks to Run and his insistence on riding around in circles from one side of town to the other. We passed the same cars numerous times, and it was obvious that a lot of people in Decatur spent part of their day doing the exact same thing.

At Run's request, we ended up at the park I had passed earlier that day on my way to the salon. A basketball game was going on, kids were playing on the swings, and there were about ten guys standing around on the corner, clouds of smoke floating in the air as they passed around blunts and took sips of beverages concealed in brown paper bags. Run had me pull up to the crowd, and instantly, all eyes were on us.

"This my mob," he said as he got and walked over to the crowd of guys.

I put the truck in park and watched Run greet each guy with a handshake that took almost ten seconds to perform. They shook, wrapped fingers, snapped fingers, touched palms and some more stuff. It was obvious gang-affiliated, and it was surprising to see that gangs existed in such a small town. Seeing that everyone probably knew where each other lived, I assumed that it couldn't be that big of a deal, and was probably something they did just to pass time.

Some of the guys were staring my way, and I could see Run look back at me as he talked, probably explaining to them who I was. After taking a few hits off a blunt, he came and got back in the truck.

"Damn." His breath was heavy with the stench of weed. "It's dry as hell around here. Ain't nobody got work, but Khalid, and he sellin' o's for fifteen hundred."

He might as well had have been talking French. Instead of asking him what he meant, I asked what gang was he in.

"I'm Vice Lord," he said, throwing up his hands. "Five poppin', six droppin!" he shouted. I was riding with a real life gang-banger. A scene from the movie *Colors* flashed through my mind.

"Hit that gas station up there," he said, licking his lips. That caused a little foam to build up in the corner of his mouth. He was suffering from a bad case of cotton mouth.

I cruised into the gas station parking lot and stayed in the truck while he went in. He came out with a bagful of snacks and was turning up a bottle of water as he walked. At that moment, the ground started shaking and my truck began to vibrate. I was thinking that I had made it to Decatur just in time for a deadly earthquake. It was like it was getting closer and closer. Then, all of a sudden, I was staring right at the cause of the tremoring. It came in the form of a black Expedition with tinted windows. The music was the loudest I'd ever heard. He parked the truck at the door of the gas station, causing people to walk around it to get to the entrance.

"This nigga," Run said, popping open a bag of chips. "Fuck he think he is?"

I had to raise my voice because of the loud music. "Who's that?"

"That's Khalid's bitch ass. Nigga think he runs Decatur."

The guy got out the truck and gazed over in our direction. The shades he wore couldn't hide the fact that we had his attention. He was sort of an imposing figure; built like a football player with skin the color of coal.

"Looks like Dark Vader." I joked.

Run laughed. "He probably trying to see who drivin' this truck. Nigga act like he the only one who supposed to get money around here."

He continued his stare down for a few more seconds before going into the gas station. It was the first time I saw Khalid, but it wasn't going to be the last.

A pool hall was our next destination. We shot a few games while Run flirted with some white girls who were playing at the table next to ours. In between shots, he would go over and hug on a different girl, talking smack like he was a real player. He seemed to be in his element.

"I heard coke was cheap as hell in Detroit," he said, lining up a shot on the eight ball.

"I guess."

He missed the shot. "You could get paid down here. It's been dry for a couple of months now. That nigga, Khalid killin' em, too."

I later learned that Khalid was, indeed, "the man" in Decatur when it came to drugs. He wasn't involved in any of the gangs in Decatur, but he was their main supplier. According to Run, when the drought came, Khalid raised the prices and only supplied a few selected people, something that caused a little animosity among some members of the local gangs. But no one dared to air that animosity towards him. There were rumors that Khalid was responsible for a murder that happened when one leader of the Disciples tried to extort him. They found the guy shot in the head in his backyard, his hand still clutching the bag of garbage he was throwing away. After that, Khalid freely sold his drugs without any interruptions.

Run missed his shot. "When you gon' have some work?"

I stepped to the pool table and prepared for mine. "I'll let you know."

My answer appeared to be good enough for him. He smiled like he was already counting up his money. I just hoped he wouldn't bring the subject up again. It probably would've broken his heart if I'd told him I didn't sell drugs.

CHAPTER 15

Since I was from a big city, I was able to appreciate all the small things that came with living in a small town. I could run in the store and leave my car running and not have to worry about someone driving off in it. Try that in Detroit and chances were you'd be walking home. People were friendlier and more cordial. You didn't have to worry about a lot of the random violence that took place in a big city. Crime happened anywhere, but I guess the odds of it happening in Decatur were slim because of the smaller population.

Decatur did have its small share of gang violence, though. But for the most part, it was isolated and didn't involve innocent bystanders getting shot or killed. It was a far cry from what was happening in places like Detroit and Chicago. I was able to relax and let my guards down a little and wasn't worried about the unpredictability that came with living in the city.

The one negative thing about Decatur was the fact that it didn't have much to offer when it came to shopping, entertainment, or good restaurants. The good thing was that St. Louis, Chicago, and Indianapolis were only two and three-hour drives away. Taj and I spent most of our time visiting those cities during my stay. We hit the Taste Fest in Chicago, stage plays in St. Louis and shopped until we dropped in Indianapolis. That's where we were when she surprised me with those three special words.

She was smiling after she'd found some shoes she had been searching for ever since she'd seen them in a magazine. Her face was lit up as we walked out the store. "I thought I was never going to find them."

"It took us three cities and seven malls, but you found them."

"I couldn't have done it without you, baby." She took hold of my arm and stopped. I thought maybe she'd spotted a store she wanted to check out, but she was looking at me, her eyes sparkling. "Kay, I love you."

I'd been waiting to hear those words ever since I'd met her. My world was now complete. "I love you more. I've loved you since that day you had Mona chase me down and forced me to pull over in that gas station."

Her laugh warmed me, soothed me, a sign that she was happy, a sign that she was enjoying herself. It was contained, though, as if it was a present meant just for my ears. She moved in for what I thought was a kiss, but turned out to be playful poke into my ribcage. "We know who chased who, Speed Racer."

"And I caught you." I sucked my teeth player-style.

She matched me with serious sass served with a smile. "And you're never letting me go."

<><><>

It was official. Decatur was going to be my new home. When I asked mom how she would feel if I stayed with Taj, to my surprise, she was as happy as I was. After the shooting, she was worried whenever I left the house, so living in Decatur was not only good for me but her nerves as well.

Taj and I drove to Detroit to get the rest of my things and to see mom before we started our lives together. It was hard leaving her and knowing that I wouldn't see her every day, but I made sure that a day didn't pass without her hearing my voice. She had done an excellent job raising me on her own, and now it was my time to step out into the world as my own man. But I guess I didn't realize that, with becoming a man, you had to make the decisions that a real man would make. Whether those decisions were right or wrong, that was another story.

<><><>

Before leaving Detroit, I went to the bank to have my money transferred to a branch in Decatur. I knew I had spent a lot of money, but I never really kept track. It was kind of irresponsible, but give an eighteen-year-old a lot of money, and they're bound to do something foolish somewhere down the line.

I was in the bank manager's office waiting while she looked over a few things on her computer. She sat back in her chair when I asked her how much money I had left.

"You've done some serious spending, Mr. Wright."

It didn't look good from the way she said that.

"Yes, I bought a few things."

"You started with a little over a hundred thousand and now you're at...thirty seven thousand."

When I thought about it, it sounded about right. The car, then the truck, the bracelet, the shopping sprees Taj and I went on, and all the other money I'd spent on day-to-day living over a couple years had added up. It was still a large amount of money for me, but after having a hundred thousand, I started to feel like I was almost broke.

<><><>

Mom eventually sold her house and found a home in Lathrup Village, a small community outside of Detroit. Taj and I went and spent the Labor Day weekend with her so that I could check out the new scenery. It also gave Taj and mom the opportunity to spend some real quality time together. They seemed to get along really well, and it was a blessing to see the two women in my life enjoy each other so much.

While in Detroit, as if it was inevitable for us to hook-up in one way or another, I ran into Jay again. I was at a car wash on the west side, waiting for my truck to be cleaned up. Jay came into the waiting area exuding money like it was cologne. Big Rick was also with him. As soon as he saw me, he walked over with a huge smile on his face.

"What's the business, Kay?"

"Just chilling, Jay. What's up with you?" I threw Big Rick a head nod.

"Trying to see why you ain't hollered at me yet. I heard you merked a nigga, got away with it and then moved to Decatur with Taj." He laughed as if killing somebody was humorous.

I shook my head. "Things happen."

"Damn right they do." He looked over at Big Rick. Rick hunched his shoulders and reached for a magazine off the desk.

"That's the best thing you could've done. That out of town money is serious. You can get rich down there. You ain't foolin' me." He shook a finger, grinning as if he was reading my mind. "Look, just holler at me and I'll make sure you get the best quality at the lowest prices. Like I told you before, ain't nobody in the city fuckin' with my prices." He went over and started talking to a lady that was behind the desk.

I assumed drug dealers were just like car salesmen. Jay was doing some heavy advertising, trying his best to get me to come do business with him, some business I wasn't into at that time.

One of the car wash attendants came in to let me know that my truck was ready. Before I left out, Jay put in the last pitch.

"Don't forget about me, Kay. I'm like the King of New York, baby! I want in!" I couldn't help but laugh. Jay was persistent and amusing at the same time.

The attendant was rubbing away at my side-view mirror while the other workers were wiping down a brand new Aston Martin. The only place I'd ever seen them were in magazines and rap videos. It was black, and seeing that Jay and I were the only customers in the place, there was no doubt who owned the luxury sports car. I looked back to the waiting area, and there he was with his face on the window, nodding his head and smiling at me.

CHAPTER 16

Life in Decatur was right up my alley. It was laid back and quiet for the most part. I eventually began to meet people, which was due to Taj being my girlfriend. She was one of the best beauticians in town, and everyone seemed to enjoy being around her. We would be out at a restaurant and people would come over to our table just to speak. Sometimes another couple would join us at Taj's insistence. I was introduced to guys who would invite me out to parties or sports events, but I never really clicked with any of them. They were cool people, but I was still the loner I had always been.

Run was the only person I hung out with on occasion. It never was planned, though. He would see me in traffic and flag me down, only to be riding shotgun minutes later. His first question was always, "Did you get some work yet?" My response was always the same, but that would soon change.

<><><>

I intended to spend Thanksgiving in Detroit, but mom had other plans. She had become real good friends with her new neighbor in Lathrup Village, a guy by the name of Mr. Frank Reeves. He had invited her to go to Las Vegas with him and she gladly obliged. I had felt kind of guilty for leaving her alone in Detroit, so I was happy that she had found someone to spend time with since I wasn't there. It was the first time she'd had a male companion since my dad passed, and I could tell from her phone call that she was definitely enjoying his company.

After finding out that I would be in Decatur for the holiday, Barbara welcomed me into her lakefront home for Thanksgiving dinner. Taj and Kim were regulars at the beautiful property, so it was nothing new to them to be at the luxurious home. I, other the other hand, was in awe of everything from the vaulted ceilings to the raised patio that overlooked the frozen lake. Two jet skis and a small boat were on trailers under a canopied boathouse, and it wasn't hard to tell that Barbara was living quite large.

I knew working as a beautician could bring in a lot of money in a big city where you had a huge clientele, but business in a small town like Decatur couldn't have been that good. The first thing that came to my mind was that maybe Barbara was pushing a little dope on the side. It was only a thought, and I guess it came from my previous run-ins with Jay.

I was beginning to think the same way people thought when they assumed I sold drugs: see somebody with nice things and they had to be doing something illegal. But Taj told me that Barbara's husband was in an accident at his job in a local foundry. A machine malfunctioned and he was crushed by a beam of steel, making Barbara a widow and a few million dollars richer. She had the shop before the accident and continued to work as a way to keep herself occupied.

Being in a house like Barbara's, only motivated me to find a way to make my money grow. But at that time, it was getting smaller and smaller by the day.

One thing that took a big chunk out of the money was the engagement ring I bought Taj. I got it in Chicago while we were doing some Christmas shopping. She was at a shoe store, so I went browsing and found myself staring down at this beautiful platinum and diamond ring. I instantly heard wedding bells. I loved her with all my heart, and I was sure that she felt the same about me. Marriage was the only thing left.

I knew my money was getting low, but Taj deserved the best. I had also become accustomed to getting something if I wanted it, and when it came to shopping for her, there was no difference. So, a week later, I drove back to Chicago and picked it up. I was almost ten thousand dollars shorter, but she was worth every cent.

Our first birthday together was when I asked Taj to be my wife. Everything closed early on Christmas Eve, so after eating a candle-lit dinner at home, we exchanged gifts and had some fun playing the new game system she bought me. She also spoiled me with boxes and boxes of clothes, but nothing compared to the two gifts she saved for last.

Every light in the house was turned off. We lit candles throughout and took a soothing bubble bath together. Taj was in between my legs with her back to me, her head resting on my chest. She was sipping on some champagne we had got to celebrate our special day.

"Baby, this reminds me of the first night we made love," she said, finishing her glass. "You showed out that night."

"Yeah, I did do my thing, huh?"

She giggled. "Yes, you did. I guess somebody taught you something."

"What do mean by that?"

"You know what I mean." She sat up and turned around, sitting on her knees with a smile on her face. "Some woman taught you how to please her and you used all that on me." Her hand went under water and stroked me gently. She always got an instant reaction from me.

"Taj." I was entranced by her touch. "You are the first woman I've ever been with."

She studied my face. "Are you serious?"

"I would never lie to you."

She didn't say anything; just reached over and picked up the bottle of champagne. After pouring her second glass, she took a long sip and then sat it down. Her hand went to her nose as if she was trying to suppress an oncoming sneeze. But instead of a sneeze, that laugh I loved so much came spewing out. It went on until, in between gasp, she was able to say. "So I popped your cherry!"

"Ha ha, very funny." I splashed her with some water and watched it stream down her beautiful body.

She was enjoying herself and I figured the time was right for me to pop the question.

"I gots me a virgin!" she yelled, laughing even more.

"Okay, calm down, calm down."

She let her last few chuckles out and then came in for a hug. "So I'm the first you've ever had?"

"Yes, and the only one I'll ever need." I reached over and took the black box from under a towel on the floor. "So will you marry me, Taj?"

She pulled back and saw me holding the box open to expose the ring. Her eyes grew wide and her mouth was partly opened as if her words were caught in her throat. All I wanted to hear her say was "yes". She didn't say anything, but her hand raised from her side with the ring finger extended further than the rest. I could see her hand trembling and tears welled up in her eyes. Then she whispered, "Yes, Kay, I will."

With those words, I took the ring out the box. It slid perfectly on her finger. "I love you, Taj."

"I love you more." She kissed me. "Well, I do have one more present for you."

I scanned the bathroom. "Where is it?"

Her stare turned downward, causing me to search the bottom of the tub with my foot. I didn't feel anything.

"Not down there, silly." She took my hand and put it on her stomach. "There's a little person in there."

That turned out to be the second greatest day of my life, runner-up to the day I witnessed my son come into this world. We were going to be a family, and I knew that we would be a loving and caring one. I promised myself that I would be the father to my son that my father wasn't to me. I would love him unconditionally and he would feel the love I had for him every minute of the day.

That night also made me realize that being the head of a family took more than just love. My childhood wasn't filled with worrying about where the next meal was going to come from. My mom made sure of that. I had clothes on my back and a roof over my head, and I was blessed to have a little more than the average kid who grew up in the inner-city. Now it was my turn to provide for my family.

CHAPTER 17

The New Year came, and we brought it in by going to the Justice of the Peace. Neither one of us wanted to wait. It was going to take some serious money to have the wedding that I envisioned us having, so we mutually agreed that we would hold off and have a ceremony later on down the line.

My mom was ecstatic when I broke the news to her about the marriage and Taj's pregnancy. I thought she would've been somewhat disappointed about us having a child, seeing that I was still young and hadn't established a career, or a job, for that matter. I had already put my schooling on hold to move to Decatur, and to be a father and husband was a huge responsibility. But I guess she knew how happy I was, and ever since I was a kid, that seemed to be the only thing that mattered.

<><><>

It was March when Taj came home excited as I'd ever seen her. I was sitting in the living room with a controller in my hand when she came through the door yelling my name.

"Barbara wants to sell the shop!" she said, kicking her boots off.

"Why is she selling it?"

I was more focused on a game of Madden I was playing until I realized that it was her dream to have her own salon. The remote was tossed to the side, and I made room for her on the loveseat.

"She's just ready to enjoy herself and do a little traveling. And guess what she said?" She didn't wait for my response. "She said she would sell it to me for sixty-five thousand. The building alone is worth that and I wouldn't have to buy anything."

I was way short of the money for the shop, and we also had a baby on the way.

"When do you have to have the money?"

"That's the other good thing. She said I could give her thirty-five thousand down and pay the rest in monthly installments until its paid off. All I have to do is come up with it by September. I have a little money saved but not that much."

I wanted my baby to have that shop just as bad as she wanted it, and I was willing to do whatever I could to help her.

Rubbing her stomach, I said, "Tell her you'll have the money by then."

"Really?" Her eyes grew wide.

"Yes, really."

A huge hug was my reward.

"Baby, I swear I'm going to save every dime," she said into my ear.

"Yeah, me too."

I began to think of a way to come up with the money she needed.

<><><>

It wasn't a surprise for snow to still be on the ground when spring rolled around in Detroit. That was something I didn't miss. The first day of spring in Decatur brought seventy-degree weather and sunny skies.

It was a beautiful day, and I got out early to go wash my truck and to get some fresh air. On my way there, I was flagged down by Run. He was in the passenger seat of a Chevy Caprice. The driver's hat was cocked to the left, so he had to be one of Run's fellow gang members.

I pulled over on a side street and Run got out the car and came to my window.

"Tell me you got some work." He had a desperate look on his face.

"Nawl, not yet."

"Man, my boy wants three o's and ain't nobody got shit, not even Khalid." He shook his head. "This fucked up right here. A nigga could get fifteen, sixteen hundred for an ounce 'round this bitch."

I thought about what Jay had said: You can get rich down there.

"What you about to do?" Run asked, looking at the Caprice.

"Hit the car wash, that's all."

"Hold up right quick. Ain't no need in me ridin' with this nigga." He walked up to the car, gave the guy their ritual handshake and got in with me. "You still ain't smokin'?" A blunt appeared in his hand.

"Nawl, but I see you still are."

"Damn right." He lit it, took a hit, and said, "Man, I'm broke as hell. I need some money."

His outfit backed up his statement. The collar on his used-to-be-white tee-shirt was almost a V-neck, and his jeans had seen better days. Gym shoes that curled up at the toe were another sign of his financial woes. He always had weed, though, which seemed odd to me. But I saw potential in Run, and he eventually became a very valuable asset to me.

At the car wash, I scrubbed and rinsed while Run stood around smoking his weed and throwing up gang signs to passing cars. While I put some shine on my tires, a car pulled in and Run went over and held a brief conversation. When he was done, he came and stood over me. "Damn, that nigga lookin' for two o's." In the time it took me to finish up my tires, that happened three more times.

"He wanted three o's."

"She tryin' to cop two o's."

"Damn, that fool came up. He wanted four o's."

While Run grew frustrated about the high demand but no supply, I was doing a little math in my head. In less than twenty minutes, at fifteen hundred an ounce, somebody could've made sixteen thousand five-hundred dollars. That somebody could've been me, I thought to myself. *You can get rich down there.*

Later that night, it was almost impossible for me to sleep. I laid next to Taj thinking about fast money, her having a salon of her own, and us living in a beautiful house like Barbara's. At that point, the only way I saw myself accomplishing any of those things was getting some fast money.

I didn't play the lottery, so that was out of the question. That sixty-five hundred dollars in a matter of an hour or two, now that could get me somewhere. I tried shaking the thought, but it wouldn't go away. A tug-of-war was taking place in my mind, each side pulling to claim victory. One side told me that I didn't know the first thing about selling drugs; the other side told me that I could learn. Then the other side told me that fast money wasn't good money. The other side responded by telling me that as long as I had money, everything was good. I tried to block that side out, but it was not to be ignored.

And as the night grew longer, it became like an army overpowering an unarmed enemy.

When Taj woke up the next morning, I told her that I had to go to Detroit.

CHAPTER 18

Taj didn't question me about why I was going to Detroit. She probably assumed that I was missing my mom, seeing that she always poked fun at me for being a momma's boy. I also knew that the weekends were her busiest days. She wasn't going to let anything get in the way of her buying the salon, so a trip with me wasn't good for her pockets or our baby she was carrying.

I had it all figured out with Taj, but I had no idea how much dope I could get with the ten-thousand dollars I withdrew from my account. I just thought it was a good round number to start with. I didn't say too much over the phone when I spoke to Jay. He was so hyped when I called, I was sure that we could work out something.

I called him as soon as I got off the highway. The noise in the background told me that he wasn't alone. He gave an address to a house that looked like it was hosting a car show when I pulled up.

Besides Jay's Range Rover, there were two more Ranges, a BMW 745, a Mercedes 600, and an old school Impala on gold rims parked in front of the house. They all looked out of place compared to the rickety shack where two guys sat on the porch. They watched my every move as I walked up to the steps and asked for Jay. The scowls on their faces told me that they weren't the friendliest guys in the world.

"What's yo' name, homie?" one guy asked.

In my best non-confrontational voice, I replied. "Kay."

He got up and disappeared through the gated door. I looked around and tried not to appear nervous while his partner continued to watch me. The guy came out minutes later and waved me into the house. As I walked in, I noticed two assault rifles lying on the porch at his partner's feet. The clips in the guns looked like they held quite a few rounds.

They let me pass and directed me to the kitchen. The house was bare except for a table and a couple of fold-up chairs. I could hear voices coming from the basement. I followed the noise down the steps and found Jay at a pool table surrounded by about eight more guys. Money was scattered around the table. A fat guy was shaking his fist, a pair a dice clicking and clacking inside. Jay glanced over at me and flashed a smile. A bar stool was in the corner, so I went over and took a seat.

It was obvious to me that all of the guys had money. Diamonds were in abundance, and expensive clothes were on the backs of everyone down there. The five-hundred dollar bets that were being called out were other signs that I was in the midst of some major ballers.

After tossing bills on the table, the fat guy released the dice. "Shit!" he yelled.

Some of the guys picked up their cash and threw some verbal jabs at the loser.

"Nigga, you ain't hittin' shit today," said a guy sporting some pink gators and matching linen outfit. "Fuck it, just gimme that money in yo' hand and save me some time."

Jay and a few others laughed. "Okay, mothafuckas, daddy got the dice now," Jay said, holding a stack of money in one hand.

Guys started soliciting bets from Jay.

"Five hundred you don't hit!"

"Bet somethin' you don't hit, nigga!"

Jay counted out his money, tossing four bets on the table. "Who got me faded?" he asked, counting out more money.

The fat guy hit a blunt and shook a wad of money at Jay. "Nigga, money got you faded."

"Buff, today just ain't yo' day," Jay said, laughing. "A gee I hit yo' ass!"

Simultaneously, both men's fingers flicked through their respective stacks. Not once did the smile leave Jay's face. He looked to be enjoying himself, and after throwing two sevens and an eleven, a lot of trash-talking came along with that smile.

"You niggas gone feel me when y'all leave here!" Jay was using both hands to sort out a pile of money in front of him. "Yo' pockets gone feel me too!"

Buff's belly jiggled with laughter. He had been the main contributor to the pile, but it didn't seem to bother him too much. From the way they talked to each other, I could tell that they met up at that dice table quite often. That day just happened to belong to Jay.

On his next roll, Jay caught a four as his point. The table erupted.

"A gee you don't hit that fo'!"

"Bet you don't ten or fo'!"

Everybody wanted a bet, and Jay took every single one.

"I gotta show you niggas what's real," Jay said as he prepared to shoot the dice. "This shit is easy!"

The dice came from Jay's hand and danced along the table. When they came to a stop, Jay was the only person talking.

"What I tell you niggas?!" he yelled, raking in more piles. "Shit is easy!"

He was laughing and enjoying what he was doing, and I smiled as I watched him. He looked over in my direction and gave me a wink.

"I pass the dice," he said, stepping away from the table and leaving his money.

They tossed insults at him as he walked over to me. "These nigga's sweet today, Kay."

"So I see." I shook his hand. "I'm ready to get money like you."

"All you gotta do is fuck with me."

"That's what I'm here for."

<><><>

I met Jay an hour later at his house. I gave him a little more time on the dice while I grabbed something to eat. He was hot on the table, so I didn't want to interfere with him getting his money. When he jumped out the Range Rover, both pockets bulging, I knew I had done the right thing.

"Thirty gees ain't bad for a day's work," he bragged, opening the door to the house.

The house contained everything I expected a guy like Jay to have. The only thing that caught me by surprise was the huge fish tank that stretched along his dining room wall. But instead of fish, the tank was the home to three baby sharks. I assumed when you got real money, you get real sharks.

I took a seat at the dining room table with Jay. He started pulling out wads of cash from his pockets. "So what you tryin' to do, Kay?"

"I need to make some money. I got ten thousand."

He sat back in his chair. "Ten, huh?"

"That's all I have right now."

"Shit, that's all you need."

He got up and went into a room in the back of the house. I could hear him moving things around. Minutes later, he came back with a duffle bag and sat it on the table.

"I just got some good shit in just for you. The big metal scale he pulled out the bag was the kind I had seen back in high school. The black square package he placed on the table had me clueless, though. I watched as he used a knife to cut into the package. He split it down the middle, causing a strong odor to escape. One by one, he began to place small chunks of the white substance on the scale, tinkering with the triple beam as he did so. I didn't know exactly what he was doing, but I continued to observe as if I was familiar with the whole routine.

"I'ma give you a half for the ten," he said, carefully reading the scale. "I charge anybody else twelve-five, but a nigga hit a lick today and you almost fam, so I'ma look out."

"That's cool."

Everything he said sounded believable. He had just won thirty-thousand in a dice game, so maybe he was just sharing some of his good fortune.

I took out my money and sat it on the table. Jay emptied the dope into a zip-lock bag and dusted off the scale while I contemplated my next move. It would've been foolish of me to leave his house and not know what to do. I didn't want to tell him that it was my first attempt at being a drug dealer, either. He had already made me out to be somebody I wasn't, and for some reason, I didn't want to make him second guess me by telling him otherwise. So instead of telling him the truth, I thought of something else.

Jay dropped the bag of dope in front of me and put my money in his pocket without even counting it. "They gone love you in Decatur when you touch down." He took a seat. "Just keep the best prices and the best product."

I touched the bag and fumbled it around in my hands. "Jay, I usually don't mess with this. Weed is my thing, but, like I said, I need to make some real money. I just don't know too much about this."

"You bullshitin'?" He cracked a small grin. "Why didn't you say so?"

Jay was more than happy to show me the ropes and enrolled me into "Dope Game-101" right there on the spot. I followed him into the kitchen, where he explained his every move in the process of turning powder cocaine into crack. Using a glass pot, baking soda, water, and a microwave, he started the transformation with me hanging on to his every word. As he poured the powder into the pot, I mentioned that there was a drought in Decatur. He assured me that I was about to make a killing, and I smiled as he took an egg-beater and began stirring the dope as if he was a chef.

"I'm whippin' it for you, Kay," he said as he added baking soda to the mixture. "You bought eighteen ounces, but when I'm done, you'll have about twenty-five of 'em. Seven extra o's and it's still gone be good."

Jay stirred for a few minutes until he was satisfied with the outcome. He held the pot up, and we watched the mixture settle to the bottom. After dumping some cold water onto it, it turned into a solid piece of cocaine in the shape of a giant cookie.

"I'm a master with this shit, Kay." Jay was smiling and admiring his work. He emptied the water out and dumped the cookie onto a piece of paper-towel. The surface was smooth and shiny. Jay dried it off and took it into the living room, retrieved the scale from the bag, and then weighed it up.

"Shit," he said, tinkering with the scale until it balanced out. "I was right on the money. You got seven extra with a gram to spare."

Jay seemed happy with it, so I had no choice but to be happy.

"I'll even cut it up into ounces, but you gotta bag 'em up. I can't do all the work." He let out a chuckle.

Jay really looked out for me, and all I had to do after that, was get it back to Decatur and sell it. He also had a plan for that. He didn't like the fact that I was going to get on the highway with twenty-five ounces of crack, so he suggested I pay Mona two thousand dollars to get it there safe and sound.

"You think she'll do it?" I asked curiously.

Jay laughed. "Mona a hustler just like me." He picked up his phone and dialed a number. "Money on the flo', girl."

Mona made it there shortly after that. She seemed surprised to see me sitting at the table with Jay. I stood to give her a hug.

"Where's Taj?" she asked.

"In Decatur. I came by myself."

She noticed the bag of dope on the table. "Oh, I see."

Jay put the plan in motion, calling the bus station to find out when the next bus was leaving for Decatur. When he finished, he ordered Mona to pack and change clothes because we had about two hours before it left. The bus would arrive in Decatur the next morning, so I had to get on the highway so I could be there to pick her up.

Jay was smoking on a blunt while we waited for Mona. "Kay, you about to make some real money."

"I hope so. I'm trying to get where you're at." I glanced at his shark tank.

"Shit ain't as easy as people think." He exhaled a cloud of smoke. "But if you stay focused on the prize, a nigga can get him some paper and turn it into some legit shit. That's what I'm on. A nigga can't sell dope forever."

Jay talked like he had a plan, and I was intending to follow that plan to a tee.

An hour had passed when Mona finally came down. When she first came in the house, she was wearing a short skirt highlighted with diamonds and her gorgeous looks. The skirt was replaced with jeans, penny loafers, and a U of M tee-shirt. A beaded bracelet was the only jewelry she wore. She looked like a college girl on her way home from school, innocent and unsuspecting. The book-bag she had on her shoulder was going to be loaded down with twenty-five ounces of crack cocaine.

<><><>

Mona and I arrived at the bus station at eleven forty-five. The bus was leaving at midnight. Mona sat in the passenger seat, fixing her hair and applying some lip gloss.

"When we go in here, we have to act like a couple," she said as she outlined her lips with the gloss. "Undercover police be in here sometimes, so we gotta be careful."

At the mention of the police, I realized how dangerous it was going to be.

Mona took the book bag while I got her luggage out of the truck. It was dark, and to me, everyone began to look like law enforcement. A woman was standing at the front door handing a bum a cigarette, her eyes locking on me as we walked to the entrance. Once inside the bus station, we stood in line to get her ticket, and whenever I glanced in any direction, it seemed like I was being met by studying eyes. The attendant at the counter could've been the police. The guy coming out of the bathroom drying his hands on his shirt could've been the police. Jay was right: being a drug dealer wasn't as easy as people thought.

Mona did a good job in helping calm my nerves. She joked and laughed as she purchased her ticket, coming off as a real pro at transporting drugs. Once she had her ticket and tags for her luggage, she took my hand and walked me over to the waiting area. I sat down while she went to a vending machine to get a few snacks for the ride. She came back with a smile on her face, planting a kiss on my cheek before sitting down.

"Stop acting so nervous," she whispered as she opened a pack of candy. "It's cool." She offered me a piece of candy by holding it to my mouth, playing the couple's role perfectly. It definitely wasn't her first time.

The station was crowded to be so late. I looked around and saw people waiting for their bus, suitcases all around. Most were black, and I couldn't help but wonder who else was shipping dope out of the city.

"There's my bus," Mona said, gesturing to door number ten.

A line was already formed, so we walked over and stood behind a lady traveling with two kids. The bus driver began taking tickets when I glanced toward the front entrance and noticed a guy talking to the bum standing outside. When the guy pointed in the direction of my truck as he spoke to the bum, the first thought that came to mind was Mona's warning of undercovers in the bus station. And when the bum seemed to look directly at me as he continued his conversation, I quickly turned my attention back to the front of the line and wondered if my drug-dealing career was about to be over before it even got started.

Mona was handing the driver her ticket when a voice behind me stopped me cold. "Excuse me, sir."

I looked back while Mona continued out the door and onto the bus. I watched her and the backpack disappear, hoping that we weren't going down together. If they didn't get the dope, they couldn't get me.

I did an about-face and was prepared to see a badge and a pair of handcuffs fitted just for me. A balding short guy was sporting a Detroit Lions tee-shirt and blue jeans. It was typical undercover police gear.

"Can I help you?" I asked, trying my best to find an ounce of moisture in my mouth.

"Is that your truck?" He looked over his shoulder, his focus on my vehicle parked outside, the only SUV in sight.

I was prepared to deny everything. But, if they were the police, and the bum was on their team, they already knew. There was no need in making it harder than it was, so I told him the truth. "Yes, it's mine. Is there a problem?" I stopped short of calling him "officer".

"Not really," he said, reaching into his pocket. I was expecting a badge, but he came out with a pack of cigarettes. He removed one from the pack and put it in his mouth. "You left your lights on."

Thanking him was out of the question as he walked away. Instead, I pictured myself running up on him and drop-kicking him in the back for scaring the hell out of me.

Mona gave me a wave as I wheeled her luggage to the side of the bus. I returned her wave and didn't leave until the Greyhound eased out of the station.

CHAPTER 19

Nothing out of the ordinary happened on my road trip back to Decatur. I made it home as the sun peeked over the green prairies of central Illinois, the thought of money was keeping me awake like I'd had ten cups of coffee. Mona's bus wasn't scheduled to arrive for a few hours, so I was going to get a little sleep before picking her up. Taj was sprawled out on the bed, unaware that I'd made it home. I smiled as I got undressed and snuggled next to her. She stirred a bit and then rolled over to face me.

"How was your trip, baby?" she asked, eyes closed and looking like a sleeping angel.

"It was alright."

"Good." She came closer and put her arm around me. Not another question was asked or another word spoken. As long as we were together, nothing else seemed to matter.

<><><>

I picked Mona up and got her a hotel room for the night, then drove straight to Run's house. He was going to play a major role in my plans. He knew everybody who was sold drugs, and I had what everybody was looking for.

Tina was sitting on the porch smoking a cigarette when I pulled up. She yelled for Run without me even having to get out. After a brief conversation with her, Run came out the house holding a blunt in one hand and a glass of juice in the other.

"'Sup, Kay?" he asked, walking up to the truck.

"Where can we get a hooptie from?"

"What we need a hooptie for?" He took a hit of his blunt.

"We can't sell dope out this truck."

His eyes grew wide. "You got work?"

"We got work," I said, correcting him.

"Shit, it's on." He opened the door and jumped in.

I reached under my seat and handed him the duffel bag of dope. "Go put that up for me."

He felt on the bag and shook it before getting out and running into the house. He was breathing hard when he returned a few minutes later, hyped-up like never before. "Oooh shit!"

<><><>

I bought an old Monte Carlo from a guy Run knew. He sold it to me for five hundred dollars, but after talking to Run once I gave him the money, he preferred to give the cash back in exchange for a half-ounce of dope. I agreed with it, and Run told him he'd bring it back in a couple hours. And that was only the beginning of our first day in business.

We got the tags for the hooptie and bought a digital scale from a guy Run knew. And just like the car, it was traded off for dope instead of cash. It seemed like crack was the new currency in Decatur.

Run volunteered his bedroom/basement as the place to cut and bag-up everything. Tina never came down there, so it was the ideal spot to take care of our business. We eventually named it the "Chop Shop" for obvious reasons.

"Whoa!" Run's eyes looked like they were going to pop out his head when I dumped the dope on the table. He picked up one of the ounces, staring at it like it was telling him his future. "You trying to take over Decatur, ain't you?"

"All I want is for us to make a little money."

"Shit, that ain't gone be no problem." He went over and reached under his bed, coming back up with a plate bearing a razor blade. "Let's get busy! Nigga's waiting on this shit!"

Run offered me the plate. I declined.

"You can do it...I'll bag. You know what people want down here." My tone was convincing.

For the next hour, Run used the razor blade like a butcher trimming meat, cutting four ounces up into half ounces, quarter ounces and eight-balls. He would cut and weigh the dope, and I would bag it up, just like with Jay. I was an expert bagger for sure.

"We can go take care of Coon and Don," Run suggested, referring to the guys we got the car and scale from. "Then we gone let this work do the talkin'."

He cleaned the razor blade off with a napkin, grinning as I bagged up the last quarter ounce. "You ain't gotta do shit either, Kay. You ain't even gotta say a word to these niggas. Just let me serve the dope and you count the money."

That sounded good to me. But I knew that in order for me to really make some money, I had to make sure that Run was happy. So I counted out four of the uncut ounces and put them into one bag. "That's yours."

A quick count was made on his part, followed by a smile of satisfaction.

"Damn, good looking out, Kay." Leaning back in his chair, he stared down at the bag, obviously amused by something. "Ain't nobody ever fronted me no dope before. Shit, I ain't never even copped nothing more than a few grams." A sincere smile came across his face. "'Preciate that, bro. For real." He stuck his arm across the table and we shook hands. "So how much I owe you? I know it's a drought and you gotta make yours..."

I interrupted him. "You don't owe me. That's yours." I stood up and handed him the bag containing the rest of the dope. "Now put this up and let's go get this money."

<><><>

We had just left Coon's house after paying him for the car, when a guy pulled alongside of us at a red light. The trunk of his Chevy Caprice sounded like he had five hostages in it. He lowered his music when Run got his attention.

"What's poppin', Los?"

He poked a dreaded head out of the window, releasing a cloud of smoke from a pair of lips that could've used a shot of chap-stick. "Shit, trying to live through this drought."

"Yeah, I hear you, but I can get you right if you need something." Run's tone was all business.

Los glanced at the light. "What them zones going for?"

Run turned to me. "Fifteen hundred?"

I stared straight ahead. "Fourteen."

The light turned green as Run relayed my response. Los didn't hesitate. "Bring me two to my spot on College."

"Bet."

<><><>

Los was sitting on the porch when we pulled up. Run got out, his strut more confident, his head high, two ounces of crack in his pocket, his usual tug at his jeans to keep them from falling down. Los got up and held the door open like Run was a VIP, giving the block a quick scan before going in behind him.

When I realized I was looking like a getaway driver waiting outside of a bank, I sat back and tried to relax. Then, a police car turned the corner and headed in my direction, killing any chances of that happening. But before I had a chance to panic, the car whizzed by and disappeared around a corner. I reclined my seat, the scene of Tony Montana's friend getting chain-sawed in the shower, playing in my head as I watched the door.

I felt a little better when Run came out of the house. Los had the smile of a satisfied customer, so I figured everything went alright. I was just as satisfied when Run got in the car and dug into his pocket.

"That nigga must've had that shit in his shoes or something," he said, passing me a folded stack of bills.

The faint odor of feet was unmistakable, but I smelled money.

When there's a drought, hustlers keep their ears to the street for any signs of dope. I learned that only five minutes after leaving Los' house, when a silver Honda pulled behind us and started blowing its horn, a petite arm waving out of the driver's side window.

"Somebody's behind us," I said, watching the rearview.

Run turned around in his seat. "That's, Dee Dee. That's Los' cousin. She be getting' money."

That was the magic word. I slowed down and turned onto a side street, coming to stop in front of a house with some kids playing in the yard. Dee Dee pulled up to the bumper and got out, exposing a short and slim frame with breast that looked too heavy for her to be carrying around. The bangles that jingled with her every step were just a small part of her jewelry collection, with her neck, literally, carrying all the weight. Mr. T would've been proud of her.

"I knew this was the car," she said, stopping at Run's window. "Heard y'all had work."

Run spoke. "Yeah, what you trying to get, Dee Dee?"

"I just need a couple o's right now."

"Twenty-eight hunnit."

She looked like she was debating with herself. "Fuck it...bring me three. How long?"

"Shit, Dee Dee, I'm comin' right back for yo' ass. Fifteen minutes. Be naked when I get back."

"Boy, I'll put it on yo' young ass." She was all confidence. "Have all yo' lil' re-up money and everything." Her titties bounced as she laughed while Run enjoyed the close-up view. "Gone and get it and come on back. You know where I stay." She walked back to her car.

Run was smiling. "I'm gone get that pussy."

I pulled off and started calculating. In less than one hour, we were about to make seven thousand dollars. And with every turn of a corner, that number continued to grow.

We were driving around Decatur, dropping off dope and picking up money like we were Domino's Pizza. Run did all the transactions while I chauffeured him around, and seeing that all people did in Decatur was drive around all day anyway, we blended in perfectly. And, we could've sold all twenty-five ounces, but Run told a few people that we had ran out just so he could go up on the price the next day. I couldn't blame him for trying to get money, either. Run was a hustler and a good one at that.

Run's basement was where we were counting up the money we had made later on that evening. I had been doing the math after every sale, so I knew the stacks of money we had on the table added up to right over twenty-four thousand dollars, minus what we paid for the car and scale.

"This five gees right here," Run said as he snapped a rubber band of the stack of bills. He tossed it to me and walked over to his hiding spot, coming back with the remainder of our supply. "And we still got seven o's left."

"Twenty-four thousand." I sat back in my chair and stared into the eyes of some of our past presidents, immortalized on that precious green paper. "Today was a good day."

"Hell, yeah, it was." Run agreed with a smile. "We can get rich down here."

I had heard those words from Jay, and now Run. The evidence was being folded up and stuffed into my pockets. The verdict was in.

"I'm going home. Taj's almost done at the shop."

"Yeah, I don't want her thinking I got you fuckin' with these hoes out here." He joked.

I shook my head and stood up, smiling at the thought of her. "She knows better. That would never be a problem."

"Right." Run studied me for a second. "Taj good people, man, so y'all make the perfect couple."

"Thanks, Runs. I think so, too." That hit me right in the ole heart. "You can have those extra three ounces in there. You deserve it, man."

There was a slight pause before he rose from his chair. "You a real nigga, Kay. On the fin..." He put his palm over his chest, all five fingers spread apart. "...a nigga better not even breathe on you or he dead."

The same palm met mine in a show of allegiance, our handshake ending with a loud snap of his finger.

"Hold up, right quick." He went over to his bed, sliding his arm under the mattress as he kneeled down. When he stood up, his hand was clutching a small pearl-handled automatic. My startled reaction seemed to go unnoticed. "C'mon," he said, turning and walking toward the stairs. "I'm on security. Niggas won't catch us slippin'."

<><><>

Mona was on the bus to Detroit the following day with twenty-thousand dollars of mine. Jay and I didn't discuss details over the phone. All I told him was that Mona was on her way home, and that's all he needed to hear.

"Say no more," was his short response.

Three days later, Mona was back in Decatur, her travel bag filled with two kilos prepared by Jay, including fourteen extra ounces. A week was all it took for us to get rid of it, and money was coming in as fast as we could count. Jay raised the ante after that, shipping in five kilos with all the extras. Mona relayed the dope and verbal messages from Jay, letting me know how happy he was about my performance. Neither he nor Mona expected a young dude like myself to produce like I was doing, but anybody who had a reliable connect could do the same thing. Dope sold itself, so it wasn't like I was out on corners hustling all day and night.

By the time the drought ended two months later, I needed a second shoebox for the tidal wave of cash that rolled in on an everyday basis. My original ten-thousand dollar investment was sitting comfortably back in the bank along with the last of my trust fund money. The aforementioned shoeboxes held a hundred and fifty thousand and were neatly stacked in a closet with other boxes of shoes in our apartment. Add the fact that Taj was just starting to show, and I felt like life was treating me pretty good at that moment.

Those cash-filled shoeboxes wouldn't have been possible had it not been for Run, though. He made it happen. The mixed eighteen-year-old who refused to wear a belt, was a go-getter if

I'd ever met one. His hustle was what I admired about him, and if the streets gave an award for "crack seller of the month", Run would've been a two-time winner. His mornings started early and his nights didn't end until late. And if he could've sold dope in his sleep, he would've.

Run's hustle was rewarded in ways he could've never imagined at such a young age. He went out and bought a 1976 Chevy Caprice convertible and put all the trimmings on it, turning it into a candy-apple red show car for the whole town to drool over. His wardrobe was updated, and he had a hat for every outfit he wore. He still wore saggy jeans, but was forced to start wearing belts because the knots of money his pockets made it impossible for his pants to stay up. And, it also supported the variety of guns he rapidly began to stockpile once the money started coming in.

CHAPTER 20

We were the "Kings of Decatur" until the drought ended at the beginning of the summer. I was kind of glad it was over because we had been making so much money it scared me at times. Run did all the hand-to-hand sales, but I was always with him during transactions. People weren't saying his name without mentioning mine, and when someone's name is associated with drugs, there's always a risk that comes with it. So, when I heard that other people were popping up with dope, I was somewhat relieved. It just wasn't a good thing to be getting all the money.

Taj was still unaware of what I was doing. All she knew was that Run was riding around in new cars, and a few of her clients had targeted him as their potential sponsor. She told me that an argument had broken out in the shop when two girls found out that both of their hairdos were being paid for courtesy of Run. I just laughed when she told me, and hoped that she didn't suspect me of being involved with Run's dealings. And when she warned me about hanging around Run so much, I knew that she didn't have a clue as to what exactly was taking place. It was something I always felt guilty about.

The two hundred thousand dollars in my stash was my justification for keeping my drug dealing a secret from Taj. I was back where I wanted to be and no longer stressing about my once-shrinking bank account. It also allowed me to do what made me happier than anything: shower Taj with gifts that I wouldn't have been capable of buying had I not found a way to better my financial situation. Of course, she loved what I did for her, but I knew that if I had just been the average guy struggling with a nine-to-five, she would have loved me the same. The material things I bought for her were merely small tokens of my appreciation for having someone who loved me as much as I loved her.

<><><>

Our family was about to expand with our child on the way, so a house was our next major purchase. When I first set eyes on Taj, I pictured us living the "white-picket-fence" lifestyle, with kids playing in the backyard and the family dog lying out in the grass licking its balls. So, after we closed the sale of a house in a subdivision on the outskirts of Decatur, I bought her a teacup Chihuahua as a house-warming gift. Appropriately enough, she named him Shorty.

After moving into our new home, and letting Taj play interior decorator with an unlimited budget, my money hovered around the one-hundred-thousand dollar mark. I didn't mind at all. My wife was happy, and I knew that with Jay as my connect, I could make that money back after a few shipments. But, as anyone who has ever been involved in the drug game can attest to, everything doesn't always go as planned.

I had Jay cut the shipments down after the streets of Decatur had, once again, been flooded with the flow of dope. We managed to hold on to some of the clientele we had built up, but it was nothing like the days of the drought. Guys who bought three or four ounces from us were now going to Chicago and St. Louis to get more bang for their buck, so two kilos was just about enough to get us through a month.

Whenever I'd get down to my last few ounces, I would call Jay. He would then set the wheels in motion and have Mona in Decatur a couple days later. But, on an early late-summer morning, my call to him went unanswered. It was unusual because regardless of when I'd call, he would always pick up, even if he was in the middle of banging some bad chick, which had happened on a few occasions. So when I left a message for him and didn't get a call-back after an hour, I got a little worried. That's when I called Mona. As soon as she came on the line, I could hear her sobbing.

My whole world seemed to crumble around me when she spoke into the phone, her voice barely above a whisper. "They killed Jay last night."

I sat speechless, listening to Mona tell me how someone had caught Jay after he had gotten out of his car and on his way into the house. She'd heard him when he pulled into the driveway, so she was about to open the door to let him in when she heard a commotion on the porch. She could hear what sounded like people wrestling and tussling, and when she heard Jay say, "Fuck you, niggas! Y'all gotta kill me right here! I'm not openin' shit," she ran to retrieve one of the many guns her and Jay had planted around the house. But as she wrapped her hands around an AR-15 that was only ten feet away from the front door, three shots rang out. When she swung the door open, Jay was laying facedown on the porch. He died at the scene from two gunshots to the head and one to the chest. His killers disappeared without a trace.

Jay's death was more than just the end of having a trusted source of drugs: it was the first time I had lost someone who I had a connection with that takes place between two men. Although our relationship had started out in business, he had become more than just my supplier. The few times we'd hung out together in Detroit, he'd introduced me as his little cousin whenever we'd come across people he knew. And during the time I'd known him, he always seemed to have my best interest at heart. From the advice he gave me, to the way he schooled me to the game, it was something a person got only from someone who genuinely cared and wanted the person to be successful in whatever it was that they did.

It was hard seeing him in a casket at his funeral. I didn't want that to be my last memory of seeing him. I preferred to remember him with that big smile he had on his face in that basement as he scooped up piles of money. He seemed to be happy then, doing what he loved to do, being who he was. And that's how I wanted to remember him.

<><><>

Only weeks later, death gave way to new life, as I witnessed the birth of my son, Dante. Well, actually, the last thing I saw was the crown of his head when Taj extracted one final push during his delivery. I passed out after that. When I came to, he was swathed in a blanket, cooing in his mother's arm. The sight of them together was a picture that was engraved into my memory from the moment I saw it. After being nursed back to walking condition, with the help of a cup of water and an orange, I was able to hold my son.

Our bond had been established before that day. I had spoken to him while his mom read books about the different stages of pregnancy. I had sung to him at Taj's request whenever the pain of him moving around became too much for her. It always calmed him down. So he knew my voice, and acted as such, the first time I whispered his name.

"Dante."

His eyes had been closed, but fluttered seconds later. All eight pounds and ten ounces of him began squirming in my arms. Streams of tears were racing down Taj's face when I turned to her. "He wants to see who the man is that could use singing lessons." The trauma of going through labor wasn't enough to contain Taj's sense of humor.

I whispered his name slowly, twice, then a third time.

"Dante…"

When his eyes fought hard enough to open, he stared up at me. And maybe I was just a blur to him, but he knew who I was.

Movement under the blanket caused me to unwrap him just a bit, making way for him to let out a big yawn. His little arms stretched out like he had just finished a tiresome journey, then he went completely still, eyes fixated on me. I took one of his tiny hands into mine and a wave of love went through my entire body. The feeling only got more pronounced when he took hold of my finger and held onto it with a grip that was surprising from a newborn.

It was a very tight grip he had, and as he stared at me with light brown eyes that were clearly passed down from his mom, I imagined what he would've said to me if he could've spoken, a message from a son to his father: "I'm here now, and I'm depending on you to be here for me; to love me, to guide me, to show me how to be a man. I need you."

As if the message was delivered and understood, he released my finger.

Words could never describe how I felt that day as I held Dante in my arms. Happiness was an understatement, and only a parent could ever begin to explain what takes place in their heart on such an occasion.

His birth also brought new meaning to my life. I was now a father, and responsible for making sure he had everything he needed, unconditional love, included. I knew what it was like to be deprived of the bond that took place between a father and son. And regardless of the fact that I was barely out of my teens, nothing was going to stop me from being the father to my son that every child deserved.

<><><>

With Jay no longer around as my trusted connect, I sat on the sideline, much to Run's dismay. But after he found a source in Chicago that kept him with a steady supply of coke, he continued his emergence as one of the premiere players on the Decatur drug scene. Whenever he'd see me, he'd basically beg me to get back in the mix. I declined every time because I was content with the money I'd saved and was happy to be able to spend all of my time with Taj and my son. And, after having somebody like Jay on my team, I was skeptical about dealing with someone else, especially since I didn't know him.

On more than one occasion, I had heard of people going to Chicago to cop drugs only to come back with empty pockets and broken spirits. A guy we had served during the drought didn't come back at all. The police found him in his car, slumped over with a bullet in his head in the parking lot of one of Chicago's roughest projects. Needless to say, I wasn't ready to cop dope from anybody in Chi-town.

CHAPTER 21

Taj had given me the greatest gift I could ask for in Dante, so for our birthday, it was only right that I give her the gift she'd dreamt about for such a long time. Barbara and I had gotten together a week before Christmas to discuss me buying the shop for Taj. She seemed to want her to have it as much as I did, so no questions were asked when I handed her a yellow envelope containing her asking price of sixty-five thousand dollars. I was going to let her and Taj take care of the paperwork, but I wanted to be the one to hand her the keys.

My plan was to make it a gift for her birthday, but the smile I expected from her was one that I couldn't hold off. Yes, I looked forward to her throwing her arms around me, holding me tight while telling me how much she loved me. Then I would respond with how much I loved her more. And yes, I looked forward to the kisses she'd give me, my favorite being the one laced with a few giggles. Yeah, I loved that one. But as much as I cherished each and every one of those things, they all came in second to her smile. To see that sparkle in her eyes was something that had become priceless to me, and nothing made me happier than to be the person responsible.

Barbara and Kim were at Taj's beck and call during the last few months of her pregnancy. After a day of implanting weaves and the latest hairstyles into the heads of their Decatur sisterhood, they would spend evenings at our house. Barbara assumed cooking duties while Kim propped pillows and gave Taj much-needed foot massages. They wouldn't let Taj scratch her booty if it was itching. That was my job. And once Dante was born, I was almost ready to start charging them rent. So, Taj couldn't have suspected a thing as we all sat around feasting on a seafood dinner arranged by yours truly.

"That boy up there is snoring like an old man," Barbara said, taking her seat at the table.

The smile on her face was that of a proud, loving grandmother, and in her cradled arms was where Dante had become accustomed. By yell, wail, or whine, he made it his business to let us know whenever his eyes got a little too heavy for him. Then Barbara would have him sound asleep seconds later, stroking his hair and planting soft kisses on his cheeks while rocking back and forth. He had taken a liking to Barbara just as I had upon first meeting her, and who could blame him? She was one of the sweetest women I'd ever met.

"He gets that snoring from his momma, Barb," I said, taking a playful punch from Taj. "I'm not lying, though, dang."

"And where he get that head from?" Kim chimed in, coming to her best friend's defense while cracking open a crab leg.

"A big head is a sign of intelligence." I pushed my plate away and stared at Kim.

"And judging from that little head of yours, it's obvious you were a genius in school." That got a laugh from everyone including Kim.

A kick to my foot got my attention. I looked across the table at Barbara. Her eyes bucked for a brief second, indicating that she was ready for Taj's surprise. She was the only person in on the secret. I shot her a smile as Kim and Taj discussed an upcoming hair show that was taking place in St. Louis.

"I think y'all should get in it, baby," I said, leaning back in my chair. I went into my pocket and pulled out a set of keys. "That would be the best way to get your shop some exposure." I laid the keys next to her plate. She continued eating, giving the keys a brief glance.

"I have a while before I have my own shop." Her eyes were on Barbara, smiling as she took a bite of crab leg. "Maybe we can enter it in a couple years."

"You won't have to wait that long." Barbara shook her head. "Give that man next to you a kiss and pick up your keys."

Taj stopped in mid chew. Her brow furrowed, and I could see that she finally understood what was going on.

Before she could say anything, Kim yelled, "You go, girl!" She started clapping as she leaped out her chair and ran over and threw her arms around Taj. "Congratulations!" she said, her head buried in Taj's neck.

My baby looked to be in a state of shock. When Kim released her, she sat silently in her seat. Her lips began to quiver as she looked down at the keys she held with both hands resting in her lap. A tear formed in her eye and trickled down her cheek. Before I could reach to wipe it away, she turned to me.

"You could never imagine how much I love you." Her voice was soft, tender. The sound of Kim snatching Kleenex out was louder. She dabbed at her eyes after passing some to Taj and Barbara. I don't think anyone was surprised when Taj found humor in the moment.

"Don't be laughing at me," Kim said, crumpling up a tissue and tossing it at her best friend.

"I'm laughing with you." Taj's voice was sincere. Her attention turned to me once again, though she was looking down in her lap when she spoke. "I mean, even before this, even before you gave me the most precious son a woman could ask for, I loved you more than I thought I could ever love anyone."

Her emotions poured out, the kind that only true happiness could bring. Turning in her seat, she faced me. I could see that sparkle I was hoping to witness. "You make me so happy, Kay, and I don't know what I would do if I ever lost you."

"You don't ever have to worry about that." I shook my head as I gazed deep into her eyes, meaning every word with every ounce of my soul.

It made her cheekbones rise, exposing that smile, my smile. She then took my face into her hands and planted a soft kiss on my lips. "I love you, Kay."

"I love you more."

CHAPTER 22

We grew another year older together, and life was dealing us a pretty good hand. Taj was living her dream as the owner of a beauty salon, and Dante was a blessing that brought sunshine to our lives every minute of the day. I had taken up the role of a stay-at-home dad, a luxury only afforded because of the money I had made with Run the previous year. Other than that, I would've been forced to punch somebody's clock, something I never planned on doing. That would've taken away all the quality time I got to spend with Dante, and I wasn't about to miss out on that for anything in the world.

Along with working at the salon, Kim had become somewhat the queen of promoting and throwing some of Decatur's biggest parties. Taj and I hadn't attended any of her parties since we'd been together, but we both felt like we had things to celebrate. Taj was anticipating on getting me drunk just to take advantage of me, and I was kind of looking forward to that.

Mom was in town spending the holidays with her new grandson, so she took care of him while we got both got razor sharp and headed out to bring in the New Year with, what seemed like, all of Decatur.

I was sipping champagne, enjoying my first buzz ever, lounging in the best seat in the house. The VIP section sat right above the dance floor, and offered a view of the entire club. Taj and Kim were among the elbow-to-elbow crowd that occupied the dance floor, everyone involved in a soulful Hustle session. It was one of those times when I wished I had learned how to move my entire body to the beat of music. I could bob the hell out of my head, so I thought it was best if I just chilled in the booth and take in the atmosphere.

There were six other booths in the VIP section, besides ours. Kim told me that they all belonged to Run, which was confusing at first. But when he came through the door with a small army, it all made sense.

He was escorted into the club like he was a high-ranking political official. A crew of his Vice Lord brethren encircled him, making it almost impossible for anyone to get within five feet of him. Our partnership had ended, but I knew loyalty meant a lot to Run, so I also knew that he was spreading the wealth with his crew. They were just taking care of the hand that fed them. Run had the money, and from the looks of it, he had the power, too.

The crowd parted like the Red Sea, as Run and his entourage made their way to the VIP section. A few people were pushed or shoved to make a path for the human caravan, but no one was foolish enough to retaliate. After throwing up gang-signs and slapping a girl on the butt, Run arrived at the steps that led up to the VIP area. When he saw me, he took the steps two at a time with his crew right behind him. I stood to greet him and showed respect to his posse by shaking about fifteen hands. Their cordial demeanors told me that they hadn't forgotten about who was responsible for putting Run in the game.

"You looking like Tony Montana up in this bitch," Run said as he slid down into the booth. "What's been up? I barely see you around except in traffic."

"Just taking it easy. Dante keeps me busy." I finished off my glass and watched Run pour me a refill. "You looking like a grown man in that suit." It was the first time I'd seen him in anything other than baggy jeans and tee-shirts.

"I kinda figured you was gon' be here, so a nigga had to represent." He slid to the edge of the booth and threw a leg up on the table to show off his brown alligator shoes. "This how they do it in the D, huh?"

I smiled. "Something like that." I put my foot up on the seat to let him see my beige alligator boots. "You're learning."

That caused him to laugh. "My nigga, Kay."

A waitress came up the steps and started taking orders. "Y'all need anything."

"Yeah," Run replied while looking to the area where his posse was seated. "...fifteen bottles of Moet for my boys back there and three bottles for this booth."

Her weight shifted to one leg. "I don't have time for the games," she said, sucking her teeth.

Run reached into his pocket and came out with a stack of money, placing it on the table. "Me neither."

The waitress quickly jotted down the order, her attitude making a quick reversal. "You need anything else?" She gave Run a flirtatious smile.

"Nawl, just go get my shit."

"I'll be right back." Run obviously was feeling himself. He looked down at the dance floor. "Which one of these hoes I wanna fuck tonight?"

The mood was slowed down a bit when the R. Kelly's "Your Body's Callin" faded in over the speakers. Taj and Kim came to the booth fanning themselves after dancing through several songs. Both had been drinking heavily and that only added to their heat factor.

"Oh shit!" Kim squealed, checking out Run's attire as he stood and gave both of them hugs. "Playa', playa'!"

"You look really nice, Run," Taj said, sliding in next to me. "Love the suit."

"Thanks, Taj." He ate the compliment up. His chest rose a bit. "Come on, Kim, let's go dance."

Kim was still standing, swaying back and forth to the slow jam. "Boy, I ain't got time to be whooping none of your hoes up in here. Then they won't come to any more of my parties."

"Gone with that bullshit, girl."

She walked over and stroked Run's cheek. "It's business, honey, nothing personal."

The waitress and three other members of the club's staff brought the champagne into the VIP area, and it seemed like every eye in the club was focused on our booth. Run didn't have to stand up to pay the lady, but it gave everyone a better view to see him slowly count off nearly two thousand dollars for the bottles. I was more impressed by the three-hundred dollar tip he gave the waitress.

While everybody was watching Run play "Big Willy", a grizzly bear caught my attention when it came through the entrance. It was actually Khalid. The full-length mink coat with the matching hat was proof that he was getting money in the town, but I couldn't tell which was darker, the coat or his face. The redbone he had with him, who was also adorned in mink, trailed behind him as he went over and took a seat at a reserved table on the lower level. Once he removed his companion's coat and pulled her chair out for her, he scanned the club as he stood behind her, his hands resting on her bare shoulders. And, if I wasn't mistaken, he was staring right at me. It was confirmed when he held the stare and flashed a grin, throwing a hand up in my direction. The touch of Taj's soft lips on my cheek broke the momentary awkwardness that I was feeling.

"Are you enjoying yourself, baby." I could smell the sweetness of champagne on her breath.

"Of course," I said, reaching under the table and running my hand up her thigh. "All I need now is to get you home and get you out this sexy dress."

She moved in for a kiss, stopping before our lips met. "We're going to get a room," she whispered seductively. "I can't let your mom hear you screaming my name."

Her tongue traced my lips, getting an instant reaction from the lower part of my body.

"We got a few minutes to countdown," Kim said, rushing back to the table. She grabbed a bottle and refreshed our glasses. More girls had made their way up into the VIP area. Most were wearing next to nothing, and I figured they wanted to be around Run when the New Year came in. If they didn't have any money, at least they could be around somebody who did when the clock struck twelve.

The d-jay lowered the volume when there were only thirty seconds left until midnight. Run and some members of his posse had gathered around our booth, bottles waving and having a good time while filling up the glasses of the girls who had just come up. And for obvious reasons, I didn't like that all eyes were on us. Speculation and hearsay ran rampant in Decatur. Although I was out of the game and no longer in a business relationship with Run, I was pretty sure everyone else suspected otherwise, especially how he and his crew were gathered around, putting me dead in the center like I was some mafia boss. That was some attention I never wanted, and, who but Run, would do all he could to bring more.

Ten seconds to midnight was when I saw him with that stack of money in his hand, counting off hundred dollar bills like a money machine. Everyone in the club was in sync with the countdown. "Five, four, three..."

Taj nudged me, her focus also on Run as he stood up.

"Two, one...Happy New Year!"

The crowd erupted, including me. That's when Run reached back like he was throwing a baseball and created his own hailstorm of confetti in the form of Ben Franklins. The bills showered down over the dance floor and sent everyone into a frenzy, both women and men. People were jumping in the air, trying to get hold of anything before it reached the ground, and during the whole episode, Run watched and laughed like he was a king who had just fed a village of hungry peasants.

"Happy New Year, Decatur!" he yelled.

It was a scene that would probably be talked about for years and years to come. I was pretty sure that was exactly how Run wanted it to be.

<><><>

"Last call for alcohol" was when a waitress came to the booth with two more bottles of Moet that I hadn't ordered. Taj was already drunk, and that was probably why she and Kim were on the dance floor busting old school breakdance moves, popping and locking like they were in a battle. I knew there was no way in hell she could drink another glass, let alone two more bottles. Run had disappeared a few minutes earlier after standing on the dance floor while some girl was grinding on him like she was a world-class stripper, so I doubted if he was the one who called for more champagne. The waitress must've noticed the confused look on my face.

"Khalid sent them over," she said while placing bottles on the table.

That was enough to sober me up just a little. When I looked down towards the table where he was sitting, I could see he had me in his crosshairs. He threw a hand up again and shot me a smile. His black ass was starting to creep me out.

As soon as the waitress left, I watched him get out his seat and stroll through the crowd, shaking hands and giving out a few hugs along the way. When he reached the steps to the VIP area, I figured I was about to finally come face to face with the man who once had a choke-hold on the dope game in Decatur.

"Mind if I take a seat, Kay?" the dark-skinned version of Suge Knight asked, a toothpick dangling from the corner of his mouth. Before I could answer, some members of Run's crew came over and started a stare-down with Khalid. I knew Run never cared for the guy, so I assumed that what Run didn't like, none of the Vice Lords liked.

"You cool over here, Kay?"

It was Roach, the guy who had sold me the digital scale. He asked me the question while mean-mugging Khalid.

"Yeah, I'm cool." I gave them a reassuring nod, not wanting to be associated with a gang-related beat-down. And if anybody was under the impression that I was somehow still connected with Run on a business level, having his security ready to put in work on my account probably only fueled the speculation.

Khalid didn't look like he was ready to beg for mercy, though. In fact, he looked a little agitated about being confronted by Roach and his boys. Considering he was in his late twenties to early thirties, he probably felt disrespected by being approached by guys who were barely out of their teens. And maybe he thought his reputation was enough to ward off anything like this from happening to him. But when money and egos come into play, anything could happen.

"I don't want any problems," Khalid said as he held up both hands, waving the white flag before anything happened. "I come in peace. Can I sit with you, Kay?"

I was hoping Roach and his boys didn't get offended about how Khalid had practically blowin' them off like they weren't standing there. The looks they gave him before they walked off told a different story.

"We never got the chance to meet, so I thought this was the best time to do so." He moved around in the booth until he found a comfortable position, even pushing the table towards me to make room for his large frame.

I adjusted the table back to my liking. "And what makes you think that?" I grabbed one of the bottles he'd sent over and poured myself a glass. He was bigger and older than me, so I was making the champagne bottle a little easier to handle just in case I had to go upside his head.

"It's called hospitality, Kay."

At that moment, he waved to someone on the dance floor. I saw Taj wave back. She continued dancing, not taking her eyes off of me. I gave her a shoulder shrug as Khalid went on.

"You know how when somebody comes into your house, you try to make sure they're comfortable and make sure they don't need anything?" He removed the toothpick from his mouth and pointed it at me as he spoke. "You know how that is, right? That's all I'm trying to do."

I knew exactly what he meant, but I didn't like how he was insinuating that Decatur was his home and I was nothing but a guest. I had a Decatur address on my driver's license, too, so it was my home just as much as it was his. It also sounded like he was offering me a chance to buy dope from him, something that I wouldn't have done had I still been selling drugs. He had rubbed me the wrong way and was somebody I couldn't see myself doing business with on any level. But just like anyone else, I let him hold on to his assumption.

"I appreciate the hospitality, but I'm good. Thanks for the champagne."

Our meeting was interrupted when Taj came back to the table. "Hey, Khalid, how are you?"

"I'm good. Just wanted to holla' at Kay, that's all." He stood. "Enjoy the champagne. I have to get back to this girl. Happy New year to y'all."

"Same to you," Taj replied. She watched him walk down the steps. "What did he want?"

I finished my glass. "I guess he's part of the Decatur Welcoming Committee."

CHAPTER 23

When I look back on it, I could never give a logical explanation as to why I decided to get back into the drug game. Maybe it was from sheer boredom; maybe it was the fact that I kind of missed the adrenaline rush that came with being in the streets dropping off dope and getting stacks of cash in return; or maybe it was the thought of that night when Khalid practically told me that Decatur was his town and I was nothing more than a guest. Maybe it was my ego that wanted to prove to him that I could come to his town and make just as much money as he could. It definitely wasn't that I needed the money. Taj's income from the shop was enough to take care of every bill we had and then some. Combine that with the money I had put away, and we weren't living too bad.

But whatever the reason was, it had me calling up Run on one of the snowiest days in Decatur's history. I hadn't spoken to him in months, so he probably knew it was something serious when he heard me on the line.

"You alright," he asked, loud music almost drowning him out.

"Yeah, I'm straight."

I was watching Dante spell out something as he sat in the middle of the living room floor. Shorty was sitting comfortably on a pillow beside him. Taj was upstairs taking a shower. "Meet me at Pop's in an hour."

He choked on the other end. I had interrupted his smoke session. "Nigga, you see all that mothafuckin' snow out there?"

"I heard you just bought a brand new Navigator. You won't have a problem making it down there. See you in an hour." I ended the call before he could respond.

"Daddy, are you going somewhere?" Dante asked while arranging letters.

I got down on the floor and stretched out behind him. "Yes, but I won't be gone long."

<><><>

Pop's Place was a staple in the black community of Decatur. Although you couldn't tell from the shack of a building it was housed in, Pop's served some of the best soul food in Central Illinois. It was probably the only soul food restaurant in that area, but people "put it on everything" that nothing compared to Pop's smothered pork chops or homemade sweet potato pie. While Taj was pregnant, she had sent me down there on many occasions whenever she got a craving for red velvet cake or the scrumptious caramel cake the restaurant served. What she didn't know was that at one point, Run and I had been responsible for supplying Pops with something that was more in demand than the tasty food he served.

The owner, who everyone affectionately called Pops, had been hustling even before I was born. He was still in the game at the age of sixty-six, serving hot orders of chicken wings with side orders of crack to customers who had stayed loyal to him ever since powder cocaine was replaced by the hard version. A scrawny little character whose stutter was sometimes comical, he told me that his long tenure in the game, without an arrest, was based on pure luck and by treating his customers with respect.

"You tre-tre-tre-treat a mothafucka wrong and they te-te-te-tell on yo' ass the fir-fir-fir-first chance they get."

There was always a lesson to be learned from Pops. He was wise and had been doing it for years, so I soaked it all in whenever I went down to his place.

"Wh-wh-wh-what the hell y-y-y-you doin' out here in all th-th-th-this snow, Kay?" he asked, standing behind the counter musing over some lottery tickets.

"I'm meeting Run." I went and sat down at the tabletop Pac-Man machine. "You got some red velvet cake back there?"

"Yeah, I-I-I got some left." He removed his glasses and disappeared into the back where the kitchen was. I slid a quarter into the machine and started playing.

I was on the second board when Run came through the door, followed by two of his boys. They were all decked out in hooded parkas looking like they were on an arctic expedition

"St-st-st-stomp y'all damn fe-fe-fe-feet before y'all track all th-th-th-that snow in here," Pops said, coming from the back.

"Fu-fu-fu-fuck you, old ass nigga," Run teased as he took a seat across from me. It was customary for Pops and Run to greet each with curse words. There was no disrespect involved on either's part; that's just the way they were.

"Get us three wing dinners with yo' old grey-headed ass."

"Let me g-g-g-go back here and sh-sh-sh-shit on yours."

We all laughed. It probably wouldn't have been as funny if Pops didn't stutter.

Run's boys picked out pool sticks and went over and started a game of pool.

"Get out so I can play you." Run took his coat off and laid a chrome-plated gun on top of the game.

I shook the joystick and put a juke move on Pinky and Blinky. "You gone shoot me if I don't?"

He chuckled. "This reserved fo' any nigga that try to run up."

I continued playing until Run said, "I got a hundred I beat you."

Gambling wasn't my thing, but when it came to video games, I wouldn't consider it gambling because I couldn't lose.

I let the ghost eat me and slid two quarters into the machine. The theme music played and I started my turn while Run looked on.

"Don't tell me you had me drive in all this damn snow to play some mothafuckin' Pac-Man."

"You don't like Pac-Man?" I asked, clearing the first board. "This is a classic."

"I'ma like it better after I take yo' money."

I went through the second board with ease, giving Run a wink as I did. Pac-Man ran across the screen as Blinky and the crew trailed close behind. The blue screen popped up and I started one of my patented patterns. I gobbled up a peach and then bit into an energizer. Two hundred, four hundred, eight hundred, sixteen hundred. I checked my score and it was perfect up to that point.

"You still got that connect in Chicago?"

"Not if you got work."

"No, I need some."

"Oh shit!" His eyes bucked with excitement. "My nigga back in the game!"

<><><>

A week later I found myself on I-57. We were trailing behind a friend of Run's, who was hauling one hundred and fifty thousand dollars in her trunk. Fifty thousand was mine. It was Run's idea to bring me along. He wanted to introduce me to his connect just in case anything happened and he wasn't able to take the trip. I had no intentions on ever going to Chicago alone, and if Run hadn't been dealing with his connect for a considerable amount of time, I don't think I would've gone with him. Those stories about what happened to people who journeyed to Chicago for drugs, lingered heavily in the back of my mind during the entire drive.

A high-rise apartment on the west side of Chicago was where our trip ended. Run retrieved the duffle bag from the other car and I followed him into the building, my eyes shifting nervously, on the lookout for anything suspicious. We got on an elevator and took it up to the seventh floor.

Run was on his cell phone calling some girl every name in the book the entire time, acting as if carrying a duffle bag full of money was no big deal. Maybe it was because he was familiar with the surroundings. But his casual manner did nothing to ease my nervousness.

We stepped off the elevator and walked until we came to apartment number seven-nineteen. Run gave the door a rhythmic knock. Seconds later it was opened by a slim guy sporting an oil-stained brown Carhartt overall with the matching skully, oil and dirt stains included. In the feds, he would've been referred to as "O.G." or "Old Head"; he was probably twice my age.

"Whats up, Chuck." Run took a step toward the door, but was denied by Chuck's outstretched hand.

"Who dat'?"

Run laughed him off. "He with me. I told Lazar."

"Hold up." He pushed the door closed, leaving me out in the hallway. I could hear Run talking to him, telling him that I was cool and so on. A third voice entered the conversation and, shortly after that, the door came open. Chuck welcomed me into the apartment with a tilt of a head. Run was standing with the duffle bag on his shoulder, giving me an apologetic look while another guy was sitting on a couch. The packages of cocaine on the cocktail table stacked-up like books, was a good indication that everything was all good.

"Sorry about that, Kay." It was the guy sitting on the couch. "I forgot to tell Chuck that Run was bringing somebody with him." He rose from the couch and took a few steps to shake my hand. "I'm Lazar. I heard a lot about you."

His grip was firm for a guy who looked like he would have a hard time bench-pressing ninety pounds. He had a few inches on me, but if it came down to it, I knew I could easily take him down.

Being from Detroit, I always pictured a connect as someone who was flashy, someone who flaunted his wealth by being draped in diamonds and expensive clothes. But the guy whose hand I shook could've been mistaken for somebody who was down on their luck. He probably hadn't seen a barber in weeks, and the faded stoned washed jeans he wore looked like they'd had their best days years and years ago. His white thermal shirt had a hole that exposed his elbow, and if the dope hadn't been sitting on that table, I would've sworn a robbery was about to take place.

Lazar returned to the couch and proceeded to conduct business. "What you got for me, Run?"

Run kneeled down and unzipped the duffle bag, placing bundles of money neatly on the cocktail table. I glanced over my shoulder and saw Chuck standing guard at the door, both hands tucked in the pockets of his overalls. I was sure he had a firm grip on a gun or two.

"One-fifty," Run said, rising to his feet. "I wanna buy six and get fronted three."

Lazar looked pleased with the offer. When he nodded his approval, Run handed him the empty duffle bag. Once he finished stuffing the packages of cocaine into the bag, there were about ten book-like packages left on the table.

"I like seein' you young boys taking care of business," he said like a proud father who was congratulating his son. "You boys ain't even twenty-five and doin' it how it need to be done. I like that about y'all." He smiled for the first time. "You see this, Chuck?"

A grunt was Chuck's only response.

"Alright, I know you boys gotta hit the highway, so I'm here when y'all need me." He rose from his seat, giving Run a pat on the back, and me another shake of the hand. His grip was firm as he looked me in the eye. "Nice meeting you, Kay, and hopefully we'll be doing more business together."

"I hope so too."

Chuck escorted us out the building on Lazar's command, making me feel safer than if we had gone down alone. We had nine kilos of coke, and in the drug game, people lost their lives for a lot less.

The dope was put in the trunk of the car driven by Run's friend. We trailed her at a safe distance back down I-57 and made it safely back to Decatur.

<><><>

The Chicago thing was going well for us, and I was literally sitting back collecting money. After each trip, I wouldn't see any more dope until we went back to get another load from Lazar. Run would take whatever I bought and front it to his boys, giving me the luxury of only meeting up with him when he had twenty-thousand to put towards our next package. He would try to get me to ride around with him while he smoked weed and flirted with girls, but our relationship was one of business, and that wasn't going to change. He was too much in the spotlight for my taste.

During our trips to Chicago, I would try to talk to him about some of the bad moves he was making. I let him know that he was only bringing heat on himself by going out and buying a new car every month like he was running a legit business. I warned him about carrying a gun everywhere he went like he was in the Wild West. He had a bunch of guys around him who would do anything he told them to do, so he had no reason to even touch a gun. And when I heard that he pistol whipped the boyfriend of a girl he was messing around with, I really put some distance between us.

The worse thing about it all, was the fact that I wasn't hanging in the streets, and Run never even mentioned any of those incidents to me. Every update on Run's activities that I had received, came by way of the rest haven for gossip: Taj's House Of Styles. And when your name is the frequent hot topic in places like that, you're most definitely doing too much in small-town Decatur. I knew trouble was coming.

The thing that led to his downfall was his appetite for the attention and drama that came with sticking his dick in almost every woman in Decatur. He always bragged about who he had slept with. It was a game to him, and he would purposely set up fights between girls by having them come to his house at the same time.

They would be out in the middle of the street fighting like pit bulls, while Run and his boys laughed and made bets on who would win. It had happened on numerous occasions. As a way to make amends with the two fighters, he would simply pay some bills or take them shopping. Maybe Run figured that money was all any girl wanted from him, but he made the mistake of embarrassing a girl who had deep feelings for him, and it cost him in the end.

Porsche was one of Taj's customers and also a good friend. Like most women do while getting their hair done, she would confide in Taj about her dealings with Run. And in turn, like most wives do with their husbands, I was sometimes force-fed a helping of what went on in Decatur's social scene.

So, unlike the girls Run usually dealt with, Porsche actually had strong feelings for him. But it was obvious that Run didn't deal in feelings when it came to women. It showed when he played his little set-up game with Porsche, pitting her against one of the craziest and toughest girls in Decatur.

Her name was Renee, and when it came to fighting, she was the Laila Ali of central Illinois. She had whooped chicks from Springfield to Bloomington, leaving trails of weave and scratched-up faces in her wake. Nobody in their right mind would start a fight with her if they had any knowledge of who she was. She had even given a few guys black eyes and bloody noses, so imagine what she did to Porsche, a girl who was timid in nature and barely weighed in at a hundred pounds.

From what I had heard, Porsche was at Run's house when Renee arrived. He and his boys were playing cards while Porsche was chilling on the couch, listening to music and smoking weed. When the doorbell rang, Run opened the door without hesitation. And as soon as Renee saw Porsche, it was on.

When it was over, Porsche, looking like she had been jumped by eight guys, ran out of the house crying and heartbroken. What made it worse was that, as she got in her car, Run and his boys stood on the porch laughing and teasing her after she had just received a brutal ass whooping. It was all fun and games until she pulled out his driveway after yelling, "That's why I'm calling the police on yo' ass!"

Run must've thought that she wasn't serious, or maybe the statement was directed at Renee. But for whatever reason, he and his boys went back inside and went on about their business like everything was fine and dandy. A few hours later, the house was raided by the Decatur police. They found five guns and a few ounces of weed. Fortunately for Run, he was smart enough to keep the cocaine in another location, but he was still arrested for the weed and guns. He ended up spending a few days in the county until he received a bond. Only two hours after bonding out, he did the unthinkable.

I knew Run could do some crazy things, but never in a million years would I have thought that he would stand outside of Porsche's house with an A-K 47 and riddle it with over thirty bullets. Porsche survived the hail of gunfire, only being grazed in the leg. Her five-year-old nephew wasn't as fortunate. He died instantly when a bullet penetrated three walls and struck him in the chest as he lay sleep in Porsche's bed. When Run found out that the child had died, he simply drove to the police station and turned himself in. Him taking responsibility for his actions carried no weight with the judge. He received a life sentence plus twenty years.

CHAPTER 24

The incident with Run didn't stop me from hustling, but I did set a goal for myself. A quarter of a million dollars was enough for me to sit back until I found somewhere else to invest my money. Lazar had been steady with supplying us with good dope, so making another seventy-five thousand didn't seem to be a problem at all. The only thing about the whole situation was that I didn't have Run. Without him in the picture, it was time for me to get my hands dirty. Roach was one of the few people I dealt with. He basically inherited Run's clientele, making it easy for him to move whatever amount I gave him. Trusting him like I did with Run was out of the question, though. I limited him to nine ounces at a time, just in case he took a loss of some sort. He did come short on a couple of occasions, but I was charging him more than usual, so in the end, I wasn't losing out. I also brought Pops into the fold, fronting him whatever he felt like he could handle. He was old school and played by the rules of the game, so dealing with him was nothing but profitable, and making my money first was his top priority. As soon as he had sold enough to pay me, he would call me up without hesitation. The money was coming in slower with just those two on my team. Because of that, I had to stay in the game a little longer than I had intended. I still was only dropping off and picking up, so I really had no reason to complain. The only risk I was really taking was hitting the highway to go see Lazar.

I didn't have anyone around me to drive the dope back to Decatur. We always used one of Run's female friends in the past. So, going against one of the things Jay had warned me about, I took the penitentiary chance of driving on the highway with a duffle bag full of dope in the back of a rental car. It was probably the dumbest thing I had ever done, but I was lucky enough to make it back safely every time.

Having a good connect in the dope game is a key factor in getting paid. Without it, success is hard to come by. I had been fortunate enough to have Jay when I first started out, and thought I had been lucky when Run introduced me to Lazar. As a connect, Jay was irreplaceable, so I never expected Lazar to give me the same treatment that I got from him; everybody was different. But I also never expected him to play me out of fifty-thousand dollars, either.

I'd been seeing Lazar about once a week. Everything always went smooth, but I hadn't gotten comfortable going without Run at my side. I didn't know anything about the guy, and it never crossed my mind to ask Run how he knew him. The only thing that mattered was that he had dope, and that was all the info I needed.

The table was stacked with dope as usual, and nothing seemed out of the ordinary when I went to see Lazar. He sat on that couch and loaded my bag with the drugs. I noticed a black "X" marked on two of the kilos but thought nothing of them. They both made their way into my duffel bag after he sorted out a few other ones and picked those two out of the bunch. I just assumed that the cocaine had gone through a lot of hands before it made it to that table, and maybe somewhere down the line, it was marked as a way of being counted.

Tina's house was still the place where I cooked and stored my dope. From the beginning, she was aware of it all, and never uttered a word to anyone about me being involved in drugs. It cost me a lot of bingo money over time, but she opened her house to me and kept everything a secret.

I was in her kitchen minutes after I made it back to Decatur, cooking up nine ounces out of one of the kilos. When the timer went off on the microwave, I removed my trusty Pyrex cooking pot and immediately knew that something wasn't right. There was no big glob of oily substance floating in the bottom of the pot like usual. Instead, I was looking at about a half ounce of cocaine as it bubbled in one small area of the pot. I had become the Chef

Boyardee of cooking up dope, so I knew that is was no fault of mine that it came back that short. I let it cool down, put some cold water on it to get it hard, and then put it on the scale just to know the exact weight. It came close to a half ounce. Something most definitely wasn't right.

I dialed Lazar's number while looking at the package I had taken the nine ounces out of. The "X" that was marked on it held my attention for a brief second. I was sure that Lazar was going to take care of the situation, so I wasn't sweating it too hard. Getting a bad batch of dope came with the territory. But, if you had a real connect like I thought I had, there was a money back guarantee on anything you bought if it wasn't up to par. The only thing I was stressing about at the time, was the thought of having to turn around and drive right back up to Chicago.

"Hey, this is not doing what it's supposed to do," I said, when Lazar came on the line.

"What you mean?"

"I did nine and didn't even get one out of it."

"Maybe you did something wrong."

"It wasn't me." I was staring at that "X". "It's the product."

Silence on his end. Then, "I only sell it how I get it, Kay." He sounded like he was getting annoyed. "I don't know what else to tell you."

It seemed as if the heat in the house had been turned up to two-hundred degrees. My temples began to throb, and I could feel sweat forming on my upper lip. My grip became tighter on the phone. I remained calm as I said, "Tell me to bring it back and you're going to take care of it."

"What am I supposed to do? Take the loss?" He spoke like I had just told a joke.

His little chuckle at the end of the statement made me feel as if he had just spit in my face. "You supposed to make this shit right!"

I was sure that he could hear the anger in my voice. It was probably the first time in my life that I had ever felt so mad, so out of control. I felt like a rape victim. I thought maybe he had hung up, then, I heard movement. It sounded like he had covered the receiver and was talking to somebody in the background. That chuckle came through the line again.

"I'll tell you what, Kay," he said, calmly but unable to disguise his annoyance with me. "Next time you come down to cop, I'll take care of you."

Take care of me. For some reason, I didn't like the sound of that. "I can be there in a few hours," I replied, not wanting to wait until the next time. "I got money to make now!"

"I said the next time!" His tone told me that he was getting a little upset at my insistence, but I was the one who was getting played.

"Look, man, I got shit to do and..."

He interrupted me before I could finish. "No, you look, mothafucka'!" he yelled through the phone. Then silence. As if he was bipolar, the angriness disappeared, replaced by a cool and collected manner. "When you come back, I'll take care of you!"

Mad or angry couldn't describe how I felt as I sat there. The guy had the nerve to act like I had sold him some bad dope, and then went off on me because of what he had done. And to top it off, he wanted to put me on hold until it was convenient for him. What part of the game was that?

That "X" caught my attention again. Suspecting some major bullshit was in the game, I cooked it up and wasn't surprised when I got the same result as the first nine ounces. Out of one kilo, only two ounces came back. And something told me I was in for more bad news with the other "X" marked kilo.

Needless to say, when the cooking process was over, my assumption was right, and I had basically paid fifty-thousand dollars for four ounces of crack. Lazar had put a wrapper over my head and stamped "sucker" on it. As hard as it was, I accepted the fact that I had been beaten out of my money. It was just that simple. I had no intentions of going back to see him, regardless of his claim to make everything right. He got me once, but he damn sure wasn't going to get another opportunity to do it again. Why he had done it, though, was beyond me. Maybe he was short on cash and I just happened to be somebody he thought he could rob without a gun. Maybe he really was down on his luck as his appearance led me to think. But whatever his reasons were, it was all second-guessed when I opened the third unmarked kilo.

The unmistakable strong stench of powder cocaine escaped the package as soon as I cut into it, something that was missing from the first two. And after removing all of the tape and plastic, a square brick of cocaine was revealed in all of its glistening glory. Just from looking at it, I knew it was the real deal. It reminded me of the dope I used to get from Jay, the kind that didn't lose a gram after being cooked. I felt a little better when I started cooking it up and it did everything real dope was supposed to do.

Using my superb whipping skills, I managed to turn thirty-six ounces into forty-eight, doing all I could to minimize my loss. But then, all the questions started coming at me. Why would Lazar sell me two bad kilos and one good one? Why would he tell me to wait until I cop again to make it right instead of letting me bring it right back to him? He had at least ten more kilos on the table when I left him, so he couldn't say he didn't have any left. And when he covered up the phone, who was he talking to and what was it about? And he changed his mind after he came back on the line, but why? At first, he was talking like he wasn't going to replace the dope. But then his tune changed and he said he would take care of me. There was a sinister tone in his voice when he said it, a tone that told me that he definitely had plans to take care of me, just not in a way I would've liked.

After Lazar removed my money from the duffle bag, I could clearly remember how he briefly stared at the three stacks of dope on the table. Instead of picking from the stack nearest him, he reached for the stack furthest away, at the end of the table; that's when I first noticed the markings. He then hesitated, like he was in deep thought, before he reached for the good kilo that was in the stack closest to him. Maybe his initial plan was to get me for all of my money, but on the fly, came up with a plan to get me for even more money when I came back. The good kilo would make it look like an honest mistake to a lot of people; it even confused me for a minute. His insistence that I wait until I came to cop again was a dead giveaway, though. If he had good intentions, he would've had me come right back to straighten everything out. But no, he wanted me to come back with more cash, and I suspected that the only way I would've left that apartment, was dead.

I let the scene of the transaction play over and over in my head. Every second, every move. Once I did that, it was obvious to me that it was no accident that I ended up with the two bad kilos.

CHAPTER 25

I never heard anything from Lazar after that. My stash had gotten shorter, and the worse part about it was I didn't have a steady connect to make up for what I had lost. The smart thing to do was to get out the game while I still had close to one-hundred and fifty thousand dollars, but I was hell-bent on reaching the goal I had set for myself. Mona was still in Detroit, and she knew all of Jay's friends who were still heavy-hitters in the game. I was pretty sure she could hook me up with someone who I didn't have to worry about selling me some bad dope. If I could've found a connect who was as half as dependable as Jay, it would've been easy for me to get that quarter of a million I was reaching for.

It was good to hear her voice when I called her. Jay was the topic of our conversation for the majority of the call, both of us recalling some of the times we had spent with him. We shared memories and we also shared a moment of silence when the emotions got a little too much for her. Jay was deeply missed.

The call lasted for about an hour before Mona said she had a few things to care of. But before she hung up, I got to the real reason why I had gotten in touch with her.

"You know anybody I could see up there?"

She didn't miss a beat. "Yeah, Kay. Just come on up."

<><><>

I set out on my way to Detroit two days later after telling Taj I had to go take care of some business. She and Dante were asleep when I left out during the wee hours of the night. I gave them both a kiss as they slept, and then hit the highway. I wanted to beat the hectic morning rush hour of the Chicago traffic and make it to Detroit by noon. That way, I could be back in Decatur in time to read Dante a bedtime story and have a late dinner with Taj. Mona had everything set-up where it would be an in-and-out process, so I planned on being there no longer than a couple hours at the most.

It was a smooth ride up until I made it to Battle Creek, Michigan, home of the Kellogg cereal company. The smell along that stretch of highway was nauseating. And, when the red and blue lights of a police car flashed in my rearview mirror, I was almost ready to throw-up.

I had my cruise control set at seventy-two miles per hour, only two notches above the speed limit. Michigan State police were notorious for hiding under bypasses in hopes of catching speeders motoring down I-94, so I knew better than to be speeding, especially with a bag holding forty-thousand dollars under my passenger seat.

"What the hell did I do?" I yelled as I slowed down and pulled over to the shoulder of the highway.

I could see the sun rising in the eastern sky over the horizon ahead. Through my rearview, I could see the door of the police car opened. A big burly figured stepped out and started walking up to my truck. The pre-dawn light wasn't bright enough for me to see his face while his flashlight danced around. He aimed it at my mirror, blinding light causing me to sit back and shake my head.

"Good morning," he said, arriving at my door. "License and registration, please."

I didn't move. "What did you pull me over for?"

"The light over your license plate is out."

I turned to look at him and noticed his Battle Creek Police officer uniform. It was unbuttoned at the top, revealing a dingy tee shirt underneath. From the crumbs around his mouth and the mustard on his top lip, it was evident that he had interrupted his snack just so he could pull me over. I grabbed my wallet and gave him what he had asked for.

"Where you headed?" he asked while studying my license.

"Detroit." I was staring straight ahead.

He pointed his flashlight in my face. Then he aimed it through the back passenger window, checking to see if anything was back there. "I'll be right back."

Enough time passed for him to run my name. I peeked in my side-view and saw him coming back. The crumbs around his mouth were gone, but what looked like mayonnaise, had replaced the mustard on his top lip. "You got any drugs or guns in here?" He tapped on my door with his flashlight.

I was a victim of DWB: driving while black. "Now why would I have any drugs or guns?"

"Hey," he said, "I just asked." The smile on his face let me know that this whole thing was amusing to him. "Mind if I search your vehicle?"

That question made me more angry than nervous. "You got a search warrant?"

"Well, I can get one seeing that I saw something suspicious in your truck back there."

I knew for a fact that the only thing in the back of my truck was Dante's baby seat and maybe a toy or two. Those were in the back seat. The rear of my truck was spotless because I never put anything back there. So, the only thing he could've thought was suspicious was the fact that I was a black man behind the wheel of a nice truck. And, that was enough for a warrant in any redneck town in America.

It didn't make any sense to get hauled off to jail and wait for some judge to give him permission to search my truck. That would've probably taken a few hours, and I wasn't ready to sit in a cell while they went through the process. It was inevitable that they would find the money anyway, so either way, I would have come out a loser.

"So what's it going to be, buddy?" he asked. One hand was on his holster while the other was gripped on my door. He was becoming more of an asshole by the minute.

Reluctantly, I opened my door and stepped out. I was met with a forceful shove that landed me against the truck, and then treated to a thorough pat down. The cold steel of handcuffs on my wrists was next.

"Just cuffing you for my own protection." He guided me to his car.

Once he had me secured in the cramped confines of the back seat of his squad car, he asked me again if there were any drugs or guns in the truck. I gave him the same sarcastic response as before.

Before he closed the door, he said, "Well, I'll tear it up if I have to."

The fat bastard waddled to my truck and opened the tailgate first. After seeing that there wasn't anything back there, he went around and opened the rear passenger's door. Half of his body went in while the other half displayed a bad case of plumber's crack. He tossed Dante's toys into the back of the truck as if he was purposely trying to do some kind of damage, causing my blood to boil more than it already was. When I saw his car seat get thrown out onto the graveled pavement, I snorted as hard as I could and hawked a glob of spit on the floor of the squad car. He continued his search of the back seats, and of course, came up empty. But when he opened the front passenger's door, I knew that was going to change.

The glove box was the first place he went, and I wasn't surprised to see some papers and the driver's manual tossed in the air and land in the back seat. It was a blatant show of disrespect for my property, but there was nothing I could do, but spit on his floor again as his attention turned to the area under the passenger's seat. He kneeled his fat ass down and stuck an arm under it, and I knew from the look on his face, that he had hit pay dirt. He was looking back at me with a smile on his face, his hand obviously holding onto the bag that contained my forty-thousand dollars. When he got to his feet, he held up the bag, taunting me as he waddled back to the police car. I held my head down and wondered what I had done to deserve such bad luck.

"So, what do we have here?" he said, getting in the front seat. The car tilted from his weight. He opened the bag and laughed when he saw the contents. "Looks like drug money to me. Smells like it, too," he said as he took a whiff.

I put my head to the bullet-proof glass just to get a last peek at what used to be mine. "It's not drug money," I replied, the sarcasm completely gone from my voice, replaced with a near-pleading cry. "It's mine."

He closed the bag and placed it on the dashboard. "I think the canine dogs will agree with me, buddy." He glanced back at me. "I'm pretty sure the Feds will say the same thing."

"The Feds?" That was something I wasn't ready to hear.

"Yeah," he said, picking up a sandwich from the passenger's seat. "Anything over ten thousand dollars and they come in and investigate. I think it's more like five thousand, but, who knows."

He took a couple of bites of his sandwich as if we were holding a casual conversation. I was waiting for him to open up a newspaper and light up a cigarette afterwards. After a few minutes passed without him saying anything or calling for backup, I sensed he was up to something.

"So what you want to do?" He wiped his mouth and then angled his rear-view mirror so that we were eye to eye.

It was then that I realized that he was going to use the money to upgrade his lifestyle just a bit. My mind started racing, thinking of ways I could get it back. My first thought was to make him take me to jail. My trust fund was a good explanation for why I was in possession of that much money. But, did I really want to get involved with the Feds if he was forced to turn the money in? Did I want that kind of attention and take the chance of them possibly investigating where every dime of that trust fund money went? And then I thought about Taj and her shop, which I was sure they would've also looked into seeing that we were married. I wasn't about to take the chance of them taking that away from her because of my mistake. And to make matters worse, I was about to lose another substantial amount of money after the Lazar incident. If I got on the Feds radar, it would've been almost impossible for me to stay in the game long enough to make that money back and reach my goal. The only option was to chalk it up as a loss and go back to Decatur a free man with my tail tucked between my legs.

I was hoping he could feel the burning stare I gave the back of his fat neck. "Let me out of here."

That made his day. He moved faster than I had seen him during the whole traffic stop. I was yanked from the back seat and the cuffs were removed in record time.

"Now you have a good trip, ya' hear." The country accent was his final taunt.

I walked toward my truck busted and disgusted. I didn't even look back at the highway bandit when his door slammed and the police car popped into gear. Tires screeched loudly as he made his getaway. That's when I noticed my license plate; it was lit up just like the law required.

CHAPTER 26

The incident with the crooked cop probably was the yellow flag, signaling for me to slow down and realize that I was fortunate to have had my freedom and my life after what I had gone through. But unfortunately, I had become addicted to the immediate gratification that came with making that fast money. And that addiction led me to deal with someone that, never in a million years, would I have never thought I would turn to as a connect.

It's basic economics to know that when no money's coming in, and money is constantly going out, Broke Avenue is right around the corner. I was a long way from being broke. But after splurging on a new truck for Taj and doing my usual everyday spending, I started to get a little uncomfortable when I fell below the hundred thousand dollar mark. That's when the feeling of being stressed out came over me. So, as a way to relieve the stress, I spent more money. I figured if anybody was going to be enjoying the fruits of my labor, it was going to be me and the people I loved the most.

A week in the Caribbean was the perfect getaway to have time to think about what I was going to do next. I invited Kim, Barbara, and my mom along to help occupy the four-room villa we rented on the island of Anguilla, a beautiful eel-shaped piece of land surrounded by the bluest water I'd ever seen. The white sanded beach, that was only footsteps away from the villa, was where we spent most of our days. It was surrounded by beautiful palm trees that seemed to stretch up to the sky.

Some smaller palm trees overlapped onto the beach and provided an ideal place for the ladies to relax and read books. Dante and I preferred to splash around in the beautiful water, and then we would often find ourselves sitting there in the sand staring out at the endless horizon. His inquisitiveness was at its peak during those times, asking about anything that caught his eye.

"Dad, where do starfish come from?"

"Dad, did they put bleach on this sand to make it white?"

I always answered as best as I could, and sometimes I would just reply by saying, "Your mom probably knows the answer; she's the Jeopardy queen."

Whenever that occurred, he would spring up and make a dash over to them as they relaxed in the shade. I'd turn around and smile as she tried to explain the unexplainable while shaking her head at me. The second day there was when we visited the marketplace that was ran by locals. They were all very pleasant and gentle people, most looking of African descent. We were greeted with smiles at every turn, and the hospitality they showered us with made the vacation even more memorable.

It wasn't surprising that Taj and the ladies spent their much-appreciated American dollars on clothes and handmade jewelry; that was expected. But what I didn't expect was to find a xylophone on the small Caribbean island. Well, of course, it was Dante who spotted the thing.

We were standing around listening to the ladies compliment almost every article of clothing that was on display at a small shed of a boutique in the marketplace. I was holding Dante's hand as he stood beside me shaking a key chain made of colorful seashells.

"How do you like this, baby?" Taj held up a white blouse, modeling it for me, waiting for my approval.

"What if I don't like it?" I teased.

She waved me off with a smile and added it to a collection she had thrown across her arm. "I know what you like."

I looked down at Dante. "Our opinions don't matter when it comes to women's fashion. Just say you like it and leave it at that. Words of wisdom for dad."

"Expert advice, huh?" Dante giggled.

"I ever tell you how smart you are?"

"No, but you don't have to tell me." He shook the bracelet and smiled up at me.

Dante inherited his good looks from his mom, but our sense of humor was one of the same. He understood sarcasm like it was a second language, and if one of my attempts at humor was off the mark, he would let it be known immediately.

"Look, Daddy!" Dante yelled.

Before I could turn to see what had gotten his attention, my arm was nearly yanked out of the socket. I stumbled before I regained my balance, as Dante pulled me along like he was a husky in an Alaskan sled race. He didn't stop until we reached a stand where an old islander was sitting at a table running sandpaper over a piece of wood. Another table was occupied by wooden carvings formed in the shape of animals, cars, and instruments. A separate table held one lone wooden instrument that took up the entire space. Dante's eyes were glued to that one particular instrument: a xylophone that was varnished and shined to pristine condition.

"Daddy, you see that?" he asked, slowly stepping closer and closer to the small table as if trying not to disturb the carvings.

"Yeah. I see it."

The islander glanced at us as he continued sanding the project he was working on. He blew off the carving and sat it to the side.

"It was my father's last creation," he said in a thick Caribbean accent. He stood and wiped his hands off on an old rag. The same rag was used to clear his face of specks of wood and sweat. "He died only three days after he completed it."

"I'm...I'm sorry to hear that."

"It's all right," he said, waving me off as he neared me. "He lived a long and peaceful life." He gestured around to the tables of art, wearing a proud smile while doing so. "This was his life."

"And now it's yours." I smiled.

"Yes, I guess you can say that."

From the look of his dark leathery skin, it was clear that he had spent his fair share of time under the Caribbean sun. He also appeared to be up in age, and I imagined his father had to have been pretty old at the time of his death. But, like all of the other inhabitants of the island, his nature was welcoming and pleasant.

"So you like that, little man?"

"Yes, sir," Dante replied as he looked up at the gentleman.

"He plays a little bit," I added.

Dante picked up the two wooden mallets and tested the notes with a few taps. He then stopped and began playing a melody that I had heard before, but couldn't remember from where. It had a tropical sound to it, and I could tell that he had caught the islander by surprise. He glanced at me with a shocked look on his face as he bobbed his head to each note. "Gassenhauer!"

I was confused. "Gas and who?"

"Gassenhauer," he repeated. "It's a very old classical music piece by Carl Orff, a German composer from the early twentieth century; though, it's been remade over and over by many people." He studied Dante as he continued playing. "Very impressive."

Before I realized it, a small crown had gathered around, lured in by the song being played by a kid who wasn't even three years old yet. I was kind of fascinated, myself, hearing him play something by some German I never knew existed. But he was my son, and I knew he was not an ordinary child.

At the end of his performance, the crowd applauded him as he laid the mallets down next to the xylophone.

"Bravo!" a few people in the crowd yelled.

His reaction when he noticed his small audience was pure Dante; he turned around with a smile and took a bow. He then came to my side and said, "Can I have it, Daddy?"

"How can I say no?"

"You can't." He giggled.

"How much?" I asked the islander.

He rubbed a chin of white stubble. "I think if my father were here, he would appreciate your son's knowledge of that instrument. So, take it as a gift. He would do the same."

I reached into my pocket as I shook my head. "No, I can't..."

Gently, he put a hand on my shoulder and stared me in the eye. His smile was endearing, and I could feel his sincerity. "It's a gift from us."

I looked down at Dante, who was beaming like the sun. "Tell him 'thank you', Daddy!"

I extended my hand. "Thanks…I'm sorry; I never got your name."

"My name is Shai, as was my father's." His grip was very firm for an older gentleman.

"I'm Kabazza. Nice to meet you."

"Likewise." He turned his attention to Dante, and in a tone that was filled with purpose and seriousness, he said, "You play from your heart, my friend. Continue to do so."

As if he sensed the seriousness of the statement, Dante nodded obediently. "I will."

There was a brief silence as we stood there, broken only when Shai spoke. "I must return to work. Enjoy your stay on the island."

<><><>

"We are going to have to ship that thing home," Taj said as we sat out on the beach later that evening.

"Yeah, I know. It'll cost a pretty penny. That kid is going to have to get a job." I said it loud enough for Dante to hear, but his new instrument had all of his attention as he sat a few feet in front of us. He was going over it like a mechanic looking for a faulty head gasket, poking and pulling at every key.

"I just can't believe you actually got it for free. That was so nice of that man."

"That man's name is Shai." I corrected her.

"Who is the Egyptian God of fate and destiny."

I cut my eyes at her. "Somebody's experiencing Jeopardy withdrawals, I see."

"Well, that is the right answer," she said as she stood up and dusted off her backside. "And, yes, I do miss kicking your butt."

"Didn't I win the last game?"

She smacked her lips. "You wish. I'm going in to see if they're done with this food. I'm starving."

"Let us know," I said, looking out at the ocean. "I think we might have a xylophone as a guest at the dinner table tonight."

She went and bent over to give Dante a kiss before sashaying away, knowing that I was watching her and that two-piece bikini. When she had disappeared into the villa, I looked out at the beautiful ocean as the sun began to set out over the horizon.

It felt good to be away from the life I was living at the time. It was actually a relief not to have to worry about where my next dollar was going to come from. I knew when we returned to Decatur, those worries were going to be waiting for me, but for the time being, I pushed them to the back of my mind and enjoyed the moment. The moment was made even more special when Dante began playing that Gassenhauer tune, soothing my mind and my spirit. I scooted across the sand to get closer to him and watched as he pelted out note after note like he had practiced it a million times. A kiss on the cheek did nothing to throw him off beat.

I stared out at the ocean again while Dante continued. "Shai," I said aloud. "The God of fate and destiny."

<><><>

The day we were leaving the island, I wanted to thank Shai again for Dante's gift. I wanted him to know how much we really appreciated his generosity. But, when I made it to the marketplace, his tables were gone and replaced by a woman selling fruit. She was also an islander, so I asked her if she knew where I could find Shai.

"Shai?" she asked with a puzzled look. "No, sir, I don't know who that is."

"He was here a couple of days ago selling wooden carvings," I said, looking around. "Older guy, with white hair."

She shook her head and again said that she didn't know who he was. I asked a few more of the merchants who I knew were out there that day, but no one had a clue as to who Shai was. It was strange considering it was a small island and everyone seemed to know each other, especially the merchants in the marketplace. But after coming up empty, I scanned the area one last time before heading back to the villa, disappointed that I wasn't able to see him before we left.

CHAPTER 27

The trip took another chunk out of my already dwindling pockets. But the sight of seeing my mom and Barbara sip margaritas on the beach while Taj and Kim splashed around in the ocean with Dante, well, that was absolutely priceless. I enjoyed myself, but knowing that my family was happy was all that mattered.

Once I was back in Decatur reality set in: I had to make some money. Mona told me that everything was still on in Detroit, but I wasn't ready to hit the highway after what took place. It was too risky and I couldn't afford to let anybody take another dime from me. So I waited and hoped something happened. And, eventually it did.

<><><>

Dante and I had just left the park after spending a couple of hours feeding the ducks and pushing him on the swings until my arms got tired. It had become routine for us to get ice cream on the way back from the lake at this little spot called Krekels. The place had some of the best hamburgers and milk shakes in the Midwest, according to most people, but Dante and I thought the ice cream stood out more than anything.

I pulled in and was getting Dante from his car seat when I saw a pearl white BMW 745 park in the space next to me. A bulking frame occupied the driver's seat, and I wasn't surprised to see Khalid behind the wheel and a chick on the passenger's side. Decatur was small, and only he had the money and the balls to ride around in a seventy-thousand dollar sedan.

Dante took hold of my hand and begin swinging it back and forth. "I want a banana split."

I checked out the paint job as we walked by the car. "But you never eat it all."

"Just get an extra-large one and we can share it, Daddy."

"I guess we can do that."

We got to the front and stood in line behind other customers. When Khalid and his companion came around the side of the building looking like they were on their way to a "white party", he didn't hesitate to speak.

"What's the deal, Kay?" He was smiling, looking like new money. Everything about him screamed, "I'm getting money", from the linen suit he wore, to the diamond stud in his ear that was as big as a skittle. The smell of arrogance overpowered his cologne. He reminded me of a villainous Jay for an instant because of how he flaunted his wealth.

"Taking it easy, that's all." I wasn't good at offering fake smiles, so I kept a neutral face.

"He is so adorable!" Khalid's companion smiled at Dante. She came over and reached down and rubbed Dante's cheek. "You are a hottie!"

Dante blushed. "Thank you. I'm Dante." He held out his hand like the perfect little gentleman he was. That got a giggle out of her. She opened her arms and Dante fell into her large breasts that were almost popping out of her white halter top.

"Okay, little man," Khalid interrupted. "Don't be trying to take my girl."

Dante stared up at him like he was offended before taking a step back. He gave Khalid a "hi" that didn't come with his usual smile. I guess he didn't like Khalid, either.

I ordered our extra-large banana split and stood to the side while we waited. Khalid went behind us and did the same. But instead of giving me a little space, he came right on side of me and just stood there without saying a word. I could see Dante peeking over at him on several occasions like he didn't trust him. The woman had gone back to the car for something, so it wasn't her he was watching.

I knew Khalid was aware that I hadn't been in business for a while. Run was doing a life sentence, and without him on my team, it was like I didn't even exist in the Decatur drug trade. But I was sure that the big bear of a guy standing next to me could change all of that. All I had to do was humble myself and start a conversation. That was most definitely the hard part.

The advantages of dealing with him ran through my mind while I wrestled with my pride. The risky trips on the highway would come to an end. If I'd ever gotten some bad dope from him, he would be easy to find because it was almost impossible to hide from anyone in Decatur. Maybe his prices would've been higher than I usually paid, but overall, the pros outweighed any con I could come up with. The only thing I was worried about was if he would deal with me after the way I shunned his so-called hospitality. But if he was about making money like I assumed he was, there was no way he was going to turn me down. So, figuring I had nothing to lose and everything to gain, I leaned over and asked, "You got work?"

He smiled as he looked straight ahead. "Do hoes trick?"

"Every one that I know." I felt a sense of relief. "What's the ticket on a key?"

"Twenty-four all day."

A car driven by a girl, who was known for her incomparable blowjobs, almost jumped the curb as she pulled into the driveway and sped into the parking lot.

"Here come this crazy bitch," Khalid said, quickly walking off without excusing himself from our conversation. He went around the building toward the parking lot. I could hear women yelling at each other, and I assumed it was Khalid's companion and the woman with the lethal lips.

"Daddy, sounds like somebody's in an extreme amount of trouble."

"Yeah, it happens sometimes, son," I said, shaking my head with a smile.

Our ice cream was ready, so I grabbed it from the window and walked to the parking lot. Khalid was standing in between the two women while they threw insults and threats at one another. When lethal lips threw a punch at the girl and it mistakenly landed on Khalid's jaw, that's when he lost his cool. The girl's neck was in between his big hands before I could turn and head in the other direction. I didn't want Dante witnessing a man beating up a woman, so we went back up to the front and waited it out. It went on for a couple of minutes. Once lethal lips was in her car and high-tailed it out into the street, we walked to my truck. Khalid seemed to be apologizing to his companion while I strapped Dante into his car seat.

He had a little trouble on his hands, so I didn't bother him. I got in my truck and started the engine. That got his attention. He came to my passenger's window with beads of sweat running down his black face.

"Hit me up," he said, in between gasps of air. "These bitches crazy."

"Ooooh," Dante whispered.

"My fault, little man." He called off his number as I stored it in my phone. "Give me a couple hours."

"Bet."

The first time I got some dope from Khalid, I expected something to go wrong; either it was going to be bad dope or he was going to short me some grams. But as soon as I opened the first kilo I bought from him, I realized that the dude was about business. The dope was A-1 and not a gram was missing. And when I was able to turn thirty-six ounces into fifty two, and sold it all without one complaint, I thought Khalid was the greatest thing since video games. But once I got to know him through our countless business deals, I soon discovered that he was the biggest asshole I'd ever met.

When people know that you are depending on them, they have a tendency to get with you at their convenience, especially in the dope game. Khalid was a prime example. I'd call him up and not get an answer, and then minutes later I'd see him riding around with some chick, smoking weed and cruising in circles. And whenever he did answer, he would have me waiting half of the day before he showed up with the dope. It was like he knew he was the man, and I was nothing more than some peon who needed him more than he needed me. I put up with his foolishness because he always kept the good dope, and really, I had no other choice. But I planned on cutting ties with him as soon as I accomplished my mission.

<><><>

"Yeah, I g-g-g-gotta chill for a while, K-k-k-Kay," Pops said, looking around at the mess the police had left behind. "These mothafuckas ain't p-p-p-playin'."

The drug task force had been busy during that time. Not a week had gone by without them running up in a place where drug deals were being made, and Pop's Place had apparently made their hit list. Being in the game for so long was his only advantage, though. He was smart enough to know not to keep any drugs in his restaurant, making the dumpster in the back of it his stash spot. They didn't find anything but they did tear the place up, leaving him to contend with an overturned refrigerator and a floor littered with the special of the day, chicken wings and spaghetti.

I sat at the counter and watched Pops light a cigarette, shaking his head at the floor. I was shaking my head, too, because his problem was my problem. He was the only person I was dealing with at the time. I cut Roach off after he shorted me five-thousand dollars on nine ounces and made no effort to pay me back. That was a lot of money to anybody, but after going through what I had been through, I came to understand that losses were just a part of the game. My mind was made up, though; I wasn't about to give anybody else a chance to mess up my money. It was then that I was forced to fully expose myself to the risks and dangers that came with being a street level drug dealer.

CHAPTER 28

There's a saying in the streets that goes, "Dope sells itself." It's true only to a certain extent, because cocaine doesn't have legs, and if you're not willing to do the running, not one gram of it would be sold. So, like any good salesman, I approached almost everybody who was putting in work on the streets, promising them that nobody could beat my prices and quality. Before long, I had a clientele that consisted of gang-bangers to grandmas. Most of them bought quarter and half ounces, with a few copping whole ounces faithfully, and I didn't discriminate against the everyday crack head, either. If I just so happened to be driving past one of them and they flagged me down, I would get that money, too. Every dollar counted, and I acted as such.

I did all I could do to hide my secret from Taj, but I knew it would eventually come to light. Decatur was too small for it not to, especially seeing that she was so well-known and a lot of people referred to me as "Taj's husband". There were times when we would be together at the mall or out to eat and I would see somebody who I supplied. They would make their way over to me and I would shake my head or wave them off when Taj wasn't looking. Sometimes Taj would notice them and they would come over and speak just to play it off. After a few of those incidences, I told everyone I dealt with that if they ever saw me out anywhere with someone, I was completely off limits. But as hard as I tried to cover my tracks, it didn't help. And when Taj found out, she let it be known that she wasn't going for it.

<><><>

I was on my way home with Dante in the back seat, listening as he went through his usual routine of filling me in on what happened at daycare. He had the ability to hold a conversation with the greatest of talk-show hosts; his expansive vocabulary was comical because of his age. He did watch a lot of television, and it wasn't limited to just Nickelodeon and cartoons.

"...and she didn't even take the time to explain why lions are the king of the jungle," he said, referring to a staff member who read books during story time. "I don't think she knows why."

I swallowed the laugh that almost escaped my mouth. Dante always asked why we'd laugh whenever he'd say something we found funny, so Taj and I agreed to appear serious when he talked to us no matter how hard it was.

"I'm sure she knows, Dante. Maybe she'll tell you tomorrow."

"Well, if she doesn't, I'm sure going to ask her."

I glanced back at him. He was looking out the window, probably thinking of all the other questions he had for her.

"That's mommy," Dante said when he heard my phone ring.

He was right. But instead of her usual sweet greeting, she said, "Come home now." The phone went dead without giving me a chance to say a word. The tone she had used was one I'd never heard from her, and something told me that I was in big trouble.

She was sitting on the porch when we pulled into the driveway. Her eyes were glued on me the entire time. I sneaked a few peeks at her while I got Dante out of his car seat, and not once did she break eye contact. She showed a brief smile when he ran up and pecked her on the cheek, but the smile disappeared when her stare returned to me.

"Go in the house and get a snack out the pantry, Dante."

As soon as the door closed behind him, she began to speak through clenched teeth.

"What in the hell are you doing selling drugs, Kay? Have you lost your damn mind?!" It came out loud enough to get a passing neighbor's attention.

"Let's go in the house, baby." I reached for her arm, but she snatched away as if she was repulsed by my touch. I had never seen her like that, but I understood why she was so upset. There had never been any secrets between us until then, and I knew that she felt betrayed and hurt. She and her brother had lost out on having their mother in their lives due to her addiction to drugs, so she had every right to feel the way she did. It was a blatant act of treason on my part.

She was staring blankly out into the street, shaking her hand whenever she wiped away a tear. "I don't understand you, Kay." She looked up at me. "How long have you been doing it?" Her eyes were intense as if she was willing herself to read my mind.

I sat down next to her and took a deep breath. "Off and on for about three years."

"Three years!?" It was a quiet yell.

I couldn't look at her, but I could feel her eyes burning a hole through the side of my head. I felt compelled to say something, anything to justify my actions. But the love we shared didn't allow excuses for what I had done. I was guilty of betraying the trust she had for me by keeping a secret from her, something that wasn't supposed to happen when you truly loved someone.

Dante came outside, a donut in one hand and a book in the other. Shorty was at his side, more focused on the donut than anything. "Mommy, can we read when you're done talking to Daddy?"

She smiled through the hurt she was feeling. "Yes, baby. Give me a minute, okay?" She turned to me shaking her head as she said, "How could you risk being taken away from something so precious, Kay? That little boy needs his daddy. I need you."

She didn't have to say another word. And, as much as they needed me, I needed them even more. We were a family, and that was more important than any amount of money. Right then and there, I made up my mind that I was done with the game.

I pulled Taj to me and gave her a hug. "I'm sorry."

"I don't want to hear that, Kay." She said, breaking away from me. "I want you to say you won't do it anymore."

There was no way I could keep another secret from her; not after this. So, I was forced to tell her about a kilo I had bought from Khalid earlier that day. Luckily for me, Dante was around. Her anger was contained to a whisper through gritted teeth and lips that barely moved.

"That shit better not be in this house."

"I've never had it around you. I know better than that."

"You have until tomorrow to do whatever it is you do." She turned to me, truth in her eyes. "After that, if I hear anything else about you and some drugs, I swear, Kay, I'll tell your mom why I divorced you."

Her words cut deep into my heart, and there was no doubt that she meant what she'd said. I wasn't about to let anything come between us.

<><><>

Dope was plentiful in Decatur, so getting rid of a kilo in less than twenty-four hours was almost impossible with the clientele I had. But Taj's threat lingered in my head, so I knew that I had to do something. I was still short of my goal by about thirty five thousand dollars, which was irrelevant because my new goal was to keep my family together.

As a way to get rid of the dope and, at the same time show my appreciation to the game and to the people who became loyal customers, I decided to give Decatur something else to talk about. After cooking up the last kilo I would ever touch, I let everyone know that I was selling ounces for six-hundred dollars a pop. They were going for a thousand at the time, and it was unheard of to get them at the price I offered. I figured it would catch the attention of a lot of people, and, without question, it did.

My phone blew up with inquiring minds: "Is it good?" "How long will you be?" "It ain't no bullshit, is it?"

I was getting calls from people I had never dealt with before, but I served them anyway because I couldn't shake Taj's words. Most of the people couldn't believe I was selling it for so cheap. They would ask me to wait while they had a crack head test it out, thinking it was too good to be true. I couldn't blame them, though. I would've been the same way had somebody done something as crazy as what I'd done.

I relived what Run and I had gone through when the drought had hit. Everybody and their momma flagged me down as I rode around like a pizza deliveryman, dropping off six ounces here, three ounces there. And, by the end of the night, I had eight ounces left out of the fifty I'd gotten from the kilo. My profit wasn't much, but I was gaining something more valuable than money.

The highlight of that night came later on while I was at home taking care of business in a game of Madden on the Playstation. Dante was in a deep sleep after his daily xylophone session that lasted for hours. Taj had gone to bed a little earlier than usual. There was no conversation over dinner or talk about the shop. She had watched *Jeopardy* alone in our bedroom and she made it clear that it would be that way until I was done doing "dumb shit", as she put it. As bad as it hurt to not be able to touch or talk to the woman I loved with every ounce of my being, I embraced the fact that she was only showing how much she really loved me.

The phone call I got while gaming capped off what had been a very eventful day. And it came courtesy of the one and only, Khalid.

"What the fuck is wrong with you, selling that shit like that?" He yelled into the phone like he was talking to one of his kids. "You ain't got it like that, nigga!"

I took the phone from my ear, my thumb going for the "end" button. If he thought he was about to get an explanation about what I was doing with MY shit, he was sadly mistaken. I couldn't believe he actually had to the nerve to dial my number with such nonsense. I found it crazy, to the point of being comical. But instead of hanging up on him, I was inclined to get under his skin just because I knew I could.

"Damn, why you mad, son?"

"Oh, you think it's funny you got mothafuckas coming at me talking that six-hundred shit, like I'm doing this shit just to be doing it!"

I kicked my feet up on the ottoman. "Well, if you can't run with the big dogs stay on the porch and lick your balls."

"Yeah, okay, nigga!" He sounded amused but angry. "If you ever need something don't even think about calling me!"

"What!? I don't need you, dog! I got connects all over this bitch! Mexico, Cali, Miami, wherever! And from now on, the only time you're going to be able to sell a crumb in Decatur is when I'm done with mine! And from now on, it's six-hundred all day long, nigga!"

I ended the call because I couldn't hold back from laughing any longer. The only thing that could've made it better was if I was able to see his face.

<><><>

I was awaken by Taj's voice. She was standing in the doorway. "We're leaving."

"Huh." I wiped the sleep from my eyes and sat up. "Where?"

"I'm going to work and Dante's going to daycare." She took her keys out of her purse. "What's the matter with you?"

"Oh...nothing. Just tired."

"Dante came in the room and crawled up in the bed. "See you later, Daddy."

He gave me a hug before leaving out of the room. I could hear Shorty follow him down the steps. Taj hadn't moved. I could see the disappointment still lingering on her face, and the silence she gave me was hard to bear.

"I hope you know how pissed I am at you."

Before I could say a word, she walked out the room. The front door slammed seconds later. It was going to be a while before things got back to normal. I fell back, staring at the ceiling, looking forward to getting rid of the last of the dope I had. My phone rung and I figured it was a customer.

"What's good, Kay?" It was a voice that I didn't recognize.

"Who's this?"

"This Wes. I need to holla' at you."

Wes was Khalid's friend, and from the outside looking in, he was nothing more than a flunky, if you asked me. I'd met him a few times when Khalid had him drop off dope to me on a number of occasions. While Khalid was driving around in new cars, Wes had been pushing the same old rusted-out Honda Accord ever since I'd stepped foot in Decatur. It was a clear sign that Khalid wasn't breaking bread like he was supposed to, considering he had the guy dropping off kilos of dope for him. There was no doubt in my mind that Wes had gotten wind of my specials, so I put on some clothes and drove over to his house. I called his phone and seconds later he came out the door.

"Yeah, Khalid told me to call you for one of his people from Springfield," he said, looking back at his house. "He said you got 'em for six."

"When did you talk to him?" I asked.

"Right before I called you."

Needless to say, I was beyond confused. After the conversation we'd had the previous night, why would he send me a customer? I checked my rearview and kept an eye out for anything suspicious. My car stayed in drive just in case I had to make a quick getaway.

"Who's in the house?" I asked, studying his every move and facial expression for any sign of a set-up.

"Nobody but dude and my two sons."

I was still leery about serving him, and he seemed to pick up on my hesitance.

"You ain't gotta worry about nothing, Kay," he said, shaking his head. "My kids in there, man, and I'm just trying to make this money. That nigga, Khalid, be on some bullshit. I been fuckin' with that nigga for years and ain't got shit to show for it." Desperation was written all over his face, and I could tell that he was serious.

"Okay, what is he trying to get?"

"Three."

A car came to a stop at the corner down the block. It waited there for a brief second, then turned quickly and headed in my direction. When it got closer, it slowed down and pulled up alongside of me. Roach was driving. One of his boys sat low in the passenger's seat.

"Hey, Kay, I'm trying to come back up, man, and when I do, I'ma clear my tab up."

"That's cool," I replied, knowing exactly what was next.

"But in the meantime, I need eight of 'em."

I turned to Wes. "Give me twenty minutes." He nodded his approval and walked back up to his house. I turned back to Roach. "I only got five left and that six-hundred was a one day thing."

"Damn!" He said in disappointment. "I missed it, huh?"

"Yeah, but since you trying to come up, I'll let you get these for eight. Tomorrow it'll be a thousand again, so you better get it while it's good." I knew I wasn't going to see the money he owed me, so upping the price on him was just a small piece of self-gratification. Either way, though, he was getting a deal so he couldn't pass it up.

"How long," he asked, after a small conference with his boy.

"I'll be right back."

I grabbed the last eight ounces from Tina's and went back to serve Roach. When I finished with him, Wes was sitting on his porch waiting for me.

"I told him a thousand a piece," Wes said as we entered his house. "Just serve him and I'll get the money after you finish."

When I saw Wes' two sons watching cartoons in the living room, I dismissed the thought of any kind of robbery taking place.

I followed him into the kitchen where a light-skinned guy with a tapered Afro was sitting at the table. Being that it was late-August and about eighty-degrees outside, the Polo jacket that he wore seemed to be a little too heavy for the weather. It kept my attention until he coughed a few times and sniffled. Then he pulled out a handkerchief and blew his nose.

"These summer cold's a mothafucka'," he said, looking directly at me. "Trying to sweat it out."

There was no need for me to comment. I just wanted my money and to get out of there before he passed his germs on.

"You got the three ounces?" The question was for me, but all I did was go in my pocket and sat them on the table. He reached over gave them a quick examination. "Is it some good dope?"

I was reluctant to speak only because he had sneezed, coughed and blown his nose, and I refused to open my mouth in fear of catching whatever virus he had. Wes noticed my behavior and spoke up for me. "That's that butter," he said, vouching only because he had twelve hundred dollars at stake.

But the guy continued asking questions. "What they weighing?"

I could tell Wes was anxious to get the deal over with. "Twenty-eight grams all day," Wes replied. "It's good dope and the grams all there."

When the guy reached into his pocket, I was relieved as much as Wes probably was. He flipped through the wad of cash and counted off three grand. "If it's good I'm coming right back."

All I gave him was a shrug of the shoulders as I reached for the money.

"Is that a Breitling right there?" he asked, referring to the watch I was wearing.

"Yeah, it's the Bentley model." It was a birthday gift from Taj, and just thinking about it put a smile on my face. I wore it proudly, and I was caught me off guard when he recognized the name, considering I hadn't even heard of it before she had given it to me.

"That's a bad ass watch. What it run you?"

"It was a gift." I was recounting the money. "My wife bought it."

"Shit, you got a good wife."

"A great one." I turned to Wes and was about to walk out the kitchen.

"Hey, Kay."

He called my name, catching me off guard because I hadn't introduced myself. I thought maybe Wes had mentioned it to him.

"Like I said, if it's some good dope, I'll be right back at you."

"Just get up with Wes." I didn't wait for a response.

At the front door, I counted out Wes' cut and gave it to him.

"Good looking out, Kay," he said, holding the money like it had been a while since he'd seen that much. "I'll call you whenever he comes back. Fuck that nigga, Khalid."

I shook my head. "It's over for me, Wes. I'm done with the game." I smiled as I walked out the door feeling like a giant weight had been lifted off my shoulders. I was thinking that I had made it out the game unscarred and was able to make a little money along the way.

CHAPTER 29

One year later

My transition from selling ounces of crack to slanging bags of weave was a move that not even I could have foreseen. Taj came up with the idea after the building next to hers was vacated by its owner, a guy who thought prosthetic limbs would be in huge demand in a small town such as Decatur. The day she found out he was giving up his business, we approached him and made an offer for the building. Three months later we had a fully stocked beauty supply store, the only black-owned store of its kind in Decatur.

There were a few other beauty supplies in the town, but all were run by Koreans. They were the kings of the beauty supply industry, but I didn't let that discourage me from putting in the work it took to run a successful business. All I did was implement the same strategy I used while selling drugs: keep the lowest prices and quality product, and the customers will flock to you. And that's exactly what I did. If the Koreans were selling a pack of weave for twenty dollars, I would sell it for nineteen. If they had barrettes for three dollars, I would sell them for two fifty. Whatever they sold, I sold cheaper, and it was the reason I was getting the majority of the business in Decatur. I even hired a delivery driver so that we could cater to people who didn't have transportation. Decatur was small enough where I didn't even have to add extra for deliveries, so all the kitchen and basement beauticians loved to call us up. It was also convenient for Taj's customers also. They didn't have to go pick up their hair before coming to the shop. We had weave on deck, ready to be stitched and sewn in all at one place.

Our doors had only been open for about five months, but in that short amount of time, I was sure that the Koreans had felt our presence, mainly in their pockets. We had the hair game on lock, and our store's future looked to be as bright as the July sun. It also appeared as if the ultimatum Taj gave me hadn't come at a better time.

Once I stepped away from the drug game, the Feds practically invaded Decatur and conducted a number of sweeps, handing out indictments like they were free movie passes. Dudes were picked up and shipped off, leaving behind wives, girlfriends, and kids. Most of the women didn't miss a beat, though. All they did was move along to the next up-and-coming star in the game, securing a spot on his roster and reaping the perks that came with dating a drug dealer.

Wes was one of the names on the list of people the Feds came to visit. He was pulled over on the highway with five kilos in the trunk, on his way back from who knows where. But one thing that everyone did know, was that Khalid probably was a little disappointed about losing a shipment.

I saw him the day after it happened. He was riding around in a brand new Range Rover with the sticker still in the window. I assumed he was trying to show the town that a five-kilo loss couldn't hurt him. And I'll be the first to admit that he did a damn good job if that's what he was aiming to do. But it wasn't a smart move on his part, considering the Feds were lurking in the shadows and probably were waiting for him to slip up. He seemed to be begging for attention, and in the back of my mind, I had a feeling that those three-letter people were going to give him all the attention he could handle.

<><><>

I was sitting at the kitchen table going over a list of new products that I had just ordered while Taj was preparing dinner. Dante was upstairs like always, playing songs that had Shorty letting out an occasional bark. I don't know if he was trying to sing along or irritated by something, but every five minutes, a yelp from our Teacup Chihuahua would echo through the house.

"He's been playing that song for a week now, nonstop," Taj said, while standing over the stove preparing dinner.

"Whenever he learns a new song he does the same thing." I was sitting at the table flipping through one of Taj's hair magazines. "You know that."

She quit stirring the rice and looked up toward the ceiling, listening. "But this one doesn't sound like the usual happy stuff he normally plays."

"Well, he is using four mallets now, and he's just advancing musically, broadening his xylophone horizon." I chuckled.

She stood there for a few more seconds before returning to her stirring. "I don't like it. It sounds kind of creepy if you ask me. I don't think Shorty likes it either."

I gave her my best *Friday The 13th* background music imitation. "ki-ki-ki-ma-ma-ma-ki-ki-ki."

"I'm serious, Kay."

The first time I heard that song coming from Dante's room, I'll admit that it did sound a little dark for my liking. But the xylophone that Shai had given him was a real instrument, and nothing like the toy xylophones that were still up in his closet. It also seemed to take his playing to another level. And when he insisted that he needed two more mallets, and was now using all four at one time, it was fair to say that he was becoming a master xylophonist right before our very eyes.

I stood up from the table and went and hugged Taj from behind while she added pepper to the rice. She really appeared to be bothered by the song that was playing like it was on repeat.

"Our son is special, baby. He's only doing what he obviously enjoys, and it just so happens that he's damn good at it."

She turned around and hugged me, her head on my chest. "I'll just be glad when he finds another song."

<><><>

"How much is your twenty-seven-inch hair, Kay?"

"Cheaper than the Koreans," I said, adamantly with a smile. "What color you need, Tasha?"

"Taj said I should get the 1B, but I was thinking about going blonde." For a quick second, I pictured her walking down the street with a blonde weave. "1-B it is." I grabbed two packs of hair off the rack. "Remember, Tasha, your stylist knows best."

"I guess you're right." She was still gazing up at the brightly colored hair as I rung up her purchase.

My driver came through the door after making a few house calls to our customers. His name was Mikey, a young kid who had just graduated high school and was on his way to college in nearby Champaign. His girlfriend was one of Taj's customers and she was also pregnant, so I hired him because he told me that he wanted to support his family like a real man should. I admired that about him because he reminded me so much of myself.

"Belinda told me to tell you that she owes you two dollars on that hair." He came behind the counter and handed me some money. "And she had three dollars' worth of nickels."

I opened both hands to receive the change. "It all spends."

After opening the cash register, I was dropping coins into their respective slots when I saw four cars pull up out front. White men in suits and ties got out of each vehicle. It wasn't hard to tell that they were federal agents; the dark-colored sedans were a dead giveaway. I continued placing the money in the register until I saw them coming up the walkway, headed right to the entrance of the building I occupied. I glanced at Mikey as he stood on the side of me. I had a bad feeling about seeing federal agents coming into my store, and something told me that they weren't looking for hair products.

They came through the door as Tasha was leaving out, business-like with not one gun drawn.

"May I help you?" I pushed the register closed. There were a total of seven agents in the store. Two were at the door, guarding it like a bank vault. Three stood across the counter from me, while the other two made sure an escape through the back entrance wasn't going to happen.

One of the agents in front of me reached inside his coat pocket. "Kabazza Wright?"

"Yeah...that's me." It died out as it rolled from my mouth.

"We have a federal complaint against you," he said, waving a single sheet of paper. "Could you come from behind the counter, please?"

"I don't understand." I was shaking my head in disbelief as I stared at the agent who seemed to be running the show. "I haven't done anything."

That's when all of the agents went for their holsters. Seven semi-automatics were pointed in my direction. Mikey reached for the sky. I could hear him whimper like a lost puppy.

"Step from behind the counter, please!" he demanded, his voice more forceful.

I did as I was ordered, walking slowly with my head in the defeated position. An agent put a hand on my shoulder and turned me around. He didn't have to tell me to put my hands behind my back; I had seen enough movies to know how the process went. Their guns were holstered once I was secured with the handcuffs. Two agents came to my side and guided me to the door by each elbow. A crowd had gathered, and passing cars slowed down to catch a glimpse of the action. Then I heard Taj. She came crashing through the doors of the shop. The look on her face was one of shock, hurt, and flat-out heartbreak. An agent grabbed hold of her before she could penetrate the circle of bodies that surrounded me. I almost broke down when she yelled my name.

The pain in her voice was deafening. My chin fell to my chest as I was led to the car and ushered into the back seat. The door slammed. I looked back one last time as the car pulled off, only to be met by Taj's tear filled eyes.

<><><>

A short drive to the county jail, and then I was escorted into the building by the agent in charge and one of his counterparts. No words had been exchanged during the ride. But as we arrived at a set of elevators, the agent in charge had something to say.

"Would you like to talk to us before you go upstairs?" He was casually rocking back and forth on his heels, giving me the side-eye as he did so.

I gave him and his buddy a glance. "Talk to y'all about what?"

"You, know." He pushed the elevator button. "Cooperate, snitch, tell, or, as we call it, save your ass."

That got a laugh out of his buddy, but I didn't find it funny in the least bit. "What am I here for anyway?"

The elevator door came open. "You sell dope in our city," he replied. "And this is where all the bad little drug dealers go. So are we taking you upstairs or do you want to talk?"

It was too hard for me to believe that they had anything on me. I had a year under my belt of being drug-free, so they had to be crazy if they thought there was a chance of me snitching about something I was no longer involved with. "Take me upstairs."

I was arraigned in federal court the next day. It was the first time hearing what I was charged with: Distribution of fifty grams or more of crack cocaine. It carried a mandatory minimum sentence of ten years to life. At the mention of "life", my legs almost gave out.

I was appointed a lawyer a few weeks after my arraignment. He visited me after I was shipped to another county jail outside of Decatur. That's when I found out why I was facing a sentence that was fit for someone who had committed a murder.

The room we were in was the size of a closet, every wall made of glass so that the deputies had a clear view of us. My lawyer sat across from me and explained exactly what I was charged with.

"Apparently, you sold a confidential source over fifty grams of crack cocaine." He raised his head up from the paper he was reading. "How much does that sell for nowadays?"

I didn't answer right off. My life was in jeopardy and he was curious about the going rate of crack. "A few thousand."

He continued reading, citing the date the offense took place and even naming the time of day and location of the transaction. I was putting dates together in my head, trying to recall anything I could remember during the time of the sale. One thing I knew for sure was that it happened around the time I called it quits.

"Whoever it was," he said, handing me a sheet of paper. "They were wearing a wire. That's the transcript of the conversation he recorded." He waited a few minutes while I went over the paper. "Look familiar?"

I shook my head as I continued to read. "Very."

The piece of paper looked like a page out of a movie script, and it didn't take long for me to recognize who was the playing the role of the confidential source.

CS: You got three ounces?
Wright: (inaudible)
CS: Is it some good dope?
Wright: (inaudible)
CS: Is that a Breitling right there?
Wright: Yeah, it's the Bentley model.
CS: Kay, like I said, if it's some good dope I'll be right back at you.

So there it was, in black and white. I had been set up and caught red-handed. The evidence was in front of my face, recorded and then typed up for my viewing pleasure. The irony of the whole thing was that, out of all the sales I had made, my luck ran out on the last one. And with that discovery, my whole thought process turned in a direction that I never imagined it would go.

CHAPTER 30

I woke up and hoped that it was all a dream. But instead of being able to roll over and put my arms around a sleeping Taj, I could only stop myself from rolling out of a bed that was better suited for a three-year-old. I knew right then and there that the two years I had left were going to be anything but comfortable.

"That top bunk is the worst."

I opened my eyes and was staring at a grungy old man in the cubicle next door. He was sitting on the bottom bunk with a newspaper up to his face. His features were hiding behind a beard that probably hadn't been attended to in years, and my first impression was that my new neighbor was doing time for a crime related to something that had to do with kids.

"It's a bitch when those lights come on," he said, peeking up from behind the paper. "You can't sleep for shit."

"Yeah, I see." It was six o'clock in the morning on my first day waking up in a real live prison, and idle chit-chat wasn't something I wanted to indulge in. I pushed myself up and moved to the foot of the small bunk. My feet swayed back and forth as I looked over the dorm.

Obviously, prison life got an early start just like in the real world. Guys were shuffling about like they had places to be and people to see. Mop buckets were commanded by other inmates who looked to be on cleaning duty, spray bottles dangling from their pockets as they moved down the aisles. There was a crowd of inmates camping out at the entrance, waiting on who or what, I didn't know. What I did know was that I was as lost as a blind man in a giant maze.

At the sight of a shiny and familiar bald head, I felt somewhat at ease. He walked up the aisle with a towel thrown over his shoulder and a shower bag in one hand. I thought about him telling me he had fifteen years left on his sentence as he came into the cubicle.

"What's good, celly?" he asked, going into his locker.

"Nothing much from the looks of it."

"The first day always the hardest. You'll get used to this shit."

He sat down at the desk and slid off his sweatpants and exchanged them for a pair of khakis, which he removed from under his mattress. They had the appearance of being straight from the dry cleaners.

"MAINLINE IS NOW OPEN!"

The announcement over the intercom caused the crowd at the entrance to disappear out the door. Other inmates dashed out of their cubicles and followed right behind them.

"Where's everybody going?"

"Chow hall," he stated, sliding into a pair of sneakers. "You brushin' yo' teeth today or do you say 'fuck it' sometimes?"

"I might pass on it today," I said, laughing a bit.

"Nawl, I can't have you hangin' around with me and yo' breath smellin' like ass." He went into his locker. "They didn't put a care package in yo' bedroll, but I got a toothbrush for you. I use it on my sneakers, but you'll be alright."

I hopped down off my bunk and, just for a second, I was able find a small sense of solace in my cellmate's sense of humor. He handed me a toothbrush still in the wrapper and said, "Go get yo' hygiene up and I'll be waitin' at the door for you. Take you over to the laundry so you can get out that pickle suit. Show you around a lil' bit."

<><><>

After waiting in line for one of the ten sinks that were shared by over a hundred inmates, I met New York out front. He was in a conversation with a bearded guy who I assumed was a Muslim because of his headgear and a khaki uniform that was buttoned up to the neck. They were talking about court proceedings and changes in the "crack laws" when I walked over to them.

"Yo, you think it's gone happen?" New York asked the guy.

He stroked his beard as he contemplated the answer. "If it's Allah's will, a lot of these brothers will be home with their families when it happens. We just gotta keep the faith."

"Word up," replied New York. "I'ma holla at ya later, though, Hakeem. Gotta go over to laundry to help get my boy his issue."

"As-Salaam-Alaikum, my brotha." They exchanged handshakes."Wa-Alaikum-Salaam."

"Are you a Muslim?" I asked New York as we began walking.

"Nawl," he said, lighting a cigar. "But after being locked up for so long, you learn all kinds of shit."

New York played the role of tour guide as we made our way to the laundry, pointing out every location I needed to be concerned with during my stay. The chow hall and the recreation areas were the two places I would eventually spend a lot of time visiting.

After getting sized up for my prison-issued uniform, I was told to come back later on in the day to pick them up. It was kind of disappointing because the green jumpsuit I was wearing cut at my balls every time I took a step. And I soon learned that nothing took place in prison when you wanted it to happen.

"Make sure you don't let them mothafuckas give you some tight ass khakis," New York said as we walked toward the chow hall. "You'll have niggas offerin' you honey buns and tuna to take a shower with 'em."

"Maybe you should give up writing music and do comedy."

His laughter died down as we approached the line that led into the chow hall. Groups of officers were standing in front of the building, eyeing down every inmate that passed.

"Pull those pants up, inmate!" one of them yelled to a guy whose pants were hanging off of him. He was in front of us, and when he took his sweet time obeying the order, the officer ran over and got directly in his face. "So you think you're a tough guy?"

"Why you all in my face?" he yelled back at the officer.

That did nothing to help the situation. The officer moved in close enough to kiss him. "Get your ass out of my line! You don't eat today, smart ass!"

The inmate slowly removed himself from the line under the officer's close watch. He headed back toward the housing unit after throwing the officer a few parting glances.

"You can't win fuckin' with these C.O.s," New York said as the line moved forward. "That nigga gon' learn."

New York continued schooling me on prison life as we inched closer and closer to being served a breakfast of cereal and a cinnamon roll. In between my lesson, he joked with other inmates who were already seated at one of the many tables that occupied the cafeteria. Most of the things he aimed at them could have been taken as an insult, but the only thing he left in his wake was a trail of laughter. I followed New York's lead and grabbed a set of utensils as we made it to the serving area. Inmates outfitted in burgundy smocks and hairnets stood behind the steel counter scooping cereal into trays and sliding it down until each order was completed. A C.O. stood close by, making sure no one got an extra scoop of Frosted Flakes or an extra cinnamon roll.

"Damn, Blue, stop shakin' the bowl, nigga!" New York said to one of the servers, who was using a plastic bowl to distribute the cereal. As usual, he was laughing when he said it.

"You know how this clown is," he replied, tilting his head in the C.O.'s direction. "Bitch ass nigga will send a muthafucka' to the hole for the dumbest shit."

"You know I know," New York responded as he eyed the cinnamon rolls. "Green, let me get that small one on the end. A nigga tryin' to lose a few pounds."

"Shit, you need to pass these sweet mufuckas up then," he said, using a spatula to place the cinnamon roll on the tray. He turned his attention to me as if I was about to make a special request. I shrugged my shoulders and he picked out one of the biggest in the bunch.

"Yeah, Green, this my boy right here," New York said as the guy handed him his tray. "Throw 'em a few extra wings on chicken day."

"Okay, just make sho' you send me some squares when I'm in the hole, nigga."

The line continued to a row of milk dispensers. New York grabbed two cups from a rack and handed me one. "The food ain't that bad," he said, stopping for a fill-up on milk. "Lunch is when they serve the best meal. Dinner always some bullshit. If a nigga ain't makin' commissary, he'll fuck around and starve in here."

The chow hall was divided into two sections, with race playing a major part in where everyone sat. Whites and Mexicans were on one side, while blacks occupied the other. I did notice a few blacks sprinkled amongst the whites and Mexicans, but it was probably because there wasn't enough room to put all of the brothers on one side.

"Might as well sit with these Three-6 Mafia rejects," New York said, heading to a table where Stop Playin' and his friend were seated. "What's up with my tear the club up homies?"

"Mane, do you eva' stop crackin' jokes?" Stop Playin' said as he looked up and took a bite of his cinnamon roll. New York sat down and patted him on the shoulder.

"It's too much material around for me not to."

"Detroit, mane, you betta' find somebody else to hang wit', mane. This nigga ain't right." He and his partner stood up to leave. "When you ready to chop it up wit' some real playas, holla' at us."

New York found the comment amusing, causing him to almost spit out a mouthful of cereal. "Get yo' clown ass outta here, nigga!"

"Stay sucka free, Detroit." He gave a gold-plated smile before walking off.

"Yo, these country niggas funny as hell."

"Yeah, that dude is hilarious," I said, surprised at the crunchiness of the Frosted Flakes. The cinnamon roll was tasty as well.

"You from the burbs or somethin'?"

"Why do you ask that?"

"The way you talk, nigga." He spooned up the last of his cereal. "You sound like you went to private school yo' whole life."

"Detroit Public School graduate," I stated proudly. "I grew up with a mom who wouldn't let me use "ain't" when I talked, so I'm stuck with the proper English thing, yo!."

"Oh, so now I'm stuck with a wannabe comedienne." He picked up his tray. "Let's get up outta' here."

My crash course in prison life lasted throughout that entire day, and by the time the sun set over F.C.I. Forrest City, I knew everything I needed to know when it came to living behind the barbed-wire fences. I had an experienced teacher; a guy who had already done eight years and who wasn't even halfway through his sentence; a guy who laughed continuously and, had he not filled me in on his situation, I would have mistaken him for someone who was on his way home real soon. But instead of dwelling on the time he had left, he seemed to be more focused on helping me adjust to my new surroundings.

I was settled in later on that evening. Taj made sure I had money on my prison account once she found out where I was going, so my assigned locker was filled with three tan khaki uniforms, two gray jogging suits, prison-issued boxers, toiletries and a variety of groceries from the prison commissary. I was also issued a pair of cheap black construction boots that I swore would never touch my feet. I opted for a pair of overpriced canvas Reeboks instead. They were also sold in the commissary. After spending close to two hundred dollars on everything, I realized that it wasn't cheap to be locked up. I also realized that the prison was probably making a lot of money off inmates.

New York was sitting at the desk, his face buried in a notebook as he wrote and then scribbled out something. I grabbed a candy bar from my locker, offering him one as well, which he refused with a shake of his head. I took a seat in a chair at the foot of his bunk and noticed how calm the dorm seemed to be. We were near the back of the dorm, so it was kind of peaceful. Most inmates were in the TV room, while a few were on their bunks reading or staring up at the ceiling. I was dying to hear Taj's voice, but that wasn't going to happen for a couple of days. Thinking about her smile was the alternative.

New York got up from the desk and went into his locker. He came out with an apple. "Shits fuck up, ain't it?" He took a bite as he looked at me.

I gave him a weak smile as I nodded my head. "Yeah, it's messed up."

He sat back down at the desk and was facing me. "How much time you got?" A crunch came from his apple.

"I did nine months in the county, so I got about two years left."

"Awww shit, you good," he said, waving me off. "You should be around this bitch smilin' and shit. Niggas in here with football ball numbers. You get less than ten years fuckin' with the feds, you lucky." He chuckled as he continued looking at me. "I'm thinking you had twenty years or better the way you over there with that sad ass face."

I couldn't help but smile as I listened to him. His positive attitude was needed under the circumstance. "I guess you're right."

"Hell yeah, I'm right. You want these fourteen years and eight months I got left? Give me them two you got and I'll do that shit in the hole."

After thinking about it, things could have been a whole lot worse. It really didn't sink in until that moment, when a stranger made me realize that I had it better than a lot of people in the federal system. He made me look at the bright side of things. If I didn't think I would have come off as a complete wuss, I would've thanked him for the encouraging words. I chose silence instead.

"You gone be able to lay around for a month, and then they gone try to throw you in the kitchen." He turned to the desk. "I'll holla at the compound officer and get you a spot on the compound."

I was confused. "What are you talking about?"

"You gotta get a job, nigga." That laugh again. "These people ain't about to let you just lay up in here without getting some work out yo' ass. You don't wanna go in the kitchen, though. That's some straight slave shit."

"What's your job?"

"I sweep up cigarette butts a couple hours a day. Walk around outside and talk shit. Ain't nothing to it." He went back to writing. "Don't trip, I'll get you in there."

Being my first time in prison, I should've been thinking that this guy had some kind of ulterior motive for being nice to me. But something was telling me that his concern was genuine.

"Thanks, man. I really appreciate that."

"It's nothing, yo," he replied with his back to me. "Just cut out the sad faces and shit."

CHAPTER 31

Two weeks later, I was getting dressed to go on my first visit. Taj and Dante flew down for the weekend, and I was looking forward to being able to touch them for the first time in over nine months. Like a kid on Christmas eve, it was almost impossible for me to sleep the night before. I was up most of the night reading, and the rest of the night I spent thinking about them. And now I was ready to hold what had been the gifts to my life.

My khaki outfit was creased to perfection thanks to a black guy who made money ironing inmate clothing, and a visit to the prison's barbershop had my tapered Afro looking pretty decent for the low cost of ten postage stamps. Stamps were the prison's currency, and it got you anything you wanted just like cash money. I even got a bottle of scented oil that was the cologne of the federal system for twenty stamps. I dabbed some on while I was checking myself out in a small mirror I had taped to the inside of my locker.

"You need to hook a brotha' up with one of your wife's friends," New York said as he sat in the plastic chair flipping through a magazine. "I ain't had a visit in six years. They moved a nigga all the way out here and the chick that was ridin' with me forgot about a mothafucka'."

I closed my locker. "I think I got somebody for you."

"All I really want to do is get up in that visiting room and see some ass or something and eat some wings out the vending machine. Look out for a nigga."

There I was, thinking about how hard it had been for me to not have had any kind of physical contact with the people I loved, and this man hadn't touched a woman in six years. I felt his pain, and for some reason, I wanted to help him in any way that I could. The two weeks I was there had been made bearable because of him, and I felt obligated to do whatever I could to make his time a little easier in return.

I leaned against my locker. "Get the visiting form and I'll give you the info you need to send it to her."

He peered up at me like he was waiting for the punchline. "You ain't got it like that, nigga."

I shrugged my shoulders. "All right then. She's fine as hell, too. But if you don't want to be up there eating wings and watching ass, that's on you, homeboy."

He didn't need to be persuaded anymore. "Okay, I'll get that visiting form and we can put it in the mailbox Sunday night." A smirk came across his face.

"Yeah, I thought so."

"KABAZZA WRIGHT, REPORT TO VISITATION"

"There you go, son," New York said. "Go see the family. Have a good visit."

"Thanks, man."

<><><>

I was nervous as I walked up to the door that led to the visitation room. Taj was my wife, but it was as if it was our first date all over again. I did everything I had done on that day: fresh haircut, neatly trimmed mustache and goatee. I wasn't sporting my favorite Polo gear, but my khaki uniform was starched to perfection, and I even had an ironed on patch bearing my name and number above the pocket of my shirt.

I checked myself out in the reflection of a barred window when I made it to the door, thinking that I looked all right for a convict. I knocked and waited until it was opened by an officer. Once I gave him my name, he allowed me into what appeared to be a small dressing room where another officer was seated at a desk.

"Wright, you're new here," the officer at the desk said, scanning a sheet of paper. "One hug when you get in there, one hug when your visit's over. You're not allowed near the vending machines; your guests have to get that. You come back here if you have to take a piss." He pointed to a toilet that was in the corner. "Don't be in there trying to finger bang or any other acts that you think might get you sent to the hole. You got that?"

Being friendly and cooperative was my only choice. "Yes, sir."

He gestured to another door. "Go ahead."

I pulled the door open and butterflies immediately attacked my stomach. There were rows and rows of chairs occupied by people visiting their loved ones. Khaki was sprinkled in among the crowd of people wearing normal clothes, and I had never been so excited to see a pair of blue jeans in all my life.

I searched the room for my own loved ones, and then my eyes made contact with Taj first, and then Dante. They were seated in the back row of the section farthest away from me. Running to them was my first instinct, but I caught myself. I was sure I would've been tackled by the three officers that were seated at a desk on a raised platform in the front of the room, fearing that I was about to make a dash for the exit. So, I calmly started toward them as they stood and waited for my arrival. It felt like I would never reach them.

Dante was wearing a smile that brought instant sunshine to my heart, and I could see Taj's beautiful brown eyes beginning to water as I neared. She had a hand over her mouth, appearing to hold back a cry that was yearning to escape. I held my arms wide as I approached them, and they both met me with hugs that I'd missed beyond anything imaginable. Dante went low, throwing his arms around my waist while Taj buried her head into my neck and wrapped her arms around me. I lost myself in the smell of her hair, the scent of her perfume, and the feel of her body finally pressed against mine. I rubbed my son's back and cherished that moment of being able to do so.

None of us said a word during our embrace, which must've gone on too long. A woman officer came up from behind me and interrupted our small reunion. She was an older black woman with a stern demeanor.

"Wright." Her voice was business-like.

I turned to her, still holding on to my family. "Yes, ma'am?"

Maybe it was my polite nature, or maybe it was the sight of my wife's tears that caused her stance to soften. She put a consoling hand on Taj's shoulder as she whispered to us in a southern accent.

"If I let y'all hug this long, everybody else gone wanna do the same thing, honey." She cut her eyes toward the desk where the other two white officers were. "I can't let them think I show favor to my people. Hey, sugar."

Dante was the target of her affectionate nature. He gave her a wave.

"Now give her a kiss and y'all have a seat," she said with a smile.

I obeyed her order as she left us to go patrol the rest of the visiting room. Taj's lips were sweet to the taste, and I managed not to stick my tongue down her throat in front our son. It was a short kiss, but any kiss from her was worth the wait.

We peered into each other's eyes. "Damn, I miss you."

"I miss you more, Kay."

Dante patted my lower back. "What about me?"

"I miss you in the most extreme way a person can be missed," I said as I scooped him up and gave him a kiss on the cheek. "I love you, son."

"I love you more, Daddy, but I'm too big for you to be picking up."

That earned him a playful mid-air bear hug. "Is that right, big fella?"

He let out a giggly whisper. "Stop, Daddy!"

I lowered him into the chair and sat between them, holding both of their hands and feeling the warmth of love. It was almost surreal to be able to touch them. The only physical contact I had before then was officers patting me down while searching for contraband.

"So is it anything like what we see on TV?" Taj was scoping out the surroundings as she asked the question.

"Not so far, baby. I haven't seen a fight or any shanks yet. No gay dudes with Kool-Aid on their lips, either."

She slapped my shoulder, giggling. "Shut up, crazy."

Sharing a laugh was something we hadn't done in a while. At that moment, my only thought was to hear her laugh as much as possible during the visit.

"You want something to eat, baby?"

"My celly told me they had good wings up here," I said, looking in the direction of the vending machine area. "I'll take a pop, too, and get us some Skittles."

"Dante, what about you?" Taj got up and my stare went right to the zipper of her hip-hugging jeans.

"I'll eat with Daddy."

"I wish I could eat something else." I mouthed, not wanting Dante to hear.

A playful lick of her lips came with a wink. "You owe me big-time."

"And you will be paid in full, I promise."

"I know."

She walked away, leaving me with a few private minutes with my son. He was holding my hand, seriousness in his features. I was sure he had questions he wanted answers to. Taj and I had agreed that I would be the one to tell him when I would be home. Regardless of his age, he had a right to know.

"Daddy really loves you," I said, feeling the emotions coming on as I held his hand with both of mine. "I have about two more years before they'll let me out of this place, and I promise when I come home, daddy won't leave again."

He spoke with his head bowed. "When I really start to miss you, a new song comes to me, Daddy. It plays itself." He raised his head, and for the first time that I could remember, a blanket of sadness covered his face. "And it hurts, Daddy, but I can never stop it."

Dante had been our rock during this whole ordeal, our ray of light when things seemed so dark. But now my time away from him was taking its toll. My heart burned with pain to see him hurting. I wasn't about to let him down by giving in to the hurt that was ready to show itself through tears.

I lifted his chin with a finger and forced a smile. "Just keep playing," I assured him. "It's your gift, and I've seen how happy it makes you when you play. Daddy will be home and everything will be just like before. We'll go feed the ducks and share banana splits real soon."

His small lips started curling up into a smile. "I should be eating the whole thing by then. You'll have to get your own."

I was seeing my Dante, my little man. "Oh, really."

His entire mood changed after that. I listened to stories about kids in his class, cupcake parties, and Shorty peeing on the carpet. When Taj came back with the food, it was like our own little picnic in the visiting room, minus a lake and beautiful blue skies. Taj filled me in on how the salon and beauty store were still going strong while we ate, and named many customers who sent their regards on a daily basis. Kim was helping her with the store and was basically brought in as a partner to keep everything running smoothly. Money was something I wasn't going to have to worry about when I got out, and I was blessed to have a wife who could hold it down while I was on my forced vacation.

Near the end of the visit, the visiting room had emptied somewhat. Dante had dozed off and was curled up under me as I ran my fingers through his curly black hair. Taj's head was on my shoulder, and I knew she had something on her mind when she started tapping her fingers on my opened palm.

"What are you thinking about?" My chin was brushing against her soft hair.

A whisper. "Who did you tell on, Kay?"

I figured the question would come eventually.

Taj never missed a court date of mine, but she never once mentioned anything about my case. When I was arraigned and the judge announced my charges and the possible sentence of ten years-to-life I was facing, she was there. And, at my sentencing, when my attorney informed the judge that I should get a departure from my sentence because of my substantial assistance to authorities, she was there. The prosecuting attorney then informed the judge that he also recommended that I receive the departure because I had given valuable information that was crucial in their investigation of an unnamed target. And when he added that I had gone in front of the grand jury and gave a sworn statement about my dealings with the unnamed target, I looked over my shoulder and was met with a look of disbelief from my wife. But, she never said anything until now.

Betrayed once by my secret, I couldn't hold anything from her. "Khalid."

She gave a one-word response without moving. "Why?"

I exhaled and closed my hand around hers. "My family."

"That was wrong, Kay. So wrong." Silence, then calmly as she shook her head slowly. "How could you do that? You put us in danger, Kay."

All along, I thought I did it for them. But, in hindsight, it was a selfish act that couldn't be justified. To know that Taj didn't approve of what I had done, was like her view of me had turned into one of being less than a man.

She sat up and glared at me as she spoke low enough so that no one else could hear. "What's going to happen when he finds out, Kay? What then?"

"The only way he'll find out is if he goes to trial after they pick him up, and dope cases rarely go to trial when the feds are involved." I tried to sound convincing. "He'll plead out like everybody else, so he'll never know."

She put her face in her hands. "I swear I could kill you."

An officer stood up from his seat at the desk. "Visitation is now over," he yelled.

The officer's voice was Dante's alarm clock. He rubbed the sleepiness from his eyes and turned to me. "Do they always yell at you in here?"

I chuckled. "Unfortunately, yes, son."

"Stop being bad, Daddy."

"Tell him, Dante," Taj chimed in, cutting her eyes at me as she stood.

Inmates began getting their last goodbyes in before returning to the housing units. After giving Dante a hug, Taj playfully puckered her lips with her eyes closed, baiting me in for a kiss. I gladly obliged, and instantly got an erection when I felt her tongue forcefully enter my mouth. The kiss told me that she'd missed the hell out of me, and it lasted until an officer yelled for inmates to line up by the door to the dressing room. When our lips finally unlocked, Taj reached down and gave my erection a gentle rub. A few more and I would've had a wet spot on my khakis.

"I love you, but I'm mad at you," she said, gazing sensually into my eyes. "You need to hurry up and come home."

"Asap, baby. See y'all in the morning."

It was hard watching them leave out of that door without me, especially when Dante stopped at the entrance and gave me a last wave. I waved back as I held my composure, letting him see a smile before he and Taj exited the visiting room.

<><><>

Another humiliating strip search took place after the visit. I had to get naked, hold up my balls, squat and cough before I was cleared to go back to the housing unit. On the way there, the kiss I got from Taj was all I could think about. It made me wish that conjugal visits had never been banned from most prisons. I needed to feel her so bad, and I was sure that she would be on my mind while I took a shower later on that night.

New York was sitting on his bunk when I made it to our cubicle, turning over cards as he looked to be involved in a serious game of solitaire. He slammed the deck on his mattress just as I walked to my locker.

"Yo, this game is some bullshit," he said in frustration. "I can't even beat myself."

"They call that the crazy man's game," I replied as I took off my shirt and hung it in my locker.

"Yeah, I see why. Shit will drive you crazy." He gathered the cards and slid the deck under his pillow.

"My dad used to sit at our kitchen table and play it for hours at a time when I was little." It was just one of the few memories I have of him. "My mom said only a crazy person could play cards by themselves for that long."

"Your parents still around?" He made himself comfortable and stretched out on his bunk.

"My mom is, but he died when I was younger."

"Damn, sorry to hear that."

I sucked my teeth. "No need to be." I changed into my gray sweatpants and a thermal shirt. The air conditioning system kept the dorm on the cool side.

"So how was your visit?"

"It was good, man." I grabbed the plastic chair and put in against my locker so that I was facing him. It also allowed me to see anybody walking up the aisle way. "It was good to be able to touch them finally."

New York exhaled. "We take all that shit for granted when a nigga out there. All the little shit a nigga can't do in here."

"Tell me about it. Never again, though."

He sat up on his elbow. "Was any bad hoes up there?"

I saw Stop Playin' come out of the TV room and start in our direction. "If there was, I wasn't paying attention. I don't think I've paid too much attention to any other woman since I met my wife."

He looked at me like that was hard to believe. "How long you been with her?"

"Almost five years."

New York nodded his head. "Damn, that's what's up. When I get out this mothafucka' I'm findin' me a chick to wife-up and sittin' my ass down somewhere."

Stop Playin' walked into the cubicle. "Ain't nobody gone marry yo' ole dusty ass, nigga." He sat on top of the desk and put his feet on the round metal seat. "What's up, Detroit?"

New York got up and shook his head as he addressed Stop Playin'. "Yo, you just come in here and sit yo' skinny ass on the place where I put in work and put yo' feet where I sit? You country ass niggas ain't got no kind of home-training."

"My fault," he said as he slid off the desk and onto the seat. "Let me get a noodle, mane. I got you when I go to commissary."

New York burst out laughing as he went into his locker. He took out two packs of ramen noodles and handed them to him. "Yo, I want my two noodles back and a tuna, nigga."

Stop Playin' had a dumbfounded expression on his face, his mouth wide open, gold teeth gleaming. "Mane, don't be doin' a real playa' like that."

It was funny to see the two interact the way they did. They always talked mess to each other, but it seemed like they had a good relationship between them.

"We been here three years together," New York said as he returned to his position on his bunk. "And you owe me about a hundred packs of noodles."

Stop Playin' laughed it off. "Mane, I got you when a playa' come up, damn."

"You need to get me one of them Memphis hoes, nigga. You twenty minutes from home and ain't had one hoe down here." New York was getting a kick out of his own jokes. "You don't have me something up in here by Christmas, I'm done fuckin' with you."

"Mane, just let a playa' work his magic."

"Nigga, you damn sho' performed some magic, because all them hoes disappeared."

I tried not to laugh, but it was nothing but a comedy show.

Stop Playin' took his noodles and walked out the cubicle. "Good lookin' out, New York."

I watched Stop him walk to the front of the dorm toward the microwave room. "Y'all two be going at it."

"I just be doing my time off that, nigga," New York said. "He cool, though. Give a mothafucka' something to laugh at. You need that in here." He let out a yawn and then rolled over and faced the wall.

I assumed he had fallen asleep after not hearing a word from him for several minutes. It was almost count time, so I stayed put and thought about how good it was going to feel to see Taj and Dante for the next couple of days.

"Yo." His back was still turned to me. "Do the chick you hookin' me up with got a fat ass?" His body shook with a quiet laughter.

"Man, you'll see." I shook my head and realized that laughter was the medicine he injected himself with to take away the pain brought on by the prison blues. It not only helped him, but it did wonders for me, as well.

CHAPTER 32

Six months later

Time seemed to fly by, and my prison bid was in full swing. Taj and Dante came down twice a month to spend weekends with me, and being in that visiting room helped me feel like I wasn't all the way disconnected from the free world. The kisses and hugs I got every other week, were almost like manna helping to feed my soul, and kept me nurtured through a time when I needed it most. It was always tough to see them leave, but I was thankful for every second I got to spend with them.

My mom, on the other hand, well, visiting her only child in prison was a little too much for her. The first time she came to see me was really tough. It wasn't only because of me; the sight of seeing so many young black men in prison uniforms was just heartbreaking to her. I spent most of the visit comforting her by telling her it wasn't as bad as it seemed, and that we even had ice cream socials on occasion. But that didn't stop her from voicing her concern about the state of young black men in the prison system. She was genuinely hurt from witnessing it for herself. Knowing how difficult it was, I told her that she didn't have to come back to see me. I had about eighteen months left, and I assured her that the visits from Taj and Dante were enough to hold me over until I came home. I loved my mom to death, but I didn't want to be up in the visiting room crying along with her.

As for day-to-day prison life, New York eventually got me the job sweeping up cigarette butts around the prison compound. We spent most of our time walking around and talking about different things to pass the time as we carried small brooms and long-handled dustpans to make it look like we were actually doing something. The job paid twenty-four cents an hour, and every month, about sixteen dollars would be deposited on my account courtesy of the United States government. There were other jobs that paid more money, but I didn't need any help, and I damn sure wasn't about to be part of the slave-like labor that the prison system was notoriously known for.

New York wanted no parts of it either, even though he didn't have a stash of money to live off of. He said his money was gone after his first five years, and his only source of income was the monthly earnings from the job and an occasional money order from members of his family. But after being gone for so long, it was almost like they had forgotten about him, and there had been many times when he couldn't even make commissary. He didn't have to worry about eating, though. Being that he was generous towards me when I first met him, my locker was always opened to him. He was also a hell of a chef when it came to prison cuisine. Whenever they served a bad meal at the chow hall, he would be in the microwave room performing miracle meals with items from the commissary and other things we bought off the prison's black market. Vegetables and raw chicken were smuggled out of the chow hall and sold for postage stamps, so we always kept a few books just for that purpose. He would make fried rice, burritos, pizzas and nachos like he was a professional chef. Meals like those were what made some days bearable, and I was glad to have him as my celly.

Since I had time to kill, and as a way to keep my promise to my mom, I paid to get my bachelor's degree in business management. They didn't have classes in the prison, so I had to do a correspondence course in order to earn my degree. It was hard starting out, considering there was no professor directing me on what to do. I would get everything through the mail and have a deadline to get it turned in. It took up a lot of my time, but time is all I had. I learned a few things that I planned on using when I got out, and it was sure to make my mom proud. She never scolded me for making the bad decision that landed me in prison, and she was nothing but supportive through it all. So, I figured it was the least I could do for her, as well as myself. By the time I was ready to leave, I would have my degree and something to show for the time I had done. It was an accomplishment that I could be proud of for once.

<><><>

The hardest time of a prison bid, as anybody can attest to who's been to prison, is during the holiday season. It was my second time around spending the holidays away from my family, and although I was able to call and speak to them, it was nothing like being there with them to enjoy their company and the food. It was during those times when I realized that there was nothing more important than family.

One thing I can say about the federal system is they seemed to sympathize with inmates during the holidays, and showed it by giving us a small taste of home during Thanksgiving. An inch thick slice of processed meat, that was passed off as turkey, watery mash potatoes, and a small portion of hard sweet peas was the meal they served us on Turkey Day in the county. The feds were on a completely different level, though. Each inmate received a whole Cornish hen, real dressing, mashed potatoes and gravy, steamed green beans, macaroni and cheese that rivaled your favorite aunt's, and a crescent roll. It was topped off by a dessert of your choice of sweet potato pie or red velvet cake, and the slices were big enough for two people.

After eating a good meal, inmates could go sign up for a chance to win big bags of snacks by entering some of the holiday tournaments held in the yard and ran by officers. Pool tournaments, chess, checkers, spades, bocce ball, horseshoes, and even a hillbilly game called Corn Hole, gave inmates a chance to win items you couldn't get at the commissary. It made the day a little better, and the mood was kind of festive around the prison. But I was sure that no matter what activities were involved, everyone thought about being home with their family at least once during that day. I thought about it every minute.

<><><>

New York and I had grown close during the first six months. We were cellmates and worked together, so we were practically around each other twenty-four hours a day. He was a real likable guy, and he was the only person outside of my family that I had ever spent that much time with. His personality and positive attitude were the things that made it fun to be around him, and he was easy to talk to and he loved to talk. So, it was only natural that we shared a lot of details about our lives outside of prison.

He was born and raised in Brooklyn, New York, and drugs were the reason he had gotten twenty-five years. A guy he had been dealing with set him up, and he was busted with four hundred grams of crack cocaine. Being that he had a prior drug conviction, his mandatory-minimum shot up to twenty years. The judge that sentenced him was known for handing down stiff sentences, and he gave New York the most he could give him under the sentencing guidelines.

I immediately felt sorry for him when he told me the story, but I also found myself respecting him even more for being the man that I failed to be when the pressure came down. Giving him the details of my case was something I didn't volunteer, fearing that it would somehow disrupt the friendship we had established over those six months. He never voiced his hate or disdain for the guy that set him up, but I was sure he had to have some ill feelings toward the person.

New York grew up in a two-parent home, and his mom and dad were still married after forty years. A car accident left his dad paralyzed from the waist down when New York was around five years old. He admitted that his dad had an affection for Christian Brothers brandy, and was drunk out his mind when he rammed his car head-on into an apartment building. Being paralyzed only caused him to drink even more, and to this day, his dad kept a fifth of his favorite drink on his lap wherever he went. And leave it to New York to have a few comical stories about his father, including one time when his father was drunk and threw his catheter at him.

"Yo, I was about twelve, and he was sitting in front of the TV watching a Knicks game," he recalled, chuckling at the memory.

"I was sitting on the couch listening to my Walkman. BDP had just come out, so I'm chillin' with my headphones on and shit, bumping' "My Philosophy". Now, I hear him calling me, but I was playing it off like I didn't hear him. He was yelling, "Von! Von!" three or four times. I knew all he wanted was for me to go to the kitchen and get him something, but I was like fuck that." He held his stomach as he started laughing.

"So, yo, I'm still ignoring his ass. Next thing I know, I see something coming right for me. I look up and when I realized what it was, it was too late." More laughter. "I see that plastic ass bottle halfway filled up with piss coming right at me. I couldn't duck or shit. The bottle hit me upside my head hard as hell, and then I felt some warm ass liquid running down my face. I thought it was blood because I was dizzy as fuck and I thought he busted my head. But then I smelled that shit. Man, I ran up out the living room crying like a mothafucka' and all I heard was his drunk ass in there laughing."

I think I laughed for a few days from just thinking about that story. According to New York, he had gotten his comedic ways from his mom. She had always been the lively one out of his parents. Taking care of four kids and a paralyzed husband did nothing to diminish her sense of humor. She was a God-fearing woman who laughed instead of cried, and never let anything get her down, not even the accident. Even when both of New York's sisters got strung out on drugs, she never let that get her down. She made light of the situation by cracking jokes about their habits whenever they did decide to come around. It got to a point where they wouldn't come around for months at a time because New York's mom showed them no sympathy for deciding to become junkies. Her door was always open to them, but they obviously couldn't handle their mom's verbal assault.

It had been years since he had heard from either one of his sisters in years, but one person he did hear from on a regular basis was his older brother, Emanuel. He was also in prison, but with two life sentences under his belt, he would never see freedom again. While New York hustled to get ahead, his older brother had been known throughout Brooklyn for taking whatever he wanted. He was a stickup kid, but instead of risking going to jail by robbing banks or liquor stores, drug dealers were his target. If it was known that somebody was getting money in Brooklyn, Emanuel would track them down and make them a victim of one of his many robberies. But after he robbed a crew of Nigerians for five kilos of heroin, all by himself, he was forced to leave town with his riches after they got wind of who he was. Not wanting his family to become casualties for his wrongdoings, he gave their mom enough money to relocate to a different area. He, himself, moved to Flint, Michigan, where an old girlfriend of his lived. New surroundings did nothing to change his ways, though. A robbery gone bad resulted in him killing two drug dealers, both dying from multiple gunshots to the head, and putting Emanuel away for the rest of his life.

"Yo, that nigga was crazy," New York had said. "But he always took care of us."

Having two children in prison and two strung-out on drugs must've been hard on his parents. One son was never coming home, while another son was going to be gone for what seemed like a lifetime. To murder someone was far different from selling drugs if you asked me. Emanuel had rightfully earned the time he had gotten, but twenty-five years in prison for selling drugs was more than cruel and unusual punishment. There had been rumors that some laws were going to change to help people who had been sentenced unfairly because they had sold crack cocaine instead of powder, and for my celly's sake, I hoped that it would happen. He deserved another chance.

CHAPTER 33

It was the week of my birthday and Christmas, and New York was going to finally get a chance to go up to the visiting room. Kim came down with Taj and Dante. She sent in the necessary visiting form to get on New York's visiting list and they had spoken on the phone a couple of times. I guess New York had a little game about himself when it came to the ladies, because Kim actually wanted to meet him. I never told her how much time he had because she never asked. I was going to leave that up to him to break the news.

Visiting hours had just started, so I went around the unit looking for New York. It had been about twenty minutes since I'd last seen him, and it didn't surprise me to find him in the bathroom checking himself out in the mirror.

"You looking like Tyrese up in here...the prison version," I joked as I watched him rub some hair oil on his bald head.

"Yo, what kind of dudes do shorty mess with?"

I leaned against one of the sinks. "Honestly, I've never seen her with a dude before. I don't know if she be creeping or what, but she's a good girl."

After a last look in the mirror, he released a heavy sigh. "What the fuck am I'm talking about anyway? It ain't like I'll be able to get out and fuck with her anytime soon."

"WRIGHT, HB, REPORT TO VISITATION! RAINES, HB, REPORT TO VISITATION"

The announcement seemed to cheer him up a bit. "Damn, I haven't heard that shit in a long time."

I smiled at him. "Let's go."

<><><>

Taj, Dante, and Kim were smiling from ear-to-ear when I spotted them in the visiting room. New York was behind me, nervous as I'd ever seen him during our walk from the housing unit. He was filled with questions, mostly about his appearance and Kim.

I was greeted with hugs from my family, Kim included. Then I started introducing New York to everybody.

"This is my wife, Taj and my son, Dante." It always felt good to say that. "And this is my boy, New..." I hesitated before opting to use his real name. "...Devon."

It kind of caught him by surprise. He smiled at me while offering his hand to my wife. "Nice to meet you, Taj."

"Nice to meet you, too, New York." Taj teased. "I've heard a lot about you."

He side-eyed me with a smirk. "Don't believe those lies."

"They were in your favor, though," she assured him with a giggle.

"Cool. And this must be the musical genius." New York reached down, extending his hand to Dante. "I heard you got skills on the xylophone."

Dante blushed while shaking New York's hand. "A little bit."

"Well, maybe we can do a collaboration one day."

A brief thought of them flashed through my mind, as I pictured them sitting with Dante's xylophone, creating a song together. It was sadly erased by the memory of the amount of time New York had left.

Taj, Dante and I took our seats while Kim and New York formally introduced themselves to each other. We looked on while Kim's eyes were fixated on the man standing before her. He seemed to be playing shy, something that had me ready to call him out on. It was funny to see the normally animated guy acting in such a way.

New York stuck out a hand. "Hi."

Kim wasn't going for it. "That's all I get after all that stuff you talked on the phone? Boy, you better come here." She laughed as she reached and gave him a big welcoming hug.

I saw New York's eyes close as he returned her hug, and I knew how good it must've felt to him to finally touch a woman again.

Taj nudged me and whispered. "She likes him."

There was a different dynamic to the visit, and most of it was because of New York. The nervousness he showed at the beginning, faded away with every passing minute. He transformed into the funny and enjoyable guy that I had come to know. And, he not only had me bent over in laughter, but Taj, Kim, and even Dante were witnesses to his humorous personality. It was never like he intentionally wanted the attention of the people around him; it just seemed to be in his nature to want anyone in his midst to smile and laugh like he did. From what I had seen, he never failed to do just that.

<><><>

It was near the end of the visit. Any other time, Dante would have curled up on the side of me and taken a nap while Taj and I talked. But, he was wide-eyed and busy keeping New York tied up in conversations about anything his little mind could come up with. It was odd to Taj and me to see him interact with another male the way he was. He was a charmer when it came to women, but he would quickly give a man the cold shoulder. It was almost impossible for a guy to get two words out of him. It was just the opposite with him and New York.

"He's a real nice guy," Taj whispered to me, watching our son go into a conversation about his xylophone. "You know if Dante likes him, he has to be. He never talks to guys."

"I told you that. If it wasn't for him, I might be in here going crazy." I glanced over at my celly. He had his arm around Kim as he continued talking to Dante.

Taj read my mind. "Kim is all in, isn't she?" A hand went over her mouth to conceal a quiet giggle. She then came closer. "How much time he got left?"

The question evoked a shake of my head as I turned to her and whispered. "About...fifteen more years."

Taj was taken aback by my statement. "Jesus! What he do?"

"Drugs. He got twenty-five years for drugs." Pause. "Don't say anything to Kim. He's going to tell her if he already didn't."

Taj gave me an agreeing nod and then let her head rest on my shoulder. "You better not ever in your life do this dumb shit again, Kay."

<><><>

"Shorty cool as hell."

The visit was over. New York and I were walking back to the housing unit, buttoning up our shirts after the mandatory strip search that took place after every visit. The cold December wind was swirling around us, biting at my face as we made the trek across the compound. The temperature was near freezing, but nothing like the winter up north.

"I told you that." I fastened the last button on my shirt and stuffed my hands in my pockets. "How did that kiss feel."

"Man, that was the best kiss on the cheek ever." He laughed. "A nigga damn near bust off feeling her lips on me. I was tempted to grab that fat ass when she hugged me, but I said fuck it."

The wind howled as we made it to the entrance of the unit. New York gave the door a hard knock and waited for the officer to let us in. His stare went to the ground as we stood there. I chose to peer up into the clear night sky and count the stars that made up the Big Dipper. "Did you write music before you got locked up?"

"Nawl. Never even knew I could make up a song until I got time to think about anything else but hustling." A pause. "I guess I found out about it a little too late, huh?"

I turned to him as the officer pushed open the door. "It's never too late."

New York had a God-given talent when it came to songwriting. The first time he did one of his songs, I thought maybe he had gotten lucky and came up with something that would get major spins on the radio. But after hearing over fifty songs that he had written, there wasn't a doubt in my mind that he was more than just a one-hit wonder. He had a catalog of over three hundred songs that he penned since being in prison, and if they were anything like the ones I had heard, he was going to be a rich man whenever he got out. He would be in his forties by then, but he would still have time to chase his dream. It was just too bad that he couldn't get out sooner.

CHAPTER 34

In a year's time, New York and I had almost become inseparable. We were two peas in a pod, one another's shadow, and we had become like brothers from different mothers. Our relationship wasn't built on business, nor was it established because of gang ties like so many other relationships that were built behind prison fences. Ours happened naturally. Neither one of us had anything to gain, but a genuine friendship. Yeah, it was me who was responsible for getting him the visits from Kim that continued even on weekends when Taj wasn't scheduled to come. And, yeah, it was me who kept us eating like kings even though his account was on zero most of the time. But everything I had done for him was straight from my heart, and I never expected anything in return. I sensed that if things were the other way around, he would've done the same for me.

When I first talked Kim into coming to see New York, I never expected anything to come from it except a little companionship to help him pass some time. The years he had left was enough to drive any woman away and into the hands of a guy who she could see outside of a prison visiting room. Both of us figured she would eventually lose interest after a while and the visits would come to a stop. And once he told her how much time he had left, we thought it would surely be the end. But, fortunately, she proved us both wrong.

I had heard of women who became pen pals with guys who were doing life sentences, which led to falling in love and marriages that were overseen by prison chaplains. I always thought a woman had to be crazy to do something like that. But I knew Kim personally, and she didn't seem to have any loose screws in that pretty little head of hers. Her physical features were comparable to any hip hop video vixen, and just like Taj, she also had the beautiful mind to go along with it. Getting a man was no problem for her, so at first, it puzzled me as to why she was so interested in New York. But after thinking about it, I came to the conclusion that, like me, she saw that he was a very good guy. He was just doing a lot of time.

There were times when he would come back from a visit from seeing her, and I could see the hurt in his eyes. He would try to mask it with jokes and laughs, but he never fooled me. I had been around him long enough to know when something was wrong. Like a friend would do, I'd only say positive things and make light of our situation. Sometimes it worked, but I knew the pain was always there. It had to be. I would feel it myself whenever I thought about him getting out of prison as a forty-year-old man, so I could imagine what he was going through. It was during those times that I'd wish that there was something I could do to help him.

<><><>

"Yo, I wrote two songs just for this young nigga," New York whispered across to me as he held up a magazine. A teenage R&B sensation graced the cover. "Man, I wish I could get them songs to him. They fit his style and everything."

I looked up and the songs instantly came to mind. "Yeah, I remember you doing them for me."

We were in the prison library. I was studying for a test for the college course I was taking. Surprisingly, I was carrying an A-average in each class. Applying myself was easy because I had nothing else to do, and I was on track to have my degree in business management right around the time I was scheduled to be released. It was going to be my coming home gift to my mom.

New York would always come along with me to the library. He kept up with everything that involved music and entertainment by reading various magazines while I studied. It was in him to be one of those people he read about, and he spoke of them like they were his peers in the business.

"All he needs is some good songs to put him on top. He got the talent, but he's lacking the right material." He was adamant about everything he said. "They lucky I'm not out there. I would be giving R. Kelly a run for his money."

It was a statement that I believed wholeheartedly. He was a hell of a songwriter.

"You'll get your chance."

"Shit, I hope R&B still around when a nigga get out this mothafucka'," he joked.

"Man, it's not going anywhere, trust me." I closed my book and starting gathering my papers. "They about to call the move. Are we going to the yard or what?"

New York rubbed his stomach. "I gotta go back to the unit. That damn lasagna we had for lunch got me with the bubble guts."

"I knew that was you over there farting."

He laughed. "It ain't healthy to hold that shit in."

"TEN MINUTE MOVE! THE COMPOUND IS OPEN!"

I gathered my things and put them neatly into my binder and waited for New York to return the magazine to the library counter. He chatted briefly with the inmate that was behind the counter before meeting me at the door.

"They said it's looking good for the new crack laws, but I can't believe it until I see it."

"What happens if it goes into effect?" I asked.

"Niggas with crack charges will be able to give some time back. I don't know how much, but anything will help." He sighed.

When we made it outside, a line of green uniforms was coming out of the Receiving and Discharge door. It brought back memories of my arrival in Forrest City. Guys were standing around watching the green suits head toward the housing units.

"Niggas leave, niggas come," New York said as we walked.

Three guys in front of us had stopped to observe the guys in green. "You see that rat ass nigga coming back from court," one of them said as they pointed to the group.

Another one responded. "Yeah, before he left he said he was going to take care of some state charges, but my people told me he testified against Rock at his trial."

"Snitch-ass mothafuckas, man."

One of the guys turned to New York as we walked past. "You see these rats, New York? They goin' home while real niggas like us doing numbers."

New York gave the guys fist bumps. "You know niggas gon' do what they do. Ain't no secret. Ain't no secret I gotta shit either, but I'll holla' at y'all later." He always had jokes.

We continued toward the unit as thoughts of being a rat caused a feeling of shame to come over me. It was something I came to terms with after I cooperated, but it was different now because of my friendship with New York. He knew almost everything about me, but that was something I hadn't shared with him.

The green suits were on the path that led right to our unit. That's when I spotted Wes near the front of the line carrying a bedroll and the answers to the questions I had for him. I didn't know where he was coming from after having been gone for a whole year, but I was about to find out. When he noticed me, he gave a solemn smile that came along with a shake of his head. It was obvious that he had something on his mind.

New York must've seen Wes' reaction to me. "You know dude?"

"Yeah, he's from Decatur."

"He probably just came back from bustin' a nigga in the head." New York chuckled. "He was upstairs in H-D. I thought he went home, but I see he's trying to get there."

"Busting somebody in the head" was federal inmate lingo for snitching. I had heard it numerous times over the past year, and it always made me think about what I had done in front of that grand jury. I wasn't alone, though. It was common knowledge that a large majority of federal prisoners had cooperated, and dudes leaving to go testify in front of grand juries and during trials happened all the time. It wasn't unusual for an inmate to be called to R&D and be told to pack his things before it was his time to go home. If he wasn't being transferred to another facility, chances were, he was going back to court to testify in some form or fashion. They would then reappear months later, just like Wes, with a shorter sentence than what they started with.

I was just hoping Khalid didn't go to trial because I would be forced to make that trip and return back to Forrest City to face the ridicule that came with being a snitch. I didn't care what anybody else would think; it was New York who I felt like I would disappoint. I didn't want it to come down to that.

I'm taking my stuff upstairs right quick," Wes called over to me. "Meet me on the yard."

I gave him a nod as he quickly went up the steps to the unit upstairs. "Take this to the cube for me." I handed New York my binder. "I need to talk to dude."

"You good?" New York asked. "You don't need no help, do you?"

I thought he was joking, but a rare look of seriousness was on his face. I smiled it off. "I'm good."

<><><>

I was standing by the horseshoe pit when Wes came up behind me on the yard. He had switched out the green jumpsuit into gray sweats and a white tee-shirt. He had lost some weight since being locked up, and the dark bags under his eyes were a sign that he had been stressing during his bid. I greeted him with the obligatory fist bump that was the official handshake of the federal prison system. With masturbation being a known practice amongst the majority of inmates, the traditional handshake had become all but extinct.

"Damn, Kay, they got you too, huh?"

I gave him a hard stare. "Yeah, and it was your boy who got me."

Wes looked confused. "What you mean?"

I began walking toward the track to get away from possibly being overheard. He was beside me at full attention as we hit the dusty track. "The dude from Springfield was wired. He set me up."

Wes' mouth dropped. "Man, you bullshitin'."

"I wish I was," I said as a jogger ran past. "I saw the transcripts of our conversation and everything. I remembered every word, too."

"That nigga, Khalid, ain't shit," Wes replied, shaking his head.

The mentioning of his name caused my ears to perk up. "What about him?"

"I told you he had me call you to serve that dude, and he had some dope. I was wondering why he told me to call you, though. I thought y'all had something going on so I didn't think nothing of it."

"We did at one point, but I was done after I sold those last two ounces."

"Yeah, but when I talked to that nigga later on that day, he said he heard dude had got caught with some dope in Springfield and he thought he was snitching." He pulled out a rolled cigarette and lit it up as we continued to walk. "I asked him why did he have you serve him and he said fuck you, and laughed about it. Dirty ass nigga."

It caught me off guard, but I then thought about how it all backfired on Khalid. "So what happened with you? Was that Khalid's dope you got caught with on the highway?"

"Hell yeah," he said solemnly. "Five keys and the nigga ain't put a dime on my books. Told my girl not to call and ask him for shit. He said fuck me, so I said fuck him."

I knew what that meant. "So you cooperated?"

Wes hesitated. "Yeah. Just came back from the grand jury. A couple of other guys from Decatur were there testifying, too. They probably about to indict him real soon. I just hope they knock something off this twenty they gave me."

I was in shock. "You got twenty?"

"Yeah, for now." He blew some smoke into the wind. "What you end up getting?"

"Three years. They wanted Khalid bad."

"Damn, you told, too, huh?" My nonresponse was enough for him. "It's a dirty ass game," he replied. "Self-preservation is alive and well in the feds."

Of course, I felt like I had gotten a small piece of revenge now that the truth had come out. Khalid had basically plotted his own demise without even knowing it by trying to purposely get me out of the picture. It probably never even crossed his mind that him sending an informant to me could come back and change his whole life. Jealousy and envy has always been the recipe for bad results, and it looked to be the reason for Khalid's soon-to-come downfall. But even though he played a major part in me being in the situation I was in, for some reason, I felt kind of bad for him. Whenever the feds did pick him up, he was going to be facing some major time.

Wes and I walked a few more laps before the next move was called. We met New York on our way back to the unit. He had changed into sweats and a tee-shirt, ready for our evening laps.

"I'll holler at ya' later, Wes," I said, giving him a fist bump before he went on his way.

New York passed him without even giving him a glance. I turned and started back toward the yard when he reached me.

"Who head that nigga bust?" A smirk came along with his statement.

"This dude in Decatur I did a little business with."

Before he could get out a joke that I knew was coming, "Brooklyn" Stew came walking up the pathway. He was from New York, as well. A gun charge got him four years in the feds, putting a halt on a budding career as an A&R at a major record label. Police pulled him over and found a .40 caliber pistol under the passenger seat of his BMW. His money wasn't able to help him; the feds wanted to be paid in time-served.

He was one guy that New York spoke to frequently, and it was always about music. Stew had connections that would've been priceless had New York been on the streets. He told me that Stew was interested in some of the songs he had written, but the price just wasn't to his liking. Stew knew his situation and was basically trying to low-ball him out of some music that could potentially make millions. My boy wasn't buying it, though; he knew what he had, and so did everyone who had ever heard his songs. Now their conversations were limited to who was "hot" in the industry and who needed a hit record.

"What's good, homey?" Stew said, bumping fist with New York, then me.

Guys were walking past while we stood to the side of the walkway. Stew was saying something about the moves he was going to make after he finished the last eighteen months of his sentence. New York listened while I thought about the conversation we were having before Stew walked up.

I realized how easy it was for me to tell Wes' business, but hadn't told him about me cooperating. Considering his situation and how he'd been set up by someone, I felt like I was withholding something that he had a right to know. I was denying him the choice of being friends with someone who wasn't a "stand up" guy like he was. In federal prison, being associated with a snitch was just as bad as being linked romantically to a homosexual. It could also cause drama if the wrong person found out and put that information out to the prison population.

There was a chance that New York would discover my secret if Khalid decided to go to trial. I would be hauled off to court, and then it would all come out. He didn't deserve to find out like that. He had already known so much about me. He'd met my family, and was becoming closer to them with every visit. Whenever I got pictures in the mail, I would pass them off to him one-by-one as he sat on his bunk. We shared everything: food, life stories, the good, the bad. I also knew a lot of things about him and his family, and just from the stories he'd told me about them, I felt like they had become like family. I also knew the details of his case and how he'd been set up. Being snitched on and then hit with a twenty-five-year sentence, was a justified reason to not want to associate with a snitch. I had to give him that choice.

"THE COMPOUND WILL CLOSE IN TWO MINUTES!"

The two guys from the Big Apple gave departing fist bumps. Stew went in the opposite direction while we entered the yard.

New York looked to be in deep thought as we step onto the dirt track. It was the same look he had after any conversation about music: one of frustration. But instead of letting him dwell on that, I gave him something else to think about.

"What if I told you I cooperated?" It broke the silence as we started our first lap.

New York went into his pocket and pulled out his Walkman. He put an earbud in his right ear and gave the track a stare. He wore a neutral expression, which was rare since I'd known him. I was hoping for that grin that warned of an oncoming joke, but he gave away nothing. He was silent. The afternoon sun hovered above as I waited for a response.

Finally, he replied. "I would say that's on you." A couple of joggers passed before he spoke again. "I already knew, though."

"How is that?"

"You told on yourself, no pun intended." He smirked as he said it. "You told me a guy was wearing a wire when you sold him three ounces of crack. That's ten years automatic."

I remember telling him. We were coming back from a visit when I gave him the rundown of my case. It never crossed my mind to leave out the details of the drug amount. My guards were let down when I was around him, and I guess I really wanted him to know the truth back then. Anybody in the feds, who was there on cocaine-related charges, knew what the guidelines were when it came to crack. I was sure New York was aware of it, so it was like I told him without giving him the whole story, leaving out the most important part.

"So what do you think?" My gaze was on the dust below my feet as we walked. The feeling of shame always caused my head to bow.

"I don't think shit." The shrugging of his shoulder and tone of his voice seemed to back up his statement. "Like I said, that's on you. You did what you did and now you gotta live with that."

I felt like I didn't deserve to talk. The guilt rendered me speechless.

"Let me ask you something." He removed the earbud from his ear and put his Walkman in his pocket. Music was his life, his therapy, so the question had to really mean something to him.

"Go ahead."

"How do you feel about doing that? How do you feel about tellin' on another nigga to save yo' ass?"

The question was laced with a seriousness that I wasn't used to coming from him. It asked for truthfulness, and I had to give it to him. There was only one way to describe it. "I feel fucked up."

I could see him staring over at me. "Damn," he chuckled. "I didn't know you could cuss."

"I guess I've been around you too long." I smiled, but the guilt quickly erased it. "Seriously, though, I hate that it came down to that. I hate that it was even an option, but the option was there. It gave me a choice to get back to my family sooner rather than later." The ten years I could've gotten if I hadn't cooperated crossed my mind, and I shook my head at the thought. "I just couldn't see myself taking that time. I couldn't imagine being away from them that long; not being able to raise my son; not being able to be with the woman that was meant for me. I mean, it happened anyway, but I was able to limit the damage."

I was remembering the moment right after I signed the 5k1.1 motion in that courtroom, agreeing to cooperate with the government in their prosecution of Khalid. My signature hadn't even dried when I told myself that it was either him or me. It was logical and rational from my point of view, and a decision that I was starting to regret less and less as the days went by.

"I snitched." Another head shake, but I wasn't looking down. Shame and guilt weren't about to keep riding me. I faced them right then and there, deciding that their ride was over. I did what I did, and that's life. "So I guess I'm not a *real* nigga." My attention was engaged with the setting of the sun. "That's what most would say. But the only thing that matters to me is what my family would say. And, I think they would say otherwise." The sunset created a scene worthy of a portrait. "There's nothing I can do about it now. I just wanted you to know."

A Mexican jogger gave New York a quick pat on the back as he ran by. He got a thumbs-up in return. "Like I said, that's your situation. Everybody's different."

"How do you feel about the guy who did that to you?"

He seemed to contemplate before answering. "I used to want the nigga dead when it first happened."

I didn't expect a smile to come behind the statement. It then turned into a small chuckle, as if he was mentally recalling some of the comical things he'd thought about doing to the guy.

"But, then I stopped blaming him; I put myself in this spot. We would've never crossed paths if I wasn't in the game; simple as that."

Years of self-reflecting came with his words. "It ain't like snitchin' just started, so I knew what I was getting into. Shit happened, and I can't focus on what role another nigga played in getting me here. I accepted my responsibility when that hoe ass judge gave me my time, and I'm good with that. Nigga could've gave me them twenty years, though, word up." He chuckled, chin up, head held high.

I let him bask in his memory. His cursing out the judge was something that he seemed to have genuinely enjoyed; mentioning it always got a laugh out of him.

"Rattin' a nigga out wasn't a choice for me," he said, returning to a serious tone. "For some people it is. But it's hard to knock a nigga for wanting to go home to his family and have his freedom, so I don't. I mean, look at this shit." He gestured to the double barbed-wired fences that surrounded the prison. A white prison pickup truck was driving slowly along the fence. "If a nigga want no parts of this, I understand. I don't condone it, but I understand."

"So, if you had the chance to do it all over again, would you..."

The shaking of his head cut me off before I could finish. "I don't fuck with hindsight. You can't change what happened already, and it's wasted energy to even think about it. I can only deal with what's ahead of me, my fate, my destiny."

The words conjured up a vision of Shai back in Anguilla. His stare of intense approval cascading down on Dante while heavenly notes escape from the keys of the xylophone. Fate and Destiny.

"You all right with me, Kay." His mood kicked up a notch. "You a good nigga with a good heart. This last year flew by because of you. A nigga getting visits and mail now, so I can't be mad at you. You folded up like a lawn chair when them people got on yo' ass, but you still a good nigga."

"Fuck outta' here," I said, elbowing him off his stride while he laughed at my expense. It wasn't an insult; it was more like a jab between friends, a harmless joke. I didn't mind it at all coming from him. Really, it was welcomed, and far better than him telling me he couldn't be around me because I was a rat, a snitch, a guy who had no integrity, no honor. And, though, I had fed him when his account was low and hooked him up with a woman who seemed to really be falling for him, I don't believe any of that factored into him befriending me. Being who he was, I think he would've been the same way with anybody. He was never the one to judge or belittle someone because of their past actions, and never boasted about taking his time like a man, like I'd heard so many other guys do. He seemed to understand how life worked, and that nobody is perfect. To him, it was like he only took into account the interactions he'd had with a person, and based that on how he dealt with you. Nothing else seemed to matter.

"You got a beautiful wife and a son that any man would be proud of," he said, turning on his radio and inserting his headphones again. "When you get out of here, you gotta be there for them. Ain't nothing worth losing them over. Don't fuck that up, Kay."

I could hear him turn up the volume on his radio. He began singing a song that was playing while I digested everything he had said. I knew I had to be there for my family, and it was then that I felt like I had to be there for him as well.

CHAPTER 35

I received some news that I knew would eventually come before I went home. The feds had picked up Khalid and a few other guys back in Decatur as part of a year-long investigation into drug trafficking in the small town. When Taj told me about it, the first thing that came to mind was him finding out that I had cooperated against him. I remembered Frazier saying that the only way that Khalid would know for certain that I had snitched on him was if he went to trial. My name would be on the witness list if that did happen, but other than that, he would only know if he could figure it out by looking through his discovery.

A discovery is basically documents that sum up the charges against you and how they came about. My discovery involved a drug deal that was a recorded conversation via wire, so it was easy for me to pinpoint who the confidential source was. In Khalid's case, I had only given information about our dealings, so if he could put together dates and locations of our deals, he would pretty much know it was me. He dealt with quite a few people, and besides me and Wes, other people had ratted him out as well. But if he did find out, and wanted retaliation for what I had done, he had the money to get something done, even from behind a prison fence. The thought had crossed my mind when I decided to cooperate, and I knew a decision had to be made for my family's safety. I didn't know how much of a gangster he was, but I wasn't about to take any chances.

Moving to Detroit seemed to be the only answer to that problem. The hardest part was asking Taj to pack up and move after she had accomplished so much with the shop and beauty supply. It was her dream to have her own salon, and I felt horrible about asking her to give it up. But, not to my surprise, she thought about our family first.

"I know how much you love your mom, and it would be nice for her to be able to see you and her grandson every day. I love your mom, too. I mean, she did give me the best thing that ever happened to me." She took my hand and brushed it against her cheek.

"So what about the house and the businesses?" I asked, regretting the position I had put her in. That's when the ambitious hustler that she was took over. She saw the whole situation as a challenge, a great opportunity to expand.

"We can rent the house out and let Kim take over the shop," she said, with a look of deep concentration on her face. "The beauty supply makes more money than the shop, so we most definitely are not about to turn that money back over to the Koreans. I can easily get a couple of people I trust to run it, and just have Kim to watch over that, too."

That wasn't the end of her plan, either.

"Baby, I want us to get a salon in Detroit." She was squeezing my hand, and I could see the wheels spinning in her pretty little head. "Barbara basically handed me the business with a clientele already in place, so I don't really feel like I made it into what it is now. I want to start new and build my own thing, with my own clients. And what better place to do it than in Detroit, one of the hair capitals of the world?"

I could see fire in her eyes.

"We've made a lot of money since you've been in here, and I've been saving every dime. I know you still have your money put up, but we don't need it. I got us, baby."

She had it all figured out, and it was better than anything I could've come up with. I was so blessed to have her in my corner.

<><><>

I only had six months left, and the other thing that worked in my favor was that I wouldn't be in Forrest City if Khalid decided to go to trial. I wouldn't have to leave to go to court and then return to be scrutinized by others who would know why I had left. It was bad enough having to live with myself for what I had done, so I could imagine the feeling of walking around with "snitch" written across my forehead for everyone else to see. I didn't know how it would work with me being home and him going to trial. I was just hoping it didn't come down to that.

<><><>

"Yo, you just about done here," New York sat up on his bunk. "You should have a halfway house date in a couple months."

I looked over the papers I had just received from the unit counselor. He'd called me to his office to have me sign some stuff that involved my release. I still had six months left on my sentence, but I was eligible to spend the last two months in a halfway house. It was the prison system's way of helping the newly-released adjust to life back in society, by giving them temporary shelter and resources for employment. I didn't need it for those reasons. I needed it as a way to get home faster to my family.

"Yeah, the counselor said I should get at least sixty days." Looking down at the papers, a feeling of anticipation flowed through my body. It showed itself through a smile. "Man, it's going to feel good to get up out of here."

"It'll be good to see you go. That means I'll have about thirteen left. Something happens with them laws and I might just have ten to go." He rubbed his hands together emphatically. "A nigga will be short then."

He was upbeat as he spoke, like the time was nothing to him, like ten years was a few weeks. His attitude was something that I admired about him.

Lopez, a Mexican who cooked in the chow hall, came by our cubicle in a hurried pace. "I got some raw chicken, New York," he said, without breaking a stride.

New York reached under his pillow and grabbed a book of postage stamps. "We eating chicken and fried rice tonight." He got up and took a plastic bowl from his locker and was on Lopez's trail.

My time was coming. Thoughts of leaving Forrest City danced around in my head. Of course, the background music was provided by a handsome young fellow bearing features of my own, and just so happened to be quite handy with a xylophone. I was anxious to be at his side again. I was anxious to give in to him whenever he asked to eat a bowl of cereal on the living room floor, and then anxiously listen for any signs of Taj coming down the steps so that we both didn't get yelled at. Yeah, my time was coming.

New York came back carrying the bowl. It was filled with chicken quarters. "Don't you got some more seasoning?" he asked as he went through his locker.

"Yeah, it's on that bottom shelf." He retrieved the seasoning and set everything up on the desk. "I need an onion and a bell pepper. I'll just go to the chow hall after count. Greene said he had a few things for me."

Two officers came into the dorm and herded everyone into the cubicles to perform the four o'clock count. Once they finished, it was time for "mail-call". Guys gathered at the front of the dorm while an officer passed out mail from a sack like he was Santa Claus. He called my name a couple of times and my letters were passed hand-to-hand until it reached me at the back of the crowd. One letter was from my mom and the other was from Taj. I immediately opened the letter from my mom first. Her letters were always short and always contained encouraging words. I kissed the letter after I finished reading it while the officer continued to call out names.

New York received an expected letter from Kim, with a few pictures included. Once he got that piece of mail, he turned and headed back to our cubicle. Before he could get a few feet down the aisle, his name was called again. When the letter made it to him, he smiled and said, "It's from Emmanuel."

He periodically got letters from his older brother. He was the only one in his family who stayed in contact with Emmanuel. It seemed as if everyone else had written him off after he committed the murders, but his little brother made sure they kept in touch.

New York took his place on his bunk while I sat at the desk and read my letter from Taj. I was surprised when it started off with her saying she couldn't wait to have me in her mouth again. After reading a few more lines, I found myself grabbing the bulge in my sweatpants. We got the chance to tease each other with feels and kisses during visits, and the sexual tension between us had grown to monumental proportions over the time I had been gone. I couldn't wait to get home to her.

The rest of the letter was devoted to Dante. He was still playing the song that Taj called "depressing" and "dark". There were times that she would be awakened in the middle of the night, and he would be playing the eerie tune. It had bothered her so much that she had actually recorded it and played it for a professional pianist in hopes of finding out where the song had come from. When he wasn't able to give her an answer, she continued her own research. She knew that our vibrant and usually cheerful son wasn't capable of coming up with such a dark and gloomy song on his own. The mood of the song didn't fit his personality or his nature, and it seemed as Taj wasn't going to give until she found what she was looking for.

I could tell that she was really concerned about what our son was playing on his xylophone, but I was sure it was nothing more than our genius being the creative soul that he was.

New York finished the letter from Emmanuel and let out a long sigh. "It's crazy that both of us locked up," he said, sitting up and putting the letter under his pillow. "If he was out, he would make sure I was straight, and if I was out, I would do the same for him."

"What's wrong?" I asked, forgetting about Taj's worries for an instant.

"He's broke just like me." He chuckled. "Being locked up ain't cheap. He in the state, so the food is really fucked up in there. We eat like kings compared to the shit they feed them. Ain't nobody sent him shit in years. Damn." He put his face in his hands and shook his head.

Having become as close as we were, I felt like his problems were my problems. Being in prison was hard enough without having other things to worry about. He had helped me just by being a friend, so I felt obligated to help him in any way that I could. I didn't know Emmanuel except from what I had heard about him, but I knew his brother. That's all it took.

New York went to go get some vegetables from the chow hall when they let our unit out for dinner. After he left, I went under his pillow and copied down Emmanuel's information. It was ironic that he was a couple hours away from Detroit, doing his time in the penitentiary in Jackson, Michigan. I had heard plenty of stories about that place, and none of them were good. He was a killer amongst killers.

I walked up to the phone area and leaned against the wall. The four phone booths were occupied, so I stood there and waited my turn. After about five minutes, one of the guys slammed the receiver down and walked away. Before I could make it to the phone, another guy came through the entrance and picked up the phone that I was headed to. I had never said anything to the guy before, but I knew he was from Little Rock. He was supposedly a member of the Crips street gang and he went by the name of "Young Gauge". But I was from Detroit, and I had never been impressed by some dudes who gangbanged over colors and territory. If he thought I was intimidated because of his gang affiliation, he had another thing coming.

He started dialing numbers when I came up behind him.

"Hey, I was in line." I was staring at the back of his cornrowed head as he acted like he didn't hear me. When he didn't turn around, I tapped him on the shoulder. "I was in line, dog."

He turned around with a snarl on his face. "Well, you still in line."

I guess he assumed since I was this quiet guy who didn't run with a crew, he could run over me like I was some punk ass dude who was going to back down.

There was a protocol in prison that if you had a problem with someone, the thing to do, so that no one got into trouble, was to take it to the bathroom and fight it out. I had never had a fight in my life, but I was ready for my first one.

I put the piece of paper in my pocket. "Dog, we can go in the bathroom and settle this."

He sucked his teeth as he put the phone on the receiver. "Nigga, you ain't said shit."

Other inmates had gathered around, sensing the tension in the air.

"Let's go then." I turned and headed toward the bathroom, my adrenaline at an all- time high. When I looked back, a small crowd was following behind Young Gauge. I went in the bathroom and stood ready by the shower stalls.

"I'll watch for the C.O.," somebody called out.

The rest of the guys came in and made a path for Young Gauge. He gave me a hard stare and took off his sweatshirt, revealing a slim frame that showcased a pair of long arms covered in tattoos. "This gone be easy," he said, giving one of the guys a wink.

I took a boxers stance and prepared for battle. I had my eyes set on his lower body. Most street fights involved going for the head, but the body was a weakness for the average person. My plan was to hit him with an unsuspecting rib shot and then finish him off from there.

"Yeah, this will be real easy," I replied, my feet taking a few steps toward him. He followed my lead, coming in slowly with his hands up.

The bathroom was dead silent until New York made his way through the crowd. He came right over to me and started removing his shirt, handing me an onion and green pepper in the process.

"My boy goin' home real soon," he said calmly, turning to face Young Gauge. "Ain't nobody about to fuck that up."

"Dee, I got this," I insisted, trying to hand him the vegetables.

He wasn't having it. "Nawl." His focus on Young Gauge. "If this nigga get a lucky punch in and put a mark on you, you'll lose some good time and be in the hole for the rest of your bid. I can't let you go out like that."

"You niggas fuckin' or something?" Young Gauge barked, stepping closer.

I didn't know New York could move as fast as did. He closed the gap between him and Young Gauge within a second. I couldn't see the punches he threw because they came so quick, but the sound of fist hitting flesh echoed through the entire bathroom. The crowd parted when Young Gauge's body fell back like he was taking the Nestea plunge. The thump of his head hitting the concrete floor was a sure sign that it was a clear knockout.

"Damn!" a few said in unison.

New York then calmly bent over and slapped Young Gauge's face like a trainer trying to wake up his fallen boxer. "Get this nigga some water," he said to no one in particular. He then walked back over to me and I handed him his shirt. "What y'all get into it about?" he asked nonchalantly.

"He tried to cut in front of me for the phone." I watched a guy throw a cup of water in Young Gauge's face. It was enough to wake him up a bit.

"Oh, okay." He put his shirt on. "That was some disrespectful shit, so he got what he deserved. I need you to cut up these veggies while I go start this chicken. Come on, I'm starving."

The crowd had cleared out while one guy was helping Young Gauge to his feet. He appeared to be a little woozy as he held onto the guy's shoulder when he made it to his feet.

New York went up to him and stuck out his hand. "You good?"

Young Gauge replied by nodding his head. I was surprised to see him give New York a fist bump. "Good shit," he replied, letting out a heavy sigh.

He staggered over to the sink area and started checking himself out in the mirror as New York and I walked out of the bathroom.

"How did you know we were in there?" I asked, thinking about what had just taken place.

"One of them Memphis niggas told me when I came back in. I knew it had to be somebody on some bullshit in order for you to wanna fight a motherfucka." He chuckled. "If you was just startin' yo' bid I would've let you handle it, but you too close to going home for that shit. Some of these niggas don't wanna see somebody else go home."

We made it to our cubicle when I remembered the call I was supposed to make. "I'll be right back," I said, putting the veggies in a bowl.

"Don't be starting no shit up there," he joked as I walked out the cubicle.

Two of the phones were open when I got there, thank God. I quickly dialed Taj's number. The phone clicked after the operator's announcement.

"Hey, baby." I could hear chatter in the background. She was at the shop surrounded by the sound of newly revealed gossip.

"I love when you call me 'baby'," I said, leaning my head against the wall. "Hey, I know you're busy, but I need you to do me a favor as soon as possible."

"Is everything okay?" she asked.

"Everything's fine. You got a pen and paper?"

"Hold on a sec, baby. Oh, did you get my letter today?"

"Yeah, I got it. I'll call back later when you get home. I got my halfway house papers too."

"Good. You need to get your butt home." She then whispered, "I need that dick."

"You freak," I said, blushing.

"Only for you. Okay, I'm ready." Once I gave her Emmanuel's information, she asked, "So what do I do with this?"

"That's Devon's brother. I need you to send him a thousand dollars."

"For what?"

"He needs it," I replied, even toned. "I just want to help."

There was a brief silence on her end, then, "That's why I love you, Kay," she sighed. "I'll put this girl under the dryer and go send it off."

"Thank you, baby. I love you more. I'll call you later. Kiss my son for me."

"Will do. Later, honey."

I decided not to tell Taj about the little incident with Young Gauge. She would've been worried about me, so I kept it from her for the time being. She also would've been mad about me jeopardizing coming home when I was supposed to.

On the way back to the cubicle, I realized how much of a friend New York really was to me. Only a friend would have done what he did. Only a friend would put my well-being before his own. It was hard knowing that I was going to be at home and he was going to be stuck in a place where he really didn't belong.

He was at the desk seasoning the chicken when I made it to the cubicle. His back was to me as he dashed different spices into the bowl. I stood there for a minute thinking about what it would be like to hang out with him in the free world. I imagined going out for drinks with him, shooting a game a pool, or just chilling at home watching a game on TV. Those were things I never had the pleasure to experience with a male counterpart, a true friend. But, none of those things were going to be possible anytime soon.

It was then that an idea came to mind. It was a crazy idea, but I thought about him taking a fight for me was just as crazy. I entertained the thought until he turned around and noticed me standing there.

"Nigga, you gone cut up these veggies or what?"

In the matter of minutes he had gone from playing Mike Tyson in his prime, to a prison Gordon Ramsey. He was most definitely one of a kind. All I could do was laugh. "I had to call home."

"Word." He got up and made way for me to sit at the table. "How's the family?"

A picture of us out on a double-date with Kim and Taj flashed through my mind. "The family's doing good. Real good."

CHAPTER 36

"Now you want to show out," I teased, as New York completed a set of fifty pull-ups.

"That ain't shit," he said, bragging. "I took a two-year break. I probably would be doing a hundred a set by now. Gone and knock-out yo' set of them little ten." He laughed, stepping to the side as I grabbed hold of the bar of the shower stall.

The bathroom doubled as a workout room for most guys who wanted to buff up. There were no weights at Forrest City, so some creativity was needed if you wanted to put on a little muscle while doing your time. The shower was the perfect place for pull-ups. After hitting a set, we would walk around to our cube and do push-ups on the floor and then come back for more pull-ups. We started the workout routine when I had about three months left. All the walking we had done over the past couple of years had my stomach flat, so I wanted to add a few cuts to my already toned physique. I can't say that I was actually doing it for myself; I was doing it, more so, for Taj. She stayed looking good for me, so I wanted to do the same for here. I couldn't wait for her to see the results the first time we made love when I got home.

I got down after finishing my set, which was the tenth and last one. New York went up to finish his out while I walked over to the mirrors and admired my reflection. "My baby gone like this," I said aloud, flexing my muscles. "I can't wait to get…"

As my time got shorter, it began to get harder to mention anything about going home. It seemed unfair. I knew it didn't bother him, but it just didn't feel right to me. I would find myself cutting my words short whenever I was about to say anything regarding freedom just to spare him of the thought.

There had been more news about the laws changing in favor of people sentenced under the old guidelines, but he would still have a lot of time to do. Ten more years was nothing to him, but it was still too long for me. I had a way to get him home sooner than that. What I didn't know was if he would go along with the idea.

He finished his set and walked by me. "Let's go hit a few laps before the yard closes."

<><><>

February in Arkansas was nothing like the winter up north. The temperature was above freezing, and our prison-issued coats supplied enough warmth to make it bearable to be outside during the chilly winter evening. The yard was practically empty except for a few joggers who braved the cold to get a piece of mind and some fresh air. We both had our skull caps pulled down over our earbuds while we listened to the Memphis radio station. I was preparing to let him in on the idea I had been contemplating, and was hoping it didn't offend him in any way. Being who he was and what he stood for, I figured he wouldn't want any parts of it. But he couldn't be mad at me for wanting to help. I tapped him on the arm and lowered the volume on my radio.

He looked over at me and removed an earplug. "Can't you see I'm over here gettin' my vibe on?"

I ignored him and focused on the stars in the dark sky ahead. "You want to go home?"

"What type of question is that? Fuck yeah, I wanna go home. Let this law change and I'll…"

"Fuck those laws. Do you want to go home sooner than that?" I continued staring ahead.

"Yeah, but I ain't trying to get five more years for trying to climb that fence," he joked.

I stopped in my tracks, causing him to do the same. "Look, Dee, you don't deserve to do all this time, and I think I can help you. I want to help you."

He was obviously confused. "What the fuck you talkin' about? How can you help me get out of here?"

I took a deep breath and exhaled. "When I get out of here, I can look into making some buys to help you get out sooner. I don't know how much sooner but it would be sooner than the out date you got right now."

He let out a snicker as he shook his head. "So you gone get out and go set-up some mothafuckas to help me get out? Kay, you crazy as hell, yo'! Gone with that bullshit."

He started walking off, seemingly dismissing the idea.

I came up from behind and grabbed his arm. "Don't you want to get out of here?" It came out more forceful than I intended. "Don't you want to go home, have a chance to chase your dream? You got a special gift, and I know you can get out of here and make a good life for yourself. You deserve that!"

"That snitchin' shit ain't me, Kay," he replied. "You know how I feel about that."

"You don't have to do anything," I said, adamantly. "Like I told you before, I'll always feel bad about cooperating with them people. Yeah, I snitched, and I did it for selfish reasons, but you showed me that it's not always about self." I watched him for some sort of reaction, but he gave away nothing. "When you fought that nigga in that bathroom, you did that for me. You had nothing to gain by doing that, and I've never had anybody who I felt had my back outside of my family."

"That's different, though, Kay."

"No, it's not," I replied. "And the only way I feel like I can have your back, is to help you get out of here."

It was probably the only time I had ever seen him with his head down. He was biting on his fingernail nervously as he stood there, and I could tell that he was thinking about what I was saying. It was an opportunity that would probably never present itself again. I was sure he knew that.

His stare went out toward the fence. "Man, I wanna go home." It came out as if he was speaking softly to himself.

"Let me help you then."

A strong winter breeze came through, causing me to turn up the collar of my coat. I waited for his response.

He pulled his skull cap down over his ears. Finally he said, "It's whatever, man."

I assumed that was his way of giving me the okay to go through with my plan. It was the answer I was waiting for. He walked off and I followed.

"I won't bring it up again," I said, my mind shifting to exactly how I was going to go through with the whole thing. And really, I had no idea.

CHAPTER 37

"Did you hear it?" Taj asked.

"Yeah," I replied, giving Young Gauge a fist bump as he walked pass and out the door. "It does sound kind of creepy. Sort of like something you would hear playing in an old music box."

"Well, he hasn't played it in a few days, thank God," she added with a giggle. "I guess he got bored with it. He's back to all happy tunes."

"That's good. He knows daddy's coming home." The thought made me smile. "I can't believe that xylophone has held up all this time without him complaining about it. Shai really knew what he was doing."

The vision of him watching over Dante flashed in my mind. It was different this time. When he turned to me, his hands were out as if he was motioning for me to come to him. He was wearing a faint smile. Fate and destiny.

"Baby…" Taj's voice brought me out of my trance.

"Yeah, I'm here."

"Did you hear me?" she asked.

I felt light-headed all of a sudden. "I'm sorry. The phone must've blinked out or something."

"Oh…I was just saying that I just can't get over the fact that we have such an extraordinary son. It blows my mind sometimes."

"Yeah, I can't wait to see how good he's gotten." I sighed. "I got a lot of catching up to do."

"You have one minute remaining."

"Another week and we won't have to hear her ass anymore." Taj giggled. "I can't stand her."

I laughed. "It's almost over, baby. Six days and a wake-up."

"Ooooh, that sounds so good."

"Sure does"

"I can throw away this dumb vibrator now."

"You damn sure won't need that," I assured her. "Okay, I'll talk to you tomorrow. I'll call after Dante gets out of school so that I can talk to him."

"We'll be waiting. I love you, Kay."

"I love you more, Taj."

The light headedness was still there when I hung up the phone. My knees buckled slightly, so I held onto the counter of the phone booth to keep my balance. If I would've tried to walk, I was sure that I would've tumbled to the floor. A few minutes went by before I was able to make my way to my cubicle. I climbed up into my bunk and instantly passed out.

<><><>

I woke up to the sound of humming and a slight rapping on the metal desk. Rolling over, I looked down and saw New York. He was working on some of his music.

"You tryin' to sleep these last days away or something?" he asked, glancing up at me.

I felt a little groggy. "What time is it?"

"It's almost count time."

"Four o'clock?" I asked, confused.

"Yeah." He reached into his locker for a candy bar. "Shit, you been sleep since eight last night. I thought you was dead or some shit until I heard you up there snoring earlier."

"I wasn't feeling good. Maybe it was that meatloaf we had for lunch yesterday."

He chuckled. "They be using three year-old meat in that shit. You see I didn't eat it."

I fell back on my bunk. "Now you tell me."

"I think I got another hit down here," he said confidently.

"Now that's something you don't have to tell me." I thought about our talk on the yard. "I meant what I said, Dee."

He didn't respond right off. Then, "You said you wasn't going to talk about."

"I know, but I just want you to know it wasn't just talk."

"Either way, you'll always be cool with me, Kay."
A drum beat courtesy of the steel desk began, and then a soulful voice followed.

First comes love, first comes love, first comes love, then comes marriage, then comes our baby in a baby carriage/
Girl, I know I'm young, but this must be love, the kind that could only be sent from up above/
So please just tell me I'll be yours for eternity, let's grow old together and have a family/
I knew you were the one when I first laid eyes on you, and the way I feel could only mean that this love is true/
First comes love, first comes love, first comes love, then comes marriage, then comes our baby in a baby carriage/

The guy was amazing. He had taken an old playground favorite and turned it into a song about young love. There were two teenage R&B singers who were on the rise, and I easily pictured both of them singing that song on stage in front of thousands of people. Devon had the gift, and it only backed up my belief that he had to be heard. I had to get him out of prison.

CHAPTER 38

The last week of my stay was filled with long days and restless nights. Time almost seemed to stand still, even while I practiced my same routine of working out and hitting the yard with New York. I found myself checking my watch like I've never had, trying like hell to will the day to move a little faster. To say the least, I was ready to run up out of there when the time came. It was almost surreal when my last day finally did come. All I had to do was wake up in the morning and I would be a free man. I had to do two months in the halfway house and complete one year of supervised-release, but that was all right with me. Anything beat waking up in a dorm with one hundred other guys and being told what to do and when to do it. The only thing I was going to miss was the companionship I had established with my friend, New York.

I had cleaned out my locker and transferred everything to his. A week earlier, I had gone to commissary and spent the two-hundred and ninety-five dollar limit on him just so that he wouldn't have to worry about anything. I planned on sending him some money as soon as I got home because I knew his situation, and I could never let him go without as long as I had it. I had over two-hundred thousand dollars stashed away and the money from our beauty supply and salon had our bank account looking pretty nice. Needless to say, I was fortunate to be leaving prison and not having to start over like a lot of people had to do.

Chef New York wasn't going to let me leave without hooking up a last meal for me. He made the best fried rice on the compound, and as he came in the cubicle with two bowls of the hearty dish, I couldn't help but to smile.

"My motherfucking boy," I said, taking a bowl from him and giving him a fist bump.

"Yo, you sounded white as hell sayin' that," he laughed. "Don't go home cussin' and shit or Taj gone think I'm a bad influence."

I took two forks out of his locker and handed him one. "I'll try not to." I dug into the bowl and took a bite. "Damn, I'm going to miss this rice. Maybe you should get out and start a restaurant."

He gave me a look as he scooped up a forkful of rice. I assumed me mentioning him getting out dampened the mood a bit.

"You want a pop?" I asked, changing the subject.

"Yeah, grab me a Pepsi," he replied without looking at me.

I got up and walked down the aisle to ATL's cubicle. He was on his bunk reading a book, his long legs hanging off the foot of his too-small sleeping quarters.

"What's up, shawty," he said sitting up. "You out this bitch first thang, huh?"

"Hell yeah. I can't wait. Let me get two pops."

He reached down into a trash can that was filled with ice, pulling up two cans of Pepsi. "Yo' boy New York gone be lost without yo' ass." He chuckled. "Y'all been hangin' since you got here."

I smiled. "He'll be straight."

"Shiddddd, that nigga ain't never fucked wit' nobody like he fuck wit' you, shawty. We been here five years together, so I know. He a real nigga. I hope something good happen fo' him 'cause he a music writin' mothafucka with some talent."

I handed him four stamps and took the pops from him. "Yeah, something will happen. I'm sure of that. When you get out of here, ATL?"

"I got six months left, shawty, then I'm back in the "A", baby! Can't wait to hit Chocolate City and make it rain on them hoes!" He laughed as he slapped his knee. "I know they miss a nigga."

"I bet. Okay, man, take care if I don't see you in the morning."

"You, too, shawty. Fuck this shit right here. This fo' the mothafuckin' birds. Enjoy that freedom."

I gave him a fist bump. "You already know."

To hear ATL's remark about me being the only person New York ever kicked it with on the regular, really made me feel honored to have that privilege. He was a good guy and everybody knew it. He was the type of guy that demanded respect without saying a word, and he gave it just the same. He accepted me despite my dishonorable action, and showed me the meaning of a true friend. They say everything happens for a reason, and I was convinced that my coming to prison had everything to do with meeting the guy who had become my best friend.

<><><>

I didn't even sleep the rest of the night. The lights in the unit came on at five-thirty, and I was wide awake when they did. I climbed down off my bunk and sat in the chair. I thought New York was sleep, but I was wrong; he had his headphones on, looking off into nowhere.

"What you doing up?" I asked, reaching into my locker for the final time.

"I was gonna walk you up to R&D."

"That's what's up."

I smiled as I took out my binder. It was full of the pictures and letters I had accumulated during my time in prison. It also contained my degree in Business Management I had received a couple of months earlier. Those were the only things I was taking with me. I then changed into my khaki uniform and sat quietly, thinking about what it was going to feel like to be free again. Taj was picking me up, so I figured she was outside anxiously waiting for me. I had twenty-four hours to make it to the halfway house in Detroit. It was about a thirteen hour drive, so Taj and I were going to spend the night letting our bodies get reacquainted.

A couple guys wished me luck as they passed the cubicle; some seemingly glad to see that someone was going home. Stop Playin' came in and climbed up on my bunk after giving me a fist bump.

"Yeah, mane, I think I might be movin' in with you, New York," he said, testing the comfort of the mattress. "Leave a playa' a couple packs of noodles or something, Detroit."

"Nigga, you gets nothing out of this cube," New York interjected. "And if you move in here, I want this floor mopped every day and waxed once a week."

"You know he's going to take care of you," I said to Stop Playin' as I laughed at the two of them.

"KABAZZA WRIGHT, REPORT TO R&D"

My heart fluttered at hearing the announcement. My time had come. New York got up and slipped on his sweats and sneakers.

"Aight', Detroit," Stop Playin' said as he sat up. He gave me a gold smile. "Keep it pimpin', homey."

"No doubt, man. Take care of my boy for me." I gestured to his new cellmate.

"I'll have some tissue waitin' for him when he come back."

"Nigga, you better have my bunk made up when I get back," New York demanded.

We shared one last laugh in Helena Bravo, and started our walk to R&D. Not even the rainy spring morning could dampen my spirits as we maneuvered our way through the crowd of inmates who were heading to the chow hall for breakfast. New York did his usual handshaking and fist bumping on the way. My mind was on seeing my family and the day ahead, especially being able to kiss my wife without an interruption from an officer.

"Kim's coming down this weekend," he said, bringing me out of my thoughts. "I thought she would leave a nigga alone once you left."

"She's not like that. Obviously, she's feeling you a lot." I watched the door to R&D as it got closer and closer.

He shook his head. "Yo', I appreciate everything you did for me, Kay, word is bond. And I don't want you feelin' like you gotta write a nigga or nothing when you out there. We about to be in two separate worlds so get out there and take care of the family. Stay away from the bullshit and enjoy life, man."

"That's the plan."

"You come back here, I swear I'm taking you to the bathroom and we boxing." He chuckled.

"You don't have to worry about that," I assured him, enjoying his humor as we came to the door that every inmate came in and waited for the day to leave out. I sat my binder down at the door. "This is it."

"Yeah." He exhaled. "You made it."

I nodded in agreement. "Finally."

"Well, this is as far as I can go," he said, his hand extended, but not in the form of a fist like he usually did when greeting people. His palm was open.

I met him with a firm handshake and pulled him in for a brotherly hug, patting him on the back as I did so.

"I'm getting you out of here, man," I said, looking over his shoulder and out to the yard. "I promise you that."

"Like I said, take care of yourself and the family."

We broke the embrace. I slowly nodded my head. "And like I said, I plan on doing that."

The door to R&D came open, signaling my time to go. A woman officer stepped out. "Wright?"

"I'm ready." I picked up my binder and turned to New York. "Keep writing. They need to hear you."

"I ain't got no choice." He took his fist and patted his heart, throwing up the "peace" sign as he turned and walked away. I stepped through the door, ready to taste freedom again.

I thought I would go in R&D and immediately be let out the front door to my awaiting wife. It always happened in the movies like that. But, I sat in a cell for almost three hours before any of that took place. After switching into clothes that Taj had sent me, I was given instructions about the stipulations of my release along with release papers. They also gave me a check for the money I had left in my account. Then, I was finally walked to the exit of the prison by a black male officer who was around my age. He hit a button and the door buzzed open.

"Good luck, bro," he said as I stepped out into the mild spring air.

I saw Taj's truck parked at the curb. "Thanks, man. I appreciate that."

It was hard to believe that it was actually happening. I began to walk freely toward Taj as she got out with a huge smile on her face. I dropped my binder as she literally ran and jumped in my arms, wrapping her legs around me as she did. My working out had paid off sooner than I expected. I held her up by palming her butt as she planted kisses on my face, leaving my lips for last. When her tongue met mine, I saw the fireworks all over again, a 'la Peter Brady.

"God, do you know how good this feels?" she asked in between kisses.

I gazed into her eyes as my erection grew larger. "Yes, can't you tell?"

She smiled, releasing her grip on me and stepping back. "I thought that felt familiar."

"We missed you." My stare went below her waist. "We got twenty four hours to get to the halfway house. How long is the drive?"

Seductively, she said. "About thirteen hours, but I can make it in eleven."

I grabbed her hand and led her to the truck. "Hmmm." I checked out her Detroit Lions hoody and blue jeans. "Did this occasion cause for matching outfits?"

"I thought it was fitting since it's our home now. Well, my home now."

Taj had taken care of everything before I was released. Our house was rented out and the salon and beauty supply were being ran by Kim. She also had hired a couple of people to work the beauty supply, keeping to her plan of not letting a penny be spent with the Korean competition. She donated most of the furniture and had everything else tucked away in my mom's basement, including my steel case that held the money I had stashed away and every one of Dante's toy xylophones that he refused to part with, even though he hadn't touched them in years. Until we found a house of our liking, my mom had happily opened her home and heart up to us. She spent most of her time with her new love, Frank, and the rest was spent spoiling her only grandchild.

As I opened her door for her, I couldn't help but to feel like the luckiest man in the world. My wife held it down while I was away. She was a go-getter and a great mother to my son. There was no way in hell that I was going to do anything to be taken away from her again. I held the door for her and waited until she was comfortably behind the wheel. I then kissed her again and said, "Thank you."

"For what, baby?"

I was feeling very emotional. "Just for everything."

"No need to thank me," she replied, caressing my cheek. "I only did what I swore to do when I married you." She kissed me back. "Now let's blow this popsicle stand."

I closed her door and walked around to the other side, giving a last glance to the barb-wired fences and watch towers. Somebody else was going to walk out that door a free man. I was going to make sure of that.

<><><>

We arrived at mom's house right before midnight. Spring hadn't quite made it to southeastern Michigan yet. A fresh blanket of snow had fallen, which wasn't too unusual for March. I got out the truck and slid across a patch of ice, arriving at Taj's door to greet her with one of the many kisses we had shared during the long drive. Dante was next door with mom and Frank, so their kisses would have to wait until the morning. I got a little giddy when I thought about seeing them. It felt good to be home.

Taj and I seemed to have the same thing on our minds. We made it in the house and headed straight up the stairs, undressing and leaving a trail of clothes in our wake. The shower was our first stop, where we kissed passionately in between "I love you's" and "I missed you's", only separating to take turns lathering one another's body with wandering hands. Once we were done, Taj excused herself from the shower and told me to wait until she called me before coming into the bedroom. When she finally summoned me, I grabbed a towel and dried myself off, wondering what she had in store. Whatever it was, I was ready.

The door to our room was cracked slightly open, allowing me to see the glimmering of candlelight shadowing off the wall. I could hear music playing softly in the background. My senses picked up the smell of roses and apple-scented body spray, my favorite. Aroused at the highest level, I slowly pushed the door open. Taj was lying across a king-sized canopied bed wearing a red laced teddy, her lips curled into a seductive smile. Rose petals littered the floor and the bed, making for an unforgettable scene of love-making. I let my towel fall to the floor and did a Michael Phelps dive into the bed. Her giggling was contagious.

"You're so damn silly," she said as she began to straddle me, her smile lighting up the room. We gazed into each other's eyes without saying a word. She then fell onto my chest as if she was listening to my heart. "You hear that song," she whispered.

It was an R. Kelly song called "I'll Never Leave" playing. I listened closely to the lyrics.

I will never leave, no
You don't have to worry, girl, I'll be right there for you
I will never leave, no
Baby, can't you see that I was born to be with you?
I will never leave, no
God put us together, nothing can't take that away
I will never leave, no
Now until forever, I'll be with you the rest of my days"

She rested her chin on my chest as she looked up at me. "I want you to tell me that, and promise me you won't ever leave me again."

It was a request that I gladly fulfilled. "I promise I won't ever leave you again. I don't know if I could ever live without you anyway."

"It hurts to even think about it," she replied, letting out a deep sigh as she came up to kiss me. "I'm holding you to that promise."

"Just hold me."

<><><>

I was awakened by the screeching voice of a six-year old and the yelping of a cute little Chihuahua. "Daaad-dy!"

Before I could rub the sleep from my eyes, he was on top of me giggling up a storm. Shorty was at the side of the bed with his paws up scratching at the mattress. I pulled Dante in and kissed him on the forehead as he threw his arms around me. Taj was standing in the doorway, happiness in her eyes.

"How's my little man?"

"I'm better now that you're home. Look, Daddy." He smiled to show me one of his baby teeth had fallen out. "Nana said the Tooth Fairy is coming to see me, but I told her there isn't such a thing as a Tooth Fairy."

I glanced at Taj. "But your Nana wouldn't tell you something that wasn't true, would she?"

He pulled at the hair of my goatee. "No, I don't think so. But I told her if I catch her putting some money under my pillow, I'll just act like I'm sleep."

Taj laughed. "You got two hours to be at the halfway house, baby. That's your closet," she said, pointing. "I did some shopping for you. Mom and I are going to cook breakfast. She's downstairs waiting for you."

Taj left us alone for some much needed father and son time. Shorty was begging for my attention, so I reached down and picked him up. He immediately began licking my face until he was satisfied, then laid beside me.

"How have you been," I asked Dante, messing up his hair.

"I've been all right. I made some friends in school already."

"I'm not surprised. You're a very likable kid." I looked him in his eyes. "You got a girlfriend yet."

He blushed. "No, Daddy. Mommy said I can't have a girlfriend until I'm eighteen. I think it should be sixteen, though."

"I'll see if I can talk her into making it sixteen." I began tickling him.

He laughed uncontrollably. "Stop, Daddy!"

The only way he was able to escape was by rolling off the bed. After his tumble, he rose to his feet and smiled at me.

"So what's this song I heard you were playing? Your mom said it was kind of creepy."

His smiled disappeared and his stare went everywhere, but to me. It was as if I asked the wrong question.

"It was nothing, Daddy," he replied. "Everything's all better now." He was looking out into the hallway, in the direction of his bedroom.

"What happened, Dante?"

Instead of answering me, he jumped back on the bed in a rushed manner and gave me the tightest hug ever. It reminded me of when he was younger, when I would pick him up while he was asleep and he would latch onto me like a magnet.

"I'm glad you're home, Daddy," he whispered, his head glued to my chest.

"So am I, son." I planted a kiss on his forehead. "So am I."

<><><>

After a breakfast with my favorite people, I arrived at the halfway house where I would spend the last two months of my sentence. It was on the east side of Detroit on Jefferson Avenue, an old building that could've used some cosmetic updating on the outside. I didn't know when I would be able to see my family again, so I gave Taj and Dante kisses and hugs like I was going off on another trip to prison.

The halfway house was exactly what it sounds like: I was halfway free, but still subject to the rules and regulations set up by the Bureau Of Prisons. I was allowed to leave for a few hours each day, but only to search for employment, and then return to the halfway house to be tested for alcohol and drugs. I shared a room with an old Arab guy who must've had a grudge against soap and water, so being in there was almost as bad as prison. Most of my time was spent in the lobby, where I searched newspapers and the internet for jobs.

When I learned that getting a job would possibly help me to leave the halfway house earlier than my scheduled two months, I began to do some serious job hunting. I would've flipped burgers if it meant going home sooner. Meanwhile, Taj was in her relentless pursuit of expanding her salon business, as she quickly found a building that was only blocks away from where we lived. She would get so excited when she would tell me all of the plans she had, and I would get excited right along with her. It reminded me of years earlier when she first told me her dream to have her own salon. That same passion was there, that same confidence and strong belief in herself. She was destined for greatness, with or without me. I was just glad to be along for the ride.

Filling out a bunch of applications finally paid off after a few weeks in the halfway house. Thanks to my degree in business management, I was offered a job as an assistant manager at a fast-food restaurant. Of course, I took it without a second thought. The pay was decent even though we were a long ways from being broke, and it also gave me the chance to be away from the halfway house as much as possible. I had a feeling I would get the job after being interviewed by one of the managers, who openly flirted as she asked questions that had nothing to do with the job.

Her name was Juanita, and she came off as one of those women who saw a challenge in conquering a married man. My wedding band was in plain view, but that didn't stop her from batting her fake eyelashes while we went over my application.

"Are you happily married?" she asked, holding her gaze as she popped her gum.

It was an awkward question, and I felt somewhat uncomfortable. I knew what was at stake, so I played along as nice as possible, smiling as I gave a very direct answer. "Very happy. I was fortunate enough to marry my soulmate."

"Oh, I see." It was obvious that it meant nothing to her, though, because the flirting continued. "So you're twenty-six..." she went on while looking over my application. "...and fine." A mischievous smile was on her face as she looked up at me. "I'm thirty-nine."

"Okay, that's good to know...and thanks for the compliment." I looked around aimlessly.

"I think you might be the man I'm looking for." The application was pushed to the side. "For this position." She added, giggling at her own joke as she stood and held out her hand. "Congratulations, Mr. Wright."

I came to my feet, happy about her announcement, but apprehensive about letting her touch me. For some reason I wasn't surprised when her thumb brushed across my knuckles a few times as we shook hands.

"I'll give you a call and let you know when I'll start training you." She gave me a wink and released my hand, then walked toward the counter, putting extra sway in hips that had more than likely bore a child or two. I knew she was going to be trouble.

CHAPTER 39

I ended up doing the whole two months at the halfway house. Thirty percent of my check was kicked back to them off the top, so they made sure they got all of theirs for as long as they could. Once I was released from there, I was finally allowed to return to living like an ordinary citizen. Besides visiting a probation officer once a month for the next year, I was a free man again.

I was close to putting that chapter of my life to an end. Bad decisions were made, but learned from as well. I couldn't change anything I had done, and I took full responsibility for all of my actions. I couldn't get back the time I had missed with my family, but I was hell bent on cherishing every single moment I was going to spend with them. The only thing that was missing was a guy with a heavy New York accent and a hell of a sense of humor.

New York and I hadn't spoken since I'd been home. Our only communication came by way of daily phone calls between Taj and Kim. Kim was still going to see him and she spoke to him almost every day, so I knew that he was doing well under the circumstances. She had given him my phone number after I had gotten out the halfway house, but I hadn't heard from him. I just assumed that he'd rather use the monthly three-hundred minutes inmates were given on hearing Kim's voice. I still made sure he had money on his books, though, and I always sent a message through her.

New York had mentioned how a couple of people had promised to keep in touch with him after they had been released. Once they did go home, he'd never hear from them again. So he probably thought it would be the same way with me. And maybe he had dismissed my conversation about getting him out as simple talk just to past the time. But, I wasn't like those other guys. He was my friend, the only friend I had, and there was no way that I was going to forget about him. It just didn't seem right not to have him around, even though a couple of months had passed since I had last seen him. More than anything, I wanted to see him home, see him enjoy the freedom I knew he was missing, see him get a second chance at life and live it the right way. I had to make that happen, more so for me than him.

<><><>

"Kay, I need you on fries."

I had just finished unloading boxes of frozen hamburger patties and fish patties off a delivery truck. My shirt was plastered to my back from sweating like I had been walking through a desert. We weren't short on people, but after casually rejecting Juanita's advances, it seemed like she had it out for me. She began working me like I was her personal slave.

Over the last couple of months, she had done all she could to entice me into giving her some dick. Her pants got tighter by the day, lips glossier by the minute, and brushing her 32C breast against me as we passed each other in the cramped quarters, became a daily occurrence. I ignored her for the most part, and that seemed to make her push even harder. When she realized she wasn't getting anywhere, she made it her business to make my time at that burger spot a living hell.

A teenaged kid, by the name of Adam, was manning the fries when I made it to the front. He shrugged his shoulders as he gave me a confused look. He then stepped aside and watched me give the basket a shake. Juanita was at a register helping a worker cancel an order. She glanced over her shoulder and our eyes locked for an instant.

"Adam, take your break," she commanded.

"I just had my break, Ms. Wilson," Adam contested.

She walked over and looked around. "Well, go run the trash."

I dumped a basket of fries and shook salt over them. "I already did that."

"I was talking to Adam."

"And I was telling you I did it earlier when you told me to do it." A smile was on my face as I continued my fry expedition, and I knew that really pissed her off. The look on her face was verification.

"Come to my office, Mr. Wright."

Before I could say anything, she stormed off to the back. Adam shrugged his shoulders and chuckled.

I walked to the office feeling like a high school student being summoned by the principal. Juanita was sitting at the desk when I went in. The stare she gave me was that of a crazed woman who had just caught her husband cheating. She wasted no time in issuing a threat that I found to be the craziest I'd ever heard.

"You either fuck me, or I'm firing you." I could see flames of fire in her eyes. "You're an ex-con who needs employment, and I'll call your probation officer personally to tell him that you have no interest in keeping a real job." She paused. "I'll also tell him that I saw you selling drugs out of the drive-thru window."

I stood there, flabbergasted at her attempt to extort me for sex. She was a long way from a beauty queen, but I was sure that it was no problem for her to catch a guy on a drunken night to give her what she wanted. I knew there was a shortage of men out there, but this was beyond ridiculous. I was just glad that I took the necessary precautions before I stepped into that office.

"So, let me get this clear," I said as I came closer and placed my hands on the desk. "If I don't fuck you, you're willing to lie on me and possibly send me back to prison for something I didn't do. Is that what you're saying?"

Her expression was as nonchalant as could be. "Yep."

I matched her nonchalant manner with one of my own while reaching into my pocket. "Man, I never thought these things would come in handy for anything but phone calls." I was studying my cell phone to make sure it was still recording. "Technology has come a long way during the time I was locked up. You can take pictures, text, and record conversations now."

I stopped recording and played it back for her. When she heard her voice come through the phone, I prepared myself to be attacked by the weave-wearing, giant eyelash batting, extortionist. But, to my surprise, she got up and walked out without saying a word.

I didn't know how she would react to rejection, so I followed right behind her to see what her next move was. When she stopped at the fryer, I stood back far enough just in case she had plans of tossing a basket of scorching hot fries in my face. The rest of the day went without incident. But, after the stunt she pulled, she couldn't be trusted, and I wasn't about to stay around long enough for her to try something else.

<><><>

"Oh, hell nawl!" Taj laughed as she handed me my phone. "That bitch is really crazy, baby!"

"I told you that when I first met her at the interview."

The trust we had for one another was unbreakable, and we always shared experiences we had when other people approached us in an inappropriate manner. There were no secrets between us when it came to things like that, so it was only natural to tell her about what had happened. We knew that we were meant for one another, and nothing was ever going to come between that.

"She's dangerous, baby, and I think you need to quit." Taj rested her head on my chest. "There's no telling what she'll do to get some of that." She reached down and fondled me as I put my phone on the nightstand.

"Yeah, I guess I'll start looking tomorrow." My eyes closed as I felt her tongue glide across my stomach. "It shouldn't be hard."

"Yes, it is," she replied, going lower. "Very."

<><><>

I was at work the next day during a very busy lunch hour. Juanita hadn't said a word to me, not even making eye contact whenever she looked in my direction. It was kind of uncomfortable because I didn't know what to expect next. Whenever she did come my way, I made sure she wasn't clutching any kind of sharp object or anything that could cause a wound. I wasn't about to spend my time at work watching my back, so I was going to give her my two week notice when my shift was over.

I was helping one of the crew members with a big order at the drive-thru when I heard someone at the counter ask for the manager. The voice was a very familiar one, and when I turned around, I was met with a big smile from none other than my beautiful wife. She didn't eat fast food, and never came out of the house wearing a head scarf, so I was kind of confused about why she came to my job. I put some a few orders of fries in a bag while I gave her a questioning look. All she did was wave and continued to smile like she was having the best day ever.

One of the crew members fetched Juanita from the back. It then dawned on me that Taj had come to put the crazy lady in check. I finished packing the order and served the drive-thru customer while Juanita approached the counter.

"Can I help you," Juanita asked Taj.

"Yes, you can."

Taj's smile disappeared as her fist came across the counter and landed perfectly on Juanita's jaw. She stumbled back and fell against the shake machine, falling to the floor from the punch. Along with me, customers and the crew members looked on in shock, some laughing while a couple ran over to Juanita's aide. I held back a laugh that was struggling to escape, staring at my wife with utmost admiration. Taj leaned over the counter, her pleasant smile back intact.

"Next time, think twice about approaching somebody's husband. Have a blessed day." She winked at me before turning to leave.

I didn't know my baby had it in her. I knew she wasn't a pushover, but I had no idea that she packed power in those little hands of hers. It was the last thing I expected her to do when I told her about Juanita, but I was giddy as a kid with a new toy as I watched my fallen manager lift herself up off the floor.

I waited for some kind of confrontation when she walked in my direction. She had never met Taj, but I was sure that she knew that I was responsible for the haymaker she'd just received.

"I'm going on my lunch break," she said, groggily with watery eyes. "I'll be back in an hour." She staggered off without saying another word.

<><><>

Taj was on the phone when I came home later that evening. It was obvious that she was talking to Kim about what had gone on earlier. Her feet were kicked up on the couch with Shorty on her lap, and I saw her reenacting the punch as I walked into the living room. The stern look I gave her caused the phone call to come to an abrupt end. I teased her with silence while I slipped my shoes off and placed them by the door.

"I'm sorry, baby." Her face was covered in shame. "But...I just didn't like what she tried to do to you."

I removed my jacket while shaking my head, then walked over to her as I pointed a finger at her like a parent scolding a child. "Do you realize how..."

She cut me off while giving me the pouty face, folding her arms across her chest. "I said I was sorry."

"But do you realize..."

Again, she cut me off. "Kay, I'm sorry, baby, but..."

When she was in reach, I kneeled down and took her face in my hands, caressing her cheeks with my thumbs. "Do you how much I love you for doing that?"

Her pout turned into a bashful smile. "I would do anything to protect you, Kay. You know that."

Words like that was the reason I fell in love with her. "And I would do the same for you."

We found ourselves in one of those deep passionate kisses that we had shared thousands of times. I could kiss her forever. Shorty's bark brought an end to our lovefest.

"Oh, somebody's jealous," I said, rubbing him under his chin.

"Get on somewhere, Shorty," Taj added, grabbing him and putting him down on the floor.

He stared at her as if he was contemplating biting her before trotting off.

"Oh, I talked to Tina earlier, so you might be getting a call from Run real soon."

"Dang, how's he doing?" I asked, suddenly reminiscing about driving around Decatur with him.

Taj opened her book. "She said he's doing good. His name is Maleek now."

"Maleek?"

"Tina said he's studying Islam."

It was normal practice from what I had seen. Dudes went into prison and turned to religion. Some seemed to do it as a way to better themselves or look for hope out of a situation that was too much to bare for most. Others did it for protection. I didn't know what Run's reason was, but, with the possibility of him dying in prison, I was sure that had something to do with it.

As I continued to think about him, someone else came to mind. Then the wheels in my head started turning, wondering if that certain person was still around, still in the game. Yeah, I needed to talk to Run as soon as possible.

"Where's my son?" I asked, noticing there wasn't any music coming from upstairs like usual.

Taj gave me a look I had come to know so well. She took a finger and began tracing my lips. "He went out to eat with your mom and Frank, and he's staying the night with them. We have the whole house to ourselves," she finished, and then seductively licked her finger.

I looked around. "Where should we start?"

"The shower," she replied, coming to her feet. "And we can finish down here in front of the fireplace."

"Sounds good. I'll put a couple comforters and pillows down."

<><><>

After an intense round of lovemaking, Taj was in a deep sleep that was accompanied by a cute little snore and crackling from the burning wood in the fireplace. The fire provided enough light for me to lie next to her and watch as she slept. She was just as beautiful then as she was awake. I studied her every feature, every lash of her eyes, unable to fall asleep myself. My love for her had me wide awake.

A feeling that I had never experienced came over me as I continued to watch my wife lay beside me. I then found myself wiping away a tear, then another. The feeling became stronger and stronger, and more tears followed. It took over me, to the point where it became overwhelming. Deep down inside of me, I could feel a forceful cry ready to escape. I quickly got up and ran to the kitchen so that I wouldn't wake her. Fearing that she would still hear me, I changed directions and ran upstairs as quietly as I could. I grabbed my chest when I made it up to our bedroom, as a way to try to delay the feeling that was roaring within me, ready to release itself.

In a frantic state, I crawled onto the bed and buried my face in a pillow just as the cry exploded like an emotional hand grenade. My heart ached as I gave in to its force, and it felt like life was being sucked out of me with every heave of my chest. I muffled the wails of hurt by burying my face further into the pillow. Then, an image of Taj penetrated the darkness, the flickering of the fire dancing off her face as she slept. The sight of her always brought me joy, but it only seemed to be an accelerant for the pain that was burning inside of me. The wails became stronger, louder, more hurtful, more agonizing.

<><><>

Cold wetness against my face caused me to open my eyes to a beam of light coming through the bedroom windows. I raised my head and removed the drenched pillow from under me. The clock on the nightstand read 6:45 a.m. I got up and went downstairs.

Taj was still in dreamland where I had left her, the fire burned out and smoldering up into the chimney. Careful not to wake her, I kneeled down and crawled under the covers beside her. She stirred a bit before rolling over. One eye open and a sleepy smile on her face, she whispered, "Good morning."

I kissed her cheek and brought her as close as I could. "Good morning."

Realizing that the feeling was no longer present, I drifted off with her in my arms.

CHAPTER 40

The environment at the fast food place was a little too tense for me as long as I worked with Juanita. She never spoke except if it concerned restaurant business, which was how it was supposed to be. But in the back of my mind, I always felt like she was up to something. Taj wasn't comfortable with me there after the incident, so I hung around for a couple of weeks after giving my notice. Being that having a job was one of the stipulations of my supervised release, I told my probation officer exactly what happened. He was cool, so he told me to do what I had to do as long as I didn't get into any trouble.

I looked for another job, but I wasn't exactly filling out a bunch of applications like I did when I first got to the halfway house. I was enjoying being able to take Dante to school in the morning and picking him up in the afternoon. I also enjoyed listening to the magic he performed with his xylophone throughout the day.

We finally accepted the fact that he was, indeed, a child prodigy. Taj and I spoke about it openly with my mom and others who were close to us, but we still weren't ready to expose him to the world like most parents of child prodigies. We knew it would eventually happen, but we wanted his childhood to be as normal and happy as possible. And it seemed like he was happy banging out beautiful songs all by himself. Until we felt the time was right, his audience would be made up of the people who loved him most.

<><><>

"So, what you think, baby?"

In amazement, I studied what was once an empty office space, now transformed into an elegant and stylish beauty and nail salon. Six styling stations were on one side, while the other side was laid out like a spacious living room where customers could comfortably wait their turn to get done up by some of the best stylist in the area. There was even a play area for kids, and two nail tables on each side of the entrance. Taj's interior decorating skills were immaculate, and everything was done in earth-toned colors, accented by beautiful floral arrangements throughout. Four flat-screen televisions hung from the corners, providing views for everyone in the salon. I was totally impressed with what she had accomplished in less than three months.

"This is sweet, baby!" I said, nodding my approval. "You did your thing for real!"

She walked over and hugged me. "I couldn't have done it without you."

"Yes, you could've, but it's easier when you get a little help." I kissed her forehead.

She didn't need the one-hundred thousand dollars that I gave her from my stash; her credit was excellent, and from the way she saved money, I thought for sure that she was part Jewish. But, I loved doing things for her, and it was my pleasure to pitch in on the cost of the continuation of her dream.

"Maybe I can hire you to be a wash guy for me." She giggled.

"So you wouldn't mind me running my fingers through other women's hair?"

"Well, on second thought."

My phone rung as she laughed and rubbed my chest. The caller I.D. read 'Unavailable'. "I wonder who this is." I answered and was greeted with a recording stating it was a call from an inmate at Stateville Correctional Facility. Hurriedly, I pressed "1" to accept the call. "It's, Run," I whispered to Taj.

She excused herself and walked toward the back of the salon. I turned and watched the traffic through the large plate-glass window, thinking that this was the start of my plan.

"What's up, Kay!"

"Damn, how you doing, Run? It's been a minute. Oh, I forgot, it's Maleek now." I chuckled.

"Yeah, man," he replied with a sigh. "Run is buried. He was out there lost in that mix we call life. But, all praises due to Allah, I'm all right."

We spent the next few minutes catching up with each other's lives, never once speaking on what had happened in the past. And, to be in the situation that he was in, he sounded like he was in good spirits. He also spoke like I had never heard him speak before, like prison had really changed him. It probably had more to do with the religion he was now practicing, because he sounded wiser, more humble, like some sense had finally been knocked into his head. It was unfortunate that it took a tragic situation for him to change his life, but sometimes things happen for a reason.

"So you good on your books and everything?" I asked after we caught up a bit. "You need anything?"

"Nawl, Kay, I'm straight, bro'," he insisted. "I still got some of that blood money put up, so moms send me whatever I need."

"That's what's up." I peeked over my shoulder to make sure Taj wasn't coming. "Hey, so whatever happened to your boy, Lazar."

"Oh, he's still out there. I spoke to him a couple months ago. I ran into his people down here and got hold of him."

"Cool. So what is he up to nowadays?"

"Ain't nothing changed with him. He's doing what he do."

That's all I needed to hear. "You got his number? I'd like to just holler at him to say what's up."

A brief silence. "Kay, don't even think about it, man. It ain't even worth it."

"It's not like that," I laughed. "I just want to check up on him, that's all."

"I hear you. Hold up a sec." I could hear pages being flipped. "Okay, you ready?"

Run called the number off while stored it in my phone. "I got it. Why don't you give him a call and tell him I'll be hitting him up."

"I'll do that," he replied. "Well, it's good to hear from you, Kay."

"Same here. You got the number so hit me up anytime."

"No doubt. Tell Taj I said hi, and you be easy out there. As-Salaam-Alaikum."

"Wa- Alaikium-Salaam," I replied with a smile.

Taj came back in as I ended the call. "Oh, so now you're a Muslim?"

"No," I chuckled. "It's just one of the few things I learned while I was gone."

She took my hand as we walked to the door. "What else did you learn?"

I pondered her question momentarily. "I learned that there's nothing more important than family."

She kissed me on the cheek. "Great answer."

<><><>

Taj had her salon up and running a couple weeks later. She hired six beauticians and two nail techs, and her business took off like a skyrocket. The salon in Decatur was still bringing in good money, but it was nothing compared to the revenue she was making from the new salon. She strategically hired two white stylists, so the clientele was mixed with black and white, something that made her salon somewhat unique compared to most salons in the Detroit area. The beauticians were some of the best around, too, and that helped in bringing customers from all over. After being open for only three months, it had become one of the premiere salons in the metro area, catering to local celebrities and women who made a living by catching themselves a baller or two. Taj was the epitome of a savvy business woman, and anything she touched turned to gold.

CHAPTER 41

I was allowed the luxury of being a stay at home dad for most of the summer until my probation officer told me that I had to find another job. I had six months left on supervised release, so I wasn't about to mess that up. I went on a search for something a little better than that fast food gig, and luckily for me, I didn't have to look too hard.

My mom's new love, Frank, was a supervisor at a Chrysler plant, giving me an inside connection to a job that paid good and offered great benefits. He had recently won a referral lottery that they held at the plant, and it was almost a sure thing that I would eventually get hired once they were in need of new employees. After filling out the application and going through a phone interview, I was offered a job a month later and was prepared to punch a clock for only the second time in my life. The only downfall was that I was assigned to work third shift, which limited my going to bed with Taj next to me, to only two days a week. It was a sacrifice that neither one of us liked too much, but it was something that had to be done for the time being. The good thing about working third shift was that it didn't interfere with me being able to drive Dante to school. Those were the times when some of our deepest conversations took place.

"Dad, what did you do to go to prison?"

The question caught me completely off guard as I watched him click the seatbelt and adjust himself into his booster seat. He let the middle armrest down and inserted a drink box into the holder, waiting for an answer as he bit into a granola bar. I knew there would come a time when he would ask; I just didn't expect it to come so soon.

"Well, I did something bad, Dante."

That wasn't good enough for him. "I know that," he replied with a smile, crunching as he did so. "But what exactly did you do?"

I was tempted to get Taj's approval before I told him. This was something we had never really discussed.

From the beginning, it was as if he understood what was going on. He probably didn't understand why it happened, but he knew that daddy wasn't there. And I guess Taj and I were hoping that time would erase any memory of that particular period in his life. But we should've known our inquisitive little son was bound to want in on the situation. I opted out of speaking to her first, and took it upon myself to tell him, a father to son moment, an early life-lesson about making bad decisions.

I kneeled down and made sure that he was strapped in safely. "Simply put, I was lazy, son. Instead of working hard and earning the things I wanted, I took the easy way out. I went for the fast money, and I paid for it dearly."

His expression told me that my response was good enough for him, but that wasn't the end. "I thought prison was for bad people." The quizzical look he gave me begged for an answer.

I formulated thoughts in my head that could end this conversation before any more questions arose. With Dante, it had to be explained clearly for his understanding so that there was nothing left for him to dissect.

"Okay, remember how you and Shorty would be making too much noise and your mom would make both of you take a timeout in your room?"

"She didn't like when Shorty barked in the house."

"It wasn't always Shorty," I teased, reaching over and tickling his neck. He giggled like a baby, using a hunched shoulder and his chin to soften the blow of the tickle. His mom's soft brown eyes focused on me through a smile.

"So you're saying you were on a grown-up timeout because you did something bad?"

"Yeah, that about sums it up."

He seemed to be confused. "But you aren't a bad person, Daddy."

"Just like you aren't a bad person, but you get timeouts." I leaned in and kissed him on the forehead, shutting the door behind me. After I buckled myself in, he continued with another observation of his.

"Uncle Dee isn't a bad person either." His matter-of-fact tone was telling me that he assumed that I wasn't aware of the type of person Devon was. "When is he coming home...off of his timeout, I mean?"

I started the truck up and thought about a phone call I needed to make. "Hopefully, soon."

<><><>

It had been almost five years since the incident with Lazar. We didn't part ways under the greatest of circumstances, so I wondered how he would react to me calling him. I was sure that Run had given him a heads up, but I didn't know how well it was received. Then I thought about that sixty-thousand he got me for. My phone lit up as I searched for his name in my contacts. I listened as the phone rang on the other end, not giving a damn about how he felt.

"Yeah."

"Is Lazar around?"

"Who this?"

"This, Kay. Kay from Decatur. Run's boy."

The phone sounded like it was being muffled. Then, "What's going on, Kay, my man?" He spoke as if I was an old friend that he was glad to hear from.

"Nothing much. I'm home now, and I was just checking up on you, seeing what's good with you."

"Right, right." A pause. "I was wondering what happened to you, then Run told me you was locked-up."

"Yeah, they sat me down for a minute, but I'm back out here."

"Dig that." Another pause. "Well, I'm here if you need me. Ain't nothing changed."

That was all I needed to hear. "I'll most definitely need you. I'm putting something together, so I'll be hitting you up asap."

"Yeah, you do that." The line went dead.

So, with that phone call, my plan was put in motion. I had another phone call to make, and once I made it, there was no turning back.

I searched the internet and found the number to the FBI office in Decatur. I didn't know if Agent Fraser and Agent Hudson were still around, but they were my only connection to the bureau. They already knew me as an informant, so I preferred to talk to them anyway.

A woman came on the line after I dialed the number. "Federal Bureau Of Investigation, may I help you?"

I stated my business and gave her my name afterwards. She informed me that Agent Hudson was no longer at that office. She put me on hold and connected to me to Agent Fraser. He picked up on the third ring.

"Fraser, speaking."

A pang of nervousness hit me from hearing his name. "Um...This is Kabazza Wright. Do you remember me, Agent Fraser?"

"Of course, I do." A chuckle. "That's a name that's hard to forget. So you made it home, huh?"

"Yes, finally."

"Well, hopefully you changed from your old ways. You didn't come off as bad as the guys we usually deal with, but I have no problem in doing my job if I get word that you're back in business."

"You don't have to worry about me," I replied with a laugh of my own. "My family would kill me first."

"Good to hear that. So, I know you didn't call just to say hi." His toned quickly turned business-like. "What's this call about?"

When I first decided to sell my dignity for a time-cut, I never mentioned anything about going to Chicago to get drugs. Fraser and Hudson showed me their hand early on. Once I realized their eyes were on Khalid, I gave them exactly what they wanted, nothing more. It never really crossed my mind to talk about

Lazar at the time, considering how we had fallen out. Now he was about to become my ace in the hole.

I stood up and started pacing the bedroom. "What's information going for nowadays?"

A sigh. "Depends on the kind."

"Kilos in Chicago."

Chi-town was a major pipeline for drugs that flooded the Midwest and beyond. The large Hispanic population made it easy for Mexican cartels to operate in the Windy City, and whenever a Mexican Cartel was involved, you could bet that there were truckloads of dope around. Promotions and bonuses were handed out after a major drug bust, so the feds' interest was always piqued when Chicago was mentioned.

The final jeopardy music bounced around in my head while listening to Fraser's silence. He replied with the right question after ten seconds.

"Where are you?"

"Detroit."

"Hmmm...give me a sec."

I continued pacing while he put me on hold. The door to Dante's room was open when I looked across the hall. His xylophone was on its stand, the morning sun glistening off of the shiny wood. Dante had taken extreme care of his gift from Shai, having given his mom the chore of dusting it weekly and occasional polishing after I went away. He was now doing it himself, keeping it in pristine condition. It was obvious that it meant a lot to him.

I was jarred from my thoughts by Fraser's voice.

"I got somebody there you can go talk to. His name is Agent Colston." He recited a number that I programmed into my phone. "He'll be expecting you."

I ended the call and lay back on the bed, questioning everything I was about to do. I can't say that I felt guilty about it, though; not how I did when I cooperated to save my own ass. An opportunity to extract a bit of revenge for my sixty-thousand dollar loss wasn't a factor anymore, either. And even if Lazar hadn't come back into the picture, somebody would've taken his place. I had spoken a thought into existence, and now it was just something I had to do, like it had been carved in stone years before.

A few hours later, I got off on the seventh floor of the Federal Building. My probation officer was two floors below, so I was familiar with the cavernous hallways and granite floors bearing the American Seal. Agent Colston seemed eager to talk to me when I called him. I thought maybe it would've taken a couple of days before I saw him, but he opened his schedule up to me and I took the next available appointment. So, at the time I would usually be in a deep sleep after work, I was about to go talk to a federal agent about some drugs.

The light on the door turned green, the knob clicked to signal me to enter. An older white lady greeted me by name as she peeked over at a note pad.

"That would be me." I gave her that quick little smile that white people usually throw on as they pass by. Not surprisingly, she returned one that was just as impressive.

Her pudgy hand reached for the phone and pressed a button in the same motion. "Your one o'clock is here to see you." She waited for an answer and then pointed a stubby pink finger. "The last door down that hallway."

I made my way down the hall until I came to the door displaying a shiny gold nameplate. It told me that Special Agent Robert Colston could be found here. Before I could knock, the door came open. When I spoke to Colston on the phone, I could tell that he was a brother, so I wasn't surprised to see a middle-aged black man standing behind the door. His short hair was littered with grey, and his navy blue suit was a little more stylish than the typical off the rack suits most federal agents wore.

"I'm Agent Colston." He stuck out a hand that was probably capable of palming a bowling ball. "So you know that joker, Fraser, huh?"

"I guess you can say that."

While shaking his hand, I wondered if Fraser referred to me as "one of his snitches".

"Crazy ass white boy." Something was amusing him. "Come on in. You can take that seat right there at the desk."

I did as instructed while taking in a decent view of downtown. Beyond a couple of buildings in the skyline, I could see the Renaissance Center. It was where Taj and I had first made love. The thought brought a smile to my face as I took my seat.

"You want coffee, water or something?" Colston called from behind me.

"No, I'm good, thanks."

I was staring at the bulletin board behind the desk where some of his achievements hung proudly: college degrees in Law and Forensic Accounting and an array of awards, including The FBI Shield of Bravery. Needless to say, I was impressed. The brother had put in some serious work to get where he was at. An article from the local paper was the thing that stood out the most about his collection, though. It was highlighted by a photo of five men standing behind a table, smiling like they had just won a national championship. Their trophy was laid out on the table that was at least twelve feet long. It came in the form of what looked to be hundreds of neatly stacked kilograms of cocaine and a substantial amount of cash that was planted nicely in the center of the table. The headline read: 100 Million Dollar Cocaine Takedown For Feds.

It was easy to recognize Colston in the picture. He was the tallest of the group, center frame, looking like he was playing power forward for the feds' version of the Fab Five. I was just hoping my little plan wasn't out of his league.

"I crushed that boy's dreams back in college." He came by me and walked around his desk. He had removed his jackets and his sleeves were rolled up. In his hand was a small plastic basketball. That's when I noticed one of those plastic basketball goals against the wall by the windows. "Five seconds left and he's in the corner, set up for the game winning three. They swing the ball around to him and he lets that baby go." The leather chair reclined when he sat down, and his reminiscing continued. "I came from the baseline and smacked that shit to the fifth row. Game over."

He probably had told that story a thousand times, and genuinely got a kick out of it like he seemed to being doing at that very moment. Or, maybe the whole basketball thing was just a prop, a good conversation piece that he used as an ice breaker in situations like this. I figured it was the latter, but I'll admit, it was a good story.

"We've been cool ever since." His laughter faded. "So, Wright, what you know about Chicago?" He started a slow and steady rocking of his chair. The ball remained in his hand.

I didn't feel any kind of nervousness or pressure as I gave Colston a brief history of my dealings with Lazar; it was nothing like before. I left out names and referred to Lazar as "this guy", omitting Run's role, as well as my last deal with Lazar. The newspaper article on the wall reminded of the times I'd walk in and Lazar would have dope stacked up on the coffee table. I was sure Colston liked seeing dope on the table, so I mentioned that.

When I was done, he really didn't look too enthused.

"So what's the most you've ever gotten from him or seen him with?" He glanced at his watch.

I did a mental recollection of the coffee table. "Nine...ten keys, but he does have more than what you see laying around."

"Ten?" The shaking of his head wasn't a good sign. His chair turned sideways, facing the basketball rim. He began practicing his shooting motion. "Is this guy a Mexican?"

"No, he's black."

That didn't seem to be the right answer. He added a slight frown to the head shake. "What's this guy's name?"

I scratched my head, thinking about what I would do after this didn't work out. "I just know him by Lazar."

"Hmmm...Lazar." He took a jump shot from his seat and watched the small ball swish through the nets, his wrist bent in the air. "Why does that name sound familiar?" He turned his chair back around, staring at me like I knew the answer, his brow furrowed in confusion. "Give me a minute."

He sprung from his chair and went into a door that was a few feet away from his desk. I sat there twiddling my thumbs, my attention going back and forth from the door to the newspaper article. Apparently, my little information about a few kilos wasn't good enough for Colston. He'd actually turned his nose up at me. But I guess it was peanuts compared to a hundred-million dollar bust. Leave it up to black people to get uppity when they move up the ladder in life.

Five minutes passed when he finally came through the door carrying a folder. He was flipping through it as he sat down. When he came to a particular page, he looked it over before sliding it across the desk. "It can't be him."

He sounded convinced as he retrieved the basketball and assumed his sitting free-throw position. A high arching shot made the nets sing again, sending Colston back into his rocking motion. It appeared to be his way of releasing tension.

I grabbed the paper. It was a mugshot. The black eyes and nappy goatee were unmistakable. He was younger in the picture, but he still had that grimy look about him. I could see him stealing cars and breaking into people's houses as a teenager.

Why Colston had Lazar's mugshot was beyond me. I wasn't dumb, though. Colston was a fed and Lazar was a drug dealer. Sometime in the past, they had obviously crossed paths. And, if I wasn't mistaken, I was now the link to bringing the two back together again. It was time to see how bad Colston wanted that reunion. I watched for a reaction as I put the mugshot on the desk.

"What if I do know this guy?"

The rocking of his chair instantly stopped. He spoke while his eyes stayed glued to the rim. "I think we could talk."

Bingo. It was a start. "Yeah, I know him."

"The guy you were just telling me about? That's him?" He turned in his chair and put a finger on Lazar's mugshot.

I nodded my head. "Most definitely."

He reached for the phone and dialed while staring at me. "Hey, buddy, hold on. I'm going to put you on speaker."

Fraser's voice came on once he pushed a button. "So what's going on over there?"

"You'll never believe it," Colston replied. "Seems your guy knows an old friend of mine." He picked up the folder and went through it as he spoke.

"Who's your old friend?" Fraser asked.

"Lamont Gordon. He was the supplier to the Campbell Brothers Organization. Nobody rolled on him after we took them down and he disappeared like fucking Houdini."

"The Campbell Brothers?" Fraser sounded confused. "That was almost ten years ago."

"Goddamn right." Colston slammed the folder down, smiling. "Bastard thought he could run forever."

I was a teenager when the Campbell Brothers were running the streets of Detroit. They ran the eastside and had crack houses that did major numbers on a daily basis. They were known for driving through the city in a caravan of foreign cars, garnering the attention of almost everyone in Detroit. It was a normal occurrence for them to drive by a high school and throw handfuls of cash out of their windows, as they rode by, earning them the respect of both young and old alike. But they were also ruthless, murdering many people during their rise to the top of the drug game.

All of the top members received life-sentences when they were indicted, and they went down as street legends because they symbolized what a real crew was because they didn't snitch.

Finding out that Lazar was kingpin status was a surprise. He damn sure didn't look the part, but I guess that's why he was able to elude the feds for so long. Needless to say, he was a smart guy. Unfortunately for him, though, the game had changed, and now he was back on the feds radar with a little help from me.

"So, how did Wright connect the dots for you?" Fraser asked.

Colston leaned back in his chair, his mind probably on another promotion and more accolades to add to his collection. "A few years ago state troopers pulled a guy over on the highway coming back from Chicago. We got called in after they found ten kilos in a spare tire. He had prior drug convictions up the ass, so it was easy to flip him. Come to find out, he was a cousin of the Campbell Brothers. He was second generation and not as tough as his older cousins. Motherfucker told on everybody and their momma." That got a laugh out of both of them. "He told us he got the dope from a "Lazar" but we didn't know who the guy was. He was looking at a life-sentence with his priors, so we couldn't take the chance of letting him out to make some buys. But, before we could start really investigating, he caught a shank in the neck during a fight in the holding facility. We don't know if it was a hit or what, but more than likely, it was.

"Lamont Gordon? Where the hell did this "Lazar" come from?" Fraser inquired.

"We figured he must've got the connect through one of the Campbell's." Colston continued, going through the folder again. "Lazar was probably a code name or some shit they used during a phone call or a visit in prison because they knew we were listening to everything. I think it was meant to be "La Czar", like the "king" or something like that."

"Well, let's take this motherfucker down," Fraser added.

Colston studied me. "Can you make some buys from him?"

The ball was in my court, and I wasn't about to turn it over. "As long as you can help me."

"What kind of trouble you in?"

Out the corner of my eye, I saw a pigeon fly by the window. He disappeared momentarily before coming back and perching itself on the window ledge. I chuckled lightly while shaking my head. "I'm not. I'm doing it for a friend."

I must've sounded like a fool as I explained the situation to Colston and Fraser. They probably thought I was crazy for even coming up with such an idea, just like I did. But Colston seemed to want Lamont Gordon, aka "Lazar", as bad as an Ethiopian wanted food. When I was done telling them what I wanted, his only words were, "Give me some time to talk to my superiors."

CHAPTER 42

The following weekend we celebrated Dante's seventh birthday by throwing him a party at an amusement center. He wasn't as introverted as I was as a child, so he invited some of his classmates along to enjoy his special day with him. I had a ball watching him play video games, ride Go-Karts and play Putt-Putt. A huge smile was plastered to his face the whole time, and there was nothing more satisfying than that.

Kim came up to spend the weekend with us, as well. She wasn't about to miss out on her godson's birthday for nothing in the world, and it also gave her the chance to see Taj's new salon. It was doing so good that Taj was only charging Kim rent for the salon in Decatur, allowing her to keep all booth rental fees and the money she made from doing hair herself. My wife's generosity was something else that I admired about her.

We were standing around while Dante and his friends yelled and screamed as they played in a giant bouncer. They were having so much fun that I was tempted to kick off my shoes and join them. The only thing that stopped me was the "No Adults" sign. I was kind of disappointed, but I sucked it up and passed the time by socializing with some of the parents of Dante's friends.

A few of the fathers and I were talking about the Lion's upcoming football season when Kim came up behind me and tapped me on the shoulder. When I turned around, she had her phone in her hand.

"Somebody wants to talk to you."

I excused myself and stepped away from the crowd, knowing who it was. "Man, what took you so long to call?"

"Nigga, say hi or what's up first." He laughed, and of course, it was contagious.

"What up, doe, with your silly ass?"

"Yo, shit just chillin'. You know a nigga only get three-hundred minutes in this mothafucka'."
"Yeah, I know. And you need them for your girl." I glanced over my shoulder at Kim as she spoke to Taj and the other moms.
"My friend," he corrected, joking, then a brief silence. "Hey, I just want you to know I appreciate everything, man, and I'm straight on my books. Yo' ass don't gotta hit me every month. My commissary ain't never been this fat."
"I know how it is. Just making sure you're all right."
"That's what's up. Oh, you know they passed the crack law, so a nigga gone be getting some action come November. I ain't too sure about how much time I'll get knocked off, but I'll take whatever right about now. Anything helps."
"Cool."
As bad as I wanted to tell him about the talk I had with the feds, I decided to keep it to myself for now. I didn't want to spoil the mood by bringing up. The talk we had before I left was enough to let me know that he didn't exactly approve of the whole thing.
"Yo, check it out."
Whenever he said that, I knew he had a song that he wanted to run by me. So, I listened as he began humming a tune, my eyes on Dante as he came running out of the bouncer and into his mother's arm. He gave her a hug and looked in my direction when she pointed to me. I smiled when he started running over, my ears taking in the sound of another one of New York's soon-to-be hit records.
"Damn, that was hot," I said, after he belted out the last note. "You're a beast, dog."
"I'm on R. Kelly's ass!"
"I already know."
Dante was almost out of breath when he made it to me. Recognizing I was on the phone, he stood by my side as he grabbed my hand and started swinging it back and forth. It was his way of letting me know he wanted to do something. I handed him the phone instead. "Say hi to your Uncle Dee."

His face lit up like the sun as I handed him the phone. "Hey, Uncle Dee! How are you?"

Whatever New York was saying to him made him giggle as he gave a lot of "yes" answers. Their conversation came to an end with Dante telling him that he couldn't wait for him to come home before handing me the phone. "That lady said there was a minute left." He went back to swinging my hand.

"That's my boy right there," New York bragged when I came back on the line. "His pops is cool, too."

"I try, man, I try. Well, I know you have to go, so keep in touch. You got my number; use it when you can. You need anything, holler at me."

"No doubt. Peace, fam."

The call ended, and I felt like I had just spoken to the only friend I had in the world. Whether it was good or bad, it was actually true.

"Come on, Daddy." Dante started pulling me along. "I want you to ride the Go-Kart with me."

Our party moved to the racetrack, where Dante and I joined some of the other kids and their parents in a competitive race around the course. I drove while Dante rode shotgun. We zoomed around the track while Taj and Kim snapped pictures every time we passed them as they looked on. The final lap around is when that feeling came over me. It was the same feeling from that night when I woke up to the soaked pillow.

We were about to pass Taj again when everything went into slow motion. She was holding her phone, that vibrant smile of hers piercing every fiber of my being, as she captured the moment. Then the tears came from out of nowhere, the wind causing them to streak coldly across my face. I lowered my head as we passed them, trying my best to hide what was happening. I could feel the pressure building up inside of me. It was laced with the hurt and pain that I'd felt before. I couldn't breakdown in front of Dante. I closed my eyes and willed the feeling away until it finally gave in, but not before it warned me that it would return.

The ride was over. Dante was excited after we came in first place, but his excitement disappeared when he looked over at me and noticed me wiping away tears. "What's wrong, Daddy?"

I reached over and unbuckled his seatbelt. "Something got in my eyes. I think it was a bug." I tried to smile it off, and it seemed to be good enough for him.

"Maybe you should bring some glasses next time," he suggested as he stood and stepped out the Go-Kart. "You're lucky it didn't fly in your mouth."

I needed that laugh. It helped disguise what I was feeling as we walked over to the rest of the group. I don't think Taj was fooled, though. She gave me a concerned look before turning her attention to Dante.

"My baby was hitting those corners like a pro," she said, giving Dante a high five.

"We were zooming, Mommy!"

"Yes, you were." She bent down and pecked his cheek while she continued her observation of me. "Are you okay, honey?"

"He got a bug in his eye." Dante answered her for me.

Taj looked me over carefully as she gently touched my face, her finger wiping away at the corner of my eye. My smile was only able to draw a faint one from her. Women seem to have a seventh sense that is almost telepathic, and I knew that Taj's was working overtime at that moment. I was thankful when Dante intervened.

"Mommy, can you go on with me next?"

She mustered up a smile while placing a hand on my chest. She didn't break our eye contact as she answered. "Yes, baby. Give me a sec."

"You better put your sunglasses on," I said, rubbing my eye.

Another faint smile before she gave me a quick peck. "I love you, Kay."

Usually those words would cause my heart to sing with joy. Not this time. I don't know how I managed to ward off that feeling as I stood before her, but I did.

"I love you, too. More than you could possibly ever imagine."

CHAPTER 43

Working third shift had turned my nights to days and days to nights, so a phone call at ten in the morning was enough to make me a little annoyed as I rolled over. I answered with my eyes closed, prepared to tell the caller to check back with me in a few hours. But hearing Colston's voice caused me to shake off the grogginess and come to complete attention.

"We're ready. How fast can you get down here?"

An hour later, I was in Colston's office seated at his desk. Three other men, who I assumed to be agents, were also there. Two were standing by the window as the other agent was fiddling with some sort of electronic device at Colston's side as he sat in his chair.

"We need to record your conversation with him setting up the deal," Colston explained. "We tracked his number and got his location. Our guys in Chicago have been watching him for the last week, so all you have to do now is play your part."

I needed some clarification before I did anything. "So Devon will get the credit for what I'm doing, right?"

"I spoke to the prosecutor and a few more of my superiors," he replied as the agent with the device handed it to him. "What you do will be taken into consideration as part of the 5K1.1 motion they'll put in once this is done. I can't guarantee you anything as far as how much of a time-cut he'll get, though."

I was very familiar with the 5K1.1 motion. It was the motion that was filed whenever a defendant agreed to cooperate. The "snitch clause" was the name some people referred to it as.

Seeing that New York was going to get a time-cut when the new laws took effect, I was hoping maybe he could be home in at least five years after I did this. It sounded much better than what he had left. Colston seemed to be playing fair, so all I had to do now was to go through with everything

"Good enough." I scooted my chair closer to the desk. "Let's do it."

The agent asked for my cell phone. He then connected the device to it and plugged some wires into another device that he sat on the desk. "Act like we aren't even here," he advised, handing me my phone. "Just talk like this was a normal drug deal."

My acting skills weren't all that good, but this was a part that came naturally. I was just hoping a drought didn't occur since the last time I had spoken to Lazar. I found his number in my phone and sat back in the chair, relaxed and ready to talk business as the agents looked on. When he answered, I went into full drug dealer mode. The device on the desk was a speaker, allowing the agents to hear our conversation.

"What's up?"

"This me, Kay."

"I been waiting on your call," he replied. "You ready to come see me?"

"No doubt. I put a little something together."

"It's all good; everything is everything. When you trying to come my way?"

Colston waved his hand and mouthed something to me.

"I'll be down tomorrow afternoon sometime. What's the ticket?"

A brief pause on his part. "Michael Jordan."

That meant twenty-three thousand for a kilo. "Cool. I'll hit you up when I get there."

"See you then."

Colston and the other agents looked satisfied with me as I handed the agent my phone. The easy part was over. They then went over the details, letting me know we would leave for Chicago in the morning. It was only a three hour drive, and if everything went as planned, I would make it home without Taj knowing I was gone. If it didn't go as planned, I was going to have a lot of explaining to do. That was the scariest part.

<><><>

I dropped Dante off at school the next morning, giving him a longer hug than usual. There was a chance that I wouldn't make it back if anything went wrong, so I held him a little tighter and gave him several kisses on his cheek. I had arranged for my mom to pick him up after school. She didn't ask any questions, and I was glad of that. Lying to her was something that I had never done, and I don't think I could've done it then.

Fridays were the busiest day of the week for Taj at the salon. It was the only day when she actually did hair herself. Her day started early and ended late, so I wasn't too worried about her finding out that I was gone. I was just hoping that she didn't call and ask me to bring her lunch or anything. I didn't know what I was going to say if that happened.

I rode in the back seat of an unmarked police car with tinted windows, along with Colston and another agent. During the ride, Colston and his buddy made small talk with each other while I sat silent, my mind focused on the task at hand. The three hour drive seemed to have only taken twenty minutes, and before I knew it, we were pulling into an underground garage in the heart of Downtown Chicago.

We took an elevator to an office on the eleventh floor, where a roomful of agents were gathered and waiting around a conference table. Fraser was one of them. He greeted me like an old friend, but I knew I was nothing more than a pawn in his mind.

"Long time no see," he said, smiling as he sat at the table. "Looks like you put on a little muscle."

"It happens when you get put behind a fence with nothing else to do." I wasn't in the friendliest of moods. I just wanted to do what I had to do and get back home.

Coslton offered me a seat at the table before going over everything. The plan was for me to buy a kilo of cocaine from Lazar while wearing a wire that would give them audio of the whole transaction. Upon hearing that, the scene in New Jack City popped in my head, when they found Pookie dead with a bomb strapped to his chest. I quickly shook that picture out of my head. Colston must have read the expression on my face.

"Don't worry about it, Wright. We got you covered." He gestured to an agent that was seated next to me. "We're the feds."

An agent, who had to be part of the fed's geek squad, presented me with a watch. "It'll record everything," he explained as he handed it to me. "Put it on, and once you get to the door, push this button."

The watch appeared to be the kind worn by your typical drug dealer, diamond bezel included. A little gaudy for my taste, but just right for the occasion. I put it on my wrist and examined it to make sure there was nothing suspicious in its appearance. The chances of me not ending up like Pookie, looked to be in my favor. The feds were some very crafty bastards.

"Here's the money, Wright." Colston walked over and handed me a backpack. "That's twenty-three thousand dollars. Go get us some dope."

They provided me with a car for the transaction, and I was on my way. I was constantly checking out my rearview mirror as I drove. They assured me that they were watching my every move, but they did an excellent job of camouflaging themselves amongst the noon commuters. When I came upon the exit that led to Lazar's apartment, not a single car was behind me. I knew they were there, though. At least I was hoping they were.

Not until I pulled into the parking lot of Lazar's building did I begin to feel a tinge of nervousness. My palms were sweating and my heart was beating faster than usual. I wasn't a smoker, but I felt like I needed a cigarette to help me calm down. I sat there for a second and surveyed the area, taking a few deep breaths while I did so. The only activity was an older lady walking across the parking lot pulling a basket. She looked to be returning from a trip to the grocery store, or she could've been an agent in disguise. I waited until she entered the building before I grabbed the backpack and exited the car.

As I walked up to the building with a tight grip on the backpack, I realized why Lazar was able to elude the feds for so long. The apartment building wasn't exactly the projects, but it wasn't a luxurious high-rise that sat on Lake Michigan, either. It was inconspicuous enough to not attract any attention from law enforcement and stick up kids, and the perfect place to push kilos out the front door without anyone having a clue. But, now I was going through that front door to cop a kilo, wearing a wire implanted in a watch courtesy of the federal government, all in the name of being a friend to a guy I had only known for a small fraction of my life. And not one time did I give it a second thought or regret the decision I had made.

I called Lazar to let him know I was at the door. The buzzer sounded seconds later. I walked in and casually strolled to the elevator, watching my back for a set-up. The lobby was empty, quiet except for an argument that was taking place in one of the apartments ahead of me. I glanced up and saw that the elevator was in use and making its way down. If Lazar was planning an ambush to finish me off like I thought he had planned to do after he sold me the fake kilos, it wasn't going to happen in the elevator. Killing me right there would've been too easy for him. If he was going to take me out, I wanted him to at least have to go through the trouble of cleaning up the blood and getting rid of my body.

The door leading to the stairwell was only a few feet away. Going with my gut, I arrived on his floor after hiking it up several flights of stairs. I used my shirt to wipe away a forehead full of sweat as I opened the door and peeked out. Nothing suspicious. I didn't hear the elevator in motion, so I headed down the hall and stopped when I made it to Lazar's apartment. The moment of truth had arrived.

I checked the time while I pressed the button on the watch. It was 1:37. A deal with Lazar never took more than ten minutes; it was always in and out. If I didn't come back out this door by 1:47, 1:50 tops, I probably wasn't coming out.

I gave the door a few knocks, my eyes shifting from left to right. Movement came from the other side, and then the unlatching of locks. It slowly came open to reveal Lazar's sidekick, Chuck. His red jogging suit was almost blinding. It didn't prevent me from seeing the bulge on his side, though. The gun was in his waistband, and I was hoping that's where it stayed. He moved to the side to let me by.

Nothing had changed since the last time I was there. The same furniture was still in place, like time had stood still inside of that apartment. The only thing that had changed was the carpet; heavy traffic had worn down the section that led from the entrance to the coffee table. I could imagine how many times a person had stood in the exact same spot where I was standing, patiently waiting for their order of cocaine to be filled.

A toilet flushed from somewhere in the back of the apartment. The creaking of a door, and then the silhouette of a man appeared in the darkened hallway. Lazar had a smile on his face when he came into the living room. A black silk-looking robe and a pair of sweat pants was his attire. Other than some greying in his nappy goatee, he still looked like the same old grimy Lazar.

"If it ain't my man, Kay." He came past the coffee table and greeted me with a handshake. I saw him take a glimpse of the watch. "Looking good, right there."

I quickly went into character, adding convincing modesty and hidden sarcasm. "Just a little something. Gotta look the part, right?"

He chuckled as he went and took his seat on the couch. "I'll leave that flashy shit to you young boys." A pack of cigarettes was on the table. He took one out the pack and grabbed a light. "Pat him down, Chuck."

Another surprise.

Before I could protest, Chuck's hands were running up and down my entire body, starting from my ankles and all the way up to my chest. He pulled on my shirt and carefully felt my chest area and down each arm. If I would've had on a conventional wire, Chuck probably would have made good use of that heavy metal he had on his side.

I let out a nervous laugh. "Can't be too careful, huh?"

"Never," he replied, lighting his cigarette and blowing out a cloud of smoke. "Shit ain't the same no more, and I ain't never been one to take too many chances."

Chuck finished his job and returned to his position by the door. Lazar sunk back into the couch, his robe opened, exposing a patch of nappy chest hair. "What you tryin' to get, Kay?"

I sat the backpack on the table. "I just got enough for one right now, but you know how I do. Just trying to get back on my feet."

He grabbed the backpack and inspected the money, flipping through each stack before putting it on the side of him. When he finished, he got up and walked into the kitchen. He was totting a department store shopping bag when he came back. From looking at it, it couldn't have held more than a few kilos.

"It's nothing but the best like always," he said, taking out one wrapped kilo as he sat down.

Hearing his proclamation triggered old memories of the day he sold me the fake dope. All I could see were those damn X's. My temper began to rise as I stood there.

He put the kilo in the backpack and zipped it up, as the cigarette dangled from his mouth as if it was glued to his lips. "This should put you back in the game." He handed me the backpack.

I knew why I was there, and it most definitely wasn't the time to bring up the past. But the more I thought about it, the more it bothered me. And for him to sit there like he had just done me a favor, well, that was a little too much for me to stand there without bringing it up.

I threw the backpack on my shoulder and stared at him through the foggy haze the cigarette had created in the room. "So, what about those two bad kilos you sold me? We never got a chance to work that out."

"Oh...oh, yeah, I forgot about that." He snapped his finger and pointed at me. "Look, I'm kind of low on product right now, Kay, but when you come back, I'll take care of you."

If my ears weren't deceiving me, he had just run the same line he used almost five years earlier. How I felt then, was how I was feeling at that exact moment. He was still trying to play me like I was some chump. I couldn't let it go down like that. "You told me the same shit last time, man! That was fifty-thousand dollars. You had me fucked up, running around like I was a fucking chicken with my head cut off. That was bad business and you got to make it right!"

I didn't realize I'd spoken almost at a yell until the last word came out. My heart began to race when he glared at me like I had just spit in his face. It only lasted briefly, and was replaced by a voice of understanding, a look of compromise.

"You absolutely right, Kay," he replied with a chuckle while nodding his head. "That's bad business." He reached over into his shopping bag and pulled out a block of dope. It was in a clear zip-lock bag and was already cooked up. "Like I said, I'm low on product, but take this in good faith. When you come back, I'll have the rest for you." He pushed it across the table. "Do that for me. It's a half of key."

I picked it up and held it with both hands while I looked it over. I had been out the game for a few years, but I still knew what good dope looked like. And what Lazar was trying to pacify me with, was some straight up garbage that was probably full of baking soda and water. He was still on some nonsense.

"You know what," I said, dropping the block of dope on the table. "You can keep that shit, dog. I'm out of here."

Chuck was still in his same position when I turned for the door. He had always worn a scowl on his face, so I didn't know how he felt about the situation. But, seeing that the gun was in plain view and no longer hidden under his shirt, I knew that all it took was a word from Lazar, and he would spring into action. When he didn't move from the door, all I could do was stand there and wait for my fate.

"He good, Chuck," Lazar said, behind me. "Let him out."

Chuck gave me a stare down for another second before grabbing the doorknob. He opened it, but Lazar's voice stopped me in my tracks.

"Before you leave, Kay."

I looked back over my shoulder. His hands were behind his head as if he was just relaxing, and I didn't sense any kind of threat until he spoke.

"Just want you to know that my momma was the last person to cuss at me. She died when I was fifteen." He paused at the memory. "You ever cuss at me again, I'll kill you."

He didn't yell, he didn't look angry, but I knew he meant every word. Little did he know, he wasn't going to ever see me again. At least not under the same circumstances.

There was no need for me to say something that could make him go through with his threat. My work was done, mission accomplished. So, I just looked him in the eye and said, "Yeah…I got you."

I turned and walked out, giving Chuck a last eye. His gun was still where it had been, tucked on his side and not aimed in my direction. When I heard the door shut, I smiled, feeling like I had cheated death, my backpack a kilo heavier and New York a few years closer to home.

A car was passing by at a low speed when I got out to the parking lot. When the two white guys in the car locked eyes with me, I knew they were part of Colston's team. They continued up the block and made a U-turn at the corner, driving slow enough to allow me to exit the parking lot in front of them as they came back. I checked my rearview as I drove off. When I made it halfway down the block, they pulled into the parking lot of Lazar's building, followed by two black vans with tinted windows and another unmarked car. I had no idea that a raid would take place only minutes after I'd left. There wouldn't be a doubt in Lazar's mind about who was responsible, either. The only thing that could have made it better, was if I could see his face when the battling ram hit the door.

My phone rung just as I turned at the end of the block. It was Colston. "Make a left at the next street. We're parked at the church on the right."

I did as instructed. Two unmarked cars were parked side by side, facing in opposite directions. Colston and three agents were standing around when I pulled up, waiting for the prized possession. They were at my door before I could put the car in park. Coslton came to my window, his eyes on the passenger's seat.

"Good job." His hand was gesturing for the backpack.

After I gave it to him, he passed it along to another agent. The agent then placed it on the hood and began talking into his phone while another one of his comrades snapped pictures of the backpack and its content. The process took less than a minute.

"You did real good," Colston said, watching the kilo of cocaine as the agent put it back in the backpack. "What else you see in there?"

I did a quick mental recall in my head. "Enough to know that I helped you out. Now you do the same."

Leaving that half of kilo of crack was quick thinking on my part. That alone was enough to have Lazar looking at twenty years without even including whatever else they found. The feds always wanted the next man up on the drug chain whenever they went after someone. That's how they operate. A twenty-year sentence was enough to hang over anyone's head as a way to get them to cooperate, and there was no doubt in my mind that they were going to do whatever they could to get to Lazar's connect. Whether he would give them up or not, was another story.

<><><>

Back at the federal building, I was in the lobby of Colston's office while he and some more agents held some sort of meeting after the bust. I was curious about what else they had found, but I knew that I would probably never know, especially if money was involved. It really didn't matter, though. All I wanted to do was get home before Taj realized I had been gone for hours without hearing from me.

I checked my phone and noticed my battery was low. Before I could put it back in my pocket, it rang, and Taj's number flashed across the screen. I answered it, feeling as nervous as I had all day.

"Hey, baby, what you doing?"

I saw Colston come out of his office, headed towards me. "Nothing, just running a few places, taking care of a couple things."

She didn't respond. My phoned beeped. I looked down at a black screen. "Damn!"

"We're just about ready," Colston said. "We'll be back in Detroit by six."

"Can I use your phone right quick." I held up my phone. "Mine's dead and I need to call my wife."

Colston gave me his phone and started a conversation with his secretary. I didn't want Taj to worry, so I had to call her back. If I acted out of the ordinary, she would catch on and not let go until she got answers.

"Sorry, baby, my phone went dead."

"I figured that," she replied. "So, I just talked to Dante's teacher. She wants him to play for his class at Show And Tell. What you think about that?"

Our son was ready to share his gift with his classmates, which we knew would eventually happen. We both understood that the magic he performed with his xylophone was meant to be shared. It would have been selfish of us not to allow others to experience his masterful taming of the fascinating wooden instrument. But we also knew that a seven-year old with the caliber of talent that Dante had, would attract a lot of attention once he was exposed to the public. Taj hadn't given his teacher a definite answer, so I was going to have a little talk with my son about the pros and cons of being a child prodigy.

The call ended without any questions about my whereabouts. My secret was safe, but I felt bad about keeping it from Taj. We talked about everything, shared every thought, but this was something I would have to take to my grave

<><><>

I made it back home in time to get Dante from my mom before her and Frank went out to dinner. It was a nice day, so Dante and I drove downtown to the riverfront. It was the perfect place to talk to my son about a few things, mainly, his upcoming performance.

We were sitting on a bench right off the water, the relaxing sound of small waves crashing lightly against the concrete seawall below. Dante was concentrating on the last of a chocolate sundae, the small cup tilted to one side while he used a plastic spoon to gather a final scoop. Remains of chocolate syrup were on the corner of his mouth when he was done. I didn't expect to get side-eyed when I took a napkin and reached to wipe it away.

"Daddy, I'm seven now."

"For real? How come I didn't know that?"

He playfully gave me a bump with his shoulder. "You can't be treating me like a baby out in public."

"You'll always be my baby, even when you're fifty-years old." I leaned over and gave him a forehead kiss.

"So, are you ready to show the world what you have?"

"It's just my friends and teacher, Dad. It's no big deal."

I smiled at his minimizing the whole thing. It was innocent, though. He was just a kid. "My son, my son," I sang, putting a hand on his knee. "You probably won't understand until you're older, but the gift you have is unique and rare for somebody your age. It's not normal for a self-taught seven-year old to be as good as you are with any instrument, let alone a xylophone."

"So does that make me weird?" There was a deep seriousness in his voice.

"Not at all." Chuckling. "It makes you special. An exceptional special. And when people hear you play, they might not ever want you to stop." I cupped his chin and looked him in the eyes. "Son, sometimes our lives are chosen for us the day we are born. It's called fate, our destiny. You weren't given this gift out of coincidence. It was given for a reason. And I believe that playing the xylophone is a big part of your destiny. It's what you love to do. I see it in your eyes when you play, and your mom and I hear it every time a note echoes through those metal things."

"They're called resonators, Dad."

"Okay, Mr. Resonator." I took his hand and covered it with both of mine. "I just want you to follow your path, do what you love to do, enjoy that gift of yours, cherish it, and share it with as many people as possible. You can make people happy with what you do, and there's no greater joy than making others happy."

I could see that my words were dancing around in his head, guiding him to understanding, and giving new meaning to his talent. If anybody could handle the job of putting smiles on faces and joy into hearts, it was him, that, I was sure of.

"I think I would like that." He paused to watch a squawking seagull fly overhead. "What do you love to do, Daddy?"

"Hmmm…that's a good question."

It was a question that had eluded me my entire life. And as I thought about it, I couldn't say that I had ever had a passion to do anything. At one point, I would've said that I loved making money. But I realized it was what I could do with the money, was what I was passionate about. Running my own business was cool, too, but I couldn't say that I woke up every morning smiling at the idea of selling weave and hair products. Those two had a common denominator, though, and it was the only answer that made sense, the only thing that I was passionate about, the only thing I was driven to do every day because it made me feel whole.

"I love to make you…your mom and nanna happy. That's what I love to do." I looked away from him. IT was coming. My hands went to my face.

"Are you crying?" He was yanking at my arm.

I had nowhere to go, no way of hiding. I could feel him slide closer to me. A gentle rub on the back was his choice of consoling. "You do an excellent job of making us happy, Daddy. What's the matter?"

His words shattered my heart, and caused the floodgates to open. I was heaving as he sat next to me, concern and fright in his eyes. He kept asking, "Daddy, what's the matter?", "Daddy what's wrong?", pleading for an answer.

Up until then, I had always been there to answer any questions he had. I was his encyclopedia whenever his mom wasn't around. I was his go-to-guy when he needed to know why the clouds were blue, or why Santa Claus came down the chimney instead of using the front door. If I didn't know the answer, I would go to hell and back to find it for him. This was something different, though.

His hand clutched my wrist. I was unmasked by a gentle pull. He took a napkin and put it to my cheek, doing his part in comforting me and trying to stop this grown man from crying.

"I know you don't have a bug in your eye this time," he said, in a whisper. "You can talk to me, Daddy."

And talk, we did. He listened, showing patience as I spoke through tears. The gut-wrenching heaves didn't startle him anymore. My expressing the love I had for him, seemed to play a heavy role in comforting him. Since the day he was born, a day hadn't passed that he didn't hear those three words from me: I love you. But, that night, I probably came close to equaling that amount in just a few hours.

Me telling him that I would do anything in the world for him, evoked only questions my son would ask. Most were his attempt to brighten the mood, to get a laugh out of his dad instead of more tears. The inheritance of his mother's witty personality and sense of humor were evident that night. They couldn't have shined at a better time; I needed it just as much as he did. It went on until the noise of the park faded into the night air, and concluded with more serious question and tears of his own. But we were able to smile as we took the ride home. His understanding of life had become clearer, and he was aware that everyone had a destiny. Some things were written in stone, while others were yet to reveal themselves.

CHAPTER 44

"Mr. and Mrs. Wright, Dante is absolutely amazing!"
Our son had just pulled off probably one of the greatest showings in Show And Tell history. His teacher, Mrs. Steinem, wasn't able to keep still in her seat during the entire performance.

Instead of one song, Dante did a medley that included everything from his enhanced version of Wheels On The Bus, to classical music that I never knew existed. Taj and I snickered every time Mrs. Steinem's mouth dropped when Dante would go into a new song without missing a beat. Along with the kids in the class, she would sing enthusiastically when a familiar tune was played, and her hands were probably sore and red from clapping. She was now showering us with praise as we congregated in the back of the classroom.

"Would you mind if I included him in our Christmas Concert this year?"

She couldn't take her eyes off Dante. He had her captivated and under his spell. His classmates gathered around him like he was a rock star, also in awe of his magic.

Taj was our spokesperson. "I'm sure that wouldn't be a problem, Mrs. Steinem. I think he would love that idea."

"Thank you so much," she cooed, shaking our hands like we had just done her the biggest favor in the world. "This will be the best Christmas concert ever!"

I was almost attacked by a group of six and seven-year-olds when I informed them that it was time for Dante to go. Luckily, Mrs. Steinem was able to keep them at bay by letting them know that he would perform again real soon. That seemed to please everyone in the classroom, and we were able to leave without getting kicked in the shin by rowdy second graders.

"How did I do?" Dante was watching as I carefully loaded the xylophone into our truck. He wasn't about to let a scratch come to that thing.

Taj turned around in the front seat. "Are you back there fishing for compliments, young man? If so, get in because I have a few for you."

"Hey, hey!" I said, waving her off. She frowned and stuck her tongue out as I closed the tailgate.

Dante was standing at attention, waiting for my response. I spoke in a low tone. "You were great, but stay humble."

"Nobody likes a show-off or a know-it-all."

"Right." I gave him a high-five and a shoulder squeeze, which didn't seem good enough for him. He hugged me, burying his head into my mid-section, his hands pulling me to him.

"What are y'all back there talking about," Taj called out, peeping in the side view mirror.

Dante released me and smiled. "Man talk, mom."

CHAPTER 45

Three months had passed without me hearing a word from Colston. I called him a few times, but he never got back to me. So, after seeing my probation officer, I stopped by his office to see what was going on. I was familiar with how the federal court system worked, and I knew it could take up to a year for Lazar to be sentenced. But I just wanted to hear something from him to assure me that everything was still in motion.

He wasn't in when I went to his office, so I left a message with his secretary. She knew who I was after taking my phone calls, and she let me know that Colston was aware that I was looking for him. I left out of his office feeling like he was dodging me for some reason, but there was nothing I could do. I just had to wait.

I was at the elevator, thinking about how I was going to really enjoy the holidays. Thanksgiving was a couple of days away, and I had so many things to be thankful for. The elevator door slid open, and Colston looked shocked to see me when I looked up.

"Hey, what's up, Wright?"

I reluctantly took him up on a handshake. "I've been calling you. What's going on?"

He came off the elevator, removing his hat and dusting off some snow as I began walking with him. "Nothing yet. You know how long sentencing takes. Gordon just took a plea. He's looking at thirty years at the least."

"So what does that mean for Devon?"

"I'm not sure. It's up to the prosecutor on his case." He stopped short of his office door, deciding to continue our talk in the hallway. "But considering you helped us catch a murderer, your boy should get a few years knocked off, that's for sure."

"A murderer?" I was confused. "Lazar killed somebody?"

"We can't prove the murders we think he did," he replied, walking over to the window and staring out over the city. "But his boy Charles got three bodies under his belt, and we got DNA evidence all on his ass, and a witness."

I was completely in the dark until Colston filled me in on Charles Harding, aka "Chuck", and it didn't surprise me to find out that he had a very violent past. Charles Harding was originally from California, and an original member of a Blood street gang called The Bounty Hunters. He committed his first murder at fourteen years old, his victim being a nineteen-year-old woman who was mistakenly shot while being in the company of a rival gang member. Chuck did seven years in California's youth authority, only to get out and kill the two witnesses that testified against him. The DNA that was recovered from the murder scene came in the form of urine. Chuck obviously didn't take kindly to being snitched on, and that was evident when he pissed on his victims after cutting them down with an AK-47. He had been on the run for over twenty years and was now back in California facing the death penalty.

Had I known beforehand that Chuck was a stone-cold killer, I would have still gone through with the buy. I may have been a little more nervous about the whole thing, but I knew I couldn't stop what was meant to be. I was just glad that I was able to keep my word to Devon.

"So, now we just wait, huh?"

"Yes, and I'll let you know as soon as I hear anything." He checked his watch before offering his hand. "I got a meeting to make. Thanks for everything."

I shook his hand. "Just look out for my boy."

He nodded his head. "I'll do what I can."

CHAPTER 46

The holiday season came around, and I could only reflect back a year earlier and be thankful. The same time the year before, I was eating Thanksgiving dinner in the chow hall with hundreds of other inmates, wishing I was home. And now my wish had come true. It was our first Thanksgiving together as a family, and I couldn't have been happier to be surrounded by the people I loved. Kim and Barbara came to spend the holiday with us, and Mona stopped by to join us, a feast that had all of us sitting around holding our bellies when we were done. Afterward, our entertainment consisted of drinks, laughs, and background music provided by Dante and his xylophone. He was playing a variety of jazz tunes that soothed our ears as we talked and played cards, never once stopping unless he had to make an emergency run to the bathroom. And during those breaks, it seemed like everything froze in time until he came back. He played for hours, and wouldn't have stopped had Taj not insisted he go to bed when she saw him struggling to keep his eyes open. I think he could've played in his sleep, though.

Mona and Kim didn't waste time pulling out their weed once my mom and Frank went next door and Barbara went upstairs to the guest room. Taj put on some R&B while I went into the kitchen for a bowl of banana pudding. When I came back into the living room, they had their own little Hustle line going, stepping in the name of love with R. Kelly. Taj loved her some R. Kelly. I sat on the couch, amused at how Mona and Kim passed the blunt back and forth without missing a step.

"Come on, baby," Taj pleaded, holding out her hands as she danced. "I'll teach you."

I was tempted to get up and try to dance for the first time in my life. The Hustle was something a man could do and still look cool, so I figured what the hell. But, just as I got up to try it out, my phone rang. I knew it was a call from either Run or Devon when "Unavailable" came across my screen.

"Give me a minute, baby." I sat back down, recognizing the call from a federal prison. I pushed "5" to accept the call. "Happy Thanksgiving, yo."

"Nigga, ain't nothing happy about it." He chuckled off the truth. "Happy Thanksgiving to you and the fam. Sound like y'all having a party over there."

"Just listening to a little music, that's all." I stopped myself from telling him how much I was enjoying myself, how much I was enjoying being free. "One day we'll be sitting around listening to some of your classics."

"Yeah, and from the looks of it, a nigga getting' them five years chopped off with the new laws. I'm short as hell now!"

"So that puts you at a little over eight to do." Of course, to me, that was still a lot of time.

"Hell yeah! It's all downhill from here!"

"It'll be sooner than that, though."

"Yeah, I'll get the full six months in the halfway house, so a nigga can say about seven and a half."

"That's not what I'm talking about, Dee."

He was adamant. "Yeah, I already added the shit up and…"

I interrupted him as I noticed light from the upstairs bathroom. "I did it."

"You did what?" He sounded clueless, and I was sure that he had dismissed everything I had told him I would do.

The light from the bathroom went out, and I thought I would see Dante peek down the steps shortly after. When that didn't happen, I figured it was Barbara.

"I did what I said I was going to do."

Just as I said it, my eyes met Taj's. She was stepping to the music, shooting me a quick smile as she gazed into my eyes.

"Yo, why you talkin' in codes and shit?" He was giggling like he was anticipating a very funny punch line. I realized he really didn't know what I was talking about, and maybe my word didn't mean anything to him. I couldn't blame him, though. It was too crazy to believe, so I decided not to tell him.

"Oh, I sent you a couple more dollars."

"Yo, I told you I was straight."

The song came to an end, making way for another slow jam. Taj and Mona went into the kitchen and came back with fresh daiquiris while Kim came and plopped down on the couch next to me, the effects of the weed and alcohol apparent in her eyes and silliness. "Is that my honey bunny?" she asked, making sure Devon could hear her.

"I'll let you talk to this goofball," I said, bumping Kim with my shoulder. "Give me a call whenever."

"No doubt. Peace."

I handed Kim the phone. Taj came over and sat on the other side of me, putting an arm around me and whispering in my ear. "We have a houseful. I'm mad."

"You're just drunk and horny."

She pushed me, laughing. "Shut up."

Mona took a seat on the floor in front of us. "You might need to hook me up with a jailbird. Look at her, all in love and shit."

Kim playfully kicked at her.

"What's up with, Devon?" Taj asked, now fondling my ear.

"He got some good news."

She didn't say anything. When I turned to her, she was staring at me with the look she always gave when she was trying to read my mind.

I bucked my eyes at her. "What?"

She shook her head and took a sip of her drink. "Nothing."

<><><>

The Christmas festival drew a packed house at Dante's school, and we had front row seats for all of the lovable and funny moments that came with a cast that consisted of second and third graders. Lines were forgotten, some songs sung comically off-key, but it was absolutely awesome. And that was even before Dante touched the stage. He had to follow a hilarious skit put on by four elves who were thinking about starting a Union for Santa's Helpers. The lingering laughter and festive chatter were still going on minutes after the curtains had fallen.

"Those kids were too cute in that!" Mom laughed in her seat, her hand patting Frank's knee.

"Elves fighting for more cookie breaks." Taj giggled.

I could see little feet running back and forth across the stage. A figure brushed against the curtain, almost coming through it before looking like it caught its balance. That caused another round of laughter. The commotion behind the stage settled shortly after, and then the curtain began to rise slowly to dimmed lights.

"Here's our baby," Taj whispered, squeezing my leg at the sight of seeing our son appear, standing behind his xylophone, a Christmas stocking on his head. "Make sure you record every second of this."

"I got this over here," I said, zooming in on Dante's smile as he noticed us.

He gave the camera a wave before taking two mallets in each hand. He was center stage, two groups of stocking-adorned kids on each side, supported by raised platforms. There was complete silence until Dante let his mallets strike the first notes of Jingle Bells, with the kids singing along. They had it rocking, and every parent and grandparent, including us, must've joined in when it came to that favorite line:

"Laughing all the way, (ha ha ha!)"

The conclusion of Jingle Bells was met with a round of applause and a scream of encouragement from a proud mom. "Go, baby!"

I let the camera zoom in on Dante's face, reading his expression like a book, laughing. "He says you're embarrassing him."

All of the kids took seats on the platform, as the applause faded out into silence. The lights then went dark, except for the spotlight that was shining brightly down on our son. "Carol Of The Bells" was next. It was one of the many songs that he'd mastered after only hearing it once. He made every song his own, and "Carol Of The Bells" was no different. I continued to record while taking a peek over my shoulder, curious to see the faces of the listeners. It wasn't surprising that they were caught up in

Dante's melodic trance, and it only confirmed what Taj and I had known all along.

"He is showing out!" Taj squealed in a whisper.

"Yes, he is. That's my son."

I couldn't have been more proud, more happy. The tears I blinked away wasn't enough to stop me from recording the moment. But, when I felt IT coming, I was forced to hand Taj the camera.

"I have to go to the bathroom."

She turned to me, quietly taking the camera. "Can it wait?"

It was dark, but I knew she saw my face. Maybe she thought I was just overjoyed with emotions, because she smiled and mouthed, "Hurry up."

The bathroom in the school was not the place to release what was coming. It would probably be heard in the halls throughout the entire building. So I headed straight to the exit, pushing the door open and out into the snowy winter evening. Almost blinded by the flow of tears, I stumbled to the parking lot with keys in-hand, making it to our truck just as the wails of heartache came rushing out at full force. Frantically, I got in and reclined the seat, letting the feeling have its way, draining me of tears and hurt until it was satisfied. It left just as fast as it came, leaving me with a heartbeat that pulsated violently enough that I could feel it in every part of my body.

I came back into the auditorium to a round of applause. The kids were lined up on stage, bowing to the crowd, Dante in the middle of it all. His eyes followed me as I clapped and walked down the aisle to my seat. I gave him a smile with a thumbs-up, and he did the same in return.

Taj was still recording while mom and Frank, along with everyone else, gave the kids a standing ovation. She didn't say anything when she noticed my return. Her head just fell to my shoulder as I stood beside her, and she turned the camera around to get a shot of us. "You've been crying," she stated, as we looked into the camera, her smile weak but caring.

I rubbed my eyes, unable to wipe away the puffiness. "Just a little bit."

CHAPTER 47

I completed my year of supervised release in March of that year and quit my job the following day. I didn't need it; money didn't mean anything to me anymore. A job or a career was now meaningless, and the only thing that mattered was spending time with my family. Most of that time was spent chauffeuring Dante around to various places to perform. He had become sort of a local celebrity after the Christmas festival, and I assumed the role of manager/driver. It was the best job I'd ever had.

"Wow! I can't believe I was actually on TV!"

I was loading up Dante's xylophone after his first televised performance. A local television station got wind of his talent after a buzz had been created from several other performances in school programs. They invited him down to the news station to showcase his magic during the morning news, and he, as always, was remarkable.

Usually, after performing, he would act like it was no big deal, like he was just doing his job; modesty was his strong suit. But, after being treated like royalty by the news staff, and getting the chance to work a real camera while the news was live on the air, he was super hyped.

"Well, your mom says everyone at the shop loved you, and she told me to tell you that your bow-tie was a little crooked."

"I blame my stylist." He straightened his tie as he gave me the side eye.

"Oh, blame it all on me," I laughed, closing the tailgate. "I don't think you would've liked it if I came on camera to fix it while you were playing."

"And embarrass me on TV? No, Daddy. It wasn't that serious."

"So what's next?" I asked, squinting from the brightness of the sun. "Water park, movies, what?"

I followed him around to the door and opened it for him. He climbed in and began to put on his seatbelt, sitting there like he was going over his options in his head. "Can we go feed the ducks?"

We hadn't fed any ducks since leaving Decatur. I thought it was something he had grown out of, but apparently not. "Of course. Ducks it is."

<><><>

Finding some of our feathered friends didn't come as easy as it did in Decatur. I circled Belle Isle Park three times before Dante spotted a small flock resting on a bank of the Detroit River. The noon-time sun was accompanied by a nice breeze. It was a perfect summer day.

"Do you ever talk to the old man that gave me my xylophone? The man on that island?"

It caught me by surprise that he remembered Shai. "You weren't even three-years-old. How could you remember that?"

He looked away, saying, "I had a dream about him last night."

"What was it about, Dante?"

"Nothing," he replied, giving me a convincing expression. "He was just there, watching me play."

It was the same dream I'd had several times since I'd been home. The exact same dream. "Did he say anything to you?"

"No, he was just standing there." He looked over his shoulder to the back of the truck where his xylophone was.

"I haven't talked to him since the island. I'm sure he would be proud of what you're doing, though."

He nodded his head slowly as he rubbed his eyes. "Let's go home. I want to take a nap."

"As you wish, sir." we headed towards the truck.

"Daddy."

"Yes, son."

"I love you."

If always felt good to hear those words from him. It was also a trigger, conjuring up that feeling deep down inside of me. The crying spells became a part of my life. They would come often, usually when I was in the presence of my mom, Taj, or Dante. The violent wails and heaving were gone, though, allowing me to excuse myself to the nearest empty room and quietly let it take its course. I had come to grips that it was just something I had to live with, and there was nothing I could do about it. But I was able to fight it off, using our bond, the love between us, as a shield.

"I love you more, son. So much more."

CHAPTER 48

Three months later—F.C.I. Forrest City
Devon Raines

"Yo, you might as well give this shit up and let's start a new one, nigga," I said, snatching his rook off the board with my queen. "Chess ain't for you country ass niggas."

Stop Playin' was watching me beat the shit out of his homeboy. "Damn, mane, I thought you could play."

His homeboy had defeat written all over his face as he studied the board. "I fucked up two moves ago. I knew I shoulda' took that pawn."

"You shoulda' never came in this TV room and sat yo' ass down at this table." I held my hand out across the board. "Let me get that book of stamps up off yo' ass."

I hadn't played much chess since I'd been locked, but the parks of New York were always battling grounds for some of the best chess players in the world. In between serving dope fiends, I would get a game in with some of the old heads, and I had learned enough to beat the average chess player to a pulp. These country niggas probably hadn't touched a chessboard until they got in prison, so it was easy money whenever one of them sat across from me.

"Fuck it." He went into his pocket and handed me a book of stamps wrapped in yellow paper. "One mo' game."

"Mane, yo' game weak as hell." Stop Playin' shook his head in disgust. "You donatin' and shit. Let's go get a joint with that book."

"Yo, how you gone try to tell a nigga what to do with his money?"

"DEVON RAINES, HELANA BRAVO, REPORT TO R&D!"

I put the book of stamps in my shirt pocket. "Fuck they want?"

"Probably a piss test," Stop Playin' replied. "Or they shippin' yo' ass to Fort Dix."

"I didn't put in for no transfer," I said, standing up. "Have the board set up when I get back. I ain't done beatin' that ass."

I ran to my cubicle and grabbed my water bottle, then headed to the bathroom. These assholes picked a fine time to make a nigga drop a piss sample, three days after I had smoked some weed. It had been four years since the last time they dropped me, and my dumb ass should've known another one was coming soon. But I was stressed, and I needed something to make a nigga feel a little better at the time.

I downed two bottles of water and prayed it would help. Going to the hole for a dirty drop didn't bother me, but getting my visits and phone privileges snatched away, would hurt like a mothafucka'. I had gotten used to seeing Kim at least once a month, and talking to her on the phone. She had a nigga's back, so I knew she would probably be mad at me for fucking up.

I looked in the mirror as I filled up a third bottle, knowing damn well it probably wasn't going to make a difference. "Stupid ass."

They usually called us to the lieutenant's office to drop, but two inmates were bringing out trash and mop buckets when I passed. I didn't see any officers, so they must've been waiting for me in R&D. I made it to the door thinking about not being able to grab Kim's ass for a few months.

A C.O. opened the door. He saw the name tag on my shirt, then asked for my prison I.D. "Step in."

Two more officers were at the desk when I went inside. One of them looked up at me. "Raines?"

"Yeah." I nodded my head, looking around for the urinal and the piss cup.

"I need you to sign this," he said, pushing the pen and piece of paper across the desk.

I signed my name and waited for somebody to lead me to the bathroom to watch me piss.

"Sign this, too." He pushed another piece of paper to me.

"Damn, y'all switched it up. I only had to sign one paper the last time."

He took the paper and put it with the other. "You got one more."

I shook my head. "Y'all taking blood, too, or something?"

"Stop bitching," the other C.O. said, looking up from a computer. "You want to go home, don't you?"

"What type of question is that?" I was tired of the bullshit. "Yo, let me piss so I can go back to the unit."

The C.O. went back to typing on the computer. His partner was finishing the paperwork in front of him. "Did you bring your property with you?"

"Nobody told me to." I was starting to get confused.

"Well, go back to the unit and pack up. You got fifteen minutes."

"Shit, all I need is ten."

I ran out R&D fast as hell.

When the new laws for crack sentencing went into effect, it knocked off some of my time, but it didn't knock off enough to have me getting out of prison this soon. Somewhere along the line, somebody had fucked up, and I wasn't about to say a damn thing.

I knew a guy who actually sent another person to do his time for him, and got away with it for the most part. The only reason he got caught was because the guy didn't report to the halfway house after doing three years. When the feds realized what happened, they went and got the right guy and gave him a few extra years for making them look stupid. It was rare for the feds to fuck up, but it happened. And, now it looked like it was happening to me.

When I made it to the unit, I went straight to my cubicle and snatched my locker open, grabbing my binder with my songs and my phone book. I stuffed some letters and pictures down into the binder and made sure I wasn't forgetting anything important.

"New York, what happened, mane?"

I glanced at Stop Playin' as he stood outside the cubicle. "I'm up, nigga."

"Where da' hell you goin'?"

I closed the locker after I got everything I needed. "Home. I left enough shit in there to last you a couple months." I gave him a fist bump. "Stay up."

"Damn, mane, hit a playa' up."

I threw the peace sign up, ready to sprint back to R&D when I made it to the door. I had a feeling they would see their mistake by the time I got back up there. Shit was just too good to be true. But when I made it back, they put me in a cell and went on about their business. And, after a couple of hours, a bus ticket to New York in hand, I was in the back seat of a prison minivan headed to the bus station. There was only one officer with me. He drove while I anticipated a call over his radio telling him to return to the prison. It never happened, though.

We pulled into a gas station in some hick-looking town, and after letting me know that it was also the bus station, he got back into the minivan and went on his way.

Shit, I can't lie; I felt lost as I stood there on the curb watching people walk up and down the street. A car drove past and honked its horn, scaring me enough to jump back a couple of feet. I laughed at myself, shaking my head at the realization that I had forgotten what freedom felt like. It felt damn good, too.

Kabazza

"What do you think about, Frank?" my mom asked, pulling from the deck of cards.

We were playing gin rummy, a game she'd taught me when I was about ten years old. We hadn't played in a while, but lately, I had been spending all the time I could with her. Our mother/son moments had been cut short after I moved to Decatur, and then prison, so whenever I had the opportunity to have her to myself, I would take advantage of it as much as possible.

I picked up the card she threw to the pile, laying down two more cards to go with it. "I like, Frank. He's super cool."

"I knew you needed that darn card." She reached for the deck again. "Well, he asked me to marry him, and I said yes." She smiled like a teenager who had tasted love for the first time.

"That's great, mom!" I jumped up and hugged her, laying my head on her shoulder as I leaned over to her.

She had been alone since my dad left, dedicating all of her time working to make sure that I had a good childhood. She deserved happiness more than anyone, and I was happy to see that she had found someone who would love her just as much as I did.

As I held her, I could feel it coming, taking over all of the positive emotions that were in me. She put her arms around me when she realized what was happening.

"Why are you crying?" She shook with laughter as she ran her hand up and down my back. "Are you that happy for me, son?"

Hearing her laugh somehow drove away the pain, and through tears, I was able to muster a smile as I let her go.

"I'm very happy for you," I managed to say as I stood there. "I love you so much, mom."

"Aww, I love you too, baby." Her endearing gaze smothered me with comfort. "Now stop crying before you make me cry."

I used my sleeve to wipe my face. "Well, I guess I'll be the one giving you away at the wedding."

She smiled. "I wouldn't have it any other way."

The ringing of my phone interrupted the moment. An unfamiliar area code was on the screen. When I answered, I was surprised to hear Devon's voice without an announcement from an operator.

"Yo, what's up, Kay?"

"Just talking to my mom," I replied, walking off into the living room and out the front door to the porch.

"You got hold of a cell phone or something in there? I didn't hear the operator."

"I'm out! Somebody fucked up and they let me go!"

Hearing his words almost caused me to leap ten feet in the air. Colston had kept his word. "Nobody fucked up, Dee. I told you what I was going to do."

"Do about what?"

"Helping you get out." I kind of regretted saying it, but he couldn't be mad at me now. "I did what I said I was going to do. I kept my word."

There was no immediate response on his end. Then, "So, you got out and set somebody up to get me out?"

The excitement in his voice was gone, and it didn't sound like he was happy about what I had done.

"Yeah." It died as it came from my mouth. "I did."

The silence wasn't what I was expecting. But it was too late to take anything back.

Finally, he said, "Yo, I appreciate everything you did for me. My bus just pulled in, so I gotta go. I'ma holla' at you."

The line went dead before I could say another word. I felt hurt. I felt like I had lost somebody close to me, and in reality, I did. But, just knowing that he was out, was good enough for me.

I walked back in the house. Mom was still sitting at the dining room table, flipping through a bridal magazine as she sipped a cup of coffee. She gave me a smile as I took my seat next to her.

"So, when is the wedding?" I asked, picking up the cards and starting a game of solitaire.

She had a dreamy look on her face. "I'm not sure, but I want to go back to Anguilla and get married on the beach. Just us, you, Taj and Dante."

"That would be nice. I know Dante would love to go back there."

When my phone rang, I was hoping that it was Devon calling back, but it was Taj. She wanted me to bring her something to eat after I picked up Dante from school. Before she hung up, I told her that Devon was out. Of course, she was surprised.

"I thought he had a lot of time left."

"Well, some laws changed and some other stuff happened, so now he's home." I couldn't lie.

"Other stuff, huh?" There was suspicion in her voice. "I guess. Well, I know Kim will be happy to hear that."

"I bet she will."

"So, where is he going?"

I paused at a question I wasn't able to answer. "I don't know."

CHAPTER 49

Months had passed without me hearing from Devon. But just like when I came home, he stayed in touch with Kim. He never relayed any messages like he did before, and I figured he was against what I had done. He was a stand-up guy that wanted no affiliation with a snitch, and it was understandable. Kim did tell me that he was in New York, though. That's all I knew. I was just hoping that he hadn't turned back to what had landed him in prison in the first place.

While at Forrest City, I had seen a couple of guys go home, only to return with new fed cases and longer sentences than they had served before. I prayed Devon wouldn't have the same outcome. No matter what, I still considered him my friend.

<><><>

I was awakened in the middle of the night by Taj and the booming thunder of a spring rainstorm. She was sitting up in the bed when I rolled over. A streak of lightning lit up the room, revealing her face as she stared at our opened bedroom door.

"He's playing that song, baby."

I rose up, my ears tuned to the music that was coming from Dante's room across the hall. It was the song Taj had told me about while I was away. The one she recorded and played for me over the phone. The one she called "creepy". And, as I listened to it in person for the first time, I had to agree with her.

"What is he doing up this late?" I asked, checking the time. The clock on the nightstand read 3:37 a.m.

"Go make him stop and go to sleep, Kay." She fell to the bed and pulled the covers over her head. "I hate that song, whatever it is."

I got out of the bed as a crash of thunder shook the entire house. It rolled across the sky and died out in the distance, followed by flashes of silent lightning. The hallway was dark. There was also no light coming from the bottom of Dante's door. Before I reached for the knob, the music stopped momentarily, only to continue seconds later. It was slow in tempo, eerily sad. I understood why Taj felt the way that she did about the song.

I turned the knob and pushed the door open slowly. Dante was a shadow, his silhouette illuminated by another flash of lightning. He was standing at his xylophone, almost motionless except for the movement of his hands. Shorty's ears were perked up as he looked on from the bed.

"What are you doing up, Dante?"

The music played on without an answer from him.

I touched the wall, searching for the light switch.

"What are you..." I flipped the light on. He was standing there playing, his eyes closed, seemingly unaware of my presence or the light. I called his name but his eyes remained closed without answering me. His face was frowned up as if something was causing him pain whenever his mallets struck a key. I called his name again as I slowly approached him. Still, no answer. When I was close enough, I grabbed one wrist while the other hand continued to strike the keys. His eyes never opened, and he appeared to be asleep as he stood there. The music stopped when I gently grabbed his other hand. I carefully pulled the mallets from his grips, but it did nothing to awaken him. The pain was still on his face as I guided him to his bed and helped him into it. He stirred as I covered him with a blanket.

"It hurts, Daddy." It was obvious that he was asleep, but the tear that rolled down the side of his face told me that he was, indeed, hurting. I leaned over and kissed him on the cheek.

"It's okay," I whispered. "Daddy's right here with you."

As if my words comforted him, the pain left his face. He then rolled over on his side and into the position he always slept in, with Shorty at his feet.

The next day, I asked him if he recalled anything about the night before. He didn't remember playing the xylophone in his sleep, and he didn't remember it occurring over the next three nights at the exact same time: 3:37 a.m. Each time, he would be playing that same song, in a deep sleep as he stood behind that xylophone. I would repeat the routine, tucking him in and leaving him with a kiss that always seemed to put him at ease.

<><><>

I got a call the following day of Dante's latest episode. It was a call that I never expected, but was glad to receive. It was Devon. He didn't give me a chance to say anything when I answered the phone
"Yo, I'll be in town today," he said, energy in his voice. "What's the best restaurant in Detroit?"
I gave him the name of a place in the heart of downtown.
"Be there at six," he insisted. "I gotta go, but I'll see you then."
And just like that, the call ended.

<><><>

Later that evening, I was getting dressed to meet Devon. I was excited to see him for the first time in the free world. I had always wondered what it would have been like to hang with him outside of Forrest City, and I was finally about to find out. I expected plenty of laughs over good food and some drinks, and I didn't intend to ruin the evening by mentioning what I had done. That was a subject that was now off limits.
The restaurant we were going to was kind of high-class and known for its expensive steaks, so I got dressed for the occasion and headed downstairs. Taj and my mom were at the dining room table going through more bridal magazines, planning the upcoming wedding. Dante was doing homework as he sat next to his grandma.
"You look nice, baby," Taj said, smiling as she checked me out.

"Thank you. You think I need a tie?" I was checking myself out in the mirror that hung over the fireplace.

Dante answered for her. "No, daddy, that's perfect. That jacket is more casual than formal."

"And what do you know about fashion?" I asked, walking into the dining room. "That homework is what you better focus on."

He put his pencil down and closed the book he was reading for a report. "I'm done."

"Taj likes this wedding dress right here," my mom said, holding up a magazine.

I went over and stood by her to get a better look. "Mom, I think that's a little too young for you."

"I think so, too, but it's not for me." Her stare landed on Taj. "She thinks we should make it a double wedding, seeing that y'all never had one."

"I told her we didn't want to intrude on her day, baby, but she's insisting." Taj's expression told me that she loved the idea.

"And I guess you're already picking out your dress?"

"Of course, baby." It came with a laughing smile.

"No, mom, this is going to be your special day." I walked back over to the mirror, instantly bringing a halt to my wife's laughter. The big grin on my face disappeared when I turned back to them. "Taj and I will have a wedding eventually."

"I think we should do it together," Mom replied, pouting her lips playfully. "I think it would be beautiful."

They probably thought that I was trying to come to a decision, but I was actually thinking about making love to Taj on the beach again.

"Okay, we'll do it?"

Smiles from everyone, and that was enough to stir up every emotion inside of me. I could feel it coming like it had never come on before. It was stronger, more powerful. My chest began to convulse, as the oncoming eruption made its way upward. I couldn't let it happen in front of them.

"I have to go," I said, quickly planting kisses on Taj and my mom. "Devon's waiting for me."

By the time I made it to Dante, the tears were starting. He noticed them when I bent over to give him a hug.

"It's okay, Daddy," he whispered in my ear. "It's okay."

"I know." I gave him a tight squeeze. "See you later."

I rushed out the door and into the truck, speeding off until I was further down the street. I pulled over to avoid crashing into something, blinded by the tears and surrendering myself to the feeling. It pushed me back into the seat and released itself through an explosion of screams and blood-curdling yells. I closed my eyes and was confronted by a flashing of the people I loved: my mom, Taj, and Dante. It seemed to drive the feeling into a violent rage. I then blacked out.

When I came to, the clock told me that it lasted more than ten minutes, and it felt like I had just awakened from a coma. The front of my blazer and shirt was stained with tears. I drove, hoping they would be dry by the time I made it to the restaurant.

<><><>

Devon wasn't there when I arrived. He'd made reservations, so after giving my name, I was escorted to a booth. It was near a grand piano that was being played by an older black gentleman, as the surrounding patrons looked to be enjoying meals that were peppered with light conversation. I took in the ambiance of the classy establishment. Candles at each table made it the perfect place for a romantic dinner, and it was also the perfect place for a future date with my wife.

The after-effects of the feeling were still lingering as I sat there. I found myself sniffling and whimpering like a kid who had just gotten a good old fashion ass whooping. Except, it was my heart that had taken a beating. A drink was most definitely in order, so I flagged down a waitress and had her fetch me a bottle of champagne.

Two glasses later, I was feeling a little better. I felt even better when I saw Devon come through the door and stop at the hostess' stand. I threw my hand up to get his attention. He saw me and walked over, smiling the whole time. Seeing him in a suit and tie, looking like a million dollars, got the best of me. I knew he would make a joke about me crying, but I didn't care. My boy was home.

I stood up to greet him, slapping hands loudly and pulling him in for a brotherly hug.

"Damn, you happy to see a nigga," he laughed, patting me on the back. "Just watch the suit, though. I don't know if they can get snot stains out this mothafucka'."

I stepped back, grabbing a napkin from off the table to wipe my eyes, smiling as he stood in front of me. "I'm fucked up, man."

He gave me a concerned look. "Yo, you aight'?"

"I'm good, man. Just a little emotional." I let out a heavy sigh. "Check you out, though; you looking like GQ's man of the year."

Composed as a mafia boss while contemplating a hit on an enemy, he reached into his jacket pocket and produced two cigars. He handed me one. "Yo, son, it's on!"

"You don't even have to tell me," I replied while silently trying to pronounce the name on the cigar wrapper.

"A hundred grand for a box," he stated while taking his seat. "The Gurkha Black Dragon."

I took a whiff of the cigar. "So you came from Black and Milds to Black Dragon, huh?"

"I didn't buy these mothafuckas. We got money but I ain't no damn fool." He laughed. "The president of the record label had a box on his desk, so I made it a party pack."

I sat across down across from him, a sense of déjà vu coming over me. The scene had happened before; though, we were wearing khakis and sitting in our cubicle when it did.

"You said you was fucked up." He quickly turned serious. "What's wrong?"

It reminded me of when I first met him in Forrest City. He did whatever he could to help when he saw me stressing, and here he was, doing it again, putting me before himself. He hadn't changed a bit.

We all need someone to talk to at times, and I was glad to have him there. It was easy for me to tell him about the crying spells, and he seemed even more concerned when I told him how often I had been having them. He suggested I go see a psychiatrist, but I knew that wasn't necessary.

"It'll be over soon," I told him, pouring another glass of champagne. "Now, what's up with you? You're suited up and that's about three karats in your ear."

"Five," he corrected, holding his earlobe to show off the huge diamond.

"Okay, five," I chuckled. "What you been doing since you've been out?"

He sat back and put his hands on the table. "What did I talk about while we were locked up?"

I took a sip. "Music."

A grin came to his face. "We did it, Kay."

Of course, he had good news; I just didn't know how good until he shared the details over dinner.

When he got out, he went to New York and chased down every contact he made while in prison. He knew A&R's from a few record companies, and he pursued them until he convinced them to give him a chance to prove that he was one of the best songwriters in the music game. It started off with him giving them two songs for an up-and-coming artist who was working on his first album. Once the record company heard the songs, they quickly offered Devon a contract as a songwriter, which he turned down. He knew what he had, so he took the money for the two songs and got in contact with another record company. After selling them a few songs, he was, again, offered a contract by them. He refused their contract, as well, and moved along to another record company and repeated the same process.

The money he made from selling seven songs didn't add up to much, but when the first song he sold hit number one on the R&B charts, it created the perfect storm. A bidding war ensued, and Devon had three major record labels bidding for his services, tossing him numbers that were beyond anything either one of us could've ever imagined. He took the best offer, and it only cost him a small percentage of the hundreds of songs he had written while in prison. Needless to say, I was proud of him. I knew he was a star from the beginning, and it was amazing to see him living his dream.

We celebrated with more bottles of champagne and an abundance of laughter that probably was a little too loud for such a classy restaurant. But, we didn't care. It was our night, one we had talked about years before.

"So, what's up with you and Kim?" I asked, feeling the effects of the champagne.

The mentioning of her name caused a boyish grin to come to his face. "That's my girl. When I got out, I was about to go spend a few days with her before I went to New York. But my dick won't even get hard when I'm broke." Our laughing caused a few heads to turn our way. "I told her I had to go get some money. All she said was she'd be there when I was ready. I'm ready now, Kay. I'm goin' ring shopping tomorrow."

"That's what's up, Dee." I nodded my head. "I'm happy for you, man. Real happy."

He gave me a serious glare. "Yo, none of this would've been possible if it wasn't for you. I don't know what you did, Kay, and really, I don't wanna know." He went into his pocket and came out with a small folded piece of paper. "I do want you to know that I appreciate everything you did for me, though. I ain't never met a nigga like you. You been real with me since we met, and it's an honor to call you my friend. Word is bond." He slid the paper to my side of the table. "It's just a lil' something for now, but I want you to have it."

It was a folded check. I slid it back to his side. "You don't owe me anything, man. We're friends, and that's enough for me."

He took his glass and turned it up, downing the last of his champagne before leaning in closer across the table. "You gave me life, Kay, and I'll be insulted if you don't take it." He pushed the paper back in front of me. "As your friend, I'm demanding you take it."

There was no laughing, no sneaky grin. I picked up the piece of paper and put it in my wallet, watched closely by a satisfied stare.

"I got a flight to catch," he said, standing to his feet. "Let's get outta' here."

I followed him outside, where we walked to the curb as he lit his cigar. I joined him after he passed me the lighter, choking instantly when I took a puff.

"You don't inhale this shit," he said, shaking his head with a chuckle. "You puff it and let it sit in your mouth, taste it, and then blow it out."

He began a brief demonstration that concluded with him exhaling a large cloud of smoke. I then gave it a second try; my results coming out just as good as his.

"There you go." He gave me a proud stare that came with a pause. "I'm on my way to L.A. to talk to a few execs. I think we got a deal to do a soundtrack for this movie."

I digested the news while savoring the flavor the cigar had left in my mouth. I had to admit that it was rather tasty. And, I also had to admit that the news he had just sprung on me didn't come as a surprise. From the beginning, I knew, if given the chance, he would make it in the music business, and big.

He took his phone out and dialed a number. "I'm out front, Ray."

Moments later, a black limousine turned the corner. It slowly pulled up to the curb, the back door, stopping right at our feet. A driver jumped out and came around to open the door.

"My boy is ball-innnn'!"

"Nawl," he said, putting a hand on my shoulder. "We ballin'."

"Right." I smiled. "So when are you coming back."

"Next week. I'm bringin' Kim and we gone celebrate like a family. I can't wait to see Dante."

"Sounds good. He'll be glad to see you."

He looked around, his gaze going to the sky as he spoke. "I missed this."

I knew he was referring to freedom. "You're here now. Enjoy it."

"Yeah, we here now." He shot me a stare. "We about to live, Kay. See you next week."

"Can't wait."

We exchanged a brotherly hug with pounds on the back. The driver made sure Dee was comfortably in the back seat before shutting the limo door. I took another puff of the cigar as I watched it drive off into the night, feeling like everything was how it was supposed to be.

<><><>

It was after midnight when I made it home. I peeked into Dante's room to find him fast asleep. The moonlight was cascading down through his window, its ghastly light glimmering off his freshly polished xylophone. I closed his door and went into our bedroom, setting the alarm clock for three thirty-six, enough time for me to go into his room before the music started. I wanted to see what caused him to wake up and play that song.

I climbed in bed next to Taj. She reached back, taking my hand and wrapping it around her. I fell asleep with my face nestled in her hair. When the alarm went off, I reached over and shut it off before it could wake her. Just as I hit the button, I heard Dante's door creak open. He was standing in our doorway when I looked up, rubbing the sleepiness from his eyes.

"What's the matter," I asked in a whisper.

He began to walk over to me, climbing in the bed without saying a word. He got in between us and put his arms around me in a hug. "I want to sleep in here with you, Daddy."

I couldn't tell him that he was too big to sleep with us. How could I? He was still my baby at eight-years-old, so there was no way that I could deny his simple request. He ended up falling asleep in my arms, and it was the calmest and most restful sleep that I'd ever had.

<><><>

"So y'all just took over the whole bed."

Taj was sitting up on her elbow when I opened my eyes, smiling at the sight of Dante curled up under me.

"Blame this guy," I said, running my hand through his hair. "It's time for somebody to get ready for school."

His eyes never opened as he put his arms around my neck. He pulled me down to him and held me as close as he could. I was surprised at how strong he was.

"He never hugs me like that," Taj said, getting out the bed. "I'm jealous."

"Don't be, mom." Dante released me and sat up. "Daddy just needed that."

"Oh, did I?"

He stared me in the eyes as he slowly nodded his head.

"I'm going down to cook breakfast. Get up out of that bed, Dante."

"I am, Mom. Can you make pancakes, please?"

"I guess I could. With strawberries?"

"That would be excellent." He gave her a sleepy smile. She left out and went downstairs.

I got up from the bed and went over to my closet. After slipping on a pair of jogging pants, I turned back to Dante. He was still sitting on the bed.

"I had another dream about Mr. Shai."

That got my attention. "When?"

"Last night." He answered while looking down at his hands.

I went back over and sat down next to him. "Was it like the same dream you had before?"

"No, but the ones before were."

Now I was confused. "The ones before? When did you have those dreams?"

"The past four nights were like the first one." His stare was aimed at the door to his room. "But last night was different. You were there with him."

I reached down and stepped into my shoes. "Did you wake up after the dream?"

"Yes. That's when I came in here."

"What was I doing in the dream?"

"You were walking with him." His eyes told me that he was trying to make sense of the dream. "We were on the beach. I was playing my xylophone. I called you when you walked off with him, but you never turned around. You just kept walking. You left me, Daddy."

When I noticed tears trickling down his face, it broke my heart into a million pieces. It was the opportune time for the feeling to rear its head. But it never came.

Dante had always been the strong one at times like these, but it was now my time to be strong for him. I grabbed him and began rocking him in my arms like I had done so many times when he was a baby. I rocked him until I heard Taj coming up the stairs.

"I'm all right, Daddy," he said, using his pajama sleeve to clear his face. "I'll go get ready for school." He jumped out the bed as Taj came in the room.

"It's supposed to rain, Dante. Make sure to put your rain boots in your backpack."

"I will, Mom." He walked by her and into his room.

Taj grabbed her appointment book off the dresser. "It's going to be a long day. I have a doctor's appointment in an hour, and then I have two city councilwomen and a state rep that changes her mind every two minutes about how she wants her hair."

I stood up and took her by the waist, kissing her lips softly. "Have I ever told you how much I love your morning breath?"

"Yes, you have." She came in for another kiss. "Yours isn't that bad, either." Then another. "Let me go finish cooking."

A final gaze into her brown eyes. "I love you."

"I know." Her hand brushed against my face. "And you know I love you. Forever."

"Go on before you burn up something."

"Okay, but can you do me a favor and stop by the bank to deposit this money. I forgot to do it yesterday." I released her hand, relishing her touch until her fingertips were no longer in reach.

"Anything for you."

<><><>

We were met by dark skies on our way to Dante's school. The rain was coming, and from the gloomy conditions, it appeared to be a storm that would last the entire day. Dante was in the front seat, buckled in tightly after convincing me to let him ride shotgun for the first time.

"I'm tall enough now, Daddy," he'd told me as he opened the passenger's door. "Just this one time, please."

While I drove, I unsuccessfully tried to recall a time when I had told him "no". And if that, alone, meant that I had been a bad father to him, I was completely satisfied with it for now.

Dante waved to some kids as we pulled up to the school. He would usually give me a hug and rush to join his friends as soon as I parked, but that wasn't the case on this day. With his backpack in on his lap, he sat there quietly, not even focusing on two of his classmates that stood on the sidewalk waiting for him to get out.

"What's wrong?"

"Can I go with you, Daddy?" he asked, looking out the window.

Dante hadn't missed a day of school since kindergarten. A flu virus was the reason, and he was virtually heartbroken when that happened. He loved school, so him not wanting to go, came as quite a shock. But this was the perfect time for me to stand up to him, and his pleading eyes, and deny him for the very first time ever. Well, I was going to compromise just a bit.

I leaned over with my elbow on the console. "What do you say about me coming to get you after school, we go get our hair cut and then go to the movies, just me and you? I'll let you ride shotgun again, and we can even get us a banana split on the way."

The mention of ice cream always worked with him. He put his backpack over his shoulder and held up a finger to his awaiting classmates. He then turned to me. "You promise?"

I smiled. "Of course."

He reached to give me a hug. It was one of those tight hugs that warmed my soul, completed with a kiss on my cheek. "I love you," he said, opening the door.

"I love you, too, son."

He jumped out and said, "Bye, Daddy." His door shut before I could respond.

The rain came out of nowhere. It was a furious downpour that caused Dante and his two friends to sprint to the school's entrance. I got out and called out to him. "It's 'see you later'!"

My words were drowned out by the sound of the crashing raindrops, as I watched him go into the building without looking back.

CHAPTER 50

I arrived at the bank under a steady rainfall. By the time I made it to the entrance, my feet were soaked and my hoodie was ten times heavier with moisture. The only thing the day was good for, was sleeping in and cuddling while watching a movie. Unfortunately, that didn't match up too well with Taj's schedule.

I wrote out the deposit slip after checking the amount on the envelope Taj gave me. Business was doing very good according to the numbers, and it was only getting bigger and better by the week. She was a master at her craft and a very savvy business woman. She always had ideas to improve her business, and even bought a few commercial spots on the local TV and radio stations. Boy, was I a very lucky guy.

The teller greeted me with a smile as I stepped to the counter. "Good morning," she sang.

"Good morning." I passed her the envelope. "We could do without this rain, though."

"Tell me about it. So you want to make a deposit?"

"Yes, ma'am." As she began the transaction, I remembered the check Devon had given me. It never occurred to me to see how much it was for. I just assumed it was a thousand dollars or so, just to show his gratitude for what I'd done for him. I'd sent him money on a monthly basis after I came home, as well, but I never expected anything in return.

I took the check out of my wallet and flipped it over to sign my name on the back. When the teller was done with the transaction, I handed her the check. Our account was already in the low six digits, so I was sure that it wasn't going to make too much of a difference, whatever the amount was.

The teller was looking the check over as I turned to see an elderly woman come through the door. In her arms was a huge tin can that she seemed to have a hard time carrying. She was almost hunched over from the weight of the thing. I quickly ran over to her and offered my help, which she gladly accepted.

"Wow!" I said, once I felt the weight. It was filled with coins. "How did you manage to even pick this up?"

"It's the strength you find when you have no choice." she let out a sigh. "But thank the Lord I saw you."

I laughed as I carried the can over to the counter. "Well, I'm happy I could help you."

"Thank you so much, young man, and may God bless your soul."

I turned to her. "You're more than…"

I was looking at Shai, his gray eyes smiling at me. He nodded his head slowly as he offered me his hand.

The teller called my name. "Mr. Wright."

I looked over my shoulder at her and then back to Shai. "Thank you again, sweetie," the elderly woman said, waiting for me to shake her hand.

I was sure my confusion didn't go unnoticed. Reluctantly, I shook her hand and was greeted by a touch that was cold and hard as stone. The chill that flowed through my body caused me to shiver slightly. "You…you're welcome."

I went back to the counter, giving the old lady another glance as a second teller attended to her.

"I think you need to talk to a manager about this," the teller said to me, waving the check.

"Why is that?"

"Tax reasons," she replied. "There are different procedures when depositing a check of this size."

"Hold up. Can I see that? It must be a mistake." She gave me the check. When I saw the amount it was for, I realized Devon was still a jokester like he'd always been. "Can you give me a minute while I make a call?"

"Sure, take your time, Mr. Wright."

I stepped to the side and took out my phone, smiling as I looked at the check. "This dude is so damn silly."

When Devon answered, I could hear music playing in the background. "What's up, Kay?"

"You and your damn jokes," I said with a laugh. "If I didn't have to come to the bank for Taj, I would probably be cursing you out right now."

"Cuss me out for what?"

"This check," I replied. "You got me coming in here trying to deposit a fake check. Man, you play too much."

Silence, and then, "It's not fake, Kay." His tone was serious. "That's half of what they gave me for my contract. It's yours."

I then knew it wasn't a joke. "Hey, I can't take this, Dee."

"Too late."

The phone beeped, signaling the end of the call. It was his way of forcing me to take the money. I looked at check in disbelief, shaking my head as I counted the zeros. Devon had gone a little overboard if you asked me. But hey, what could I do?

The teller was waiting for me, so I walked back up to the counter and handed her the check for three million dollars. "Well, I guess I need to talk to a manager."

<><><>

I was in the bank a couple of hours getting everything taken care of. It was going to take a couple of days before the check cleared, but I had no use for the money. It was just going to be there for Taj to invest however she liked. I knew she would turn it into more, so she and Dante would never have to worry about anything. I did withdraw fifty-thousand dollars from our account, though. I was going to use that to buy something really nice for my wife, something she would always remember me by.

The rain was still coming down as I got on the freeway. The jeweler I went to when I got my trust fund money was located in Harper Woods, which was near the east side of Detroit. Years had passed, and I didn't know for sure if the store was still open or not. I had nothing else to do, so I headed east on I-696 while thinking about all I've been through during my short lifetime. And, looking back on it, I can say that I was blessed to have made it as far as I did.

I switched the windshield wipers to full blast when the rain picked up at even a faster pace. The speed limit was seventy, but some drivers were driving like the roads were dry, darting in and out of lanes as they sped past me. Checking my rearview mirror, I noticed a car coming quickly up on my tail. I was in the middle lane. When he got closer and began flashing his high beams, I hit my blinker to jump in the right lane. Just as I angled the steering wheel to begin to get over, the loud blaring of a semi's horn caused me to yank the steering wheel back to the left. I must have yanked it a little too hard, because the SUV began to spin out of control.

I don't know why my hands came off the steering wheel, but they did. I took my feet off the gas, and instead of lightly tapping the brakes, I just sat there and went along for the ride. If it was my time, I was content with the outcome.

The first spin around, I could see headlights of other cars as they all seemed to slow down behind me. I caught a glimpse of the semi in the right lane on the second revolution, but it appeared to be traveling at the same speed. That's when I realized I was drifting off into the right lane, and directly into the path of the eighteen-wheeler.

I could feel the SUV losing speed on its final revolution. The lights of the semi caused me to squint as the spin died out, and I knew it was coming straight for me. I then saw the grass of the embankment, and then a loud thump jolted the SUV, knocking me around in the front seat like a human pinball. Two more blares of the semi's horn caused me to wait for the impact. I closed my eyes. I was just hoping that I would die without suffering too much pain.

I felt the front end of the SUV elevate and come to a complete stop. Horns were sounding off behind me, but the distinct sound of the semi's horn was moving further and further away. I opened my eyes to the green grass of the embankment, my wipers still moving at high speed. If I had been going any faster, the SUV would've driven right up the hill.

There wasn't any damage to the truck when I got out to investigate. The front end had made a dent into the dirt of the embankment but that was all. I was able to back out and drive away with everything intact except for my nerves. I got off at the next exit and took the main streets to Harper Woods.

To my surprise, the jewelry store was still there. A security guard was standing at the door when I went in. They obviously knew the risk that came with having a jewelry store on the border that separated Detroit from the suburbs. My browsing started under the watchful eye of an Arab woman who was seated behind the counter. There was a variety of bracelets, rings, and watches in the cases, but I didn't see anything that was worthy of my wife.

"Are you looking for anything in particular?" the woman asked, in a thick Arabic accent. She stepped to the counter and leaned on one of the glass cases.

I continued to search the inventory. "I need something big."

"Hmmm...how big?"

I made my way around each case until I was in front of her. Not wanting to alarm her, I went into the pocket of my hoodie very slowly, pulling out five stacks of fresh one-hundred dollar bills still with the bands on them. I put the money on the counter. "This big."

At the sight of the money, she nodded her head at the security guard. He went and turned the locks on the door. "Give me one minute."

She went into a door that was behind the counter, returning minutes later carrying a tray covered in white felt. On the tray, were several rows of diamonds of various colors and sizes. A smile was on her face as she laid the tray in front of me. "Now we talk."

I was given a quick lesson in the four C's of diamond purchasing: karat, color, clarity, and cut. She did an excellent job of explaining what I would be paying for while letting me examine each stone with the jewelers' eyepiece, which is called a loupe. Once the lesson was over, I made my choice.

"I want this one," I said, pointing at a four-karat canary yellow diamond. It was heart shaped, and the perfect symbol for the love I had for Taj.

"You have good taste." She used some tweezers to hold it up for me. "So, would you like it set for a ring?"

The only ring I ever wanted her to wear was her wedding ring. I wanted something she could keep close to her heart, something she could hold whenever she thought of me. "What about a pendant?"

She gave me an agreeing smile. "I can set it in a platinum setting, and it would be beautiful with a nice 16" inch platinum chain. Very classy."

"Sounds good. When will it be ready?"

"A couple of days, maybe tomorrow. I'll get right on it." She put the diamond back on the tray. "I am going to need a deposit today and you can pay the rest when you pick it up."

I shook my head. "No, I'll pay for it now, but I want the receipt in her name. I'll give you her information and you call her to come pick it up when it's ready."

"That's fine." She grabbed a calculator and punched some buttons.

"The total is forty-eight thousand, but I will knock off five thousand. You seem like a very nice gentleman, and I know your wife will be pleased."

"Yes, I hope so."

I broke a band off one of the stacks and counted out three thousand dollars while she wrote out the receipt. As I gave her Taj's information, I noticed a display of cards behind the counter. "Do you have any blank cards that I could write something in?"

"Yes, I have some small ones that come with all of our jewelry." She reached down under the counter and handed me one of the cards and a pen.

I was never good at writing out my thoughts. But, as I pictured my Taj, the words came naturally, unforced. And, from the time I'd met her, everything between us had been that way.

Satisfied with what I had written, I paid for my purchase and bidded the woman farewell.

CHAPTER 51

The clouds that blanketed the skies appeared to be retreating as I drove down Eight Mile Road. The rain had let up significantly, but after the incident on the freeway, I decided to take the long way home. I had an hour left before I picked Dante up from school, so there was no need to rush.

I was coming up on Van Dyke Avenue when my gas light came on. It had been a while since I'd been in that area. There were gas stations on both sides of Eight Mile Road, and it would've been easier if I had gotten to the right side of the street and pulled into the gas station up ahead. The house we used to live in was only a couple of miles down, and about a mile away, was where I had almost become the victim of a car-jacking. It was a memory that I had somehow tucked away in the back of my mind, long forgotten about up until that very moment.

The city of Warren was considered the suburbs, populated by mostly whites and much safer than Detroit, which was, literally, right across the street. But for some reason, I found myself going past Van Dyke and getting into the furthest left lane to make a Michigan U-turn. I then made a right turn and headed south down Van Dyke Avenue, the east side of Detroit. The gas station was a block off of Eight Mile. When I pulled up to the gas pump, I was immediately approached by a face riddled with despair and need. His assault began with the opening of my door.

"Young buck, I'm tryin' to hustle up on a drank." He held my door as I got out, flashing a smile that Leon Spinks would be proud of. His valet routine broke the ice. "All I need is some change."

My mind was already made up about helping him out. I reached in my pocket while he closed my door. He then reached into his, coming out with, possibly, his life-savings. After a brief count of some coins, he came to a conclusion that he seemed to be sure of. "A dolla' can get me right where I need to be."

I pulled out a hundred dollar bill, handing it to him and then proceeded to the gas station's entrance. I didn't say a word, and I didn't even look back after he proclaimed that God was going to bless me.

It took me less than twenty seconds to pay for my gas, and I wasn't surprised to see that my valet guy had disappeared when I came back out. He was gone in the wind, and the last of the rain had gone along with him. I started pumping the gas while the sun finally decided to show itself. The last of the clouds were moving out, making way for blue skies. It was hard to believe that a day that started out so gloomy was actually looking like it would end on a pleasant note.

A car in desperate need of a muffler parked on the opposite side on the pump I was on. It was so loud that I could barely hear my phone ring. Taj's number was on the screen. I answered as the car's engine shut off.

"What you doing, baby?"

"Pumping gas," I glanced at the pump, thinking it shouldn't have taken that long to dispense forty bucks worth of gas. It was only at fifteen dollars and moving slow enough to where I could count along without missing a number. "How was your doctor's appointment?"

"It went well. That's why I called you."

The driver of the noisy car walked by, giving me a stare that was a little too long for my liking. I didn't blink until he broke eye contact. He then looked back again before going into the gas station. I checked the pump. Twenty dollars and counting, slowly. "What happened that made it good?"

She giggled. "Dante's going to be a big brother. I'm pregnant, Kay."

I almost lost grip on the phone at her announcement. An attack of mixed emotions came over me, and I didn't know whether to jump for joy or break down in sadness. "Th...that's great, baby."

I was watching the driver of the loud car as he exited the gas station. He was watching me also. When he came to an abrupt halt at the front of my truck, my senses went on high alert. He began staring as if he was trying to recall something, snapping his finger as if it was helping him to remember.

"You don't sound too enthused," Taj replied. "What's wrong?"

The guy took a few steps toward me, his finger still snapping. "Hey, don't I know you?"

"Hold on one second, baby?" I took the phone away from my ear, giving the pump another glance. The handle on the nozzle clicked and the pump read thirty-three seventy. "I grew up around here." I was watching him as I placed the nozzle back on the pump. "I didn't hang out much, though."

"Did you have a drop-top mustang back in the day? A candy-apple red one on chrome twenties?"

"Yeah." I screwed the gas cap on, thinking about how the car stood out when I drove it. "That was mine."

It seemed to satisfy his curiosity. "Oh, okay, I thought that was you."

I brought the phone back to my ear and watched him go into his waistband. Time slowed down, and his every move was made in slow motion. Running never crossed my mind. This was it. I whispered into the phone. "I love you, Taj."

She responded as his hand wrapped around the handle of a black pistol. "I love you more."

The barrel of the gun revealed itself, rising slowly until I was looking into the blackness on the hole. I could see the veins bulging in his hand as he gave the trigger a squeeze. Then another. And another.

The impact of the last bullet was enough to push me backward and onto the concrete behind my truck. I landed flat on my back, my eyes to the sky, admiring the sun as it began to shine through the last of the parting clouds. I couldn't move. All I could do was think.

They say that some people, in rare instances, can predict their own death. So, I guess I was one of those people who were privy to such information. There was no way to know exactly when or how it would come about, but I knew it was coming.

When I experienced the first crying spell, I thought it was just me being emotional after being away from my family for so long. I thought I had missed them that much. Seeing them, and even the thought of them, began to hurt as time went on, and it was something that I didn't understand in the beginning. Not until the dreams I had of Shai, was I able to put the pieces together. Shai, the god of fate and destiny, was calling me home.

Meeting him on that island was the introduction to what was ahead. His first warning came the week before I was going to be released, when he came to me while I was on the phone with Taj. Then, once I got home, the crying spells started. And it had everything to do with me being emotional, but only because whenever I looked at, or thought about, the people I loved most, I knew how much I was going to miss them after I met my fate.

The dreams about him watching Dante, as he played the xylophone that came as a gift from him, was his way of telling me that the time was near. He used my child's talent to relay his message, a message that came in the form of a song befitting of death. And, as I lay there on the ground, I prayed that Shai, the god of fate and destiny, would continue to watch over my son like he had done so many times in those dreams.

My eyes started getting heavy. I could feel the burning in my chest. I was choking, gasping for air, drowning from my own blood. A crowd of people formed around me, but all I could hear was Taj's screams. I turned my head and followed her voice, resting the side of my face on the concrete. My phone was still in my hand, but I couldn't feel it, I couldn't bring it to my ear to tell her that everything was going to be okay. I couldn't tell her that I was sorry that I wasn't going to be there for our wedding. I couldn't tell her to kiss Dante and my unborn child for me. That was the worst part.

The sun was blocked when a figure kneeled over me and began to calmly give me instructions. "Don't try to move, just breathe."

The crackling of a radio drew my attention to a shiny badge pinned to the police officer's uniform. He pulled it from his side and relayed his location to a dispatcher, then looked down at me. "The ambulance is close. A minute away."

Nothing could help me, though. I responded with a cough that was followed by the taste of blood. It filled my mouth instantly, while a tranquil feeling came over me. I became relaxed enough to spit out some of the blood, letting it roll down the side of my face. The officer had lifted up my hoodie and pulled it back down after he probably realized that he couldn't do anything for me. But there was something that he could help me with.

"What..." I took a deep breath and spit out more blood. "What...time is it?"

His hand was on my chest as if he was trying to stop the bleeding. He was applying pressure, a look of panic on his face. "The ambulance is right down the street!"

I felt my lips curl into a smile. "Can you tell me the time, please, sir?"

He granted my final request, looking down at his watch as he continued to apply pressure to my wounds. "It's 3:37."

I stared up at the sun, shining in all of its brilliance. "Yeah, I thought so."

CHAPTER 52

Devon

I was in a meeting when I got the call from Kim. As soon as I heard her crying, I knew it was bad news. After she said Kay was dead, I was waiting for him to get on the phone and laugh to let me know it was all a joke. I fucked with him all the time when we were in prison, so I was hoping it was his sick way of paying me back. But I knew it wasn't a game; just wishful thinking on my part.

My trip to L.A. was supposed to be a three-day thing, but there was no way in hell I could focus knowing what his family was going through. While we were locked-up, a day didn't pass without him talking about them, so I knew how much they meant to him. The least I could do was be there for them because I knew that's what he would want.

I couldn't remember the last time a tear rolled down my face, but I let a few go during my flight back to Detroit. And, as I listened to Kay's mom sit in the front row at his funeral, moaning her grief away, I couldn't help but let a few more go for my boy.

It was hard to believe that the church was as empty as it was. Besides the choir and his family, there were only a few others there. Kim and her cousin, Mona, were seated next to me, while Taj, Dante, his mom and her fiancé filled the rest of the front row. Behind us was Taj's grandma and her little brother, along with some more people who came from Decatur to pay their last respects. In all, there were about fifteen people, and it struck me as being strange that somebody like Kay didn't have many friends. He was a great dude, always smiling, always trying to help. But he was the quiet type, so people who weren't close to him, probably never knew how good of a guy he was. And to me, that was their loss. But after knowing him, and spending time with him in Forrest City, I believed that he felt like all he ever needed was his family. And when it boils down to it, family is all that matters.

When it came time for people to go up to the podium to talk about the times they shared with Kay, a woman named Barbara was the first to speak. She spoke highly of my boy, too. According to her, he was different than anyone she'd ever met at his age. She described him as respectful, approachable, and an all-around beautiful person. She called him an angel, a heaven-sent man who swept Taj off her feet. Mentioning how Taj talked her ears off about Kay when she first met him, caused Taj to crack a smile, and it felt good to see her do that under the circumstances.

Tina was another woman who got up to speak, and she also had some good things to say about Kay. Apparently, Kay hung out with her son while he was in Decatur. He was in prison, but she said Kay turned him into a man and showed him how to make things happen. She said she was grateful for meeting a guy like Kay, and I knew exactly how she felt.

After Tina was done speaking, Kim patted my leg. "Go ahead."

It was my turn to speak about my friend. I knew it was going to be hard, but it was something that had to be done. I walked to the podium, not wanting to look at him lying in that casket. I looked, though, and thought about how bad things always happened to the best people.

When I began to speak, I felt a lump forming in my throat. It wasn't a good time to breakdown, so I started telling them about how I met Kay. I told them about meeting him on the track the first day he got there, and how he looked a little uncomfortable wearing a tight green jumpsuit. And I told them how we walked that track every day just talking and sharing different things about ourselves and our families. I mentioned how generous he was to me, and how he introduced me to my fiancée, Kim. The more I talked about him, the more choked up I got. The last thing

I was able to say was that he was my friend, and how much I was going to miss him. I walked back to my seat in tears.

Dante got up and came and sat between us, as his grandmother was helped to the podium by Mr. Reeves. She was weeping, but somehow found the strength to say some last words about her son. Dante rubbed me on my back. "It's okay, Uncle Dee."

Kay had always said that Dante was the strongest while he was in prison. I hadn't seen him cry not once after Kay's passing. He was eight-years-old and smart enough to know the situation, so everything Kay told me about him seemed to be true. But I knew losing his father had to hurt, especially knowing how strong of a bond they shared. I had no intentions on interrupting that bond, either. But I was going to make sure that Dante had a great life, and I was going to be there for him as much as I could. No matter what Kay had said, I owed him, even in death.

During her speech, Kay's mom said that Kay was now in a better place. That was something I didn't agree with. And I was sure that if it was left up to us and Kay, there was no better place for him to be, other than here with his family, heaven included. Her speech ended when she was overwhelmed with emotion. She and Frank walked down the aisle and out of the church as the choir stood. Her only child was gone, and that had to be devastating for her.

The choir went into a song called "Goin' Up Yonder", led by a young lady with a very powerful voice. At her first note, Taj began shaking with grief.

If you wanna know
Where I'm going
Where I'm going soon...

The dark shades she wore weren't able to hide the tears and pain she was going through. Kim was the first at her side, taking her best friend in her arms and rocking her as the choir sung. Barbara was behind her, massaging her shoulders and doing her part in consoling her. Even over the thunderous voices of the choir, I could still hear her cries. It had to be the worse day of all of our lives.

The hardest part of the funeral came as the choir ended the song while the piano continued to play: saying goodbye before the closing of the casket. It was something that I didn't want to do, and Dante must've noticed when the line began to form. He took me by the hand and led the way, seemingly not even bothered by the sight of his father in a casket.

There were flowers and wreaths lined all around. Dante grabbed a rose and broke off part of the stem. When we got to the casket, he stepped up on a small staircase that was put there just for him. He looked at his father for a moment, then kissed the rose before sticking it in his lapel.

"I'm going to miss you, Daddy," he said, touching his father's hand. "But I'm being strong like you told me to be. You told me not to cry, and I'm not. I'm going to be a man and take care of Mommy, too. I'll protect her and make sure she's all right. You don't have to worry about that. I promise."

Watching Dante speak to his father, almost killed me. I reached for my handkerchief.

"Oh, I'm going to take care of Nana, too, Daddy. She's been crying every day, but I told her that you said you'll be watching over us." He looked over at me. "Uncle Dee wants to talk to you, so I'm going to go now."

When he leaned over and hugged his father while lying his head on his chest, I had to turn away. "I love you, Daddy."

He stepped down and walked over to his mom. I don't know what he said to her, but whatever it was, she reacted by taking him in her arms. Kay left behind a beautiful family.

It was hard to look at him. It was hard to accept that he was gone. I would've done anything to be able to laugh with him again. He was too good of a person for shit to play out like it did, too good of a person to die at a fucking gas station, surrounded by people who had no idea who he was.

"Yo, don't think I'll ever forget about you, Kay." My voice began to crack and it felt like I had sand in my mouth. "I ain't never had a friend like you. I'ma make sure Dante's straight.

He'll never have to want for nothin', that's my word. You did a hell of a job raising him into a little man; that boy's strong. I'll do whatever I can to help him be as great of a guy as you were."

I couldn't take it anymore. I put my hand on his shoulder, and that's when it hit me. "Shit ain't fair."

Kim came to my side. Both of us had tears in our eyes. "This is horrible," she said, putting her arm around mine. "Let's go outside. Give Taj a few minutes with him."

Dante and the rest of us left out of the church, leaving Taj alone to say her last goodbye.

CHAPTER 53

Taj Wright

My loving husband, my best friend, was in a casket a few feet in front of me. *Why my, Kay?*

They were waiting for me so that they could put my baby in the ground. This was going to be the last time I saw him, the last time I would be able to see and touch his handsome face. *Why my, Kay?*

I walked slowly over to the casket, wishing I could see his eyes, see his smile, feel his kiss. It was almost inconceivable to think that I would never be able to enjoy any of those things ever again.

There were many nights when I would watch him as he slept. He would always have this look on his face as if he was enjoying the dream he was having. I would kiss him on the cheek and thank God for putting him in my life. And, as I stared down at him in that casket, I kissed him one last time and thanked God again for putting him in my life.

I was hurting bad. Real bad. If there was ever such thing as a perfect husband and father, my Kay was him. And I knew for a fact that I would never love another man again. After having him, I could never settle for less. I knew that no other man was capable of loving me like he did. He was my soulmate, and a love like ours only comes once in a lifetime.

I touched my husband's face, and even though I knew he was no longer there, it still felt good just to be able to touch him. I reached for a yellow diamond pendant that hung from my neck. "I'm wearing it for you, baby. I wasn't going to go pick it up, but I knew you would've wanted me to be wearing it when I saw you. It's beautiful just like you." I reached into my purse. "I love this card the most, though."

They say that diamonds are forever.
But my love for you will outlast any diamond, any stone.
Love, Kay

I held the card to my heart and knew that he'd meant every word. He knew how to make me happy. Our time together was filled with memories that I would hold onto forever. And those memories were enough to fill the emptiness that I felt when he left me.

"If it's a girl, I'll name her Kaye Marie," I said, rubbing my stomach. "And I'll name him after you if it's a boy. I know you would like that." I kissed him again. "Dante will be happy to have someone to boss around finally." The thought caused me to laugh a little. "Kay, I'll make sure they know who their father is, and they'll always know how loving you were. I promise." One last kiss. "I love you. See you later."

Devon

We were standing around outside on the steps of the church. Because Kay didn't have any male friends, some members of the church volunteered to be pallbearers along with me. I had been stressed the fuck out ever since Kim called me to tell me what had happened. Now I was really feeling it, as I watched Dante stand with Kim and the rest of the ladies. Dante was Kay's world, and it hurt to know that he wasn't going to be around to see his son grow into a man. "Damn."

Taj was still in the church, but nobody was in a rush. We all understood what she was going through, so the pastor gave her all the time she needed. It wasn't until Dante looked up at the entrance of the church, did we notice her standing at the top of the steps. She removed her dark glasses, showing the tears and puffy eyes. She looked like royalty in mourning, dressed in all black.

She wiped her eyes and exhaled deeply, then said, "You can go in there and get my baby now."

CHAPTER 54

The burial ceremony was over. Kim, Taj, Dante and I were the only ones left at the cemetery. When Taj made the funeral arrangements, she made it clear that she didn't want Kay's casket lowered into the ground until everyone was gone. She said she didn't think she could handle seeing his casket covered in dirt.

We were sitting under a tent. Kay's casket was in the center with a huge wreath on top of it. We were all quiet. Dante was sitting next to me, our eyes looking straight ahead. Taj's head was resting on Kim's shoulder. She wasn't crying anymore. She had been crying for the last six days, so she was probably all out of tears. She just sat there, fingering the yellow diamond pendant.

Dante went over to the casket and circled it twice, then stopped. He ran his hand across the top of it. "Uncle Dee, daddy is going to heaven, isn't he?"

I smile at him. "No doubt. That's where all the good people go."

I just couldn't understand how Dante seemed to be holding up like he was. As close as he and Kay were, I would've expected him to be crying for days. He had to be feeling messed up. It would probably hit him later on, but for now, he was being a soldier, a little trooper.

"Come on, Dante," Kim said, standing up and walking to him. "Let's go get some ice cream."

She winked at me as she took Dante's hand. They walked down the hill and got into the limo. Taj broke the silence as it drove off.

"He used to talk about you all the time while y'all were in prison. He would call me and tell me about his boy, 'New York'. He talked about you so much to the point I thought my baby had gotten a boyfriend in prison."

Her giggling cheered me up a bit. I laughed. "That's my nigga, right there," I replied, nodding at the casket. "Word up. You don't find too many dudes like him."

"Oh, don't I know." She turned in her chair, legs crossed, the pendant never leaving her touch. "How did you come home so fast, Devon?" Her voice wasn't filled with blame. She sounded sincere, just in search of the truth.

The question caught me completely by surprise. I didn't know exactly what Kay did, but I had a feeling Taj knew something. We didn't know who killed him, and if it was because of what he had done to help me come home, the shit would be on my conscious forever. I would've been to blame for him not being around for his family. I hoped that wasn't the case.

I was trying to figure out what to say, how to tell her that her husband risked his life to help me get out of prison. I still couldn't believe it, so I knew it would sound crazy to her. But before I could say anything, she answered for me.

"I know he did something; I just don't know what exactly." She looked toward his casket. "My Kay would do anything for the people he loved. And, honestly, he seemed to love you like a brother."

It was good to hear that. We had been like brothers since we'd met, and she had just confirmed that he and I looked at each other the same way. I felt guilty, but I also wanted to know if she knew any details about what he had done.

"How did you find out?"

She shook her head. "He called me one day from a strange number, saying his battery died on him. I didn't think anything about it. I trusted him with all of my heart, but the woman in me got curious. So, three days after that, I called the number back. A guy answered, addressing himself as Special Agent Colston."

The dark sunglasses hid her eyes, but her smirk was the kind that women make when they know when they've outsmarted somebody.

"I watch enough TV to know what a special agent is, so I played it off and told him who I was. Then I asked him if Kay had made it down there to see him, because there was an emergency and he left his phone at home. He fell for it, and said he hadn't seen him in a few days, but if he came down to his office he would give him the message."

Yeah, she knew, so there was no need for me to play dumb. "So, he never said anything to you about it?"

She shook her head. "No, but one time you two were on the phone, and I read his lips when he told you he "did it". I didn't know what he was talking about at the time, but just knowing who he was, it wasn't hard to figure out that he was only doing whatever he could to make your situation better." She was wearing a broken smile as she spoke to his casket. "He had this thing for showing his love by any means necessary. It came in words, backed up by a whole lot of action. I'm sure you understand that now."

It wasn't up for debate. It was just still hard to believe that he went to the extreme to help me.

"Some laws changed and other stuff; he told me that's how you got out." Her gaze went to the casket. "I never questioned him about the other stuff, because I knew it was his way of telling me there was more to it. He wasn't going to keep another secret from me; he probably prayed that I didn't ask more questions, and I didn't. And, now you're home."

"Taj, I didn't know he was…"

She cut me off. "It's fine, Devon. Really, it is." A sigh. "That was just Kay being Kay."

A calm breeze whipped through the trees above us. I took a second to appreciate being able to hear leaves rustle in the wind. Then my mind wandered back to those days on the track with him, just talking. It was hard knowing that we would never have another conversation.

The limo was pulling up when Taj finally spoke. The driver came around and opened the door for Dante and Kim. Dante got out holding a banana split, licking his finger before taking Kim's hand. Taj was watching them as they walked across the grass. "That boy is going to miss his father. I thought he would be crying his eyes out, but he's taking it better than I could've imagined."

That made me think about what Dante had said when he was talking to Kay at the church. *I'm being strong like you told me to be. You told me not to cry, and I'm not.*

"Even when I told him that his daddy was gone, all he did was hold me, telling me everything was going to be all right." She raised her glasses to dab at her eyes with some tissue. "I cried for three days, Devon, and he didn't leave my side. I cried for Kay but I cried for my son just as much. And I don't know what kind of shape I would be in if I had to see him hurting. But, it's like he's just concerned about me."

I looked at the casket. "He got it honest."

"You're right about that." Taj giggled, her tissue still at work.

Dante came under the tent and stood next to the casket. He held out a spoonful of ice cream. "You want some, Mom?"

"No, thank you, baby."

"I would offer you some, Uncle Dee, but Auntie Kim said dairy products don't agree with you?"

I eyed her as she came and sat next to me. "Oh, so you telling all of my business now?"

Taj let out a laugh, and it seemed to be a much-needed one. Kim kissed me on the cheek. "He was going to buy you something, so I had to tell him."

The three of us were watching Dante. He ate a spoon of ice cream and then smiled as looked over at the casket. Taj got up and went over and put her arm around him, sharing their last moment together as a family.

"This just ain't right," Kim whispered.

Taj affectionately touched the casket, letting out a heavy sigh. "I'm ready, y'all."

This was the last time I would be in Kay's presence. I went and got as close to him as I could, touching the casket before I walked off with Kim. I could hear Taj's last words to Kay.

"Okay, baby, I guess I'll see you later."

CHAPTER 55

**One Year Later
Devon**

I never liked flying. Shit was for the birds, for real. If it wasn't born with wings, it had no business in the friendly skies, especially a piece a metal that weighed tons and cruised at thirty-thousand feet. But sacrifices had to be made, and life on private jets wasn't all that bad. Butter-soft leather seats, good sound system, and a few shots of Hennessey, always helped take away the fear of the plane's motor giving out and falling from the sky.

I had two songs in the top twenty on the R&B charts, and one was still climbing at number eleven. A song of mine was recently given to one of the biggest names in pop music, so things were about to get even crazier. People wanted my songs, and all I had to do was go into my stash and find one that fit the singer. It was one of the keys to a hit record; I knew what it took. Ain't nothing like the feeling of hitting number one, and I wanted to feel it again, and again, and again.

I had just left Atlanta after a meeting with my new manager. I got tired of my phone blowing up while I was in the studio with artists, so I hired one of the best in the industry to manage the business side of things. Kay would've been perfect for the job, and if anybody deserved a percentage of the money I was making, it was him.

The jet took a dip. I raised my seat up and looked out the window. The familiar Detroit skyline and the surrounding lakes and rivers were coming into view. Kay should've been waiting to pick me up when I landed. That's how it was supposed to be. I could only imagine how it would've been had things not gone the way they did. The money wouldn't have changed him at all. He probably would have taken Taj and the kids everywhere he went because he was always about family.

They caught his killer two weeks after the funeral. His name was Michael Moseley. He was the older brother of Carlton Moseley, a guy who was killed while trying to carjack Kay. In the police report, Kay and other witnesses said that the carjacker got out of another car, but the driver got away. More than likely, it was the brother. They bumped into each other at a gas station after all those years, and he took his revenge out on my friend.

Finding out that he actually killed someone came as somewhat of a surprise to me, even though it was in self-defense. I mean, he was a real laid-back type of guy, quiet and good-natured. Of course, he wasn't a punk; him in the bathroom ready to get it on with Young Gauge was proof of that. But Kay wasn't a killer. He would save people if anything. I knew he only did it because he had no other choice.

What didn't surprise me, though, was the fact that he never once mentioned it, let alone brag about it like the normal street dude would do. Being known for catching a body carried big weight in the streets, but not in Kay's world. And I guess that's why I got as close to him as I did, because he was different, different in the best way possible.

I learned about the carjacking during the preliminary hearing for Moseley: I didn't miss a court date. The prosecution used it as the motive for Kay's murder. They also had video surveillance of the whole thing, and Moseley ended up copping out to twenty-five-to-life.

I got twenty-five years for selling drugs, and it was a possibility that a killer could get out one day if he kept his nose clean while doing his time. In the process, he had taken the life of the one friend I had during the worst part of my own life. That shit wasn't fair, and I took it very personally. The only satisfaction I got came when I searched for him on the internet and found out where he was doing his time.

Ionia Correctional Facility

I hadn't seen my brother, Emanuel, in over fifteen years. While I was locked up, we would write each other every now and then, but he hadn't heard from me since I got out. Everyday life had a way of taking up a lot of my time, so I never got a chance to sit down and write him a letter. I did make sure that he was straight on his books, and when you're doing a couple of life sentences, that's really your only concern.

Being in the position I was in, made it possible for me to even visit him. Prisons make it hard for convicted felons to visit their facility, especially when your conviction was for drugs. But, all it took was a phone call from the president of my record company to get me on Emanuel's visiting list. He spoke to the Warden and I signed my name on a letter they had typed up for me. Now, I was sitting at a table waiting to see my big brother for the first time in years.

The visiting room was more like an extra-large jail cell. There were six tables in all, but I was the only person there. I imagined lifers didn't get many visitors. Most probably had forced themselves to forget about the outside world because it was something they would never see again while they were alive. The reality of Emanuel never getting out had set in years ago, but it was still hard to believe. In his letters, he never complained or said anything about his time. He had faced the reality of dying in prison. He was my brother, and I will always love him, but prison was the only thing that could contain him. I can't lie, either; he was an animal, a stone-cold killer. If anybody was meant to be locked in a cage, it was him.

The steel door came open and in walked a fucking mountain of a man. His arms were so big that he couldn't put them at his side. He had always been tall, but years of weight lifting made him look like the meanest WWE wrestler ever. His dreads were pulled back and hung past his broad shoulders. He was twelve years older than me, but his dark skin was glowing and he looked as young as I did. Prison had a way of preserving youth, and it definitely showed with him.

He kept a serious look on his face as he walked up to the table. Not until the C.O. closed the door behind him, did he show a hint of a smile.

I stood up and hugged him. His arms felt like steel when he grabbed me. "Damn, bro, you lookin' good." I patted his back, glad to finally see him. "You big as a fuckin' house."

He stepped back, a hand on my shoulder. "You don't look so bad yourself. How the hell you get out?"

I shook my head as I took my seat. "Long story. I'll tell you about it one day."

"Nigga, I got double life; tell me the secret."

A sense of humor ran in our family. Not even his time could take that away. I couldn't remember the last time we laughed together, and it was good to share one with him again.

"So, I heard you were in the music business," he said, studying me with a deep stare.

"Huh?" I hadn't talked to him, so I didn't know how he found out.

"You got a deal, didn't you?"

"Where you hear that from?"

"Your boy, Kay. He came to see me and told me about it."

Now I was really confused. "Kay came to see you?"

He nodded his head. "Yeah, about a year ago, but that's the last I heard from him. He told me you got out and everything. I was just wondering why you didn't hit me up sooner."

"Hold up." I was trying to make sense of what he was saying. "So Kay came to see you?"

"Yeah, it was strange at first. Somebody sent me some money a while ago. I saw the name but I never knew who it was. Then, the first time Kay wrote me, I saw that he had the same last name as the person who sent the money. He told me who he was and said he wanted to come down to see me." He yawned, stretching his arms in the air. His forearms reminded me of Popeye's.

"I wasn't about to turn down a visit, so I put him on my list. He came down and told me you had just signed a deal. He also told me it was his wife who sent the money the first time. After that, money would just pop up in my account. Five grand popped up in it about six months ago, so I thought it was him."

"Nawl, that was me." I was thinking about what a hell of a guy Kay was.

"What else did y'all talk about when he came to see you?"

"Family shit. He was telling me about his family, and about the time y'all did together." He shrugged his shoulder. "It really just seemed like he wanted somebody to talk to. He's a cool brotha'. What is he up to?"

Finding out he had looked out for Emanuel just made it even harder when I thought about him. I didn't want to drop a tear in front of my big brother, but it came anyway. "Kay's dead."

"Damn, you bullshiting?" Shock was on his face.

"Nawl, that's why I came down here." I reached down into my waistband and pulled out the folded copy of the mugshot I got off the department of corrections website. I slid it across the table as I watched the door. "You ever saw this guy before?"

He studied it for a second, and then slowly nodded his head. "Yeah, he got here about a month ago. Got a murder case."

I looked Emanuel in the eye. "He killed Kay."

The veins in his neck began to bulge as he looked back down at the paper. He seemed to transform right in front of me. I didn't see my brother anymore; I saw evil. There was a gleam in his eyes that said it was time to feed that evil, and the only way its hunger would be satisfied, was if someone paid the ultimate price. The visit ended right there.

"Don't even worry about it." He tapped his chest with a closed fist, and then stood. Without saying another word, he turned and walked to the door. It was feeding time.

10 Years Later

Hi Baby,

It's a beautiful day out. The sun is shining and there's just enough of a breeze to keep me from sweating lol. You know I hate to sweat. Well...except for when we used to make love. (Sigh) You'd be on top of me, sweat rolling down your forehead...right down to the tip of your nose...and then land right in my eye, lol (I really did laugh out loud just now), It would surprise me and sting a little, but I would keep going without missing a beat (Extra-long sigh)...

We did really good today! The auction was a huge success! We raised over $300,000 for the foundation. Dante had Tylar Elizabeth-Greer paint every last one of those xylophones from his closet, with her own designs. You don't know who she is, but she's an amazing artist. She's like the female Picasso of our time. Anyway, not one of them went for less than $10,000 (yay!) They ate those xylophones up, baby, lol. Imagine if I would have donated those things when Dante started piling them up! The Kabazza Wright School of Arts & Music is shining today!

I'm looking at your son now. You probably get tired of me telling you how much he reminds me of you, but he does, even more now that he's a young man. And his heart is so big, Kay. Just like yours. He just gives and gives. Looks like he's passing down everything he learned from you, too. The twins adore their big brother. Kay Jr. is working the video camera. I think he might be a director or something; he records everything and then tries to edit the footage, lol, he's learning. Kaye Marie, on the other hand, is sitting next to me in this lawn chair, tapping away at her phone as always lol. She keeps a lot of her poetry in there, so I just assume she's being creative. She has a slam tournament coming up next month. I know her butt better kill it.

Kay, he's doing it big now, orchestra and all. It's the 7th and 8th graders, and they are truly marvelous! On the first day of school, not one of them knew anything about the instrument they were playing. Those boys have really come a long way. If only you could hear them, baby. Oh, and they're playing Lionel Hampton's "Flying Home". Groovy jazz

He told me everything about that talk on the riverfront, and how much it meant to him to do what you asked. And he's done everything, baby. I'm glad that you talked to your son. I think that's the reason why he's the beautiful young man that he is now. And he says without that talk, he wouldn't have come this far. He's been a man ever since you left. A strong and gentle man.

I remember that night. You two came home real late, and I saw how puffy your eyes were. I wanted to say something, but if it was meant for me to know, you would've told me. I just don't know why he decided to tell me about the "man talk" you two had, minutes before the biggest show of his life, which was to play in front of the President of the United States at Carnegie Hall. Geesh lol.

I cried when he told me. I kissed him and told him how proud I was of him, and how proud you would have been. He started crying like a baby in his dressing room, but it was a happy cry, Kay. It was because of you. I will admit that I felt left out, because we shared everything, Kay. It did answer a few questions I had, but one still has gone unanswered after all this time. I guess I'll never know. I guess you had your reasons to cry. I'm not mad at you anymore, by the way. After thinking it over, it was for the best. I don't think I could have handled it anyway. I guess it's not important. Okay, let me stop. This is a happy day☺

Devon did more than his share, as usual. The state-of-the-art music department for the school has most definitely been a blessing for the kids. They love it, and are excelling, Kay, in every aspect. The million dollars he donated today will just help more kids when they go on to college. Our other donor's contributions haven't even been added up yet, so it's going good.

Kim can't have kids, baby. She just found out yesterday. I feel bad for her. I thought it was probably something wrong with Devon, at first. Thought maybe he had spent too much time in the shower when he was locked up lol but it's her. She said something about adopting, so we'll see. Until then, they'll just keep being the wonderful tee-tee and uncle they've been all this time. They're here now. Devon is near the stage with several of his artist that performed earlier. He has some of the hottest acts signed to his company, and they come to the school to mentor the kids all of the time. Kim is mingling with some of our clients that showed up. I should be doing the same, but I just wanted to talk to you for a minute.

I miss Shorty. He lived a long life for a Chihuahua, but I miss him staring up at me with those puppy dog eyes begging to sit in my lap. Kay Jr. wants an English bulldog, but those things slob over everything, lol. I might let him get it, though. He'll just have to be the one to clean up after the little monster lol.

Your mom just texted me. She and Frank are still in Paris. I think she likes it there. It's been a month now and she says the only reason she's coming home is to see her grandbabies, lol. We'll probably all go there in a few months. Some organization wants Dante to come and perform over there, so it'll be a nice family trip.

Oh, and your son told me about you giving me your blessings to get married again when the time comes. But, Kay, that'll never happen. I guess you were too good to me. You loved me like I know I could never be loved again. I would compare every man to you, and they would always come up short. That's a disappointment that I can live without. So, it's not going to happen, buddy! I'll see you again, and maybe we'll be butterflies, like Ms. Badu said lol

Okay, your son is hitting the last notes, and now it's time to announce the total of the donations. I'm down to the last pages of this notebook, so I'll be starting a new one when we talk again. I think this makes an even 30 that I have. I keep them in a safe, along with some other things that remind me of you. Maybe I'll use them to write a book one day. I don't know Okay, talk to you later, baby.

Eternally Yours,
Taj